Seen Her Year

Baylin Wing

SEEN HER YEAR

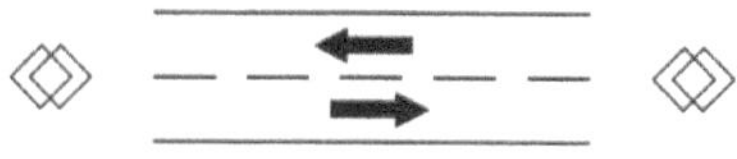

BAYLIN WING

ISBN: 978-1-964680-00-2 (ebook)
ISBN: 978-1-964680-01-9 (paperback)
ISBN: 978-1-964680-02-6 (hardcover)

Library of Congress Control Number: 2024913846

Cover Art by Tanjibo
Interior Illustrations by Tanjibo
Proofread by Krista Dapkey
First Edition October 2024

Visit the author's website at: www.baylinwing.com

To all the what ifs and what could have beens,

this one's for you.

I wanna go home.

My arms are tired. My feet hurt. I lean against a nearby rail, sighing as weight eases up from my legs. Much better. Suddenly, someone looms over me from my right, taking me by surprise. I retract a little until I see who it is.

"Wipe that look off your face, you're ruining the mood," Dad mutters. "It's your sister's graduation. You should be happy to be here."

He walks away before I even get to respond. I didn't even— I wasn't— What the heck! That's just my face. I swear I wasn't glaring or anything. My chest starts to heave, my eyes getting warm. *No. Not here, Kayla. You can't. You should be used to this by now. That's not his first time misunderstanding you.* Getting off the rail, I put on a decent smile. Let's face it, you're only here for picture duty today. What else are you good for if not a silent coat rack and a table rest? Maybe even a *supposed* extra armpiece of a daughter—if I'm even considered either of those.

Mom and Dad are busy talking with other surrounding adults while Josslyn's preoccupied with gathering another batch of friends to take pictures with. Her hands are full—her graduation cap, diploma, and phone in her left hand and a massive flower bouquet taking up her right. I switch my sister's two smaller bouquets to my other arm to stretch out my stiff one. I had offered to hold the last of her flowers but she'd insisted on carrying them herself. After all, *Simon* gave them to her.

Can't say I didn't try.

Wait. When am I *not* trying? I put on a smile so Dad can be happy. I hold the flowers so Mom wouldn't have to worry about my sister or do so herself. I changed my dress so Joss wouldn't feel like I'd outshine her—at least, color-wise.

But none of that matters.

Joss had debated between a black bodycon dress that added ten years to her or a white one-shoulder dress that a jealous ex would wear to crash a wedding. I wasn't a fan of either so I encouraged her to wear the one she *wanted* to. She liked the white one better—I know she did. Mom saw potential in both but leaned towards black after Dad kept insisting on it being the better choice. My sister ended up choosing the black one all because Dad said, "This one looks good. Very classy."

So much for *my* opinion.

She could've at least stuffed that phone in the pink floral dress I liked. The one I'd caught sight of when we went shopping last month. It was simple. Pretty. Looked comfortable. I remember the excitement I had felt grabbing the flowy dress off the rack and rushing past five other girls sifting through the dress department, to show her the treasure I had found. All for what? A mere two seconds of a glance and a scrunch on her face. She didn't even give me a chance to tell her about the *pockets*!

What's the point of trying if all I'm gonna get is rejection? Shame! To feel like it's my fault whenever they're not happy. They're never satisfied. With how I act. With what I say.

With me.

Thankfully, the depressing thoughts and memories gets pushed back when Joss's friend hands me her phone before walking back to the group to pose. I do my job and when I give them a thumbs-up, they break out of their poses to give each other hugs, saying all their goodbyes.

"I'm gonna miss you so much!"

"Don't forget to send the pics!"

"Girl, you are looking fire."

"Keep in touch, okay? I'll text you later!"

It's déjà vu, except with different faces. Like in all the other photos I've taken today, everyone's picture-perfect. Yet, there's always one who stands out the most. Her black formal dress might not be as flashy as the others, but it does one heck of a job emphasizing her decorated neck. Sashes. Gold cords. Money, candy, flower leis. Her whole ensemble practically screams intelligence, popularity, and accomplishment. It's hard *not* to notice my sister. I chuckle. And she still doesn't see why so many boys in her class like her.

When I return the phone to its rightful owner, the friend doesn't bat an eye before she turns away to find someone else to take a picture with. I swallow the lump in my throat for the umpteenth time today, trying to understand where the thirst was coming from when I haven't even uttered a word since the ceremony started. Movement from nearby makes me scoot aside for a man and his wife to walk past me freely. In the midst of fixing my hair from a gentle breeze, Dad looks over at me.

Is he gonna comment on my face again? Attitude? Shit, shit, shit! He's coming over. *Hurry, look happy. Smile or he'll give you a lecture when we go home!*

"Kayla, be a doll and take a picture of us and your sister." Dad shoves his phone in my hand before hurrying to his position next to Josslyn and Mom.

Holy crap. He didn't say anything. Yes! I let out a breath of relief as both Mom and Dad get ready to pose, one on each side of their daughter. Shiny jewelry. Glossy purse. Sharp suit. Fancy watch. They look like they've just stepped out of a luxury magazine. Oh, and add in the golden child. The three of them look so prestigious. For a moment, I forget I'm related. As my sister smiles widely, showcasing a perfect set of teeth, I take the photo of a flawless family.

Must be nice to matter.

"Take some the other way too!" Dad's voice booms over all the other noisy people crowding the area.

Oh god.

As if he hadn't turned some heads around us, he calmly returns to his proud dad pose as quickly as he broke out of it. I shrink a little as I bring his phone up, fitting the three of them in the screen—vertically this time. Out of nowhere, a few individuals walk by in front of me, blurring the camera.

"Come on," I hiss. "Focus." Panic ensues as I look to Dad. Not mad. Thank goodness.

After snapping a few photos that would be good enough, Dad retrieves his phone as another round of graduates come to greet Joss. Some parents around the area approach us. Mom and Dad proceeds to entertain them, boasting about the so-and-so awards my sister had received and the reputable colleges she'd been accepted into. Joss looks like she'll wave me over for another picture soon. I walk to her before she gets the chance to, ignoring the sharp pain shooting down my heels.

Smile, Kayla. It's bearable. *Don't ruin this.*

I stand nearby idly, trying to somewhat dry my clammy hands on my dress discreetly. The sun's glaring, people are too close for comfort, and everyone's talking over each other. Waiting quietly, I shiver. *Really? Not a good time, Anxiety.* I swallow as I shake a limb here and there to get some blood flowing. Suddenly, my body grasps onto something familiar. A brooding feeling under the obvious ones.

It's cold. It's crowded. It's loud. But worst of all, it's lonely here.

I feel lonely.

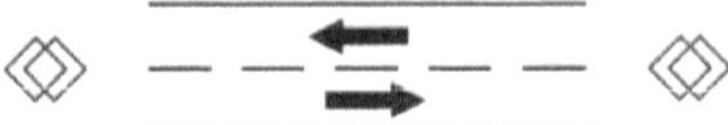

Deep breath. In and out. The silence is beautiful when I walk down an empty staircase and through a doorway to the outdoor plaza. The loud hustling and bustling of the pushy crowd last weekend creeps up my mind.

Wipe that look off your face, you're ruining the—

Stop. It's already over. Just listen. Rustling tree leaves. Chirping birds. It's nice. The plaza is so big, the other students dining outside are nothing but spread-out faint noises. It's peaceful. You're okay here. *Relax.*

As I reach my regular spot, Franny easily opens her lunch thermos and digs in with her spoon. "Can you believe it? One more class left before we're officially seniors!"

Pat takes another bite of her PB&J sandwich. "Don't forget finals."

As a member of East Line's speech and debate team, Franny's quick to retort. Soon, the two honor-roll students begin to argue what technically determines the end of junior year and the actual moment we turn into seniors. The discussion gets so intellectual that it attracts the attention of Rex and Leif, two smart lanky boys who hang around at one of the nearby tables. They join in to take sides and are so serious about it, I stifle a small laugh as I take another bite of my turkey salad.

Out of the corner of my eye, Tracy heads towards us. *Strange*. I've known her since kindergarten. Even from a distance, I can tell something's off. She sets her backpack down on a neighboring chair as I quickly swallow the last of my lunch and pack it away.

"You okay, Trace?" I ask softly, desperately trying to shoo away the sense of impending doom.

"Yeah." She sits herself on an empty chair next to me and looks down dejectedly. Her eyes are red. Eyelids puffy. If she's attempting to hide her face, she sure is doing a bad job at it. She sniffles. Ah, as I suspected.

"Trace?" I lay a gentle hand on her back. "What's up?"

As if I had just said some trigger word, Tracy bursts into tears and I stiffen. Oh dear, what am I supposed to do? M-My hand! I start to rub her softly but my good intention takes a turn for the worse. She bawls even harder. I retract my hand immediately, only to give her sympathetic pats now.

"I-I'm . . . I-I'm going to miss everyone so much." She wipes away a tear. "W-We're going to graduate and then we're not going to s-see each other anymore!"

Miss everyone? She's barely been with us this whole year! My brow furrows as Tracy tries to get ahold of herself with more sniffles, failing miserably. Soothing her back with soft rubs again, I let out a soft chuckle in attempt to lighten up the mood. "Trace, we're not even seniors yet. We still have another year. It'll be okay."

"But we're *going* to graduate. Everyone's going to separate and we're not going to be together anymore." She's covering her face now, occasionally wiping away her water streams.

Ironic. Isn't that how it is now? It's not often she comes to our spot during lunch and for the times that she does, she's off somewhere else the second she's finished eating. Off to see her other friends, I suppose.

"Well" — *careful with your words, Kayla* — "we all got our own paths to take and sometimes, we have to take them ourselves. But that doesn't mean we're never seeing each other again. We can always meet up when everyone's back in town." I nod, silently approving of the uplifting words that came out of my mouth. Not too bad.

"It's not going to be the same!" she cries, grabbing the attention of our friends around us.

Never mind then! I switch to patting her back again, feeling jittery all of a sudden. "Just because we won't be seeing each other that often doesn't mean we're not friends anymore. P-Plus! You're gonna make many friends in college. There's nothing to worry about, Trace."

"It won't be the same," she whimpers.

Again, my words are tossed aside. I hold my tongue as I watch Tracy wipe another round of tears, followed by some hiccups. Of course it's not going to be the same. Isn't that how life is? It'll move on, with or without you. *We used to be best friends, but you found another bestie to add onto your ever-increasing circle of friends.* Isn't it *you* who moved on? Without *me*? Things aren't the same anymore. They will never be. Did she not see that? My hand continues to pat her back, but I keep my mouth shut now. I know better than to say anything. At the rate I'm going, she's gonna cry me a river. Shivers run along my skin. Something burdensome begins to weigh me down; like I'm sinking in my seat.

Rex sits himself on the other side of her, putting a reassuring hand on her shoulder. "It'll be okay, Trace. We can always FaceTime each other."

Tracy nods, still sobbing but recovering now. "Y-You're right."

I draw my hand away, watching in horror. My so-called best friend since fourth grade, is being successfully consoled by this guy—she's known probably in a shorter amount of time—with FaceTime? It might be a solution to keep in touch, but that doesn't make it *the same*. If she was going to accept that so easily, why . . . why did I try so hard?

"We can always meet up when we're on our breaks." Rex is rubbing the center of her back now. The very same spot I worked on earlier.

Tracy's tears seem to be clearing up now, reacting positively to his comforting words. I hold in a scoff. Oh my god, did she not hear me say the same thing at first? The boy continues to suggest more ways of staying in touch. He even says something that makes Tracy laugh a little. I don't hear it as I stare in silence. Both Franny and Pat decide to chime in with a few words of encouragement that I also don't catch. Just like that, Tracy's emotional fire—that I had apparently *fueled* with my extinguishers—is finally dying down now.

I should've never cared. Never said anything! I should've just let her cry until someone else decided to cheer her up. My body feels heavy, and only now do I realize my limbs are cold.

Move.

Take a walk or something! Get out of here. *Now.*

Everything feels so rigid. I get up stiffly. Tracy's in good hands, so I don't worry if I leave them to it. I make up an excuse about needing to use the printer for my next class before grabbing my backpack and walking into the school building as if everything's fine.

It's not.

I can't do anything right, can I? Why is it always me *ruining* things and *saying* the wrong things? Is there something wrong with . . . *me*?

I shrug away the shivers creeping up my spine as I prance up six flights of stairs. Before I know it, I'm in the library, standing in front of the printer. A boy looks at me strangely when he sees me walk away with nothing. I would be so angry right now if it weren't for the burning sensation in my legs distracting me successfully. Huffing a little, I go down the flights of stairs and head towards the other side of the building, eventually reaching a small L-shaped hallway where the vending machines are.

It's quiet here. Peaceful. I don't have to worry about ruining anything. I turn into the dead-end, stopping in front of my favorite machine. A classic brown bag of milk chocolate M&M's catches my eye.

Perfect.

Maybe *you'll* get rid of the bitter taste in my mouth.

A picture is worth a thousand words. Yet, nothing come to mind when I stare at a picture of my girlfriend leaning against a wall of some poorly lit room. Her arms are wrapped around the neck of a guy she's making out with. A guy that's *not* me.

Only his back and a small angle of his face were captured. It would've been hard to identify him if it wasn't for his hair. Those brown curls were familiar enough. Kai Williams is in our grade. Varsity soccer. Talks a lot. Loves attention. Look at the way he's pressed up against her; one hand clutching her waist and the other groping her butt. But that's not the worst part. The worst part is the way Em looked while he ate her face.

She was *enjoying* it.

Why am I not surprised? Our relationship might've soured over the past few months, but there's no way she would do that to me. I trust her. I . . . *trusted* her.

"I'm sorry, bro." Nick's hand rests on my shoulder, a gesture of comfort I would've appreciated more if it didn't just confirm the truth I've been trying to deny. "You okay?"

"I'm fine." I swallow hard as I give my friend his phone back, trying to get as far away from that picture as I can—for now. *Calm down. Keep it together.*

He takes his hand back, his eyes still on me. Is that worry I see on his face? Or pity? Before I think to, my hands start to stuff books from my backpack into my locker. I continue in silence, not shoving the books in too hard or too light as though I had been affected.

"It's from Jessica's party last night. Kyle sent it to me. He said he thought you should know."

"Thank him for me."

Nick nods. "So . . . what are you going to do about it?"

I zip my bag and swing it onto one shoulder, closing my locker with a slam. *Damn, too hard.* Nick seems indifferent to it and I let out a sigh of relief. "Can you send that to me? I'm going to talk to her."

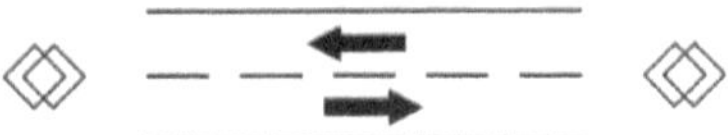

I run through my plan again. *Get her out. Confront her. Don't cause a scene.* I can do that. Inhale. Hold. And exhale. My heart skips a beat when I storm my way through the hall, towards the nearest doors leading to the cafeteria. The sound of the push bar gets drowned out by the countless students around me. There she is. The all-too-familiar blonde catches my eye, and I'm closing in on her table within seconds.

"Nells, look at them! Even I can do better!" Em extends her hand, showing her fingers to her friend. Her back is facing me, so she doesn't notice me. *Yet.*

Nelly looks at her friend's bright pink nails, giggling. "Bet you're never going there again, huh?"

"Are you kidding me? Of course not. The woman there had no idea what she was do—" Em notices Nelly's attention shift from her and she turns in her seat. Our eyes finally connect and she brightens up. "Hey, babe!"

She's smiling. For someone who just cheated on her boyfriend, she sounds remorseless. Did she plan on pretending like nothing happened? As if I wouldn't find out?

"Babe?" Her brow furrows as she tilts her head a little.

It's not cute. Not anymore. How did I ever think that was cute? Blue eyes search mine. They certainly look like the ocean, except now, I can see them for what they truly are: *full of secrets.* My mouth gets dry, not yet ready to speak to this traitor.

"Earth to babe," she drags on the nickname, taking my hand into hers.

Was that the one that ran through Kai's hair? *Disgusting.* It takes everything in me to not fling her dirty hand away. I clear my throat. "We need to talk."

Eyes widen around us. Funnily enough, Emma mirrors them. Surprised. Like *she's* the victim here. Someone, give her an Oscar.

"Okay?"

I ignore the confused tone in her voice and turn to lead the way out of the cafeteria. From the corner of my eye, I catch her shrugging to her friends. *How silly.* I turn away and proceed on with her on my tail. This time, the sound of the push bar echoes through the hallway. It's less noisy here compared to the cafeteria. Blood shoots through my veins as I walk towards an empty area decent enough to carry a heavy conversation. Emma follows me to a stop in the middle of the corridor where the vending machines are. It's just the two of us here, but the silence is cut short when her already low patience level becomes nonexistent.

"What's wrong?"

There's a hint of accusation in the way she asks her question, but I shake it off. *She didn't like that I embarrassed her in front of her friends, is that it?* She crosses her arms as she watches me pull out my phone.

"Why don't you take a good look at this" — I face the screen towards her — "and tell *me* what's wrong."

She glances at the picture I opened up and it takes her a moment to register what it is. Suddenly, her face drops. I almost chuckle at her pleading eyes when I put away my phone.

"It's not what it looks like! H-He came onto me!"

"Seriously, Em? Cut the crap."

"I'm not lying! He kissed me first!" she shrieks.

"So what? Did you stop him?" She doesn't answer my question and I know my assumptions are correct. "You were kissing him back. You were into it as much as he was."

"W-We had a fight and it was a moment of weakness." She tucks a loose strand of hair behind her ear before softly murmuring, "I was drunk."

Of course she was drunk! She'd pick up any drink she could get, given the chance. Just how many times do I have to tell her to stop drinking? Who's the one that has to pick up after her?

"It was a mistake. I'm sorry. It won't happen again."

I stare at her, wishing she'd hear how stupid she sounds right now. "That's the thing, Emma. It's not supposed to happen in the first place."

"I shouldn't have done it. I'm sorry, okay?"

She's said that before. During the car ride home after I held her hair back when she was throwing up. The very first night I witnessed her drink. She was so drunk, she'd climbed up on a table to sway her hips to the music, putting on a show for everyone there. There would've been living proof if I didn't knock down a guy's phone in time. That wasn't the last time it happened. Unfortunately.

"Babe!" She sounds almost mad I'm not responding to her nor accepting her half-ass apology.

"Don't call me that." I glare at her, hoping my furrowed brow look more angry than hurt. "'Sorry' doesn't change anything. Tell me, what am I doing wrong? What is it that I don't have, that you were all over Kai last night?"

"Aiden, don't do this."

"Say it, Emma. You owe me that much."

"We've talked about this. You're too *nice*! You never *say* anything when I'm around other guys. You don't even *do* anything."

She says it like it's a no brainer. I hate it.

"Hanging out and making out are two different things!" I let out a sigh and bring down the volume a notch. "I know you hang out with other guys just to spite me. You don't think I can see through your games?"

She crosses her arms, her left eye twitching. "I wouldn't be playing games if you'd just show some feelings for once. I want to feel wanted. Be a little possessive over me. It's not that hard, Aiden!"

"Do I need to punch a guy for you to know that I'm jealous? Flip a table? Not all of us need to act out like that."

Emma jabs an accusing finger at my chest. Her nail sharp. "What you need to do is to *act* like my boyfriend! *Act* like you care about me." She takes that ridiculous finger away. "What are you so embarrassed about that you always have to hide our relationship?"

I know better than to think it was a question. It's a statement. Most of the time, she'd complain about how I avoided her kisses or attempts to sit on my lap. This is the first time she's put it into words. But she's wrong. I'm not embarrassed. I've never been. Everyone knows we're dating. What she doesn't understand is that it's uncomfortable. Everything feels wrong. Forced. Fake. Like the poses she'd made me do for the pictures she'd post. Or the answers I *should* be giving to her trap questions. Or how I'm *supposed* to react when she'd pull those stupid pranks on me.

"I never hid us. It's *you* who wants to share every single little thing with everybody else. But I don't want that. I don't want everyone to know what we do all the time. Why can't you be happy with . . . just me?"

"Grow up, Aiden. You need to get out of your comfort zone and live a little. It's called being fun."

"Maybe for you, but not for me. I don't like it."

"Oh, come on. It gets boring when you play it too safe!"

Ouch.

She knows she crossed the line because she looks away quickly. Her face softens. "Look, that's not what I—"

"You should've just told me. You could've broken it off before you decided to be with someone else."

"I don't want to be with someone else, I want to be with *you*!"

"If you did, you would've thought of that last night."

She has the audacity to throw me a look of disbelief. It makes me sick. I turn to take a step towards the exit. To my dismay, she's quick on her feet and steps in front of me. I stop myself before I walk into those filthy hands.

"Aiden, please. We can work this out."

She's begging now and I don't feel anything from the broken voice she makes. Rather, it's getting annoying. "Don't. If I can't give you what you want, then go find someone else who can. I'm sure Kai would love to continue where you two left off."

"What's *that* supposed to mean?"

"It's over, Emma." I lean down a bit. "We're done."

"A-Are your breaking up with me?" Her eyes widen.

I can't make myself any clearer than that, dammit. Walking around her, I manage to get a few steps away before she turns to me.

"Aiden, wait." Her hand grabs my arm, stopping me in my tracks.

It feels like poison. I turn my head only enough to catch a glimpse of her in my peripheral. "Don't touch me." The words come out softer than I want them to, and I curse myself for not even letting myself be what I am right now. Hurt.

"Fine." She lets go. "Don't say I didn't try in our relationship. You'll regret this."

She walks past me, not sparing me another glance before disappearing into the hallway. I stand still, running her last few sentences in my head. The sound of the push bar is faint from here, but I still hear it. Emma's back in the cafeteria. Before my brain can react, I slam my arm against the vending machine next to me. A loud bang echoes within the area.

So much for not making a scene. But it's fine. No one's here, and I don't give a damn anymore. I needed that. Warm tingles linger in my arm as I let out a long sigh. The only one who actually tried in our relationship was *me*. How dare she—

The lunch bell goes off.

You've gotta be kidding me! The timing could not be worse. Class is the last place I want to be right now. I want to be alone. I need to be. Soft echoes of talking students start to fill the hallway.

"Dammit." I run a hand through my hair. I can't be so affected by this. So *weak*. Reluctantly, I trudge out of the corridor. Just one more class.

For now, suck it up and be a man.

Holy shit! I swear it wasn't on purpose. I didn't mean to hear it. He should've walked out by now, right?

Doors. Footsteps. Chatter. Students are heading back to class. I let out a breath I didn't know I was holding and take my hand out of the vending machine. It squeaks—almost as bad as Emma when she tried to defend herself.

Crap! If only the M&Ms didn't get stuck. If only I shook the machine harder. If only it had fallen faster! Then maybe I wouldn't have had to worry about this squeaky panel thing ruining their moment. I might've made it out before they—

I shake my head. *Stop, Kayla. You still have a class to get to.* It's been a good minute since the bell rang. I'm pretty sure he isn't there anymore, but just in case, I peep out from the dead end with caution.[1]

Empty.

---

[1] See Appendix A for more details

"Thank you," I mutter as I stuff the bag of candy in my bag before speed walking to the corner of the corridor. Good. No sign of a giant with chestnut hair anywhere. One, two, three, go!

I walk out into the hall and head to class without looking back. The pounding of my heart starts to slow when I pass through the classroom doorway with two minutes to spare. Settling into my seat, I take a moment to set up my things and register what just happened. Interestingly, the whole Tracy thing seems so insignificant now. Adrenaline simmers down and worry takes over.

W-What do I do? I just witnessed my classmates' breakup! Definitely didn't see this coming. Or *hear* it coming? Maybe I should've left right after I got the M&Ms? But I couldn't just leave in the middle of their argument. That would've been so weird and awkward! Staying quiet and letting them finish was the right thing to do, I think. Even if it was, I still feel like I've wronged Aiden somehow—he made it clear he values his privacy. He was being chewed out for reasons I couldn't comprehend. I would feel bad for invading Emma's privacy as well but I don't. She was the chewer. The cheater. I don't feel like I did her too wrong. I'm not gonna expose the whole cheating thing to anyone, but why do I feel so bad about this?

Great going, Kayla. You really can't do anything right, can you? You literally didn't even have to do anything this time; just stay put and listen. I shake my head. No, stop blaming yourself. It was just an accident. They don't know about this, and they can continue living their lives without ever knowing. We can all live in peace. That's right. No one needs to know that I witnessed it. The most important thing is if . . . if Aiden's doing okay. He should've made it to his next class by—

Wait a minute. Holy crap, I can't believe I forgot! I turn to my right and look at the empty seat by the window. Of course! That makes sense. Who would want to come to class after all that? Dang it, it's the last class of our junior year. He's not really going to skip, is he? But with whatever happened moments ago? Yeah, can't say I blame him.

The bell rings and I turn my attention to the board only to catch a guy who barely makes it through the doorway on time. *Aiden.* He walks past the front of the class and into his seat. Yup. Definitely the guy who just got his heart broken ten minutes ago. He looks so sad, it makes my heart ache. Not wanting to look like a stalker, I shift my focus back to Mr. Halls. He pulls up the study guide for the history final and continues his lecture from where he left off last class. I try to focus on everything he's saying, but the words go in one ear and out the other.

A strange sensation begins to bother me. Hold on. What is this? Anger? If anyone should be angry, shouldn't it be Aiden? He's the one who got cheated on. How come I feel like I'm being wronged too?

Maybe now is a good time to acknowledge that you liked this guy.

Remember? It all began two years ago in geometry, my little crush on the Aiden James McLaren. *Seriously, are we really gonna do a flashback right now?* Yes, yes we are. Don't bother fighting because (1) we both know you're not gonna listen to this lecture—sorry, Mr.

Halls—and (2) this *is* a nice memory. I roll my eyes. *Fine, you're not wrong. Proceed on.* Thank you.

Mr. Sanders had put me in charge of collecting the papers from every row—probably because I sat at the very back of the row closest to him. Not sure why didn't he pick the first person from my row since everyone passed their papers to the front, but I'm glad he didn't. Aiden sat at the front of the furthest row, so he was my last stop. I had just collected the pile of papers from the row before his, when he got up and handed me his pile. Maybe it was because he was at the very last row, but no other person had done it. It was a small gesture, and I appreciated it nonetheless, so I thanked him.

"You have a game today?" he asked quietly, his hazel eyes noticing my game-day attire.

Taken aback, I only nodded with a polite smile. And then he did the strangest thing. *He wished me luck.*

Maybe it was his words of encouragement. His thought to even notice. The warmth in his voice. Or how he made my heart skip a beat when he flashed me a grin. It made my day. *He* made my day. For a moment, I felt seen. I felt like *I mattered*. The funny thing is, I won that tennis match. Not like I told him or anything. Never planned to. We weren't friends, and he probably wouldn't recall ever doing that in the first place. I mean, why would he?

I sigh. Oh, I remember, all right. Aiden's well-liked. Somewhat popular. Plays football. Cliché, I know. But to me, he's a big teddy bear. Strong and tough-looking, yet kind and approachable. I'm surprised a guy like him initiated a conversation with me. Wait, did that even count as a conversation? I only said two words to him—both being "thanks." He didn't seem to mind though. I grin. The guy's got these cheeks that gets chubbier when he smiles. It's cute. I get why I liked him. What's there not to like?

Well, that was before I found out he was dating Emma Costner. Felt kinda wrong crushing on a guy who was taken after that. Emma's the student council vice president and captain of the lacrosse team. She's smart, athletic, and pretty. They were perfect for each other. Or at least I'd thought they were.

Oh my god, is that it? Am I annoyed that I gave up liking him just so she could break his heart in the end? Of all things, it had to be cheating? Because she was drunk? And the worst part is—if my assumptions are right—she cheated on Aiden with Ramen Hair! That douchebag kicked a soccer ball between my legs once when I was walking. I didn't trip or fall, but that doesn't make it any less dangerous. He and his friend were too busy celebrating to even care about my safety. I wonder what Emma sees in Ramen—I mean Kai. Then again, I don't understand half the logic she was using earlier. She doesn't like that Aiden's nice? She thinks he's "boring" and "safe," yet still wants to be with him? And what did she mean by him hiding their relationship? The fact that someone like me—one of the last ones to ever hear something juicy—even knows that they're dating is a feat itself. Geez, I'm so confused. Team Aiden on this one.

Team Aiden? What the heck, Kayla! What right do you have to take sides? Okay, fine. Sorry. I don't know Emma enough to know her story. But I do know that she doesn't really acknowledge other people unless they're her friends. Speaking from personal experience, that is. When she does interact with other people like me, she's not particularly very nice either. So, there's that.

But *Aiden.* My cheek muscles work on their own. I catch myself smiling. *Stop that!* The sight of my notebook brings me back to the present. Right, we're still in class. Mr. Halls is pulling up a timeline that is definitely gonna be on the final. I'm copying it down without a question.

Okay, I might be a little biased but I have good reason to be. Aiden's nice and well-mannered. He's not a bad guy. And Emma should know she's only the main character in *her* story. Oh, and cheating is never a good thing. The sound of her pleading suddenly comes to mind. The edges of my lips curl up.

Don't! You can't be happy about this.

I don't know why *happy* was the first term that came to mind to describe what I'm feeling, because I'm definitely not happy about how it played out. All of a sudden, a tiny question creeps up in the back of my mind. Oh no. No, no, no! I push it away, trying to delete it from existence. It's no use though. It makes its way to the front headlines.

Are you sure you're not happy because he's single now?

I swallow softly and look up at Mr. Halls. The timeline's gone. He's moved on to something else. I attempt to catch up with his lecture, making a little note next to my unfinished timeline.

Don't be so selfish, Kayla. My head shakes a little. I'm not being selfish. I'm glad he's not in a bad relationship anymore. I'm glad he didn't decide to stay with a cheater. That he didn't give her a second chance. He might be sad now, but it's the right decision. This breakup can be seen as a good thing. But . . . But what?

You still like this guy.

My shoulders sink. So what if I still do? It's not like we're gonna get together just because *I* like him. That's not how it works. The feeling needs to be mutual. That's not gonna happen, so stop dreaming. Even if he so miraculously did, I'll probably ruin it somehow. I have a knack for that. Not to mention, he's not really in a place to start looking for another girlfriend right now, is he?

Coming to terms that I've won yet lost the battle, I rest my head on the palm of my left hand. Y'know, I could've enjoyed admiring him from afar for one more year if it weren't for Emma. What a waste. Aiden deserves better than that. I just hope he's okay. Extending my resting elbow on the desk, I open my angle more towards the right. In a very subtle manner, I glance through the window, at the trees outside. Ha, who am I kidding? My focus on Mother Nature instantly shifts to the boy who's literally kept me preoccupied with my thoughts this whole class.

His thick eyebrows are crinkled, empty eyes staring down at his notebook. Even from two seats away, I can tell he's not reading it. His eyes are motionless, lost in that one spot like it's the most interesting thing on earth. How long has he been like that? Skipping over his deep frown, I look down. Pencil. Hand. At least he's still taking notes. Wait. Are those white knuckles? How do you even write when you're gripping the pencil so—

Oh.

He's not writing.

He's *shaking.*

My face softens as I feel my heart ache again. I want to give him a hug right now, but that'd probably be useless and totally weird so I throw the thought away.

You're gonna be okay without her, Aiden. You'll be okay.

As if he's heard my silent message, he blinks a little; eyes finally taking a break as he puts his pencil down. He shifts in his seat, and I catch his Adam's apple bob up and down before my eyes land on someone's back. Someone in the rows between us, so it would look like I was just casually looking around. Crap, I hope he didn't see me. In my peripheral, Aiden looks to my direction, and my eyes immediately return to his. *Why, Kayla? You're not supposed to—*

Shoot! He's staring. Without thinking, I give him a soft smile—one not too wide or happy because it's really not the occasion right now.

I don't know if it's a look of recognition or surprise, but his brow unknits and that detestable frown upgrades to a straight line. His lips twitch a little and I quickly look away before I can be accused of staring. From the corner of my eye, he also looks away and picks up his pencil again. When I know for sure he isn't looking, I sneak a brief peek at him before returning my attention to the board, giddy with the result.

It was small but . . . *he was smiling.*

There's not much I know about Kayla Summers. Just that she plays tennis. The tennis courts are right outside the football field, so I see her walking by sometimes when her team finishes practice before we do. She doesn't talk much in class and seems a little on the shy side. No. Not shy. *Reserved.* I've seen her cheering for her teammates and goofing around with her friends before. We've also spoken to each other a few times in class. She's nice, I can say that much. Friendly. I may not know much about her, but there's one thing I know for sure: I didn't know smiles could be so sweet . . . until I saw *hers.*

"How you holding up?"

"I'm okay." I turn to my friend and give him a slight smile, but Nick scans me like he's doubtful. When we turn towards the parking lot, I give him a pat on the shoulder. "Seriously, don't worry about me. I'm glad it's over."

The heavy weight on my shoulders has left ever since our last class ended. It's finally summer break. I should be celebrating, not moping around. I breathe in the fresh air and let out a satisfied sigh.

Nick looks at me in bewilderment, face contorting suddenly. "What happened in history?"

I laugh. "I thought about it, Nick. It was doomed from the start."

He grins, one of his eyebrows arching up. "Let me tell you something. For someone who has nothing to offer, she expected way too much. That girl can't even take responsibility for her own actions. She's self-entitled and a total bitch."

"She's not—" I swallow. "She wasn't always like that. It's just . . . she's got a lot going on and doesn't handle stress very well."

"That doesn't excuse what she did to you, Aiden."

"I know."

We get quiet, walking past parked cars. Nick's not wrong. The cheating is unforgivable. But I think our relationship was done for, long beforehand. Things started going south six months ago, when she failed her driver's test. Emma only missed it by a point, which made the blow even harder. It was devastating. For someone who doesn't fail. She turned all that disappointment and rage onto her academic life. Studies, student council activities, managing football and lacrosse; she had to be good at everything she did. It kept her busy—feeling accomplished in some way—but I knew it took a toll on her. She'd get annoyed easily. Nagged me for "forgetting" things she never told me. Made a big fuss when I'd ask for her opinion on where she wanted to go for our date. The stress of ACTs, SATs, and college applications didn't help either. She couldn't keep up, so she took it out on partying and drinking. Eventually, it became a habit.

She got tipsy one time and tripped on some stairs, spraining her wrist. I thought it would've been a good wake-up call since lacrosse was important to her, but it seemed to have worsened it. My dislike for her drinking only caused more friction between us. She needed to "let go" and didn't like me holding her back from "having a little fun." The time we spent together gradually decreased, and when we did spend it together, it wasn't the same.

To make matters worse, her desire for perfection not only applied to herself anymore. There was me. There was winter ball. There was that look on her face when she watched a guy dip his lady and kissed her passionately. And finally, there was that look she gave me after witnessing that.

The expectation. The disappointment. The *shame.*

Maybe I wasn't smart enough to catch on to what she wanted me to be. Maybe I wasn't able to fake the way I show my feelings the way she wanted me to. But I was fed up. She'd get frustrated, but never tell me what I should've done because I "should've already known without her telling me." What I should've done was to end things there. But I'm an idiot, that's what I am.

I thought that waiting for her to get over whatever she was going through was the way for things to go back to normal. She didn't need to be all that. She was fine the way she was. No matter how many times I tried to tell her, it was no use. Waiting gradually became the new normal. Just hoping to get back the Emma I liked before all the perfect expectations. Before *not being enough*. I thought I was happy because I was with somebody I liked. And for once, Dad was finally proud of me. Dating his friend's daughter—a football fan and one of our football managers—was something he boasted about all the time. Mr. Costner did the same. But now, having spent a whole class thinking about everything, I'm not even sure if we dated to make *us* happy or *them* happy. When did it start feeling like a chore?

Nick and I come to a stop when we reach his car, and he gives me an understanding look. "I'm not gonna lie, bro. These past few months, you looked pretty miserable with her. I just didn't want to say anything."

I nod quietly. Honestly, the past half year has been emotionally exhausting. But has it really been that obvious? Did I not see how bad it had gotten until *now*—until she cheated on me?

Nick pats me on the shoulder. "She's wasn't worth it. You'll find another one in no time."

"Please, no more girls for now. I'm done."

"You never know. Plenty of fish in the sea."

I chuckle. "I'll be okay without any fish for a while."

"Fine, but never say never!"

He laughs and I can only roll my eyes when he hops into his car as I walk to mine. There was a time when I'd felt lucky Emma even looked at me. She had boys lining up for her, and when she chose me out of everyone, I thought she saw something in me. That she liked me for me. Now . . . I don't know anymore. She knew me well enough before we got together. She got into this relationship knowing what

I had to offer. Shouldn't she have known what to expect from me? What about me did she even like? What did she—

No. What's the point in wondering now?

It's over.

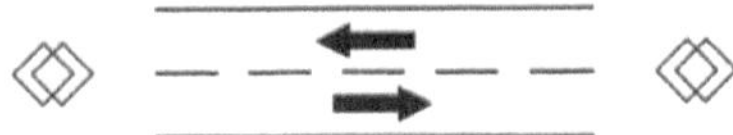

Two weeks. That's all it takes for rumors to spread like wildfire. Once they're out, they're out. Once spread, there's no way to un-spread them. Whether it's about me being the son of East Line's varsity football coach or how Emma and I got together over the summer; it's all the same. Doesn't matter if they're true or not, people eat them up.

When news got out that Emma and I broke up, it was followed by a rumor that *she* had dumped me. Word was, she didn't want to be with me because I had cheated on her. I remember how quick Nick was to relay the message to me and how he almost flipped when I didn't react the way he'd expected me to.

"You're not gonna do anything about it?"

"Nope."

He looked at me in disbelief and I smiled at my friend, shifting the gear to park and turning off the car. It was amusing. He was more affected by the rumors than I was. To be honest, I had a pretty good idea who spread the rumors. Only two people could've benefited from it—the cheater and the one she cheated with. It's only a suspicion, but I'm quite certain it was one of them. Possibly both of them. Nick didn't need to know though; he'd actually do something about it.

"But *she's* the one who cheated on *you!*" he burst out before gesturing to our three other friends who sat in the back seats. "We all know the truth!"

Evan, Luke, and Jack all expressed sounds of agreement, and I only laughed in return. "And that's what matters. I don't need anybody else," I said before turning towards them. "We playing ball or what?"

The boys could only laugh and howl before getting out of the car. That was how I got them to stop talking about the rumors. Don't get me wrong, the guys are like brothers to me. They only have good intentions, and I appreciate it. But all I want is this to blow over already. Thankfully, there isn't that much of a commotion compared to the previous rumors I've had. The end of the school year and finals week kept everyone preoccupied.

The only time I had to deal with the rumors was during summer conditioning. It was never spoken outrightly, but it was obvious the team had heard about it. There were the guys who were unaware or didn't care much about it. Some guys acted the same but lost whatever approval they had of me. I could see it in their eyes. Some got all chummy with me like I'd done something they respected. It was disgusting. It all felt too similar to when they found out who my dad was.

Tired of waiting for Nick to arrive at the gym, and not wanting to loiter with the team, I walk up the stairs to sit on one of the nearby benches. At least now, I don't need to be reminded about how they see me. But fate likes to play. I can't run from tomorrow. The very thing I'm trying to hide from comes for me. Just around the corner, one of my teammates is giving in to the rumors at the nearby water station.

Kevin's had something against me ever since the start of freshman year; when I dealt with my very first rumor. He's with his friend, Donny, who happens to be a friend of Nick's as well. They go way back. Donny and I don't talk much because of Kevin, but we're cool with each other. Even though I appreciate his words of defense in their conversation, I know better than to listen in. I pull out my phone and scroll through anything that can keep me occupied, glad I'm out of their view.

Like any other instance, I do my best to ignore it. To wait it out until it's over. To run away. After all, that's what I'm good at.

The girls and I exit the gym from the lower level. One by one, we all go on about our ways. I bid Franny and Pat a goodbye before heading towards the nearby water station to refill my empty water bottle. Pulling up, I twist open the cap as a bunch of rowdy boys head down the same staircase we'd just left from. I take a quick glance. Football guys. I turn back to mind my own business, hiding my grimace as I straighten my back, mentally dispelling all the testosterone close by. *Relax, you're okay.*

"Dude, did you hear? Emma and Aiden broke up."

My ears perk up. Not just to the taboo words that came from behind, but also because I can recognize that smooth-talker voice anywhere. Kevin Colvin! He's been in at least one of my classes since freshman year. That guy gets away with everything, whether it's arriving to class late or getting an extension for homework he *totally* "did not have the time to finish" because of his lame football excuse.

It doesn't matter who they are, Kevin is the ultimate charmer with both classmates and teachers. I don't know whether I should hate him more or admire him. I put my water bottle on the platform for the auto filler to do its job, not turning around because I know full well he isn't talking to me.

"Yeah?" His friend doesn't sound surprised. I can't pinpoint who it is right away.

"You know what that means, Donny?" Kevin is excited and doesn't wait for his friend to respond. "Emma's back on the market."

Emma's not really on my good list, but she's a fellow girl. Not some meat he can buy off the market. I roll my eyes in disgust, glad that it's my back that's facing them. The vision of Kevin wiggling his eyebrows at his friend is so vivid, I have to remind myself it's my imagination.

"Seriously?" Donny asks in disbelief, and I applaud him for his tone. "Give the girl some time to move on, bruh."

"Move on?" Kevin scoffs. "I heard she dumped him because he cheated on her. If she was with me, I'd know how to show her a good time."

My blood pressure shoots up and I do my best to grab my now-filled water bottle calmly. I twist my bottle cap, trying to keep it together and not lose myself to the disrespect. The only thing here that's keeping me in check is Donny semi-defending Aiden's honor.

"Are you sure, man? Aiden's not like that."

He sounds skeptical, and I appreciate it. Good job, Donny. That's your best line yet! Maybe I can actually leave before this conversation annoys me for the rest of the day.

"He's a damn player and you know it, Donny."

That's it.

I whip around so fast it catches the attention of both Kevin and his red-headed friend. "Excuse me," I say with bitter politeness. Cold blue eyes meet mine, and I hold my stance. "The only *player* he is, is a darn good football player. And you know it, Kevin."

Truth is, I've never watched Aiden play, so I don't know if that's exactly true. But I would assume so since Aiden has been on varsity since sophomore year. Though he's not as lean as Kevin, he's built bigger and bulkier with his own muscles. Don't even get me started with his thick arms. They can carry the weight of the world. Honestly, I think he can tackle Kevin down with no effort. Kevin's speechless for once. I'm elated by a sense of accomplishment, but I don't relish it for long. I'm not finished yet.

"I would appreciate it if you'd stop talking bad about your teammate. And quit treating Emma like she's some object you can have. Because she's not." From the corner of my eye, Donny looks like he's just seen a ghost. Quickly, his attention shifts from me to his friend.

Kevin snickers, running a hand through his hair as if whatever I just said didn't slap him in the face. "Who are you? Aiden's fangirl?"

I laugh. Fangirl? I know football is a popular sport here, but is he serious right now? My brow knits harshly from genuine confusion.

"You don't remember me? I was in your biology class in freshman year. English during sophomore. Kevin, I was also in your math class this year. The one that ended *two weeks* ago?"

He lights up as if he's recalled something until his face returns flat just as quick. "You must've been a nobody. I don't remember unimportant people."

Is he joking? Look at him act all high and mighty. If I didn't like Kevin before, I loathe him now. I don't need to be important to him, but I literally picked up his eraser one time and he even said thanks! This guy is unbelievable.

"Makes sense," I blurt out, "coming from someone as narcissistic as you. I mean, it's not like we've seen each other almost every day for the last *three years*."

A laugh escapes from Donny before he can cover it up with a cough. The dirty blond shoots daggers at the poor boy, and I'm starting to wonder how Donny even befriended this jerk in the first place. Kevin straightens himself and I tilt my head upwards to adjust for his height. "You're lucky you're a girl."

His sentence is short, but I can take a hint from that menacing voice of his. It's a threat. He wouldn't hit a girl, of course. Especially on school grounds. Neither will I. I wouldn't hit anybody. Unless for self-defense, that is. But what's so lucky about being a girl? If you look past all the double standards, sexual harassment, gender disadvantages, and all that great stuff, then maybe we're lucky? I mean, luck should be person based, not gender based. Because being a guy isn't all that lucky either. But at least they're born stronger?

They're the ones with a higher chance of fighting off robbers and kidnappers. The only thing *we* should do is *run*, or so Dad says. Except, I've always been a bad runner. So I guess I'll just stick to fighting.

No one in their right mind is gonna target Kevin. Unless they know they can overtake a five-eleven lean-yet-muscular football player, the chance is slim. He won't ever understand how safe he is. How free he is. But that's okay, I can have some fun with this.

"Yeah, you're right. I'm very lucky." I nod with self-reflection. "I've always wanted to cramp in pain and bleed every month with the possibility of ruining my favorite pair of pants."

Donny's a good sport and turns away to contain himself. Kevin's staring at me in disbelief. Maybe he's shocked by my sarcasm? Maybe he's disgusted by menstruation? I don't know, but I go on.

"I also love it when people pressure us to get married and have kids because that's our job! We're alive to bring babies like you into the world." I say each sentence with the utmost sincerity I can muster, trying to keep a straight face on while saying the most ridiculous things I've ever said in my life. Kinda cringe at this point, but hey, I'm not gonna let him pick on me.

Unlike his friend, Kevin's not impressed. "You think you're funny?"

"Sometimes." I shrug shamelessly. "But humor's in the eye of the beholder."

Steam is practically coming out of Kevin's ears. A thick silence quickly takes over. It's intense. Maybe I overdid it. Donny is back to facing us, and I don't need to see his face to know that this has gone far enough.

"Oh, look at the time!" I take a quick glance at my wrist before looking back up at the boys in front of me. "Don't wanna keep Coach P waiting, do we?"

Blue eyes glare at my empty wrist, returning to my eyes when I step aside from the water station. I turn to Donny and give him a sincere apologetic smile. "Sorry for keeping you. Please." I gesture a hand to the water fountain, hoping he'd understand that I'm also sorry he had to stand there and witness whatever was happening between his friend and me. "Good day, gentlemen."

Nodding a little, I send myself off with a two-finger salute. As I take a step backwards, Kevin follows with a step forward and his index finger pointing at me, but Donny's quick. He's instantly holding his friend back, keeping him from taking another step closer.

"Get back here, you little bitch."

"Last I checked, I'm from the human species!" I smile at how Kevin's face scrunches up.

That's not funny, I assume he'd say if Donny didn't speak up. "Calm down, Kevin. She's just kidding. Come on."

The redhead pulls his friend towards the water station. To my surprise, Kevin is actually getting dragged along. Whether it's because Kevin is letting him or not, props to Donny. He may be a few inches shorter than his friend, but he seems like he's been keeping Kevin in check his whole life. The devil himself is giving me a death stare now. I return the favor with a wink before I turn around and walk away from the scene.

What is wrong with you, Kayla? That was mean, you shouldn't have said all that! I know, but I couldn't help it. He was spreading false rumors. Trash talking Aiden! Being a misogynistic mess. He even threatened me—ish. He deserved it. Oh, *and* he called me a bitch. Ha! If that's what I am for telling the truth, so be it.

I shake my head in disapproval and walk faster. Letting myself dwell on my actions another time, I get closer to the area leading to the lower-level gym and see a figure standing there. Probably another one of the football guys. Shouldn't he be downstairs by now? Being the safety-conscious person I am, I size up my opponent, and instantly regret it. He's a big guy. I mentally curse myself when I catch his sturdy arms connected to those god-dang beautiful shoulders. Crap! If I look away now and keep walking, he'll know I didn't wanna get caught staring. But I'm already looking. Might as well go all the way now, right? He's probably not even looking anyways. My eyes finally settle on a familiar pair of hazel eyes.

Well, shit.

He's staring straight at me.

Kayla Summers. Of course it's her. Her doe eyes go wide when we make eye contact. Like a deer caught in headlights. I swallow a laugh when she quickly sends me a smile, bringing up a hand to acknowledge my existence. Without thinking, I return the gestures. She gives a little nod and looks away as I watch her speed walk towards the school entrance, disappearing behind a corner.

For a second, I don't move. She caught me by surprise. I didn't think the girl I heard talking back to Kevin, was *her.* I'd actually gotten up to take a peek from where I was at, but Kevin and Donny's bodies blocked my view of the girl. Though I didn't see her at all, I heard her. Mystery girl was very soft-spoken, but every word hit as hard as rocks. Not only did she hold her ground, she was almost intimidating. Kevin didn't stand a chance, no matter how tall he towered over her. She blew my mind.

Suddenly, there's an instinctive pull, and I follow it. I run for the entrance doors, hoping she hasn't gotten too far. Keeping a hand on the open door, I turn to my left, glad that was the first direction I chose.

"Kayla!" I call out, catching the attention of the girl walking up the incline.

She pauses for a moment before turning around to see me, her eyes blinking in surprise. "H-Hi Aiden." She clears her throat. "What's up?"

I let go of the door, taking a few steps forward so I don't have to yell. We're around ten feet apart when I stop moving closer, too afraid I'd scare her. Or maybe, vice versa. "Thanks for sticking up for me back there." I point a thumb over my shoulder. "Takes guts to talk to Kevin that way."

She looks to the side. "Oh, that's nothing you need to thank me for. I just didn't like how he was talking about you." When she meets my eyes again, there's a slight pause before she jolts a bit in panic and quickly adds, "Or Emma! You don't deserve any of that."

Strangely, the mention of my ex doesn't sour my mood this time. Maybe it's the gentle breeze or the smile that Kayla has on, but it's calming. My face softens at the girl in front of me. "I appreciate it."

Her smile widens and our eyes linger on each other's before she looks away again. Hesitantly, she steps forward, closing the distance between us. When she stops a few feet away from me, I realize we're at eye level.

"Before you go, I" — she adjusts her bag on her shoulder — "I . . ." She's itching to adjust it again, but persists to grip on the strap instead, sighing. "I have a confession to make."

It's my turn to blink in surprise now. Before my brain can form the question, she shakes her head a little.

"No, sorry!" She brings a hand up to clear up a misunderstanding. "I mean, I have something to tell you."

Her correction doesn't clarify anything, because I'm still so curious as to what this girl has to say to me. What is there for her to tell me? We barely know each— No, this can't be. I've never been confessed to before. And more importantly, why would she? *With someone like me.*

"I was there," she says abruptly. "The day you and Emma were talking near the vending machines . . . I was there."

My heart drops. I'm speechless as I try to register what she had just said. But she doesn't stop there.

"I was at the little corner area getting my M&M's, and then out of nowhere, I heard the two of you talking. My hand was in the machine and the panel thing was really squeaky. And before I knew it, things got really intense, and I didn't want to ruin the moment," she rambles rather quickly, before letting out a sigh. "So I stayed there and heard the whole thing. You could say it was a wrong-place-at-the-wrong-time kind of situation."

Flashbacks of Emma. Her insults. Her jabbing finger. My defenseless questions. *Weak.* I feel blood rushing to my face. But one look at Kayla cools the heat building up inside me. She looks flustered. Almost ashamed. I'm confused. Shouldn't *I* be the one embarrassed here? She witnessed me pour my heart out that day. All the things I said. What Emma said. The way I felt. She must think I'm—

Boring.

Too safe.

Pathetic.

"I'm really sorry," she says in a soft voice.

There's concern in her eyes. So much so, that I have to look away when I straighten my back and clear my throat. I may not have been in my best state, but I don't need anyone to pity me. I don't want it. "It's okay. You don't have to feel sorry for me."

Her eyebrows furrow and her look of disbelief turns into one of horror. "No, that's not what I meant!"

What else would she mean by—

"What I mean is . . . I witnessed you in a vulnerable moment. I'm sure anyone would've liked to have kept that private. But because I chose to stay still, I took that away from you." She speaks slowly, carefully putting her thoughts into sentences. "So for *that*, I'm sorry."

She's not sorry for me. She's sorry because she feels like she wronged me? It's like my breakup didn't concern her one bit. Even now, when I think about it, Kayla has never spoken anything *about* my relationship with Emma. Everything she's said has been neutral, if not factual. Judgement free. It's refreshing. I feel almost silly for thinking how she had thought of me earlier.

"It's none of my business, and I didn't tell anyone anything. I just wanted you to know that," she adds in to help her case.

As if there *is* a case to begin with. It's obvious she didn't tell anyone about it. The rumors would've been different from what they are now. She has no reason to lie to me. No reason to even tell me she'd heard anything at all. But here she is, telling me everything. Confessing her "crime." It's not her fault she was there at the same time I decided to bring Emma there. She didn't have to leave the area when we arrived. Even if she had, things would've been awkward. Emma and I would've been too embarrassed to finish our conversation. We probably wouldn't have broken up at that moment. The thought of staying in that relationship any longer . . . scares me.

"I don't know what to say." I'm at a loss for words, but Kayla offers me a comforting smile that somehow validates my feelings.

"You don't have to say anything. I'm telling you because you have the right to know. It wouldn't be fair if I kept that from you." She looks down and speaks her next sentence in a smaller voice. "And mostly because I feel guilty about it."

She's frowning now.

"Don't be." That comes out of nowhere, surprising the both of us.

Kayla looks back up quickly. There's a glimmer in her eyes. Like some sort of puppy.

It's kinda cute. I brush away the thought immediately, running a hand through my hair. "That's on me. I was so caught up in the moment, I didn't bother to check the area. It means a lot that you're telling me this. So, thank you."

"Thank *you*." Her pout curves upwards, and my shoulders loosen up a little. She looks away, smiling as if my words relieved her from a huge burden.

I smirk. Glad we're both on the same page now. Kayla gets a little awkward suddenly and reaches a hand to the back of her head, bringing the rest of her ponytail over the front of her shoulder. Long black hair ends around her elbow, a big contrast to the white shirt she has on. I can't put my finger on it, but there's something about the way she carries herself that makes her so easy to be around. Comfortable. This girl witnessed me in a humiliating situation, and I'm not mad about it. Not even a little.

"I don't want to be rude, but" — she shifts her feet — "don't you start conditioning after us? I don't wanna make you late."

"Right," I say but my feet don't move. That completely slipped my mind. If I head back now, I should still make it on time. She's looking at me expectantly, waiting patiently but the look on her face doesn't rush me at all. Instead, it's understanding that I have to leave abruptly. It actually makes me want to do the opposite.

Her eyes are on the darker side of brown. I only notice it now. They look almost melancholy. It makes me wish I didn't have conditioning right now. If I had more time, I'd probably ask her if she played tennis. That would be stupid because I know she does. Her shirt literally says ELH TENNIS. But I would've asked just for the sake of asking. To be here a little longer and to hear her talk about herself. Maybe she would've laughed about it and asked me if I played football—even though I'm also wearing a shirt representing our football team. But I think she'd ask anyway, just to reciprocate my question or out of courtesy. I'm sure of it.

Her kind smile never leaves her face, and I know it's time to go. Reluctantly, I raise a hand to say goodbye, but the words get caught in my throat. *Bye* sounds like I won't see her again. "It was nice talking to you"? That's not exactly false, but I'd rather talk to her about anything other than my breakup. Maybe we can some other time? My brain shoots out line after line until—*Clap!*

Kayla gets back into her position after giving me a high five. I'm stunned, and she sees it on my face. Realization hits her. "Sorry! I thought you were— That that was a— Never mind."

She's mortified and looks away with an awkward chuckle, but my eyes don't leave her. Kayla bites her lip, yet manages to keep a standard smile on to save face. I find myself grinning and trying my best to hold back a laugh when I set my hand down. *Put her out of her misery already.*

"I'll see you around?"

"Y-Yeah." She's the verge of laughing at herself before she manages to say, "See you around."

After giving me a small wave, she turns around quickly and walks off. Did she just facepalm herself? A small snicker escapes me as I see her shake her head. Before I can linger any longer, I jog towards the entrance and back to the lower-level gym.

"Where were you, bro?" Nick asks as soon as I walk up next to him. "And why are you smiling like that?"

"I was talking to someone."

He looks at me strangely and almost asks me about it but shakes it off, as if there was something else more important to address. Nick nods to the direction diagonally across from us. "You just missed it. Kevin got roasted by some girl, minutes before you came actually. I wonder who it was."

I follow his gaze and meet the sight of Kevin leaning against the wall with his phone in hand. He's scrolling through it like there's no tomorrow. Donny is at his side, entertained by his search.

Kevin pats his friend urgently, but his eyes never leave the screen. "Which class was she in again?"

"Math?"

Clicking some buttons and scrolling down some more, Kevin's thumb stops, and I stiffen. He's found her. He puts his phone away as Coach P walks by. Few by few, our team trails after him, making their way into the weight room.

"Let's go, Donny." Kevin gets off the wall and Donny follows suit, rolling his eyes. They walk by, passing us without a glance. "I've got you now, Kayla Summers."

For some reason, hearing that makes my blood boil.

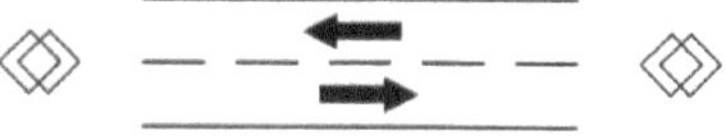

Ding! I look at the notification. Dad. Two digital tickets for a movie I've seen advertised on posters around town a month ago pop up. I look to my right and catch Dad sitting at the kitchen table, reading the newspaper.

"Something came up, your mom and I can't make it tomorrow." His eyes don't leave what he's reading. "You should go with Emma. I haven't seen you two together in a while."

I look away. Despite the rumors circulating, Dad doesn't know what had happened between Emma and me. No one from the team had said anything about the breakup or the cheating when he was around. They're all too intimidated by him. I wasn't worried about them spilling the truth. If anyone were to talk, it would been Emma herself.

She and I haven't met up since our breakup. Or since I've blocked her—to ignore her stupid texts and calls—but she's been trying to find any chance to contact me. Unfortunately, I still see her during summer training since she's one of our team managers. Ms. Perfect acts as if nothing happened. While I try to avoid her as much as possible, she'd made subtle attempts to come and talk to me. Though there hasn't been many due to time restraints, it still annoys me. It would be worse if Nick didn't step in sometimes. If the interaction was absolutely necessary, I try my best to be indifferent about it. I don't need the whole team feeling like they're walking on eggshells.

Hearing Dad's comment just now, he must've noticed something's been going on. For a moment, I want to brush it off with another *she's busy* excuse. But it's no use, I've delayed this for too long already. "We broke up."

Dad slams his newspaper on the table, causing me to look back at him. He's horrified, but suddenly, I have his full attention. "Why? She's a good girl, and I'm friends with her dad! How am I going to face Robert now?"

"You've been friends with him since high school. That shouldn't change just because we're not dating anymore." I put my phone away, watching him get up and make his way towards me.

"Well, how does it look? When my son hurt his little girl? What's he going to say about that? That I didn't raise you properly?"

His thoughtless assumptions are nothing new to me, but why does he have to take her side again? Why does it have to be my fault? Something snaps in me, and I'm on my feet in seconds, facing my father. "She's the one who hurt me! She cheated on me with some immature soccer boy."

The grimace Dad has on barely softens. "What did you do? Emma's a sweetheart. She wouldn't do that for nothing."

I grit my teeth. "I didn't do anything."

He scoffs in disapproval. "Precisely why. If she wasn't happy, it's because you didn't treat her right. You let her slip out of your hands! How many times do I have to tell you? Be a man! Take charge and chase after her. Women love that. Even if you don't mean it, if you apologize now, it might not be too—"

The telephone goes off at the perfect time. I can't stand another minute with Dad yelling at my incompetence—for lack of a better word. We're staring each other down in utter silence until he sighs, pinching the bridge of his nose. I can't believe he landed someone as great as Mom with that advice. The phone rings again. Dad furrows his brow and turns around for the phone in the kitchen.

"How can you lose to a soccer boy?" he mutters.

My fists ball up, shaking. I didn't "lose" to Kai. Nor did I lose Emma. And there's no way I'm going to go after that cheater. I don't want anything to do with her. Not after all she's done to me. "I'm not going to apologize for her mistake."

Dad stops in his tracks and turns around to look at me, repulsed.

"How you handle your friends is up to you, Dad." I grab my keys off the coffee table and give him a hard stare. "Don't drag me into it."

I turn around and walk out the room. Of course, this is how he reacts. It's always about winning and being a man. The phone goes off again. I hear Dad answer it with a raised voice and when he suddenly apologizes to the caller, I know it's Mom who's calling. She's the only person who can keep him in line. Not even my grandparents can do that.

Unlike with Dad, I'd broken the news to Mom shortly after my little conversation with Kayla—which strangely helped me feel more ready talking about it. Mom surprisingly took it very well. In fact, if I didn't know any better, I'd say she was happy about the end of my relationship. But upon hearing why it ended, however, she started throwing shade and using profanity in her sentences. It's not often Mom swears, but when she does, it's quite a thing to hear. She must've been furious. I knew she never liked Emma very much, but I never knew why until I asked her.

"All she cares about is herself," Mom had simply said.

I was confused at first, but she followed her statement shortly with her vexation of the girl. Mom shared the many times that she had to ask Emma for help on something she was obviously struggling with, instead of her offering it out of the goodness of her heart. During the times Emma had voluntarily helped Mom, it was in front of people. Better yet, in front of my dad.

"She's so fake." Mom snarled while cutting an orange. "And she parties too much."

I choked on the orange she gave me only to laugh it away. It was true. Mom had hit it on the mark. And to think she's felt this way the whole time Emma and I were a thing. Had I really been so blind till now?

"I'm proud of you. You made the right decision," Mom said. "You might not see it, but you look a lot better these days. Trust me, no one would've even known you've been through a breakup recently."

"Actually. . ." I chuckled when the image of a doe-eyed girl popped up suddenly. I gave in, telling her about how Kayla overheard everything and how she confessed out of guilt. Mom had a great laugh that day.

I smile at the memory, closing the front door behind me. Mom said she wasn't going to tell Dad anything so I could tell him when I was ready. I'll always appreciate her for being on my side. Even now, she miraculously saved me from Dad's lecture. Mother instincts *are* real.

If only Dad could be half as supportive or sympathetic as Mom. Sighing, I run a hand through my hair and walk down the front steps of the porch. Dad might be upset, but at least he knows the truth now.

I don't have to hide it anymore.

Ten minutes. I look at the time on my phone, sighing. A digit goes up. Tracy and I were supposed to meet at the lobby eleven minutes ago. Tired of standing idly waiting for her, and feeling too awkward wandering around in the hall, I texted her that I'd meet her in the movie room instead. As I slump back into my seat, a cute couple walks in from the left of the theater room and makes their way to their seats a few rows in front of me. They settle in happily and I look around. There's a group of friends sitting near the front, whispering to each other and eating popcorn. On my left, sitting in the row in front of me, there's a guy on his phone. I wonder if he's waiting on someone too. Settling my arms down on the armrests, my attention shifts to the big screen in the front of the room. Quickly, I pull out my phone and send a text.

Me

Hey, u coming? Previews r starting

Tracy

yes omw!

Ok cool

I click my phone off and feel my anxiety die down a little. She's the one who decided on the meeting time for today and she's late? Funny. Unexpectantly, my phone vibrates.

o btw

There's the typing bubble. When her message finally comes through, I'm horrified.

bringing along 2 friends

hope that's ok

cya soon!!

My eyes are ready to bulge out, but I blink back the urge, too focused on typing up a response to my friend.

No that's not ok. Y didn't u tell me sooner?

My thumb hovers over the send button, but I decide better. Delete, delete, delete. The message eventually disappears. *Don't reply, Kayla.* Remember, the whole reason why you're meeting up with her today is to redeem yourself for her crying fiasco last time. To *mend* our seemingly broken friendship. Not *end* it.

Breathe. Patience. *That message would've done nothing to help you.* Honestly, this isn't a surprise. *You should've known better.* She's always been a social butterfly. Of course she was gonna bring more people along. She did the same to our group hangout last time.

"You're my best friend!" Tracy once said in fourth grade, hooking an arm around mine.

I scoff at the sudden intrusive memory. *You're no exception, Kayla. You should know that already.* Tracy has always been the well-liked, smart, and bubbly girl that solved everyone's problems. She's energetic and athletic—having led both the basketball and volleyball teams in middle school. Students and teachers—both young and old—she befriended them all. Even boys from the upper grades liked her. It was kinda weird yet kinda amazing, because it was obvious they liked her for her outgoing personality.

Maybe it was because she was the youngest in our class—being born a year later—or maybe it just came natural to her, but she never really had any trouble getting people to like her. Everyone just seemed so comfortable with her. Myself included. Not that *that* matters anymore. We don't talk as often as we used to. Then again, I never went out much or stayed after school for anything unless it was absolutely necessary. The only times we talked were at school, during recess or lunch. And that was when Tracy wasn't too busy playing basketball with the boys. She'd be back for me by the end of the break though, barely managing to get a few words in before it was school time again. I liked to think that I was something similar to a *home base.* And that was okay because she was someone I could turn to since she always seemed to know her way around everything. She made me feel okay when school and extracurricular activities got overwhelming and confusing. As much as I hate to admit, *I relied on her.*

But high school was a slap in the face and a good wake-up call. I was overjoyed when I learned we were attending East Line together. I thought it was gonna be another four years with my best gal, but I was wrong. Freshman orientation showed me just how little I knew. I remember sitting in a table uncomfortably, surrounded by a bunch of other students talking to each other. Everyone seemed like they knew one another while I practically knew no one. It was intimidating, to say the least. Tracy was one of the very few—including myself—from our middle school that went to East Line. But she was too busy talking to some guy I'd never seen in my life. Some other guys recognized her and quickly came to greet her. Everything seemed to unfold as I watched in silence, among the rowdy students in the cafeteria. Just how many friends did she have? That day, even though it was obvious I was uncomfortable and alone, she barely made time for me.

She didn't go back to her home base.

It was only during one of those final stupid freshman-orientation-break-the-ice exercises, we were finally close to each other and partnered up. I wouldn't have seen it coming when I noticed her attention was everywhere other than me. *Dead weight*. That's what I was. A *burden* she had to entertain. The bored expression on her face told me all I needed to know: she wanted to do the exercise with anyone other than me. I guess I was just convenient for always being there, but inconvenient when it tied her down. Holy crap! *Had it always been like that?*

"Hey, sorry I'm late," someone whispers from my left, cutting my train of thought.

I turn towards the voice and immediately see Tracy sitting in the seat next to mine. Like a switch, I put on a small smile and assure her that it's okay. I catch a glimpse of the two friends she's brought with her. *Why couldn't she at least bring girls? This is so weird!*

"That's Fred and Derek," she whispers to me.

Nodding, I lean out a little of my seat so they can see me better and bring up a hand to greet them with a whisper. "Hi!"

Fred and Derek don't respond, too busy on their phones. I could almost feel a blood vessel pop, but I don't let it happen when I lean back into my seat. It's okay. *They probably didn't hear you. You could've repeated yourself, but you didn't because it's too much of a hassle if they didn't hear you again.* One of my eyebrows twitch. Sure, but they could've and probably should've said hi too. I'm pretty sure that's basic manners, right?

Sighing quietly, my eyes return to the screen as they air their probably-fourth trailer. I try to enjoy what's showing but I can't. This was supposed to be a one-on-one hangout. Why did she bring these boys here? This isn't a double date. I don't even know them. And they look like babies! Oh my god, please don't tell me they're freshmen. I- Is that what she's into? Knowing Tracy, anything's a possibility. I take a glimpse at my friend who's leaning towards Fred and whispering something into his ear. He nods and she giggles softly. I don't even wanna ask. Thankful that none of the boys sat next to me, I rule out the double date theory. *You might be safe for now, but nothing's guaranteed after the movie.* I shake my head. Maybe I'm overthinking this. There's no way she's trying to set me up. She would've asked beforehand, wouldn't she? Who am I kidding? She didn't even ask about bringing Fred and Derek here in the first place!

My head turns to glance at Tracy, who's leaning over Fred to whisper something to Derek this time. Somehow, I'm not even surprised anymore. *This isn't gonna change, is it?* No matter how many times we meet up, things aren't the same as they used to be. Tracy's changed throughout the years. But so have I. The old Kayla would've stuck with this, clinging on desperately to the thought of being a good friend. But I know better now. Even though it's just a casual hangout at the movies, she shouldn't have brought them. It was uncalled for. She should've asked me if it was okay ahead of time, not ten minutes prior. It makes no sense. They aren't from our grade and they're probably not even from our school! Last time was okay because Franny and Pat were there. But not this time. I'm not going to stay here and go through something I know I'm going to hate. I can't do it.

I won't.

Tracy's attention shifts back to the screen, and my eyes dart there as well. Must be the last trailer now. *Now or never, Kayla. I don't care what you have to do, just get out of here.* Quickly leaning towards her, I bring a hand to cover a side of my mouth as I whisper into her ear. Something about me not feeling well. She leans away to look at me in sympathy. Just then, the screen goes black. The room darkens.

"Sorry, Trace. I gotta go," I whisper to her. Before she gets to say anything, I quietly get up and send a small goodbye wave to the three of them. Tracy waves back with a pout, and surprisingly, Fred and Derek finally notice me. Fred brings up a hand to say bye and Derek looks at me confused. I turn around, walking down the stairs and out the room as the opening credits roll.

A comfortable silence takes over me as I stride along the empty hall and make a turn to another hallway towards the escalators. I could take one down and leave the building, but I don't. I did not go out of the house today just to go back without doing anything worthwhile. So instead, I sit on a nearby bench, just a short distance away from the end of the hallway. Occasionally swinging my legs, I let it all sink in.

I might be a terrible friend for lying to her. But still, why did she have to bring those boys to our hangout? Am I not fun enough for her? My eyes loom over the eccentric scratch patterns of the purple carpet. Maybe it's finally time to admit it. I was never her bestie. Only a friend. Someone she could go to when she had nobody better to hang out with. I let out a bitter laugh. It's never gonna be like how it used to be, is it? I used to feel happy when I was with her but now, it's just bitter and heavy.

I sigh. It's not that I hate being around Tracy. She's fine as a person. It's just frustrating to think that this is what our friendship really was to her. It's annoying that I was the one who thought different. She probably doesn't even know it. And it's not something I can end either. I've known her for almost twelve years. Am I really gonna pour it all down the drain just because I didn't know any better? I pout, relaxing my shoulders when I lean my hands on the bench to support my weight. When it's not meant to be, it's not meant to be. I shouldn't fight it because things happen for a reason. Right?

"Hey, stranger."

A raspy voice takes me by surprise and I finally register the white kicks on the carpet in front of me. I lift my head up, meeting a face I wasn't ready to see so soon again.

Her innocent eyes look up at me and I can't help but grin at her surprise.

"H-Hi, what are you doing here?" She looks away quickly when a sudden grimace takes over her face. Her eyes are back on me when she lets out an awkward laugh. "Sorry, you're obviously here to watch a movie. Don't answer that. I mean . . . hi!"

"Hi," I say back, grinning even wider than before.

Kayla automatically utters another *hi* before turning away in embarrassment. She looks like she's seconds away from giving herself another facepalm. I try my best to hold in my laughter when I take a seat next to her, glad I took Nick's advice and went to the movies today.

"I was heading there but had to grab some sweets on the way." I hold up a Crunch chocolate bar as my head gestures to the direction of the escalators. "I was about to go up, but then I saw you."

Kayla stares at me with an unreadable expression.

Just a minute ago, she'd been sitting here all alone with such a sad look on her face. I can't figure her out. But at least now, she doesn't look so down anymore. *I'm glad.* "Something on your mind?"

Her lips press into a thin line before she turns away, her gaze returning to the carpet. This is the first time I've seen her look so glum. *Why did I ask her that?* I look at the carpet too, hoping the gesture will give her some space. "Sorry. You don't have to tell me if you don't want to."

"No, it's okay actually," she says rather quickly. She's so earnest. I can tell by the tone of her voice that she didn't want me to feel bad about it. "It's just silly . . . and kinda embarrassing."

"I know a thing or two about embarrassing."

Our eyes connect with a zing of recognition. We're both thinking about the same thing—the little incident regarding my breakup. She looks away, breaking into a chuckle, and I feel my shoulders relax.

As if thinking carefully on how to explain her story, she starts off slowly. "I was meeting my friend on a one-on-one today. But at the last minute, she brought along two guy friends I don't even know." She swallows—as if recalling the event—before she turns to me shyly. "It made me feel *uncomfortable*, y'know?"

My heart tightens, grateful for how vulnerable she's willing to be with me. Yet, there's a sense of anger inside.

Anger for her.

Anger for me.

I completely understand what she's talking about. Being put into an uncomfortable position is never a fun thing. Unwanted memories of Emma and feelings I've longed to forget cross my mind, but they vanish immediately when Kayla laughs dryly.

She stares into the far distance, lost in thought. "I've known her since we were five. Friends drift apart sometimes, I get it. But I was there to hang with her, not her and her other friends."

There's hurt in her voice, but there's also acceptance. I catch my lips from hooking upwards. *Her self-regard is very admirable.*

"So, I made up an excuse and left. I lied and ditched her," she admits shamefully, finally looking me in the eyes. "I'm a horrible friend."

"You're not." My almost immediate retort takes her by surprise, and my brow furrows at the thought of her truly believing that. "I tend to worry about maintaining the relationship, that I never really thought about how I felt." I recall all the mixed emotions I've felt from recent situations with a certain blonde. "It's hard always being the one that steps back. That's not how it works. Relationships are complicated. They're . . ." I look away, trying to find the word I'm searching for. It doesn't come to me and I'm about to give up when Kayla's gentle voice breaks the silence.

"A two-way street?"

I look at her, almost excited. "Exactly. You stepped away instead of stepping back today. You're able to respect yourself and your feelings. I respect you for that."

She blinks as if she's never thought about it that way. *Funny, she's like an open book.*

"Thanks. Me too." Her sweet smile is back and I mirror it. "Um, I mean I respect you too for respecting me . . . for respecting myself . . . for that?" She looks at me, doubtful, either not knowing if that made any sense or if I even understood her.

"Thanks," I simply say, wondering if she confused herself with that one.

Dark brown eyes hold mine for a few seconds before Kayla bursts into a soft laugh. It's contagious. I find myself joining her. It all ends too quickly when she clears her throat to collect herself.

"Sorry, you should probably head back to your movie," she says with a jolly expression. "I don't want to make you late, listening to me rant about my problems and all."

"Not at all, there's still time." It looks like my effort to put her worries at ease works when I notice her lean against the wall for support. *I actually like listening to you rant about your problems,* I almost say but bite my tongue before it gets the better of me. She looks like she's in a better mood now and my heart warms at her look of relief. An idea forms in my head, and I like it so much I don't think twice before blurting it out. "I have an extra ticket." She looks at me with curiosity but doesn't ask me anything. Only waits for me to go on. "It's a long story." I say, not wanting to dive into the conversation I had with Dad or the fact that Nick couldn't make it today. "If you're okay with it, do you want to join me?"

"Me?" She points to herself.

For the second time today, I've caught her by surprise. I break into a smile at her bewilderment. It makes me feel accomplished. Yet, saddened in some way.

It doesn't take much to amaze her, it seems.

"Yeah, you. Who else am I asking?"

She looks to her left then to her right. I follow suit and see nothing but an empty hallway. It's just the two of us here.

"Right," the girl mumbles quietly, slightly pouting in embarrassment. She takes a good moment to think about it carefully, and I start having doubts.

It gets boring when you play it too safe!

Emma's words replay in my head, and I let it get the better of me. She turned me down almost every time I asked her out to something. Is that why she'd always rather do something else—something only she enjoyed? Due to a lack of interest? And that was when she was my girlfriend. What makes me think Kayla—a classmate—would even agree to it? Swallowing hard, I prepare myself for a rejection. But before I can get consumed by regret, Kayla flashes me an excited grin, lifting all the heavy weight away.

"I would love to."

Her voice is sweet and gentle. It's music to my ears. Maybe it's the lighting, but I think her eyes twinkled a bit. I bite back from smiling any wider. "Then let's go," I say, before she can change her mind.

We get up together and walk towards the escalators. This is my first time walking side by side with her. She's a whole head shorter than me, barely reaching my shoulders. *I wonder if it's her height that makes her look so harmless and cute.* I scrap that thought immediately. Emma's only an inch or two taller, but there was nothing harmless about her. We step onto the escalator and my body moves on its own. From next to her, I stand on the stair below hers and set a foot on the one that she's on when I lean against the rail. I stiffen.

Old habits never die, huh?

Instead of shifting positions, I let it be. Emma never understood why I did this. She never asked. But the answer's simple: I like to look at the person I'm talking to. As for the foot on the same stair, it's so she won't feel left out.

Kayla turns to her left, looking over my stance before meeting me at eye level.

Recognition.

Well, this is a first. Maybe even gratitude starts to show through her shy smile.

"Can I ask you something?" she speaks carefully.

"Shoot."

"Are you really okay doing this?"

"Doing what?"

"Having me join you? We barely know each other and I also, y'know," she hesitates before whispering, "overheard the *thing*." Her focus shifts to the escalator step in front of us. "It's not weird for you, is it?"

"Not really."

"Oh, okay." She keeps her gaze down when we get off the escalator and take a turn to step onto another one heading up.

I don't know why, but something about her expression makes me correct myself. "Okay, yeah. It is kind of weird. What's also weird is" — I rub the back of my neck — "I don't mind that you heard everything."

Kayla looks at me like I'm crazy. I don't blame her. *I sound pretty crazy.* "It's kind of nice having someone know the truth without needing to tell them. A few people know what happened, but none of them were actually there to witness the words she said or the way I felt. As strange as it sounds, you make it feel less . . . alone."

She's holding my eye contact with a careful yet understanding look. Her expression's soft. I want to tell her more, but when we reach the end of the escalator, it brings me back to reality.

"It feels like you're on my side." I clear my throat before I spill out any other weak words. "So, about your question, I wouldn't have asked you to join me if I wasn't okay with it."

"Oh, okay."

They're the same words she'd uttered a moment ago, but it's different this time. Her tone. That smile she has on her face. A soft shade of pink takes over her cheeks. I look away, proud that I came clean to her. I'm glad she knows how I think of her, regarding this situation. *Did she ask because she still felt guilty about it? That I'd hold her accountable?* I'm about to ask her until I realize we're a few steps away from the ticket collector. We enter the theater room and settle into our seats.

Not a second later, Kayla leans in close to whisper, looking all excited. "So, what are we watching?"

Suddenly, I don't remember what I was supposed to ask her anymore. I whisper back, worrying a bit when she says she's never heard of the movie before. *What if she doesn't like it?* I should've thought this out more carefully. As if she read my mind, she shrugs casually like it didn't matter. Her hand signals an okay then a thumbs-up before she shifts her attention to the screen with a smile, just happy to be here. The trailers start going off, and we don't talk for the rest of it. It's a rather comfortable silence between us. Almost as if we were friends before this.

Action comedies aren't what I normally watch. All I have to say about it so far is that it's campy. Absurd. We're probably a quarter into the movie when things take a turn. To my surprise, it gets even more ridiculous but I'm eager to find out what happens next. I look to my right and see Kayla giggling at something the main character says. A warm wave of relief washes over me. *She's enjoying it.*

Peeling back the wrapper from my chocolate bar, I offer her some. My hand movement catches her eye and she looks back at me, almost hesitant. I give her a nod, hoping she'd take some. Smiling, she mouths a thanks before reaching for a square of the bar. Something sparks inside me. In a subtle manner, I shift my wrist a little to the side.

Her hand misses the bar. Barely. She blinks in confusion, and I can't help but grin. *This girl has too much faith in me. Did she not suspect me at all?* She goes for the bar again. I flick my wrist forward this time. Her pinch misses it by a little, grabbing nothing but thin air. Kayla turns to me in shock, and upon seeing my face, grins back. She knows

I'm messing with her. Rolling her eyes, she puts a hand on mine to hold it in place, shifts it upright, and—with her other hand—swiftly breaks a piece of chocolate before retracting away.

Her touch was quick. Short. Still, I can't forget the feeling of it. She was colder than me. But somehow, she felt warm on my skin. It wasn't forceful. Just soft. Kind. In some way, it was almost . . . pleasant. I didn't hate it. Not at all.

Kayla flashes me a wider grin before stuffing the whole square of chocolate in her mouth. Her attention shifts back to the screen as she chews happily. She's so engaged in the movie, her chewing slows down. Until she stops. Her brow furrows. The fight scene finishes up and the film's main character says something cheesy. Kayla giggles. Then—as if she'd just remembered the chocolate in her mouth—she continues to chew. She's so absorbed in the moment. She doesn't notice me staring. Nor my smirk.

I didn't know someone could look so content next to me. It's at this moment—with this classmate I barely know—that I realize something.

I like being around this person.

In a blink of an eye, senior year started. I was all excited because that meant a new tennis season. Not only that, but a new school year meant seeing Aiden again. That unintentional and *totally* platonic date with him at the theater had me all excited for the new school year. I wanted to see him again. Maybe pass by him in the hallway. I was happy to just say hi. But I got lucky, he sits right behind me in precalculus! I never appreciated assigned seats as much as I do now. Bless your soul, Mr. Cadman.

The first two weeks went by relatively quickly. Things were busy, we never got to talking much aside from greeting each other from time to time.

I sigh. The sound gets drowned out by all the other students, staff, and family leaving the gymnasium. The fall sports meeting finally wrapped up and most of them are heading out or helping themselves to the free food at the cafeteria. I walk alongside Franny and Pat when we leave the gym.

It finally dawns on me that I never got the chance to tell Aiden I had fun that day. *Can I tell him that? Or is it too late to say it now? Hold on, should I even tell him?* It's not weird to thank someone. Yeah! I mean, the guy treated me to lunch after the movie and no matter how much he insisted that *he* was the one who asked me to join him, it's only right to treat him back. Right? *That's not an excuse to hang out with him again, is it?* No, I don't think so. That's pretty legit, actually. I should probably ask him sometime. However it happens, I hope he agrees to it.

"Guess who's going to hang out with Alek now?"

Franny's excited voice pulls me back to reality. I'm suddenly intrigued. She's mentioned she's had a crush on a guy named Alek for some time now. I ask just to confirm when we walk down the stairs. "Alek from photography club? The guy who transferred here last year?"

"Yep!"

Pat gives Franny a knowing look. "Did you finally introduce yourself to him like you said you would?"

"Uh . . . no. But Tracy knows him through a mutual friend. She said she'll help set me up with him."

My ears perk up at the mention of Tracy, and flashbacks of her wild love life in middle school floods my brain. Tracy . . . being a wingwoman? *Ha! I don't think so.* My neck does a little twitch involuntarily.

"That's a start," Pat says, taking what she can get.

We've reached the end of the stairs and enter the hallway near the cafeteria when a honey voice pops in from the side. "Hey, guys!"

Speak of the devil. I turn to the all too familiar, perfect girl next door. She's wearing a pair of leggings and a loose long-sleeve that is almost short enough to count as a crop top. Tracy's style usually leans more on the loose tomboyish side, so it's a little different seeing her wear something that hugs her figure. Or at least the bottom half. Maybe it's because I haven't seen her outside of school often enough or something, but I take note that she's dressing more feminine now. Come to think of it, she'd worn a pink top at the theater that day. *Huh, that's funny. She once said pink was too girly, that she would never wear something like that. Time does change people.*

Both Franny and Pat greet the girl excitedly, but I barely manage to say a "Sup." *Yeah, I'm still bitter about the theater incident.*

"You ready?" Tracy turns to Franny. "Alek's waiting over there. He's in the beanie."

She turns to point in the direction of two guys loitering around the front entrance, just a little farther ahead of us. I spot the guy in the beanie and try to store him in my memory. Alek's tall. So tall, he stands above the crowd. Even from my angle, I get a good look at his face. He's got a long one with feminine features. On the thinner side. A soft boy. Strangely enough, this guy looks a lot like what Tracy would go for. Some of her exes also had similar vibes. If I didn't know she was playing wingwoman, I would've thought *she was seeing Alek herself.* I shake my head. *You're overthinking this, Kayla. Franny once mentioned she liked pretty boys too.* Right, my bad. That market is a big one.

"Who's that with him?" Franny's question makes me shift my focus to the other guy standing next to Alek.

"Just a friend. Alek wanted to bring him along because he thought it would be awkward if it was just him and two girls," Tracy says without much thought.

I understand the awkwardness on Alek's end but still find it kinda weird that Tracy's tagging along when she's the wingwoman. *Do wingwomen usually go on the date too or just make the date happen?* Franny tries her best but doesn't do a good job hiding her disappointment. *Oh? I guess she wasn't expecting Tracy to tag along either.* This supposed-date-turned-third-wheeling just became a double date. Suddenly remembering the theater incident, I look away and do my best to not gag in front of them. From the corner of my eye, Pat's very amused by all the drama enfolding in front of her. *Bet we're both wondering how this is gonna play out.*

"Let him get to know you better! I'm sure there'll be a chance for some alone time."

So she knows the point of a date and what being a wingwoman means. I wonder if this is all part of the plan then. Maybe during their group date, Tracy will hype Franny up with compliments and step aside with the friend, so that Alek and Franny would be able to get closer? Not my area of expertise, but that sounds about right. Franny nods, feeling a little better by her words.

"Okay, let's get going. The cafe is about to open!" Tracy says happily, turning around and leading the way towards Alek and his friend.

Franny bids a goodbye and Pat follows them out as she's going that direction too. I give them a wave before heading towards the cafeteria. Heck yeah! I manage to snag the last two double chocolate white chocolate chip cookies from the sweets section. Leaving the cafeteria, I take a turn to a less crowded hallway, only to come across a sign advertising the lantern festival that's coming up soon. I pause, taking my time reading it. *Did Aunt Gwen say that she was going to perform in the lantern festival this year?* Geez, I never remember these things.

"Hold it right there, Summers."

The voice comes from behind me, and I roll my eyes. *What is he talking about? I'm not even moving.* "Kevin." I turn around to face the culprit knowingly. "To what do I owe the pleasure?"

"That's my cookie you took over there." With his chin, he points toward the chocolate pastries I'm holding before sighing. "Of course it had to be you of all people."

"It's first come, first served, Colvin."

"Don't call me that."

"Oh, don't be a hypocrite," I respond too fast, completely forgetting to play nice.

He's glaring, huffing in irritation, and I start to feel bad. Why? I don't know. But I understand the frustration of wanting something so badly only for someone else to take it before you, all because of bad timing. Also—I'll admit—I hadn't exactly been nice to Kevin during the whole water fountain situation. Then again, he never really gave me a reason to. It might've felt justifiable at the time, but I never felt good about hurting people's feelings. Giving in to my own conscience, I sigh. "Okay, fine. You can have one if you want. I didn't touch it yet." I wrap a cookie with an extra napkin and offer it to him. "Here."

Instead of being grateful, he sneers. His arms cross. One of his eyebrows raise. "What? This a peace offering? After that note you gave me?"

Ah, yes. The note. My response to his little joke of a note I found in my locker some time ago, reading:

Watch out Kayla

Summer's over

-Kevin

His warning didn't go unanswered. I wrote a little something back on the bottom half of the piece of paper saying:

Cuz it's FALL NOW Kevin

<3 your favorite season

P.S. congrats, you finally know my name

I remember stalking him one day to find out where his locker was, just so I could slip him my masterpiece of a pun. Too bad I never got to see his reaction to the little gift I left him. He must've been furious. He probably crumpled up the paper and threw it on the floor. A little chuckle escapes me.

"I liked your pun, couldn't help but respond with another one." I shrug and move the hand offering the cookie to him. "Anyway, do you want this?"

"First you insult me, then you challenge me, and now you're offering me a cookie?" He scrunches his face and looks away. "I don't get you."

"Well, if you're mean to me, then I'll be mean to you. If not, then I'm gonna try to be nice," I say before mumbling something about the golden rule. He looks away, rolling his eyes. *Like he doesn't even believe me.* I hold myself back and move the cookie in front of him to catch his attention. "You gonna take the cookie or not? My arm is getting tired."

"Yeah, gimme that." He snatches it a little too rough for my liking.

I don't say anything about it because it's too much trouble. I just want him to leave.

He takes a bite of the cookie, speaking in a softer tone now. "You say that, but what did I ever do to insult you?"

An instant comes to mind. He was able to get his quiz postponed to the next week with his football excuse, yet the very same teacher wouldn't grant me a one-day homework extension with my tennis excuse. My blood boils. Kevin chews on the cookie as he looks away into the distance. Glaring and sneering like he hated being here; talking to me. I want to tell him it's unfair. That he's so lucky to have everything work out for him. But I can't say anything. The more I think of how to put it in words, the more it doesn't make sense. *Why?* Aside from the water fountain incident and his note, I can't recall a time when he *actually* insulted me. *Come on, think! There must've been a time he—*

It finally hits me. It's not Kevin's fault he knows how to use his personality to his advantage. And if it's in the classroom, it should've been the teacher's fault for playing favorites. *Have I been bias against Kevin without me knowing? Have I been blaming him this whole time when I should've blamed the teachers instead? Or have I just been blinded by jealousy?* Crap, I've made a big mistake. I shouldn't have said the things I said to him at the water fountain that day. Even though they're kinda true, I could've just left it there when I told him to stop talking about Emma and Aiden. Ugh! *Why am I so stupid?* I should apologize. I mean I *need* to apologize! As I open my mouth to begin an apology, Kevin turns to me with a pointed finger.

"This isn't over, Summers."

Well, there goes my chance. I sigh. "It never is," I mumble jokingly.

He turns around and starts walking away. Guess I'll have to catch him at another time. It's probably for the better. I need to let this sink in and give him the proper apology he deserves. Suddenly, he pauses and turns just enough so I can see the side of his face. "Thanks . . . for the cookie."

With that, he walks off, not sparing me another glance. Like he hasn't said anything at all. I'm frozen in place, still shaken from the fact that I've done him wrong and that he actually thanked me for the cookie.

Munching on my cookie, I shift my feet a little and turn back to the poster. *Seriously, Kayla? You're always going on about being good and doing the right thing, but look at how unfairly you treated Kevin just because you're bitter about the influence he has on people! Shame on you.*

My shoulders slump, and I immediately straighten my back, trying to correct my posture. It feels a little better, but I can still feel it. The guilt is heavy.

"Congrats. I knew you'd make it into varsity."

The low voice comes from behind me, and I recognize it too well to turn around. We briefly talked about it being my last year making varsity when he treated me to lunch that day. *I can't believe he remembered.* Swallowing down my bite of cookie, I give him a reply without looking back at him. "Thanks. And I knew you'd make it again."

He pulls up on my right, standing next to me with his body facing the wall and hands in his pockets. Like me, he's got his eyes on the lantern poster.

"It's not a big deal." He shrugs. "I've been on varsity for the last two years. It's pretty much expected."

In no way did his last statement sound cocky. Not like, it's pretty much expected he'd be on varsity because he's so good. No. Rather, he said it in a kinda dejected way. Like it's pretty much expected he'd be on varsity because he *had* to be on varsity. It's the tone someone uses when they're carrying the weight of expectation and trying to live up to it. Something I can resonate with. I wonder what Aiden's going through right now. *Don't assume anything, Kayla. You think too much.* But what if? It won't hurt to say something, just in case.

"Hey, you know what they say." I turn a little to look at him. "Getting to the top is hard, but staying there is a lot harder. Or something along those lines." I give him an encouraging smile before taking another bite of my cookie.

He blinks, deep in thought, before a small smile comes across his face. "Yeah, you're right." He stares at the poster blankly. "I guess some people tend to forget that."

Aiden must've been referring to the person whose expectations he's trying to live up to. But taking a look at his semi-surprised face, I think there's another person who's forgotten too. "Yourself included?"

He takes a moment before facing me again with a gentle smile. "That obvious, huh?"

It's my turn to shrug. "We're a little too hard on ourselves sometimes." That came out way sadder than I'd expected it to, but I don't regret it when Aiden's expression softens. As if we planned it, we both shift our attention to the poster at the same time. For probably my fifth time today, I skim the poster again, staying quiet so that he can take his time to read it. If he was reading it.

"So," he begins out of nowhere, "are you going to the lantern festival?"

"Maybe? I think my aunt is performing there. Are you?" I clear my throat. "Going I mean, not performing."

Seriously, Kayla? Of course you meant going! Why would he be performing? I put the last bite of cookie in my mouth to play it cool.

He gets a little quiet, as if he's thinking long and hard about an answer.

Crap.

Whatever it is, please don't think I sound stupid or anything.

Chapter 10
Aiden

I went to the lantern festival once, with Nick and Luke a couple years back. We played a few of the game booths, ate some food. It was pretty fun until Luke got bored and wanted to go the arcade instead. Nick could never refuse the arcade, and I didn't mind as long as I was with them. So having only spent an hour there, we left the festival early and met up with Evan and Jack at the arcade. We stayed a good three hours until we were finally satisfied with beating *Zombies, Aliens, and Dinosaurs* with the highest score on the game system. After that, we made it a tradition to visit the arcade every lantern festival to try and rank another high score.

The town festivals and holiday special events consisted of mainly carnival games—something I prefer over arcade games, but only by a little bit. Of course, I never told the guys that. It's not that big of a difference to me. But standing here next to Kayla, looking at this festive poster, it seems like my preference is more apparent than I remember. The idea of playing games and eating with her sounds fun.

I'll go if you go.

W-Why did I think that? What about the ZAD tradition? Deep down, I know that the guys wouldn't mind if I skipped out. Especially if it's because of a girl. After the whole Emma thing, they'd probably even urge me to go. I clear my throat and settle with, "Maybe."

It's the first word I can think of, so I sounded a little unsure of myself. Thankfully, Kayla doesn't catch my dilemma and nods at my response, probably thinking I haven't decided about going yet. There's a pause of silence. *What's the point of wondering?* If I *were* to go, that doesn't mean she's going to go *too.* Just because she agreed to watch a movie with me last time, doesn't mean she'd agree to go with me this time. *If* I were to ask her. There's a slim chance she'll agree, a higher chance she won't. *It's like dealing with Emma all over again. Except this time, I've learned.* The decision sinks in; ZAD tradition it is. The brothers would be proud, hopefully.

"Hey, I know this is out of the blue, and a few weeks late, but I never got to thank you for that day." Kayla's looking down at the floor, fingers fiddling. "For listening to me and being so understanding. I had a fun time."

Did she mean the day at the theater? I almost laugh at how silly she is for thanking me when it was *her* who lifted my spirits up that day. If it weren't for Kayla, I think I'd still be as miserable as I was when I finally told Dad about my breakup.

"And you probably know this already, but I'm gonna say it anyway." She turns to face me with an angelic smile. "You're really cool."

Her words catch me by surprise. My heart stops for a second. *Did I hear that correctly? Did she just say I was cool?* I'm hit by a wave of happiness and I don't know what to do but stare at her. I don't think I would know how to respond if I didn't catch sight of a few chocolate crumbs on the side of her chin. *That must've been from the cookie she was eating earlier.* I want to thank her for her praise, but the sight of those cookie crumbs on her innocent and oblivious face is just too damn funny. Suddenly, I look away and start chuckling. This is not how I planned on responding to her nice words. But I can't help it.

Kayla looks concerned, pouting in confusion. "What? What's so funny? I'm being serious!" She whines like she's mad but that smile on her face says otherwise. Like she wants in on the fun.

It's cute and I want to keep her in the dark a little longer, but I know better than to make her hate me for it. It doesn't matter anymore because when I look back at this moment, I can remember her cookie face clearly.

"Sorry, it's just—" I purse my lips to stifle another laugh and look at her carefully. Her puppy-like expression sends me turning away again and I give it everything to force out my words. "You . . . You've got some cookie on your face." I cover my mouth to keep my composure.

She's horrified, eyes bulging out like a cartoon character. "Oh my god, where?"

Her flustered look makes me feel a little guilty and I clear my throat to be serious for once. Unable to keep myself from smiling, I look at her and run a thumb over the right side of my chin. "The right," I say, signaling the very same spot on her face.

Kayla hastily brushes the other side of her face with the napkin in her hand before asking in a hopeful voice, "Did I get it?"

"No, I said the right." I grit my teeth with a big grin when I show her my demonstration again. *If she doesn't get this, I might just burst.* "The right side," I say firmly, but it's not very good as we both can hear I'm at my limit.

Kayla wipes the same spot again in a small but fast manner. Like a squirrel cleaning itself. Panicky. "This *is* my right side!"

I freeze, eyes widening. "Sorry! I meant *my* right." Unintentionally, I start to snicker.

She flashes me a playful glare, wiping the cookie crumbs off successfully this time and I give her a thumbs-up to put her mind at ease. As I'm having the time of my life burning off calories over here, Kayla huffs out in frustration and facepalms herself. "Please delete that from your brain."

"Never."

She looks away, grimacing. *I think I'm enjoying her mortification more than I should.*

"Ugh, this is so embarrassing," she groans, rubbing her head.

I don't know what comes over me, but all the constant holding back on the laughing did it. The string snaps. My laughter turns up a notch. I can't even control it at this point. With her arms crossed,

Kayla looks at me, unamused. Some seconds go by, and when I don't show any signs of stopping, her angry pout curves into an embarrassed smile.

"Stop laughing!" She elbows my arm with a light push as she chuckles a bit herself. "I was giving you a compliment too!"

"Alright, alright. I'll stop." Putting my hands up in the air to surrender, the giggles finally seem to be coming down. I clear my throat a few times to make sure I stop efficiently. To my dismay, I end up coughing out a few more snickers before they finally stop.

Kayla doesn't seem to mind it when she huffs out another time and turns her attention to anywhere but me, mumbling a thank you.

Clearing my throat for the last time, I put a fist against my mouth to make sure the snickers are gone. They're gone. For sure. I take my hand away and stuff it in my pocket, eventually remembering what she was talking about before my whole laughing fit. Reaching out, I tap her arm lightly with my other hand. Her eyes catches mine.

"About that day, I had a great time too." Kayla's lips curve up a little more at my words. *You're really cool*, she'd said. I grin. *Damn, I haven't felt this good about myself in a while.* "And no, I didn't know that." She looks confused so I elaborate. "No one's called me cool before."

She teases me with a small sneer like she doesn't believe me. "Maybe just not to your face."

"You'd be surprised with what I hear. I can tell you all about it sometime."

Kayla has a small grin on. As if she liked that idea.

Do it.

Ask her.

"Maybe we can—"

"Aiden!" Nick's voice interrupts my sentence midway, and I realize something. *I was about to make a big mistake. I was being swept away by my emotions again.* Grateful for the intervention, I turn to my friend who's approaching us from a distance. He reaches us shortly and brings a hand up to point a thumb towards the direction he came from. "Your dad wants you to meet someone."

Must've been one of the football scouts Dad's been connecting with lately. Or a coach of some sort from one of the colleges he wants me to attend. The thought of it all sours my mood, and I run a hand through my hair to avoid a grunt. *Hold it in.* Nick might be used to it, but Kayla's right next to me. Not to mention, she's seen way too much of my bad side already. I don't need to show her any more than that.

I give Nick a small pat on the arm. "Alright. Thanks, man."

He sends me a nod of acknowledgement before his eyes wander down to the girl next to me. Nick sounds pleasantly surprised when he greets her. Kayla responds politely, throwing in a gentle smile to which the brunet returns. When his eyes return to mine, his grin gets wider.

Goddamn, Nick. Why don't you just tell her I told you everything already?

Suddenly, he smacks my back lightly and backs away like he's fleeing a crime scene he's just stumbled upon. "Okay, I'll see you later." He looks beside me and does an upward nod. "Bye, Kayla."

Without a word, Kayla nods back with a soft smile and a small wave. The both of us watch Nick disappear nearby in silence. Kayla's the one who cuts the tension first. "Sorry, I didn't catch that. What were you saying?"

Her harmless question holds me still as I think back to what I was about to ask her earlier. "It's nothing," I murmur. "I'll see you in class?"

She looks at me intently, though only for a short while. In those few seconds, I think she's seen right through me. Was she *expecting* something? If she was, she didn't show any sign of it.

"Yup, I'll be around," she confirms with an easygoing smirk. "Take it easy, Varsity."

I chuckle at the nickname she gave me. "I'll do my best."

Kayla gives me a small goodbye wave before leaving me to do the same. When she turns a corner, my smile gradually sinks into a thin line. I run a hand through my hair, sighing.

"Sorry, bro." Nick comes out of nowhere and puts a reassuring hand on my shoulder. "I didn't mean to ruin the moment."

"You didn't, Nick. You caught me just in time. I almost asked her to hang out."

Mr. Dramatic over here pulls his hand away to cover a gasp. "Why do you say it like it's a bad thing?"

"Because it is." My answer is almost automatic and his expression makes me want him to understand. To understand how easy it is to make the same mistake over and over again just because you had hope in someone, only to be let down every time. But he wouldn't be asking if he knew. "I'm always the one who reaches out first and look where that got me. I almost forgot how much it hurt every time she turned me down when I tried to . . . try." I sigh. "And suddenly, I'm boring and playing it too safe! I don't want to go through that again."

"You don't have to. No one is forcing you to get into another relationship. But I can see that Kayla's a good person and she has a positive effect on you." Nick pats me on the back. There's a soft expression on his face before he offers me a smile. "I like it when you're around her."

"Why?"

"Because it's nice seeing you be yourself again."

That catches me off guard. *What does he mean by that?*

Nick slumps an arm around my shoulders. "C'mon, your old man's gonna kill me if we take any longer."

"Okay, okay." I stand straighter, smirking when I shrug his arm off. "Let's go."

As we make our way to the cafeteria, each step feels a little lighter than the previous one. Despite the normal pace we're walking, my heart rate picks up. *Why am I feeling so excited?* Definitely not for whatever Dad has planned for me. I look to my side and see Nick wave at a friend.

What he said earlier is still running through my mind. Nick's right though. No one's forcing me into another relationship. So, would it really be okay to hang out with her? Or the better question is, does she *want* to hang out with me? She did say she had a fun time. But that doesn't exactly mean she'd want to do it again. Does it?

I sigh, rubbing the tension in my neck. *Why am I so afraid of reaching out first?* Kayla and I aren't even in that kind of relationship. She's just a nice classmate who's kind and considerate. Someone who's witnessed me in a bad moment but treats me with respect nonetheless. A girl who can make me laugh and who happens to be cute. She's just a friend.

Fuck.

That's not wrong. But at the same time, the term didn't quite sit well with me.

Not as well as it *should've.*

What the heck, Kayla? First, it's Kevin with the cookie and realizing that you're the one who's been acting unfair towards him this whole time! Then, you just *had* to eat that cookie and embarrass yourself in front of Aiden! Dang it. I can't even give a compliment without getting laughed at. Way to at least be decent looking.

I push open the bathroom door and make my way in, tossing my napkin in the trash and standing in front of a nearby sink. My eyes travel up to the mirror, fingers running across the area where I wiped off earlier. The place where those cookie crumbs were at.

"How the heck did that even get there?" I mutter. I roll my eyes at my stupidity and proceed to wash my hands to get rid of any cookie residue stuck on my hands. Hopefully, washing away some of the embarrassment too. Keeping busy with lathering soap in my hands, I calm down a little.

Did you see his expression earlier? I swear he was about to suggest something! Like to hang out or to see each other again. A heavy sensation takes over my body. I scrub my hands a little faster. What is this? Disappointment? *Woah, woah, woah. Stop right there, Kayla. Before you get too ahead of yourself. He definitely wasn't. Why would he ask a girl like you to hang out? Especially not after that embarrassing cookie thing.* He asked me to join him at the theater, didn't he? *Yeah well, that's probably because he pitied you about that whole ditching-friend thing and felt like he was obligated to entertain you. Especially since you have something to hold over him.*

I rinse the soap off my hands. Wow. Is it really that hard to accept the fact that he actually had a great time? And that he actually *wanted* me to join him? He did say he was okay with hanging out despite me witnessing the whole breakup thing. Maybe I should—

"Hey, you," a familiar voice calls out to me as the faucet automatically turns off. "It's Kayla, right?"

I look up in the mirror and catch two pretty girls behind me. Ah. Definitely *not* a coincidence. I flick my hands over the sink, ridding them of any dripping water. "Yeah?"

"Look, I don't know what you're trying to pull here, but I don't like it. Lay off or you're gonna get what's coming."

Well, well, well. If it isn't my second threat this senior year. I didn't expect this one to come from the vice president herself. Emma's arms are crossed and that menacing look on Nelly's face isn't helping either. The only time these girls would talk to me—willingly—is probably for a group project. And neither of them is in any of my classes this year. Which only means one thing.

This is about Aiden.

I turn to grab a paper towel and wipe my hands when I finally face them. "I don't know what you're talking about."

"Don't play dumb. You've been eyeing Aiden since the start of the semester. I know you've been flirting in class. And that little stunt you pulled earlier? I saw that. Give it a break."

What the heck is she going on about? First of all, he'd caught my eye a long while ago—not like I'm gonna correct her on *that*. Second, does saying hi in class really count as flirting? And third, what stunt? Having cookie crumbs on my face was not planned! Has she been stalking Aiden at school? Geez, she's the one who cheated on him. Why is she getting so worked up and all?

Stay calm Kayla, there's nothing to be scared of. You did nothing wrong. I crumple up the paper towel and toss it in the trash before I reply in a relaxed manner, "You've got it all wrong. Please don't misunderstand. Everything's just a coincidence."

"That's bull," Emma spits out. "You might've fooled Aiden with your innocent look, but you can't fool me. You obviously like him, and you're making your moves. But he's mine, so back off."

"What?"

"You heard me."

The thing is, I did hear her. But everything she said is so unbelievable, I'm at a loss for words. Suddenly, those dramas I've watched where girls bully other girls out of jealousy for the affection of some guy, comes to mind. *Is this it? Is she gonna smack me while Nelly pulls my hair?* I'm not sure if I should be laughing or crying at my imagination right now.

Emma scoffs. "To be honest, you should thank me for saving you in the long run. It's not like he'll ever go for someone like you anyways." One of her eyebrows arch up as her eyes look me up and down. They're back up again.

My face remains flat with confusion. Seriously? I think I'm supposed to be offended by this, but I'm not. I already know Aiden's not going to go for someone like me. What's there to worry about? *I'm not a threat.* Did she really need to go this far?

The blonde smirks a bit, thinking she's done something to my self-esteem. Then she shrugs, proceeding to speak in a sweet voice. "He's just going to break your heart."

Oh?

"Like how you broke *his*?" There's genuine curiosity in my question, and I applaud myself for biting back a snicker.

The smile on her pretty face suddenly falls into a straight line, eyes blinking in shock. I can just imagine what she's thinking right now. *What? How did she know? Did Aiden tell her?*

How I want to take a picture of her face right now and send it to Aiden—not like I have his number or anything, but still. A small win is a win nonetheless, right? Confronting the cheater for her crimes?

Nelly's face contorts in confusion and it catches me by surprise. "How can you say something like that? He's the one who—"

"Nells, it's fine."

"But Em!" Nelly turns to look at the lacrosse captain.

Emma shakes her head, stopping her friend from defending her any further. The frustrated scrunch doesn't leave Nelly's face. She seems discontent with how things are playing out and my heart is slightly moved by the sight. I've always thought Nelly was cool. Seeing her stick up for her friend, well, I guess I wasn't wrong. Her ebony skin looks so shiny and smooth in this bathroom lighting, I'm left staring in awe.

No. *Don't get distracted, Kayla. Nelly doesn't know Emma's the cheater!* Does she really not know or is she pretending not to know? Because if she really doesn't know, then that means Emma lied to her. To her own friend! And if that's true, then that means the one who spread those rumors was—

Holy crap! That only makes sense. Of course *she'd* turn the tables first before the truth comes out. Before people shame *her* for cheating. Smart. But despicable! Because of her, Aiden's got dirt on his plate now. And knowing him, he's too nice of a guy to correct it. He probably let it happen too because he's the type to think it's better for him to be tainted than her. Especially because she's a girl and someone he liked before. That gentle giant would totally think that. He's too lenient for his own good! *How, Aiden? Just how did you even end up dating her?* A small laugh escapes my mouth at the ridiculousness.

"What's so funny?"

The ex-girlfriend sounds like I've offended her or something. I want to tell her off to her friend. Confront her on how unfair she's being to Aiden. The way she spoke to him when she hurt him that day. Her affair with Ramen Hair Kai! Those stupid rumors. Everything. Anything! Anything I can think of to make her feel bad for the things she's done so that maybe—just maybe—she can finally acknowledge her wrongdoings and own up to her mistakes.

But one look at that conceited face tells me everything I need to know. No matter what I say, she won't listen. She won't admit to any of it. At least, not in front of me. It'll be useless. So instead, I sigh and give her a defeated smile. "The grass is always greener on the other side, huh?"

Emma frowns, jaw muscles tightening. "You don't know what you're saying." Her voice is dangerously stern.

Good. Seems like I hit a nerve. She's glaring, and I keep my face soft to tick her off even more. "I know enough," I say confidently. "You and Aiden aren't together anymore, yet you're talking like he's still yours. No?"

Silence.

"Look, I've explained myself. It's your choice whether you wanna believe me or not." My eyes flicker over to Nelly before returning back to Emma. "But I don't appreciate you coming in here, falsely accusing me of things I did not do just because you're jealous."

Emma's facade breaks into a flustered one. "I-I'm not jealous!"

"Then why do you care so much about who he sees and talks to?"

"I don't!"

I snicker. "You were just telling me to stay away from him."

If looks could talk, Emma's probably saying that she hates me so much right now. I never intended on making her mad, but there's nothing I can do if I'm out here spitting facts and she's the one losing her temper. *Maybe this is what she gets for all the times she's had Aiden all riled up. Serves her right.*

Emma stands straighter with a scowl. "I was giving you some advice."

"And I never asked for any. But you know what? I'm feeling really generous today, so I'll give you some *real* advice. You may not feel it now, but pretty soon, it's gonna eat you up." I don't say what. I just look at her. Knowingly.

The guilt.

It was a split second. If I hadn't been paying attention, I wouldn't have caught it. But there was a slight falter in her eyes as she blinked. *So she knows.* Maybe she's experiencing symptoms already. Emma decides to hide her feelings through that glare of hers while Nelly gets more confused by the minute. She's about to defend her friend again, but the ex speaks up.

"Let's go, Nells." Emma turns around to leave. "Don't waste your time on her."

A wisp of blonde hair disappears behind the door as it closes and despite what Emma said, Nelly stands in front of me. "How could you be so insensitive? She was cheated on. She's hurt!"

Yup, that confirms it. *You can tell her the truth and maybe do some damage to their friendship?* No. I'm not that type of person. And it's not my story to tell. It would also be better if she finds out the truth from Emma herself. Find out what kind of friend she really has.

That'll probably give that cheater some sort of punishment, right? "Nelly, if she was cheated on, then why does she still want him?"

"You don't know anything." She shakes her head in disbelief, curly hair dancing. "I don't know what Aiden sees in you," she says and I mentally disagree, as Aiden doesn't see anything in me. "You can't even compare to Emma. Except what? Long hair?"

I keep a dead smile on, tired of all this drama yet still kinda amused by what I keep receiving. She continues to ignore my question as she scans me up and down, scoffing. Nelly clicks her tongue in a disapproving tsk.

"What a letdown." With that, she spins around. Like her friend, she grabs the door handle and pulls on it aggressively before storming out.

"I mean that was a legit question," I mutter in the now-empty bathroom. Guess my attempt to steer Nelly in the right direction was a bust. I turn around and catch myself sighing in the mirror.

Long hair, huh? If there's one thing I hate the most, it's being compared to other people. Because no matter what I do or what I say, *I know that I'll never be enough.*

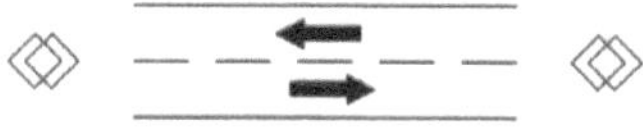

My drooping eyes zap awake when the bell rings. Precalc is over. Finally! Sorry, Mr. Cadman, but your voice is just too soothing. *Pack your things, Kayla. Let's get out of here.*

"Aiden." Mr. Cadman's soft voice is almost inaudible in the midst of all the students packing and leaving. I hear it because I'm in the row closest to his table. Discreetly, he gestures Aiden to come over. Aiden walks around the other side, and I focus on packing so I can give them the privacy they need. Doesn't exactly work 'cause I still hear them talking.

"What's up, Mr. C?"

"Aiden, I'm not calling you out or anything but I was looking over your past few pop quizzes. At the rate you're going, I'm a little worried. You're going to have to study a little harder if you want to do well on the test that's coming up. I'm available after school if you need any help. I don't want you to fall behind."

"Yes, sir."

"I know you have football, but midterms count as a large percentage of your grade. You know you have to keep your grades up to continue playing on the team."

"I'll step it up, sir."

Go, Kayla, go. Mind your own business. I zip up my backpack and start to head out.

"If you can't make it to my open hours, I suggest you study with someone if you can. Someone who knows the material . . . Ah, Kayla!"

I stop walking, with just three more steps to the doorway, and look over my shoulder. Mr. Cadman gestures at me like he did Aiden a minute earlier. *Oh god, is this really happening right now?* I hurry over to stand next to Aiden, acknowledging him before looking at Mr. Cadman. "Yes, Mr. C?"

"Kayla, you've actually been doing really well, despite always dozing off in class. Don't think I don't see you." Mr. Cadman raises an eyebrow at me.

Out of amusement, I hope. Embarrassed, I smile. "Sorry, Mr. C."

Our precalc teacher clears his throat. "Since you play sports too, that makes you the perfect candidate. Your schedules should be pretty similar, right?"

I freeze. *He plays football and I play tennis. In no way does that make our schedules similar. That's not how it works.* Aiden and I look at each other, stunned. Before either of us can correct him, Mr. Cadman speaks up again.

"You think you can help a boy out? Maybe go over some material together, answer his questions, share some notes? From one athlete to another."

I turn to see Aiden staring at me in silence. His face is still, and I can't read his expression. What if *he's not okay with it*? I can't even ask with Mr. Cadman in front of us. Whatever, I'll let him decide later! Quickly turning to Mr. Cadman, I nod a little. "Sure, of course I can."

"Perfect. Thank you, Kayla. I knew I could count on you. And how convenient, you two sit right next to each other. Aiden, don't be afraid to ask questions. Kayla doesn't bite."

His little comment gets a grin out of Aiden and before I can look away, Mr. Cadman shoos us out when a few students come in for retakes. The next thing I know, we're both standing idly outside the classroom. Aiden rubs a hand on his neck. "That was embarrassing."

I chuckle. "I think we're past embarrassing."

"You don't have to help me with this. I don't want to impose."

Impose? I already said I was gonna help him at first. Did he think I only said yes because we were in front of Mr. Cadman? Or is he making sure *I'm* okay with it? Wow. If that's the case, that's very thoughtful of him. It's making my heart all mushy. And the way he says it! It's so gentle, it makes me wanna help him even more. I smile, glad I can actually do something for him.

"It's totally okay. I'd love to help." It's not a big deal, really, so I give him a little tap on his arm, trying to assure him it was nothing. Woah. Was that his skin? *He's warm.* It was only for a brief second, but I can still feel my fingertips tingling from the sensation. I clear my throat. "Plus, it'll help me review for the midterms. It's a win-win."

My attempt to free his burden seems fruitful when he finally gives in, nodding. *So I guess he's okay with it after all.* It gets quiet, but before it can get awkward, I try my best to make the first move.

"Should we exchange numbers?" My question throws me off, and suddenly I'm panicking. *What if he doesn't want to give me his number? There are other ways of communicating too!* I shake my head. "Or we can do email, I'm fine with any." *Geez! Did I just say email?* That was stupid, I shouldn't have said that either. It's too late to unsay it now, so I smile shamefully, doing my best to hold in the cringe.

"You're funny." Aiden snickers before pulling out his phone.

I chuckle nervously when I do the same and open it to a new contacts page, glad that he finds my stupidity amusing. We exchange phones and digits before returning them to each other. I quickly save my new contact and see him saving my number on his phone. His eyes aren't looking at me now, so I finally relax a little. *Now's your chance, Kayla. Say it. Say it now!* "Let me know when you need help or wanna go over anything."

Aiden looks up from his screen and smiles at me, making me all warm inside. "Thanks, I'll text you."

My heart flutters. Or is that my stomach? I don't know! But his words get me all giddy inside. I don't think I've ever been so grateful for having a phone before.

"By the way, Kayla . . ."

"Yeah?"

"I like the new look," he says, giving me an upward nod.

"Thanks," I say, though not immediately registering what he's referring to. New look? *Is he talking about my hair?* I chopped off a good eight inches all because of Nelly's little comment. It was a decision made on an impulse; one I started to have second thoughts about after realizing I couldn't braid my hair anymore.

But now . . . Aiden just said he liked it. Oh dear. Blood rushes up my cheeks, and a smile forms on my face. So wide it almost hurts.

Braids can wait.

A pair of familiar arms wrap around my waist from behind and I stiffen.

"I shouldn't have cheated on you. I'm sorry. I was wrong. Give me a second chance." Her face presses against my back. It's sickening. I don't move. Body feeling rigid. She doesn't take the hint and continues to plead. "Please Aiden, I miss you."

My mind is screaming, but I remain silent and take a deep breath. There was a time we play-wrestled and I accidentally pushed her too hard. Her head barely missed the coffee table. Gritting my teeth, I carefully take each of her wrists and untangle her from me. She must be joking. It might've been the first time she cheated on me, but asking for second chances were nothing new. If she really did want a second chance, she wouldn't have lied to everyone about being the one who was cheated on.

I turn around and face the girl I used to call my girlfriend. Her hair looks duller than I remember. Eyes haggard. She was probably back to her bad habits again. For once, I don't feel annoyed. I don't feel the urge to tell her to do anything. I don't have to. She's no longer my responsibility and honestly, it's a relief. It's liberating.

"You hurt me a lot, but I forgive you." I'm bewildered at her hopeful face and when her shoulders slump down, she has the audacity to smile in relief. She's about to say something senseless. "It's over, Emma. I don't want to do this anymore. I want to move on, and I think you should too."

Her brows furrow. "Aiden—"

"Please, let's not do this." It gets silent between us and I think she finally understands. There's a subtle look of surprise on her face. I wonder if she thought I'd take her BS forever. A soft echo of a closing door breaks the silence, and I'm grateful for it. It may be after school hours, and football practice might've ended early, but we're still on a stair landing that's usually crowded between classes. Anyone could walk by us at any moment, but I'm not that bothered by it. Maybe because our previous conversation already had a witness or because that conversation was overall much worse than this one. I don't care anymore. I just want to get out of here. The sooner, the better. "Don't touch me again. Don't make it harder than it already is."

Her face contorts with hurt—something she doesn't have the right to feel. I hold in a tsk. She's the one who said I was gonna regret ending our relationship, but look at us now. It was always like this.

Her saying cruel words was always more a reflection of herself than me. I sigh. *Why did I ever tolerate all this?*

"Goodbye, Emma." I walk away without ever looking back, muscles relaxing when I get far enough. As I reach the front entrance, I stop at the glass doors. The ground outside is wet, and I look up to see it's raining. "Great. This day just keeps getting better and better."

My gym bag has nothing but shoes and a sweaty change of clothes. No umbrella. I should make it a habit to check the weather ever so often. *Whatever. Getting a little wet won't hurt.* I push open the door a few inches but pause when I hear quick footsteps coming from behind me.

"Wait!"

A female voice stops me in my tracks and I'm flooded with horror again. I thought she didn't follow me. From the corner of my eye, I see a hand reaching out to stop me. Before she can touch me, I let go of the door and bring up a hand to catch her wrist.

"I said don't touch me," I growl. The door drops on its close and my eyes go from the grip I have on her to her cold blue eyes. Except they're not blue.

They're a warm shade of dark chocolate.

Fuck! Immediately, I let go—hoping I didn't grip her too hard.

"Sorry!" we say together.

I look at her in confusion. Why is *she* apologizing? I'm the one who grabbed her.

She looks to the side, blinking a few times. "Sorry, I shouldn't have—"

"No," I cut her off quickly, before she gets any ideas. "You're fine. You can touch me."

Her eyes meet mine again, and I'm glad my words put her worries away. But why did I say it like that? I sound like a creep. She cracks a smile, and I almost think she's laughing at me. I swallow hard. *Should I say something else to clear it up, or would that make it worse?*

Before I decide, Kayla reaches out with her index finger and pokes my arm softly. "Boop." She retracts her hand and I look at her in awe. There's a goofy smile on her face, and we stare at each other in silence. A few seconds pass before we break into a fit of giggles.

Somehow, I'm no longer embarrassed about what I said anymore. When the laughter wears down, I rub a hand on the back of my neck, feeling grateful she can make a joke out of this.

"Sorry, I didn't mean to grab you. I thought you were—" I clear my throat. "I thought you were someone else."

"It's okay. At least you've got a good grip! Must come in handy in . . . your field of sports." Her eyes widen a little as she looks away awkwardly, wishing she'd disappear right then and there. I like how easy it is to read her.

"Thanks." I chuckle a little. *Good to know I'm not the only one saying weird things today.*

Kayla clears her throat before looking back at me with a newfound confidence. "Anyways, here." She holds up a yellow umbrella that I hadn't noticed until now. "I think you need this more than I do. I have this." She lifts her arm a bit to show off a light pink rain jacket she's carrying.

Is she always this prepared for the weather? Even so, a mere rain jacket won't cover as well as an umbrella. I smile at her kind offer. "It's alright, thanks. I'm just heading to the parking lot."

She blinks in surprise. "Oh, so am I."

I stare at her in silence, not knowing what to say. But before I can even think about what to say, she offers up another suggestion.

"We can go together . . . if you're okay with it?"

She looks unsure as her round eyes look up at mine, searching for my answer. Or maybe a sign of discomfort. I wonder if anything about me gave off that impression. It's like she genuinely cares about my thoughts on this. It's not that big of a deal, but it somehow means a lot to me. I feel my stomach take a leap. *Are these butterflies? I haven't felt this way since—*

"Only if you're okay with it," I say, forcing down a lump in my throat.

"Well, I'm the one who asked you first. Of course I'm okay with it." Kayla laughs a little, and it makes my heart skip a beat. "Let me put this on real quick. Give me a sec." She starts to unravel her jacket with one hand. The other one occasionally helps as it's busy holding the umbrella.

"I can take that," I say, extending a hand. To my surprise, she hands me the umbrella, thanking me. I'm not sure what I was expecting, given how much of a fight she put up for the bill I paid last time. Or how easily she offered to give me the umbrella, while she planned to head out in that small jacket of hers. *Kayla tends to do everything herself.* It makes me happy to know she's relying on me, even just for a tiny thing like this. It feels like she's letting me in. If that's what it is.

As she zips up her jacket, I pop the tie wrapper open, letting the umbrella flaps swing loose. Kayla settles into her jacket and extends her hand out, only to look at me in surprise. I'm leaning against the push bar, biting back a smile at her silent offer. "Ready?"

I'm not exactly sure how she planned on holding the umbrella over the both of us. She's a whole head shorter than me, so she'd need to raise her arm and hold it there to keep me covered. She blinks before hurriedly nodding.

"Ready!" she chirps before scurrying next to me as I open the door and her umbrella.

It's clear she didn't quite think it through. I'm holding the umbrella over us and the handle is around my shoulder area. The thought of Kayla holding the umbrella like the Statue of Liberty makes the corners of my mouth turn up.

"Are you covered enough? It's not that big of an umbrella." She's looking over at my side while stuffing her hands in her jacket pockets.

I don't get to reply before she suddenly scrunches her arms to herself, making her frame smaller than it already is, and scoots a little closer to me. I end up tilting the umbrella back upright, in the middle of both of us. Rain droplets stop wetting the side of my arm. *Did she notice that?*

"I'm good, thanks," I say, not needing to lie. If there's one thing about Kayla, it's that she's very considerate. Maybe she really was planning to hold the umbrella for the both of us. And that's because she didn't expect me to do it. Something stirs within me and I realize that instead of feeling relieved, I'm *bothered* by it.

We're barely touching. I start to wonder if she's even comfortable in that compressed position. I want to tell her that I don't care about getting wet. That I planned on walking out uncovered anyway. She didn't need to move for me. But I don't tell her any of it. I know she's just going to say that it's fine. Telling her would only make it hard for her to respond, and I don't want to make her any more uncomfortable than she already is. Not to mention, I literally yanked on her arm earlier. *Did it hurt? Did I scare her at first?* I take a quick peek at her. She's still scrunched up, staring blankly ahead as her little legs scurry along to keep up.

"I . . ." The word escapes my mouth before I even comprehend what I'm about to say. Kayla looks up at me, and I grab the chance to take smaller steps now. I clear my throat. "Nothing, never mind."

Looking ahead, I distract myself with the rain. *What was that? What was I going to say?* Kayla turns from me to the road in front of us, shifting a little in that scrunched up form. *Is she cold? Or are we too close? Maybe I should give her some space.*

"Hey, Aiden?"

Her soft voice stops me from inching away. Instead, I look at her. She's not saying anything, attention focused on the floor. Aside from the pouring rain, it's quiet. I can't see her face, but she looks like she's thinking really hard. Or maybe, something is troubling her. Did she actually say something or did I imagine it?

"Would you . . ." Kayla finally looks up with a hopeful smile. "Would you be interested in going to the lantern festival with me?"

My mouth opens, but I can't get a word out. I don't know what to say. Her question surprised me. I must've been quiet for too long because she looks away shortly.

"I'm just asking. You don't have to if you don't want to." She laughs it off. As if it's not a big deal.

But it *is*.

She just asked me out, didn't she? For someone who's always been the one asking, this is a first. The feeling is so foreign, I don't know what to feel. *What about the ZAD tradition?* Nick and the others weren't too happy about Emma getting in the way of our plans last year. They might not have outrightly said it, but I knew. If I skipped it for Kayla, I don't think they'll mind. Even so, I'm not going to let another girl take my time away from the boys again. Not this time. Kayla may be nice and easy to be around, but it's always fun and games in the beginning. *She's going to change for the worse too.*

Emma did.

Say no. It's not going to end well anyway.

"I don't think I'm—" She looks up at me again, and my plan gets foiled when I see those eyes. "I . . . Can you give me some time to think about it?" Maybe it's my imagination, but it takes her a second longer than normal when she responds with a nod and a small smile.

"Of course!" She sounds optimistic and is back to looking at the ground. I'm glad she's so understanding. Before I can think of something to say, we stop in front of a black car. "Well, this is me."

"Here, your umbrella."

Kayla smiles softly as she waves her hand. "It's okay, keep it for now. You still have your car to get to."

"What about you?"

"I've got a rain jacket." She smirks and pulls her hood over her head. As if she's showing off something amazing. "You can give it back to me next time."

It's a nice offer. My truck is further down and I'm not going to lie, I would be drenched without this umbrella. *But Kayla doesn't need to know that.* And I don't want to take advantage of her kindness more than I already have. When she notices my hesitation, I decide to return her umbrella.

"It's okay. Really," she says. Like she's urging me to take it. "You're in the middle of your season. I don't want you to catch a cold."

Why? Why is she so nice to me? Why is it so easy for her to say something and change my mind like that? So casually too. *Don't give in. Just say I don't need it. I don't need it. I don't—*

"Okay, fine." I huff. "You've got a point."

She makes a wide grin at her victory. I officially give up with this girl. It doesn't matter how well I build my brick wall. Kayla can seep through it with that smile of hers. *What is wrong with me?* Letting a girl in is the last thing I should be doing right now. But Kayla is like the cool breeze in the middle of a summer heat. Hot chocolate on a cold rainy day.

She's comforting.

She turns around and unlocks her car. I'm holding the umbrella over us, making sure she stays dry as she opens the driver door. Before she steps in, I feel the urge to say something. "Hey, Kayla?"

"Yeah?" She faces me with a concerned look.

I want to laugh. *As if there's anything else she can help me with.*

"Thank you," I tell her sincerely, "for everything."

To say "thank you for everything" is a little vague, but I didn't want to bring up the breakup again. I want her to know that I'm grateful to her. Not just for her honesty, but for being nonjudgmental and forgiving when I showed her the parts of me I don't like. For all the times she's made me feel better, intentional or not. For all the smiles she's given me in class. Waves in the hallways. *For always being there.*

Kayla doesn't say anything when she looks at me. She just smiles. And then, I don't feel the cold air anymore.

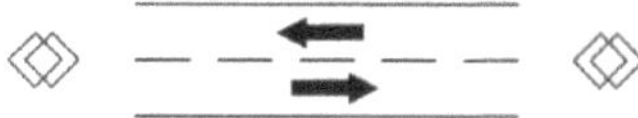

Nick pauses the game and looks at me like I'm an idiot. So does Evan, Luke, and Jack.

"What? Why are you guys looking at me like that?"

"Aiden, bro! You should've said yes!"

"Exactly, you lucky son of a gun!" Evan shakes his head. "What I would give for a girl to ask *me* out."

On my left, Luke puts his controller down on the coffee table. "Dude, if you're thinking about us and our ZAD tradition, don't."

"I'm not going to make the same mistake and let a girl get between our plans again." A pillow gets thrown at me, and I pick it up from the floor. "Seriously, Evan?"

"Sorry, my hand slipped."

"Is this Kayla, Kayla Summers?" Jack walks out the open kitchen with a bowl of popcorn, his free hand measuring right below his shoulder. "Asian, yea tall?"

"Yeah, the one who cut her hair recently," Luke says.

"Oh, her! She was in one of my classes in freshman year. Nice girl." Jack sits himself on the couch. "Mixed?"

Luke shakes his head. "Doesn't look like it."

"Does that even matter?" Evan takes some popcorn and throws it in his mouth. "She's pretty. Not Emma pretty, but in a plain and sim—" Nick clears his throat and whacks him. Evan rubs his arm, looking confused. "What? Did I say something wrong?"

I'm a little bothered that Evan brought up Emma, but I'm not mad because he's not entirely wrong. Kayla *is* pretty. She's got soft features, so she might not be the first one you'll look at when you enter a room. But when you see her, you won't look away. *You can't.* Because the more you look at her, the prettier she gets. And that smile of hers—she can make *you* feel pretty. I don't care what people say. Emma can shine all she wants.

Kayla radiates.

Jack swallows his bite of popcorn before clarifying. "I was just wondering 'cause her last name's Summers."

"It's from her step-grandfather," I say. The boys expect more from me, but I stay silent and grab some popcorn for myself. I don't say any more as I recall Kayla sharing her story with me at the diner.

"My grandma met him at the café she worked at. And they bonded over having the same last names. His—you can probably guess—was Summers. And hers was *Haa*, which means summer in Cantonese," she said with a proud look on her face. "She was a single mother at the time, but it didn't matter to him. They fell in love. And Grandpa treated my dad like his own."

Kayla looked so happy telling me that. I don't even remember how we got into the topic, but I smile. She and I spent a good minute or two saying *Haa* to each other until I got my pronunciation right. It was funny. It sounded like we were laughing. In tones.

"Aiden." Luke stares at me intently. "You want to go to the festival with her, don't you?"

"I . . . I don't know."

"Man, what are you so afraid of? Just tell her you wanna g—ow!" The pillow I throw drops to the floor as he stares at me in disbelief. "What was that for?"

"Sorry, my hand slipped."

Evan snarls as the others only laugh at him. Jack puts the popcorn bowl on the coffee table and takes a nearby pillow to smack him. I get up and head to the kitchen as Luke joins in on the fun. There's a bag of cookies laying on the counter, and I open it. Nick approaches me slowly.

"Luke's right." He takes a cookie from the bag I hold out. "You don't have to worry about us or the ZAD tradition. No one's been able to top our score anyways."

I chuckle. It's true. We're practically trying to beat our own scores at this point. "What if it doesn't go well, Nick? Kayla's nice. Funny even. I like being around her . . . but it was like that with Emma too. Until it wasn't." I put the bag down and lean against the counter. "Good things never last. Emma didn't. Kayla's not going to either."

"Don't say that." He takes another cookie and stuffs it in his mouth. "That was Emma. This is Kayla. She's not her, you know?"

"I know, but—" I sigh. "I know that."

Nick looks at me with skeptical eyes. I know what he's saying. And I agree. Kayla is in no way like Emma. Not even close. She's honest, for one. And two, she's kind. Kayla has always made sure I'm comfortable with an idea before actually pursuing it. She's continuously kept her distance, never even coming close enough to cross the line. *Ever.* Sometimes, she feels so far away.

And I wonder why.

Nick gives me a light smile before grabbing the last cookie out of the bag. "If there's a tiny part of you that wants to go, you should go. She took the chance and asked you, didn't she? The question is, are you willing to take a chance on her?"

You shouldn't have asked him, stupid! You knew he wasn't gonna agree, so why did you ask him? I don't know, I thought he would be somewhat interested. Who doesn't like carnivals? And I mean, he said he had a great time last time. So I thought that maybe he'd . . . he'd—

He'd what? Say yes?

Yes . . .?

He was gonna say no! I know, I heard him. He didn't want to hurt my feelings so he asked for some time to think about it. That's pretty much a no, I get it. Wait. What if he wanted to say no but couldn't because he thinks I have something over him? Not that I do because I'll never use that breakup information against him. But what if he thinks I will?

I hope he doesn't actually think that. He did thank me last time. Though I don't know what for. Not telling other people that he was the one who was cheated on? Or tagging along for a free movie and lunch so that he wouldn't be alone? That makes no sense. It was him who helped *me* during those times. Whether it was for forgiving me or cheering me up. *Man, what was he thanking me for? The umbrella?*

"I can't believe we made it to semi-finals, Kay!" Tracy's chirpy voice puts an end to my Aiden thoughts as I finish changing into my practice gear.

Badminton intramurals. Right. We won our last match yesterday against two junior douchebags. They were losing points on purpose to catch up later in the game all because they "wanted a challenge." Oh, we gave them a challenge alright. Tracy didn't understand why I was playing so hard during the match, but that's because *she* didn't overhear them talking trash about playing against girls that day. She was too busy talking to that Alek guy. Probably doing her wingwoman duties.

I come out of the bathroom stall to wash my hands. "Right? I hope we make it to finals."

"We can do it! But I'm not sure if we'll win because we might be going against the Sharks," Tracy says, busy fixing her hair in the mirror.

"Are they good?"

"Really good. Jonah and Rico are on that team."

"Oh." I grimace at the mention of their names. Suddenly, Tracy has a mischievous smile on her face.

"I bet he wants to play you."

"Who?"

"Jonah."

"Why?"

"Because he likes you, duh."

I groan as I dry my hands. "Don't talk about it. Paisley told me three years ago. I mean I had a hunch, but it's been so weird and awkward after she confirmed it. I don't even know why he likes me. We don't talk that much."

Tracy shrugs. "I don't know why he likes you either."

Wow. I know I just said that. But when she says it, it sounds like I don't have the qualities for someone to like me. No Kayla, that's not what she meant. She's just agreeing with you. *Well, that tone of hers didn't sound like it.* I clear my throat. "I mean, it's flattering. Thank you, but no thank you."

"That's a little harsh, Kay."

"Harsh? Just because he likes me, that doesn't mean I have to like him back. Plus, it's not like he told me personally, so there's that."

Tracy chuckles. "Why don't you like him?"

I hold in a laugh when I think about my answer. To put it plainly, it's his personality. I don't feel comfortable around him.

I hit a bad badminton shot one time, and he gives me advice on how to improve my strokes? I understand it's supposed to be a nice gesture, but I never asked him for it. I was playing around. I'm happy with the way I hit. I've hit shots he couldn't counter before. But no, he spends a minute or two showing me how to hit properly while two other people were waiting on us! I just wanted to get on with our rally. He thinks he's all that just because he's good at it.

Another time, I carry a few things and he comes over, trying to take some from me when he's got way heavier things in his hands. Even despite me telling him that it's okay and that I've got it—because it legit wasn't heavy—he doesn't stop insisting, eventually taking the box from me without my consent.

He's so intrusive.

Always trying to play the hero when there's no need for one! He thinks he's helping or saving me, but all he's doing is making me feel like I'm *incapable.* I huff out a little just thinking about it. "He's . . ."

Tracy looks at me with a curious expression. *Crap, don't say it. They've got mutual friends. This might circle around.* "He's what?"

I swallow. "Forget it. I just don't like his vibes."

"Kay!"

She thinks it's a ridiculous reason. A harsh one. But I really don't care, so I shrug. "Gotta go, see ya."

Tracy bids me a goodbye when I exit the bathroom. After putting away some books in my locker, I'm about to head out the nearest exit until I spot a certain someone down the hallway. *This is it. This is your chance! When else do you see him? Alone too!* I want to walk away, but I don't. There's no better time than now to do this. *Come on, Kayla!*

I take a deep breath in and out before making my way towards my target. *This has been weighing on your mind since that cookie incident. You got this girl. You can do this! You have to, it's the right thing to do.* I stop and station myself by an opened locker with a busy boy behind it. He doesn't see me and I'm internally grateful to the piece of metal blocking his view—even if it's just for a few more seconds.

"C-Can we talk?" *Geez, way to start off confidently.*

The dirty blond shuts his locker and turns to look at the source of the question. Our eyes meet, and he's stunned. To my surprise, he doesn't scowl or anything. He doesn't even speak. Kevin is as still as a statue. I wonder if he heard me or not. Before I debate about repeating myself, he nods in the direction of the open space around us. *I guess that means lead the way?* I slowly walk towards a more private area where we can chat, but not before turning around to make sure he's following me. He is. When we reach an appropriate area, I face him and dive straight into it.

"About what you said last time . . . you're right. You never offended me. I shouldn't have called you narcissistic. That was uncalled for." It's subtle, but there's a shift in his expression. Shock. *Heck, I'd be shocked too if I didn't plan for this myself.* "I didn't like how you were talking about Aiden and Emma, but I shouldn't have let my feelings get in the way and made it personal. I was being immature. I'm sorry."

Kevin swallows, brow furrowing. He looks away momentarily, trying to process my words as I stand there quietly, patiently waiting for his reply. At least he's not spouting random remarks right now.

"So" — he crosses his arms — "what do you have against me?"

For a second, I consider not answering his question. Or simply outrightly denying it. But I decide against it. I'm gonna own up to my mistakes wholeheartedly.

"You get to class late, don't do an assignment, and it's okay. You get along with practically anyone, and teachers adore you. You get away with things without even trying. It's unfair. Especially for someone who struggles to raise their hand in class."

He opens his mouth—

"But, but, but! Everyone's got problems, and that doesn't exclude you. I realized I've been blaming you for their mistakes. You're not the one playing favorites."

Kevin closes his mouth. Speechless. Beyond surprised, I suppose. I am too. Not by my words, but by how stupid I've been to dislike Kevin just because he's naturally charming. That sounds so silly when I think about it now. I accidentally let out a nervous chuckle—interrupting the awkward silence between us. *Crap, he probably thinks I'm joking or something.* I stare at the floor to gather myself and hopefully appear serious. Because I am being sincere.

When I make eye contact with the boy in front of me again, he looks away with a stern expression on his face. He's been real quiet so far. *Oh man, this is so not like him.* I prepared myself for a bunch of scenarios, anything I thought he would come up with. But this silence? I wasn't expecting this kind of reaction. He finally looks back at me, wearing an expression that I can't read. *What's that supposed to mean? He's not saying anything. Why isn't he saying anything? This is so awkward!*

"Look, forget it. I just came over to apologize. You don't need to forgive me, but I want you to know I had my reasons." Kevin doesn't move or speak. I feel weird. And a little stupid. *Why on earth did I think this was a good idea?* "Thanks for listening."

I give him one last look before walking away. Geez, I try to do the right thing but it never goes right! I swear I'm not gonna try next time. I was so prepared too! Why didn't he say anything? It's fine if he didn't like my apology. At least say something. I have no idea how to respond to that. Maybe I should've asked hi—

"Hey, Summers?"

I stop in my tracks, thinking I heard wrong. Hallucination, maybe? Just in case, I turn around and take a peek at Kevin to make sure. He's staring at me steadily with a softer expression now.

"Thanks. I needed that." He mumbles the last part, but I still catch it.

It's not forgiveness, but that's all it takes for my doubts to vanish. His calm demeanor brings me a sense of relief. Maybe this is what it feels like to bury the hatchet. Grateful for his words, I give him a smile.

Probably the first genuine one I've ever given him.

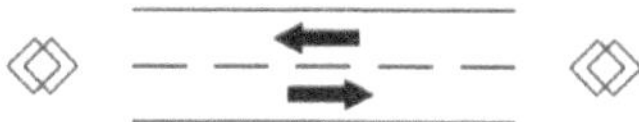

Aiden's lefthanded. I mean, I noticed it way before all of this, but the thought is more prominent today. Sometimes our elbows touch when we do our work, and it sends electric shocks through my body. And every time, I'd scoot my arm back to recover a safe distance between us. Not immediately, of course. I don't want him thinking I *don't* like it or something. Thankfully, he doesn't seem to pay much mind to it. That, or he doesn't even realize it. Maybe it's because I'm the only one feeling this way, it drives me a little crazy. I have to try to carry on without thinking too much of it.

Aside from this minor thing, I can see why he sat me on his left. It's much easier to lean in and look at his progress. Or check on his work without him bringing his notebook to me every time. We went over the previous quizzes before catching up to the current material. It didn't take long because Aiden's a quick learner. At the rate we were going, I'm not even sure why or how his grade was falling.

Mrs. McLaren visited us halfway to give us some of her potato salad to try. It was mouthwatering. I had no idea what Aiden meant when he said she was trying to perfect a recipe when it's already perfect. I finish a homework problem and pet the asleep pug on my lap. I still can't believe the look on Aiden's face when he said he forgot to ask me if I was allergic to dogs. Priceless! And so sweet, because he actually did look concerned. I almost feel bad for liking it.

I lean a little to my right to check on Aiden's progress. He gets the problem right with the correct formula this time, and I smile in content. He probably doesn't need to hear this, but I'm just so proud of him. "There you go, you got it."

"Thanks, I don't know why I couldn't do this before. You make it sound so easy."

I rest my back against the chair, gently stroking Pilly's head. "That's all because of Mr. C's worksheets. They're simple and to the point. Weird, because his lectures aren't."

"They must be pretty boring for you to fall asleep." Aiden flashes me a toothy grin.

I look away, embarrassed. Focusing my attention on the pug in front of me, I give his little ears a soft massage. Pilly unconsciously scoots himself closer to me. The motion calms my nerves a bit.

"I can't believe you remembered what Mr. C said." He faces me, resting an elbow on his book, then his head on the palm of his hand. The movement makes me look at him.

"You must've forgotten you sit right in front of me."

My face drops. Oh, geez! He's probably noticed me fall asleep many times before Mr. C called me out on it! I turn away when I feel my face heating up. Aiden breaks his stance and chuckles a bit. *Is he teasing me right now?* Oh no, I can't stop it. My lips curve up.

I like this.

Man, what is wrong with me? I give him a *Ha ha, you're funny* look before we continue studying and working on the homework. Things begin to slow down when Aiden starts to mix up formulas. It happens more than twice, and I can tell it makes him a little upset. With himself, I'm assuming. Because he hasn't stopped being nice to me. It's strange because Mom and Dad speak with frustration a lot when they're stressed out or irritated. Dad especially when he's upset with how I can't be more like Josslyn.

"Did I get this right?" Aiden asks softly, scooting his notebook closer.

"It's good."

He breathes out a sigh of relief before returning to work on the next problem. I watch him quietly as he's reading it with a serious face. Aiden looks tired but he's persisting. It makes my heart ache a little, so I give his arm a gentle tap.

"Hey, let's take a break."

He's surprised at my suggestion, and then there's a little glint in his eyes. He catches on to what I'm doing. Before he can say anything, I give him a soft smile before going all shameless-mode.

"I need one. I think I'm gonna fall asleep if I do another problem."

Upon hearing that, he nods. His face softens into a beautiful smile.

It's selfish, I know. Probably even stupid.

But I want to think that . . . *I did that.*

I haven't felt this much fun throwing a football in a while. Kayla catches the ball, and I feel a deep sense of pride as she celebrates a little. We've been doing this back and forth for some time. Her throw is getting better. I can't believe she's never touched a football before. Not even a foam one. I catch her throw and back up a few steps. She does the same.

"You ready?" I call out to her, gripping the neon-green foam ball.

"Go for it!" she yells back with a fighting spirit that makes me excited.

The second it leaves my hand, I know I overthrew it. Kayla seems to see it too, so she runs back until she gets closer to the ball. It's still a little high. I don't expect her to catch it, but she jumps with a hand reaching up. It touches the tips of her fingers before tipping over. She doesn't give up. Her hand fumbles for the ball, keeping it alive for a few bounces before finally getting a grasp on it. She caught it! I'm elated, but the moment is short-lived.

I'm running towards her the next second. The jump. The catch. The momentum. Whatever it was, she loses balance when she lands her jump, falling onto the grass. *Is she—?*

"I'm okay! I'm okay!" I hear her say as she waves a hand up. She sits up so fast, I get surprised. But then *she* gets surprised when she sees me approach her. "Did you see that? I caught it!"

I smile and nod at her enthusiasm. She looks down to her hands, confused. They're empty. Her head turns all directions, searching for the ball. I bite back a laugh when I offer her my hand.

Without much hesitancy, she takes it, chuckling. "Thanks."

I help her up, unintentionally noticing the size of her hand. *It's kind of small. Cute. Like her.* I let her go and swat the thought away.

She quickly bends to pat down the dirt and grass off her clothes before standing up again. There's a loose piece of grass on her hair. Without thinking, I reach out and take it, letting it fall to the floor.

Kayla stiffens, looking at me with widened eyes.

Damn. I forgot to ask befo— *Wait, is she blushing?*

"T-Thank you." She smiles before turning away and clearing her throat. "I wonder where the ball went."

Out of nowhere, Pilly runs past us with the football in his mouth. I chase after him and grab the little pug off the ground. Kayla catches up, laughing from behind us. I manage to get Pilly to let go of the ball, but it's all slobbery now. "We should probably head back."

She chuckles, nodding in agreement as I clip the leash back on the dog and set him down. We walk out the grassy field, and just when we get on the concrete sidewalk, Pilly plops himself down into a Superman pose.

I tug on the leash lightly. "Come on, Pilly. You were running all over the place just a second ago."

He pants heavily before closing his mouth and resting his head on the sidewalk. *What is up with him today? He's never acted this needy before.* I sigh. From my side, Kayla walks toward him and scoops him up into her arms. Pilly doesn't fight it, casually enjoying the ride.

I unclip the leash as we head back to my house. "You spoil him too much."

"What, you jealous?" There's a little playful look in her eyes before she turns away giggling. "Just kidding!"

I gaze straight ahead and try to hold in a smile—failing horribly. This girl can sure joke around. The few minutes spent walking are in a comfortable silence. She shifts Pilly to a better position before we walk up the stairs to the porch. I open the front door with her following closely behind.

Fuck.

I come to an abrupt stop. "Dad."

Kayla bumps my back lightly. I bring a hand around in an attempt to steady her, but I don't turn around. I keep my stare on those glaring eyes. His arms are crossed. Jaw clenched. *He's upset.* Kayla touches my back a little, murmuring a small apology. From the corner of my eye, she steps a little to the side to peek at what's in front of me.

Dad takes a glance at her before returning his focus on me. "What do you think you're doing?"

I freeze. His tone is harsh, even in the presence of a guest. Kayla stiffens a little but recovers quickly as she sets Pilly down. Dad has the audacity to stare at Kayla with those hateful eyes when she turns around to close the front door. Pilly's soft panting fades into the distance, leaving the three of us in silence until Dad speaks up again.

"When you told me you needed time to study, I expect you to study. Not mess around with some girl!"

"Dad, we were studying. We were just—"

"Don't lie to me, Aiden. I saw you two in the park when I was coming back."

"I'm not lying, we were—"

"I did not give you a day off just so you can waste it on her!"

That's the second time he's said something rude about Kayla. I want to turn to her and apologize, but I can't even face her right now. I'm too ashamed to.

I grit my teeth, trying to think of something to say. Something that can end the conversation quick. To get Kayla out of this situation. Suddenly, I feel a soft reassuring hand on my arm.

"Mr. Mc— I mean Coach James, we were just taking a break," she says calmly, cutting the silence. Taking away the hand on me, she gestures to herself. "It was my idea. Please don't blame Aiden, it's not his fault."

Dad snarls. "He's a grown man, he can speak for himself."

"He *can.* Maybe if you stop cutting him off, you can actually listen to what he has to say."

"I was talking to him. Not you, young lady!" Dad steps forward, pointing a finger.

I take a step in front of Kayla, bringing an arm up to scoot her behind me. "Don't talk to her like that."

"I'll talk to her any way I want. This is *my* house!" His voice bellows, and I can only hope it's not scaring Kayla.

"What is going on here?" Mom comes out of the kitchen, walking into the scene with an incredulous look on her face. Scanning the three of us, her eyes land back on Dad. "Richard James McLaren! What are you doing? Why are you yelling at them? She's our guest!"

"Honey! You won't believe it. I caught them playing outside when *he* said he needed the day off to catch up on his studies. I told you I needed to be harder on him. Do something about this." Dad rubs his face, mumbling something about a headache.

Unexpectedly, I feel Kayla peek out from behind me again. "Sir, with all due respect, working hard does not mean to overwork."

Dad sends her a hard glare. I'm about to cover Kayla from his view again when Mom puts a hand on his shoulder. His gaze softens before turning to her.

"She's not wrong." Mom sends me a soft smile before facing him again. She takes his arm, dragging him upstairs. "Now come on, let's go. *You're* the one that's getting in the way of their studies."

Mom's got the situation under control as they disappear up the stairs. So I take my shoes off and head to the dining room. Kayla follows suit, but I don't say anything. Still unable to face her after whatever had just happened. She's already seen me as some pathetic guy who got cheated on. I don't need to add daddy issues on the list. I still can't believe Dad went off at her like that. He can intimidate *me* all he wants.

But not Kayla.

She sits down next to me, and we get back into precalc like the whole thing never happened. Aside from studying questions and answers, she's quiet. Once in a while, I sneak a few glances at her. She's got on a blank expression as she works on the math problems. Like the whole Dad thing didn't affect her. *She always wears her feelings on her face, but is she really okay?* It's not that I don't believe her. It's just that Emma once cried when Dad said something *interpretively* disrespectful in a very calm manner. Not only had he shouted just now, but he outrightly insulted Kayla. To her face. *Did he scare her?* Damn. I should've done more to stop him. To protect her. But *she* was the one protecting me. From my own dad. *What does she think of me now? A coward?*

"I'm sorry." Her voice is soft, but it's clear and firm among the silence of the room. I look at her, dumbfounded. She puts her pencil down and covers her clenched fist. Our eyes connect for the first time since the incident from earlier. "I had no right to butt in. Especially not between you and your dad. I didn't want to put you in a bad position but when he started yelling at you because of me, I just . . . I got mad."

Mad? Out of the three of us, she was the most composed—even when talking back to my dad. She looks away at her book, thumbs fidgeting. I swallow. "Kayla . . ."

"But if anything, I'm not sorry for saying all that to him." Her eyes return to mine with a sad smile. "He needed to hear it. He needed to know."

I turn my body so I can face her fully. "Kayla, if anyone should be sorry, it's me. He shouldn't have spoken to you like that. And I should've done more. I shouldn't have let that happen in the first place."

She gives my hand on the table a soft boop. The little gesture cuts some of the tension in the room. "You're not responsible for what he does. And you did so much already. Thank you for standing up for me."

"I should be the one thanking *you*. No one's ever talked to him like that before. Especially for me. You're amazing."

"Thanks." She smiles widely, the air between us lightening. "So this might be a weird time to say this, but I didn't know Coach James was your dad."

I raise an eyebrow. "*James* didn't ring a bell?"

She looks surprised. "I thought that was his first name. And isn't that your middle name? I don't know, no one tells me this stuff!"

That would explain how she addressed him at first. Funny. I thought the whole school knew about it. Her face looks flushed and

I chuckle. Because of this talk, we finish our study session on a better note. It's mid-afternoon when she starts to pack her things, and I excuse myself, a little disappointed that she's leaving. When I return, she's already standing up with her bag, all ready to go.

"Here."

"Thanks." She takes the yellow umbrella I hold out to her, and we walk out the dining room, discussing meeting up again after the upcoming test. We're at the front door and Kayla's just finished putting on her shoes when we hear little pitter-patters heading our way.

"Pilly!" Her voice goes up a pitch, just like all the other times she's spoken to my pug. It makes me smile. Pilly's in her arms again, and she rocks him like a baby. She must like dogs a lot.

"He likes you. Pilly's usually not this clingy with people. Definitely doesn't sleep on just anyone."

"Really? I'm honored. He's a really good boy." She pets his head, and when she starts to put him down, Pilly shifts in her arms—preventing her to do so. As if *he* didn't want her to leave. "Sorry, buddy. I gotta go now."

He doesn't calm down, so I take him from her. I hold Pilly with an arm, and he finally settles down when Kayla strokes him lovingly. Streaks of sunlight shine through the glass door and onto the side of her face. Her eyes glow like honey in the sun.

How alluring.

I clear my throat when she notices me staring. "I'll see you on Monday then?"

She nods and says a goodbye to us when I open the door for her. Kayla walks out the house and down the porch stairs, but slows down on the last few steps. Suddenly, she turns around and skips up the stairs, meeting me at the doorway.

"Did you forget something?" I sidestep to check for her, but her hand on my arm stops me from moving.

"No, I—" She lets go of me when I step back into my original position, facing her. Her hand is gripping the umbrella, eyes avoiding me. "T-Tomorrow is the final match of the badminton intramurals. I'm playing on one of the teams. Just letting you know, if you wan— I mean, if you're interested in watching."

"I'll be there."

Kayla looks up quickly, and I finally see her eyes again. Surprise. *Delight*. "Okay, then." She tucks hair behind her ear with a wide smile and brings up a shy hand. "Bye."

I wave back at her, and she walks down the steps—with confidence this time—disappearing down the corner.

Mom approaches me from behind. "I like her."

"Me too." I close the door and catch her giving me a knowing look. I have to resist rolling my eyes. "Not like *that*, Mom. You know what I mean."

"I do."

Her grin says otherwise.

Chapter 15
Kayla

Tracy's annoyed. Her eyes are almost glaring after I miss the birdie that landed on *her* side of the court. I swallow, not knowing if she was blaming me or herself for not anticipating that shot. Since she didn't seem like she was getting it from where she was standing, I guess maybe I could've gotten it if I were faster?

I sigh. "Sorry."

"It's fine."

Her tone of voice and that look on her face doesn't seem to think so, but I try to shake it off and be hopeful for the next point. Jonah and Rico are up a few. It'll be their set if we keep messing up. Or more like, if *I can't cover for her mistakes*. From my left, someone steps forward and tugs on the sleeve of my shirt. I'm about to pull away until I recognize it's Kevin.

"You've got nothing to apologize for, Summers." He leans in and speaks in a low volume. "It's your friend who keeps messing up."

He lets go, and I look at him, surprised. I appreciate his sentiment as it lightens some of the burden. But it doesn't shake my stress away. Unable to respond properly, I give him a weak smile. We've been good ever since my apology. Tracy and I even won against him and Donny last week. He was cool with it. So it's not a surprise that he's here to watch the final match of badminton intramurals. Many of the other players—mostly those who lost at the semi-finals—are gathered around to watch as well. To see who would win, most likely. But at this rate, it doesn't look too hot on our side.

And I'm right. Without much trouble, Jonah and Rico win the first set. When we switch sides, some guy from the audience catches my attention. Who is that waving me ov—

No way. He came. I can't believe he's here! I mean, I know he said he'd be here, but when he didn't show up for the first set, I assumed he'd forgot or something. I jog over to greet him, trying not to take too much time away from the game.

Aiden flashes me an apologetic smile. "Hey, sorry I'm late. Got held up."

"It's okay. I'm just glad you made it." I gesture to the scoreboard, a little embarrassed. "We just lost the first set. So, not much of a show here."

"Oh?" His brow raises in a pleasant surprise. "Did you *want* to put on a show for me?"

What the— I look at him, flabbergasted. This guy. I swear he's a serial teaser.

He snickers. "Just do your best, that's all that matters. And" — he gives me an uplifting tap on my arm and sends me a wink — "go get 'em."

Instant dopamine.

That's what he is. A power-up. A boost. His little encouragement is all I needed. A newfound sense of motivation comes over me, and my best is what I did. My smashes were smashing. Returns were returning. I even got the ones Tracy missed. The birdie comes my way, and I take the chance to jump and smack it down as hard as I can.

Oh, shit. It hits Jonah's crotch.

Most of the boys watching react to the hit while others clap for the point. I step close to the net towards him. "Sorry, sorry! I didn't mean to do that! Are you okay?"

Jonah nods and turns around in embarrassment. Feeling awkward all of a sudden, I look away and catch Aiden silently laughing at me. Nick's next to him, nodding in approval. Nearby, Kevin's clapping, and Donny sends me a thumbs-up. *Dear me! What did they just see?*

Not my proudest shot, but it earns us the second set. I feel kinda bad about it, but then again, it's Jonah. So, not *that* bad. Due to time constraints, we're told to play a tiebreaker of ten points. Win by two, ideally. If not, first to ten is the winner. Meaning, every point matters.

The match—which was heated already—becomes even more intense. Every time we play out a point, no one speaks. The gym gets so unusually quiet. Just the sound of strings hitting the birdie.

Sometimes, shoes squeaking. And occasionally, some mumbling communication among us players. There's so much pressure.

Jonah smashes the birdie, and it lands inside the lines—on Tracy's side. *Crap. That was one of his slower ones.* She could've gotten that. If we had gotten that point, we would've won the game. But it's 9–9 now. Deciding point. *Don't mess up, Kayla. Don't mess up.* I take in a deep breath. Jonah's fired up. Rico too. I look at Tracy. Not good. Her drive is dying.

"We got this," I encourage her.

She nods, but it doesn't look like she heard me at all. I don't know why, but my eyes travel over to Aiden. He gives me a reassuring nod and a smile that makes everything feel okay. Like he believes in me.

Just do your best, that's all that matters.

That's right. If we lose, we lose. At least this was fun. I'm proud with how I played so far. I really am. The weight of the pressure seems lighter now. I smile back, getting into position.

Go get 'em.

Rico serves. Tracy returns. Jonah backhands. I smash at Jonah. *Crap, not fast enough.* He returns it. Tracy hits. Rico returns. It goes over me. I back up and smack a long shot. *Good, down the middle!* It's going to Jonah's forehand so it should be him, but Rico backs up as well. *He's going for the shot?* Both of them are in the back now. *Yes, an opening!* We have to hit one near the net. I run back into mid-court position as Jonah—after a silent miscommunication with Rico—returns it. It's coming over to my side, near the net.

Hit it mid-court and we risk a longer rally before either of them ends us with a killing smash. But a drop shot. We might just win this if they don't run up fast enough. What if I can't do it? What if it doesn't go over the— Wait! How do I do a drop shot again? I run towards the birdie. This is super risky! Probably a bad idea! I'm not sure if I can—

Don't think, just do.

I loosen my grip on my racket as the birdie bounces off of it. It flies up and hits the top of the net. Jonah and Rico are racing up to the front, shoes squeaking. But it's too late. The birdie lands on the floor before either of them can reach it. I swear it was so quiet for a second, I heard the birdie bounce off the floor.

It . . . it went over.

Suddenly, the crowd around us erupts. They're cheering. Clapping. Tracy squeals and runs over, hugging me. "We did it! We won!"

I return the hug and can only hum in agreement, still speechless about what had happened. That drop shot *barely* made it. That was so lucky! Tracy lets go of me before running off to somewhere else. I don't pay attention because Aiden comes over.

"You did it!" He gives me a high five.

"Thanks!" I'm smiling so hard, my face hurts. "And thanks for coming! I couldn't have done this without—"

The bell rings, and as if on cue, the crowd disperses.

"Sorry, I still need to wrap up over here. You can go first, I'll see you later!" I give him a wave as I jog towards Jonah and Rico, extending my racket. "Good game."

They look at me and clink my racket with theirs, returning the words. No smiles. No lingering looks. They just turn away like nothing even happened. Coach Dan—the intramurals instructor—congratulates Tracy and me, then announces us as the winners of the upperclassmen badminton intramurals.

There's no prize. Tracy's a little disappointed when we put our rackets away, but I laugh nonchalantly. No prize? We just beat Jonah and Rico. Nothing's better than this sense of accomplishment. *I don't think Jonah will be giving me any more advice after today. Man, the satisfaction!*

As Tracy and I grab our things, I see a familiar guy lingering nearby. Franny's crush, Alek, stands there semi-awkwardly. Well, he's definitely not waiting for me. I turn to my friend and see her brighten up. Tracy bids me a goodbye before she and Alek quickly walk out of the gym together. *Someone's taking her wingwoman job very seriously.*

I exit the gym alone and suddenly see Aiden around the corner. He's leaning against a rail, looking towards the direction Tracy and Alek are heading off to. "Hey. What are you doing here? I thought you left already."

He walks by my side. "We have precalc next. Figured we could just go together."

Aiden waited for me so we could walk to class together? We reach the stairs, and I smile, feeling like my heart just melted.

"Was that your friend who just left?"

Oh.

Did he wait for me just to ask me *that*? Of course he wants to know about Tracy. Everyone does. He probably likes how cool she looked playing badminton, huh? That she obviously doesn't look half the sweaty mess I am right now. Even after that intense match, she probably still smells like strawberries. This is it. It's over. Aiden must've noticed how amazing she—

I clear my throat. "Yup. That's Tracy."

"Tracy," he repeats, as if memorizing her name.

His voice is so deep. And that rasp. Ugh, so attractive. But why did he have to say her name like that? Why is he asking about her? Is he *interested* in her? If it's because he saw her today, then that would mean I—

I bite my tongue.

You should've never asked him to come.

Shivers run up my spine.

"Is she that . . . theater friend?"

I catch myself slowing down a step before I match his speed again. "She is."

He nods, soaking in the information. We reach the bottom of the stairs when I take a good look at his face. *What is he thinking about?* For the rest of the way—luckily or unluckily—we walk to class in silence. Harbored thoughts spill out, and my head gets the best of me.

It's not fair. I knew him first. I liked him first. I—

Stop! Stop being bitter and calm down. Aiden's not even her type. And he referred to her as the theater friend. He knows how uncomfortable she made me feel. Shouldn't that be a good thing?

It *should* be. But why does my heart feel like it's—

No. No. No! Not again. *Haven't you learned by now? You know he doesn't see you that way. He's not interested. He doesn't like you.*

I know! And he doesn't have to. I'm okay with this being unrequited. I just like spending time with him. Can't I have *that*?

Not when a certain someone has caught his eye now.

I hold in a sigh. It's not a competition. I know that. But even so, I feel like I've lost something; something I never really had in the first place.

I feel defeat. I can't help it. So, I accept it.

Congratulations, Trace.

You win again.

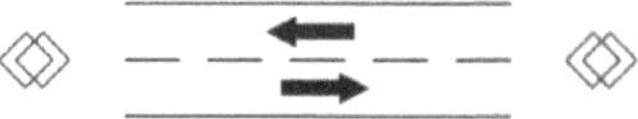

Tennis practice always does wonders. It's fun playing with my team and getting to use all my strength when hitting the balls. It tires me out. The good kind of tired. It helps me forge— *Accept* reality. It's good it turned out this way. He wasn't gonna like me back anyway. *What was I freaking out about?* I guess it was just nice being around someone who knew *me*—without Joss or Trace in the picture.

"Okay, girls, huddle up! I've got an announcement to make," Coach Aubrey calls out, and the team does as told. "As you all know, the fall rally is coming up soon and guess what? They're changing it up this year. Instead of student council members, the class representatives participating in the games will be from fall sports teams. We've been very lucky to have two of our girls chosen for the rally. So let's give a big cheer to Allana and Kayla! We wish you luck, and may the best team win."

I freeze as the team claps for us. We're all dismissed, and some of the girls congratulate Allana and me. Janella gives me a high five and wishes me luck. I thank her and flash her a grateful smile before she leaves. My stomach is turning in circles, but I manage to hold a straight face. *This isn't good. What if I do bad? I can't do this.* Next to me, Franny and Pat are celebrating.

Franny nudges me playfully before we all grab our things. "Represent us seniors, Kay! Win for us!"

Pat claps excitedly. "I can't wait to watch you play!"

"Thanks guys, I'll" — I laugh nervously and fist bump the air — "do my best."

"Great! I'd love to chat some more, but I gotta go. Bye, girls!"

Pat and I bid Franny a goodbye in unison, waving to her disappearing figure.

"She's in a hurry."

"Speech practice," Pat simply says. "So she can spend the first half of the lantern festival with Alek."

"What about the second half?"

"No can do. That's when the competition starts. What a shame."

Spending the first half together doesn't sound very long, does it? I wonder if they can even enjoy themselves with the limited time. Wouldn't that be a lot of pressure on Franny? I don't bother to ask all these questions aloud but I do give Pat a response. "I hope it works out with Alek."

"Don't worry. Tracy's her wingwoman, remember? What can go wrong?"

A sudden shudder runs up my body. "Right . . . What can go wrong?"

Kayla's been acting pretty anxious lately. I wonder if she's hanging out with that friend of hers too much. Tracy, was it? She was the one making most of the mistakes during their badminton match. Yet, she had the audacity to make those faces at Kayla? I don't like her. Not one bit. If Emma hadn't bothered me, I would've showed up earlier and told that Tracy to get her act together. Kayla kept going like it didn't bother her but it infuriated me. That girl needs to learn it's not okay to take your frustrations out on people. If it hadn't been for Kayla, they wouldn't have won. I'm glad Kayla ditched her last time. *She's no friend.*

I sigh. But if I'm wrong and it's not Tracy causing her nerves, then it must be Kevin.

Nick told me he saw Kevin and her talking last week. "It looked serious. You don't think he's picking on her again, do you?"

"What do mean *again?*"

"Donny said Kevin left a note in her locker after failing to flip her lock. Don't you remember? After the fall sports meet— Wait, that's when you disappeared to Kayla herself!" Nick said, laughing.

I was hoping it wasn't him since Kayla seemed fine in the beginning of the semester and Kevin has been quite tame lately, strangely enough. If that's because he's found an outlet—picking on Kayla—to blow off some steam, then it has to be stopped.

Football practice ends and I tell Nick to wait for me outside while I linger around for Kevin to pass by. He doesn't say much, just nods before walking ahead. From a short distance away, I spot Kevin and Donny coming this way.

Donny straightens his neck and speaks in a softer tone, like he's reenacting someone, "You don't have to go easy on us next time. We like a little challenge."

Kevin laughs. "Did you see the look on their faces?" They both gape at each other, laughing about it afterwards. Not a second later, Kevin spots me, and his amusement disappears.

I walk up to him, stopping them in their tracks. "I need to talk to you."

"Well, I don't." He scoffs. "For fuck's sake, why does everyone want to talk to me lately?" He takes a step forward, and I take one to stop him.

It's utter silence between the three of us. The faint noises of our teammates in a far distance only adds to the tension. Donny catches on and clears his throat. "I'll see you outside."

Kevin grits his teeth as he watches his friend disappear from the scene. When Donny is gone, he's back to glaring again and speaking in a murderous tone. "What do you want, *James*?"

"I don't know what you have against me, but whatever it is, it's between you and me. Leave Kayla out of it."

"Summers?" His brow loosens up as he smirks. "Jealous much?"

I feel my body burn up. This has nothing to do with my feelings for her. It's about him dragging her into this mess between us. I do my best to ignore his remark and steer him back on topic. "You wouldn't even have looked her way if she didn't defend me. It's *me* you want to get back at. Don't take it out on her."

"You don't know anything, James." He points a finger at me with a dark look. "And you don't get to tell me who I associate with. *You* of all people!"

"What does *that* mean?"

"Seriously?" He shoots me a dirty look. "You stole Emma from me and still act like you're the victim? You knew I liked her!"

"Stole her? You and Emma were never together, Kevin. And . . . I had no idea you liked her."

He sneers. Anger burning in his eyes. "Come on, James. You gotta do better than that!"

I hate the way he calls me by that name. I hate the way he's provoking me. It reminds me of Dad. I ball up my fists, holding it in. "I didn't know. You never told me."

"Why would I? Unlike you, I don't need everything handed to me on a silver platter, *Coach's boy.*" He spits the last two words, disgust in his voice.

"You don't know what you're talking about." My voice gets deep and there's a silent pause between the two of us. I tried to be understanding when it was about Emma. But this? *He's crossed the line.*

Kevin scowls. "The same goes for you. So stay out of my business." He walks past me, bumping my shoulder on the way.

I'm about to let it end there, but then I remember why I came to talk to him in the first place. I turn around and call out, "Kevin, please." He stops in his tracks. "Don't blame Kayla because of me. I'm asking you. She has nothing to do with this."

He sighs, eventually turning around compliantly. "I don't blame her. Not anymore. I admit I was wrong to mess with her in the beginning. I was angry and . . . immature."

Kevin never admits fault. *Just what happened between him and Kayla?*

"She came to me to sort things out. If you don't believe me, ask her yourself." He doesn't elaborate further. He just walks away.

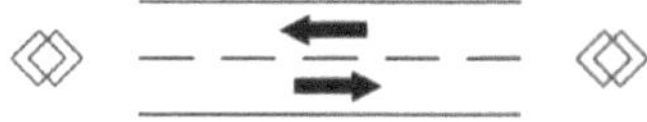

Dad is clapping systemically, yelling me to go faster. Sprinting. Cutting corners. Ladder steps. Drill after drill. *Faster, Aiden. Faster. Focus. Not sharp enough! Put more power into it!* His comments are endless. In the middle of a single leg hop, my ankle gives out for a second. I stumble a bit before recovering and finish the drill with a sprint.

"Come on Aiden, these are simple drills!"

I rest my hands on my hips, exhaling deeply and trying to even out my breathing. Dad pinches the bridge of his nose before sighing. I wipe the sweat dripping down my face with the hem of my shirt.

He shakes his head in disappointment. "When I was your age, this was nothing. I used to run all over the place and not get tired."

I don't say anything. Too tired to. *Did I mess up a drill earlier today or did I underperform during practice? Is that why he's drilling me right now?* It's already dark and the last person at the park left twenty minutes ago. My feet are getting sore, muscles burning.

Dad sighs as he adjusts the cones on the grassy field. "Your grandpa used to drill me harder than this. Come on!"

I almost want him to keep lecturing so I can catch my breath. I take my time getting into position before we do a few more cone drills. Relentless comments, one after another. Not one "good job." By the time I finish, the cold night air is a blessing. Dad picks up the cones and heads to the pile of equipment he'd brought over.

"You're getting slow, Aiden. I expect you to do better tomorrow."

"Yes, Coach." As he grabs the rest of the equipment, I walk over to pick some up as well, thinking we're finished.

He shoos me away with a wave of his hand, stopping me from helping him. "Get two laps in before doing your weights tonight."

I stay silent as I let out a quiet sigh, glad his back is facing towards me. My frustration may be barely audible, but my face is a different story. I feel it loosen up a little when I look away.

Dad turns around with his hands full. "Got it?"

Not looking at him in the eye, I turn to his direction and nod. "Yes, sir."

Dad turns around to head home without me. I start running my laps and watch him walk onto the sidewalk as I do a turn. When I know I'm out of his vision, I slow down to a jog. Getting to the end of the second lap, I sink down onto my back with bent knees. My shirt's probably going to get dirty, but frankly, I don't care right now. I need to lie down. I'm finally catching a much-needed break while on the grass, admiring the full moon tonight.

Unlike you, I don't need everything handed to me on a silver platter, Coach's boy.

I chuckle a little, letting my limp legs sprawl out to rest on the ground. My breathing finally steadies from the panting. If this is what he means by silver platter, then I don't want it. I never did. What's so good about being *Coach's boy* when he can't say one positive thing to me? Not a single word of encouragement. Not even one of his typical default lines he uses for the whole team during practices. I'm doing my best. *Why can't he see that? Why can't he be satisfied with that? Am I really that lacking or is it something I'm doing wrong?* My body tenses up until another familiar voice plays in my head.

We're a little too hard on ourselves sometimes.

Kayla's words replay again and my body starts to relax. She's right. I know she is, but what if? What if I'm really not—

You're really cool.

She'd said that with such a bright smile. Somehow, the image of her shuts down all my doubts. My worries. I can't believe Kayla actually said that. I'm the guy who got cheated on. The guy who can't even talk back to his dad. What does she see in me that's cool? Being able to find the fun in the little things and to laugh off anything is what's admirable. I snicker. If anything, *she's* the cool one. A few peaceful minutes pass before I quickly sit up and grab my phone. *It's just a question, there's no harm in it.* Not wanting to have any second thoughts, I send my message.

Me

Hey

R u still goin to the lantern festival this Saturday?

I don't expect her to answer right away, so I'm about to click my phone off. But suddenly, typing bubbles appear. My heart starts to race.

Cookieface

Not sure, it depends

On?

On y u're asking 0.0

What if I said I want to go?

Typing bubbles again. But it's taking longer this time. Excitement turns to anticipation. And anticipation turns to fear when the bubbles disappear. *Why did I say that? Maybe I scared her off. Or maybe she made plans already? Am I too late?* This was a bad idea. I should just tell her to forget it. *Ding!*

Do u?

I let out a laugh of relief. Did it really take her a whole two minutes to type three letters? *That scared me.*

I do

I'm still going

Typing bubbles. They disappear again. No messages appear this time. *What am I waiting for? I should be the one saying something.* I never even gave her an answer last time. *Suck it up and ask her already.* I start typing out my reply but sending it through text doesn't sit well with me. Before I think to stop myself, I press the call button and I'm up on my feet in seconds. Too late to back out now. The call rings. And rings. And rings before it cuts off.

"H-Hello?"

The sound of her sweet and surprised voice makes me smile. "Hey, Kayla. Sorry for calling so late. I thought . . . it'd be easier to just call you about this."

I pace around but come to a stop when she chuckles. "Okay."

"What you asked me last time, about going to the lantern festival with you. I never gave you an answer." I rub my neck. "Is . . . that offer still on?" It's silent on her end. I look at the screen. The call's still connected. "Hello? Kayla? You there?"

"H-Hi! Yes, I'm still here!" She clears her throat. "It is. The offer's still on."

I don't need to see her face to know she said that with a smile. My grin widens. "I want to take you up on it if that's okay."

"Yeah! I mean yes. That's totally okay. I'd like that."

"Great . . ."

"I'll text you," she says, cutting the silence.

I don't realize how tense my shoulders were until they relax. "Great." *Damn, is that all I can say?* I clear my throat. "It's getting late. I should get going. I hope I didn't bother you too much."

"No! Of course not. This was fun. I liked hearing your— *Ahem*. I mean, yeah, this was fun."

She liked hearing my what? My voice? I feel my cheeks warm when I chuckle. "I'll see you tomorrow then. Good night."

"Good night, Aiden."

Her three words are so pleasant to the ears, I'm standing still to savor the moment until the call ends. There's a cool whisp of air that breezes by, but I can't feel it on my face. Suddenly, tonight doesn't seem so bad anymore. I can get through this. I grab my things before jogging back home to get started on the weights with a newfound energy.

Thank you, Kayla. Thanks for not letting me down.

He wanted to join me. *Faster, Kayla. Run!* I dart past the crowd and head towards the tree I was waiting in front of twenty minutes ago. *Please be late, Aiden. At least, later than I am.*

What if he's not late and was there all along? What am I gonna say? "Sorry, my aunt (the singer) was running late, so my friend Janella (the assistant stage coordinator) asked me to cover for her"? Yeah, that was me who opened the first song five minutes ago. Yup, that was a bunch of people.

No! If he's been waiting this whole time, that meant he saw *and* heard me sing. How embarrassing! I wanna crawl in a hole and disappear right now. Why did I— *No, Kayla. Janella lent you her racket when your strings broke during that one match. You were returning a favor.*

"I was just kidding about the favor thing! The whole team offered their rackets to you, remember? I only said that because I knew you'd feel bad and do it for me. That was evil of me. Sorry Kayla!" Janella said just moments ago.

If I didn't have someone waiting for me, I probably would've stayed and complained to her. *Whatever, it's over now. You did a good thing. Janella needed you, Aunt Gwen needed you, and you showed up. That's all that matters.* Four minutes of humiliation and anxiety were worth it, I guess. It doesn't matter if you were shaky or swallowed too many times. You still got through the whole song with no lyrical mistakes. *Give yourself some credit, you should be proud!*

I sigh as I slow down at the big tree. No one. Not to the left. Not to the right. Not behind the tree. *Yes! He's not here yet.*

It's six minutes past our meeting time. No notifications yet. Should I text him? Would that be rude? Or just wait for four more min—

"Boo!"

I involuntarily shriek, whipping around to see the source of the sudden noise and catch someone familiar. Unfortunately, in the process, I back up and unknowingly step onto something uneven. *A tree root,* I think as I lose my footing and tilt backwards.

Aiden lunges forward, grabs my arm, and pulls me toward him. I grasp onto the nearest thing I can get my hands on. It all happens so fast. Before I know it, his arms are secured around me. Our feet stumble from the jolt until finally, we find our balance.

I didn't fall. I'm safe! I'm . . . *I'm being smothered into his chest?*

Holy moly, he caught me! Still high on adrenaline, I stiffen—accidentally clutching onto him tighter. I-Is this his torso? So sturdy.

So warm. *Shit, shit, shit. Get it together, Kayla!* When I try to relax myself, he loosens his grip on me, giving me the chance to pull away from the unintentional hug.

"Are you okay?"

"Y-Yeah, thanks for the save. You scared me!" My tone isn't accusing and I make sure he knows it when I laugh a little.

"Sorry. I got a little too excited."

"For what? Halloween?" I jokingly ask, rubbing the jitters off my chest.

There's a slight pause before he clears his throat. "Well, it is right around the corner."

He's brought up a good point, so I nod. *Play it cool, play it cool, Kayla.* I adjust the strap of my bag and brighten up.

Aiden fixes his hair. "I hope you didn't wait too long."

"Not at all! I just got here."

"Cool, me too."

I let out sigh of relief. At least that means he didn't witness me on stage. That would've been weird. I swallow. "So . . ."

The words get caught in my throat. He agreed to come, so I thought I'd make it fun by throwing in a guess-each-other's-lanterns game. We'd agreed on doing a prompt about our favorite something. I doubt we're gonna spend the whole day looking at lanterns though. Playing carnival games wasn't on the schedule, but it's the only thing I could think of to spend more time with him. It won't hurt to try, right? I give him a smile, hoping to convince him to say yes. Aiden looks at me curiously, patiently waiting for me to go on. *Come on, girl. Spit it out!*

"I . . . I got us a stack of tickets. I thought that maybe we could go play some games before we do our little guessing game."

"You did?"

"Yeah." He looks taken aback. *Maybe this was a stupid idea. Keep your composure, Kayla.* "We don't have to, of course! I was just asking."

"No."

I nod understandingly. *Honestly, I should've seen that coming.*

"No," he repeats, sighing in defeat. "I mean no, I want to."

"Really?"

"Yes." He chuckles. "I was just . . . You surprised me, that's all."

I nod, not understanding what he meant by that. Surprised him how? Whatever, I'm just glad he said yes.

As we head towards the carnival booths, he suddenly turns to me with a confident smirk. "You better get ready. I'm going to win this lantern guessing game."

I grin at his feigned arrogance and declaration of war. Who knew Aiden had a competitive side? I cross my arms and give him one of my own confident smirks. "Oh, really? Game on. Good luck with *warm*."

"That's your hint? Good luck with *motivated*."

My confident demeanor dies down a bit, and I swear he's restraining himself from laughing. "That's so vague!"

"I'm willing to give another hint, but . . ."

"But what?"

He flashes me a grin. "It'll cost you."

He's so mischievous. And so cute. Gosh darn it. *Look away, Kayla. Don't get swayed.* I keep a smile on as I glance ahead. "No, we agreed on one hint only. I'm not complaining." I'm adamant with my words, and I'm proud.

His brow raises, almost looking slightly disappointed when he breaks into a smile. "Then" — he extends a hand towards me — "may the best guesser win."

"May the best guesser win," I repeat, doing the same.

He wraps his fingers around my hand, and oh my god. It *does* feel like electricity. We give it a shake as I try to keep the blood from rushing up my cheeks. The sensation starts to fade away when we let go and debate about what games to play. I do my best to focus, but I can't stop thinking about how his hand felt.

So welcomed. So grounded. So warm.

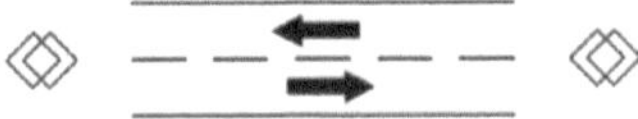

We played a bunch of games. Aiden's got a knack for these carnival games and I . . . well, I'm not bad, thankfully. Each game went pretty well, except for the basketball booth. Shooting hoops is my weakness. I wouldn't even have played if Aiden hadn't *asked* me to. Oh, and aside from that other game where you have to knock the floating beach ball out the air vents with a beanbag. I knocked it down easily, but because I threw it so hard, it bounced back into the air vents and returned to their floating position. Aiden laughed hysterically. I felt cheated, but at least he was enjoying himself. It was all very fun.

They sold Hong Kong street food in one of the booths. I was so happy 'cause it gave me the chance to introduce Aiden to eggettes and curry fish balls. Luckily for me, he was more than keen on trying it. He was so eager, he even stuffed a fish ball in his mouth without a second thought. It was hot, so he had to spit it out on the napkin I offered him. He's so silly. We ate dinner together after having scavenged all the hanging lanterns around the area.

Time flew by so fast, the next thing I know, we're throwing our trash into the bins. Before we can idly stand around, I turn to him. He does the same and says something. I don't hear it because it's so loud in this crowd.

"What?" I give him a shrug and a confused look, making it obvious that I didn't hear him. I think he understands because he starts to look around. For what? I don't know. I look around, too, but all I see are people. Suddenly, he takes me by my wrist and gently tugs me along behind him. I don't question it, I just follow.

After a few steps, he slows down and turns to me. "Sorry."

I don't hear but see him briefly mutter it as he loosens his grasp on my wrist, and gently moves his hand to hold mine. *Oh dear. I did not expect that!* He doesn't seem to pay much mind as he turns around and continues to lead the way—*holding* my hand now. *Crap! You should've just kept it on my wrist. My heart's gonna burst!*

Too bad he didn't take my left hand. That one doesn't have any calluses. Wait, can he even feel them? Before I internally sulk some more, we come to a stop and luckily get into a . . . a Ferris wheel? Not good. This cannot get any worse! I know I kinda wanted this to be a date, but I was fine with it being a friendly hangout. But could it be? *Does he maybe possibly like me too?* I mean, it's a Ferris wheel! And if it's just the two of us, doesn't that make things kinda romantic? *Stop overthinking it and pull yourself together, Kayla!* Friends can ride a Ferris wheel together. Right!

He lets me go in first, still holding my hand to help me step inside the cart. Only when I sit, he lets go. I clear my throat as I settle into my seat and he into his. The Ferris wheel operator closes the cart door and we're making our way up in seconds.

There's an awkward silence before he decides to break it. "Do you want to rock paper scissors? Winner goes first?"

"For what?"

He laughs. "The guessing game. Figured this was quiet enough to hold a conversation."

I laugh back. "Yeah, sounds good." *Right, of course that was it. I was reading too much into things.* A girl can dream though. We do a rock paper scissors and he wins with a paper covering my rock.

"Ready to be blown away?"

I chuckle. "Surprise me."

He takes out his phone and pulls up a picture before handing it to me. The center of the lantern displays a drawing of the French dish ratatouille. *It's mine.* I take a moment before I hand his phone back.

"H-How did you know?"

"I had a feeling this was yours." He shrugs, shoving his phone back in his pocket. "And there wasn't much related to *warm.*" I look at him in shock, still surprised he got it on the first try. "It's *Ratatouille*, right? When the food critic gets a massive flashback of his mom's cooking? The dish that turned his frown upside down?"

"Yes! That's exactly it. That was my favorite scene in the movie. His ratatouille is like my chicken alphabet soup!" *Why on earth did I say that?* He breaks into a laugh and I look away, smiling sheepishly and making sure I call him out playfully. "It makes me happy, don't judge me."

"I would never." His laughter dies down, and I look at him suspiciously. "Mine's mac 'n' cheese."

My embarrassment suddenly vanishes. Who would've guessed that? And Aiden shared that piece of information willingly! I turn away, unable to keep myself from giggling. *It kinda suits him.* The thought of this big guy getting sentimental over mac 'n' cheese makes me weak. I can't with this. He's adorable.

Come on, Kayla, it's no time to admire his comfort food right now. He clears his throat and I catch him looking away bashfully. Aiden's got a smile on and . . . is he blushing? Holy crap! Never in my life, would I have thought I'd see this. Is this the first time he's told someone that? My surprise fades as soon as it comes. No, that's not possible. I'm sure he's told that to other people before. But still, it makes me happy he's told me this. It makes me really happy.

"Alright" — he nudges my foot lightly with his — "your turn. Let's see what you got."

Gosh darn it. How can I even guess properly now? *Is he gonna be disappointed if I don't get it right?* I don't . . . I don't want that. I sigh. "To be fair, there were a lot of motivational lanterns out there. It was hard," I warn him as I pull up my guess on my phone. "I'm not confident with this one, but here goes nothing."

Don't be disappointed, I want to say. I don't think I can handle it if I let you down too. Aiden only nods with a smile, waiting patiently for me to guess. I hand him my phone, and he reads the quote on the lantern I took a picture of.

He laughs, giving it back to me. "How does that make you feel motivated?"

"To be a better and understanding person. I don't know." I start to laugh now, too, as I put my phone away. "Hey, I was looking for a needle in a haystack! Cut me some slack."

"Okay, not gonna disagree with you there. Do you want to give it a few more tries?"

"Ha! And embarrass myself some more? No thanks. I know when to accept defeat."

As if expecting my answer, Aiden chuckles and starts to pull up something on his phone. "Here." He hands it to me, and I see a picture of his lantern.

"'The same boiling water that softens the potato hardens the egg. It's about what you're made of, not the circumstances,'" I read aloud, skipping the unknown author reference line. "I saw this one near the bridge." He gives me a small smile when I look up at him. I hand him his phone back, and he puts it away swiftly. "So, that's your favorite quote?"

"It's a parable, actually. About a girl who complains about how miserable her life is and how she doesn't know if she could handle it anymore because problems keep coming one after another."

I shift in a better position to listen more comfortably before he continues on.

"Her father's a chef. So he boils three pots of water, puts the potatoes in one, the eggs in the other, and ground coffee beans in the last one. He lets them boil for half an hour until he finally takes them out to show his daughter, explaining we can get soft and weak like the potato, hard and jaded like the egg, or . . . we can change our circumstances instead of letting them change us like the coffee beans."

I grin, completely amazed and immersed in his storytelling.

"Moral of the story—it's what happens within us and how we choose to respond that's important."

When he finishes, the atmosphere gets a little serious for some reason. So much so that I can tell he truly values the meaning behind this story. My want to know more and understand why it's so important to him gets the better of me. I don't think before I ask, "Which one are you?" *Crap. Why did I even ask that? It sounds like a sensitive topic. Hurry, I need to tell him he doesn't need to an—*

"I want to be coffee beans, but most of the time I feel like I'm a potato. Sometimes an egg, not like that's any better. I don't know. It's . . ." He laughs bitterly as he plays with his fingers.

A knowing feeling washes over me, and I regret ever asking him my question. I never want to be the cause of that kind of face again. *I should've just kept my mouth shut.* But I can't take it back now, can I? How do I fix this?

Physical touch reduces stress and anxiety.

I read that somewhere on the internet a while ago on my search to help lower my anxiety. But physical touch seems like one of Aiden's love languages. I don't wanna touch him without permission. Wait. Didn't he say I could touch him though? After the whole arm-grabbing mishap? Maybe . . . maybe I can try?

Just do it.

Not letting myself think about the consequences for now, I extend my hand. I try to put it on his softly. The sensation seems to snap him out of his thoughts and he looks up at me, confused.

"You . . . You don't have to tell me anything you don't want to." One of my thumbs unconsciously caresses his hand when I think of what to say. "In my opinion, they might each react differently, but they all taste good. Am I right?"

I let out a chuckle after hearing how silly I sound. Aiden doesn't laugh though. Instead, he looks at me with this expression I can't quite figure out. *On second thought, maybe this was a dumb idea.* I'm carefully retracting my hand when one of his hands breaks away from the fidgeting and rests on top of mine. Holding it there.

His hands are big and rough, yet delicate somehow. He's so unusually warm, I hope I'm not making him cold. Hold on. This was supposed to be an attempt to comfort *him*. Why do I feel like *I'm* the one being comforted here? At least he looks like he's in a better mood. I clear my throat.

"I guess what I'm trying to say is. . . there's no rainbow without rain?" My statement turns into a question because I don't know if that makes any sense or if he could make any connections to that.

Aiden nods his head a little. "I never really thought about it that way, but I get you. You're right."

He looks at me with a newfound confidence, and I feel like I did something right for once. Smiling, I let out a sigh of relief. If he didn't get that, I wouldn't know what to do. Suddenly, my failed attempt to console Tracy comes to mind. *Ugh, don't think about that right now.*

From the corner of my eye, something bright catches my attention. I turn to take a look and see a handful of candle-lit lanterns floating in the sky—some, reaching around our height. They're beautiful. It's like a scene from a movie.

"Look, look! A lantern!" I point out the window with one hand while the other shakes his hands violently. Wait, his hands? *Oh. His hands.* I catch him smiling, politely hiding his surprise. "Sorry!"

I let him go and pull my hands together onto my lap. It's not like I intended to do that for so long, I just got distracted. He collects himself, rubbing his hands onto his pants. *Oh dear, did my hand sweat too much? I hope he didn't feel that!*

"I read that physical touch reduces stress." *Stupid mouth.* Aiden looks at me intently and I can only cringe at my assumption of his feelings. "Not that you were stressed or anything!"

Just a little down, I think. Unconsciously, my eyes dart down to my own hands. Squeezing one with the other, I start to mumble, "I don't know, I just thought it would help or something."

Geez, this is so embarrassing. I totally blew it. Did I just make things awkward? He probably didn't like me touching him. But he did touch me too, right? Screw this, my head's all over the place. I don't know anymore. *You really stepped out of line this time, didn't you Kayla? I swear when this cart lands, you'd better hurry on out of here!* Suddenly, my mind gets quiet as I feel something.

Something warm.

It's Aiden. He's covering my hands with one of his. When his thumb rubs my hand softly, I look up at him speechless. "It did, thank you."

His smile wipes all my worries away, and I think time stops for a moment. Well, at least for a very short moment because he takes his hand away too soon. A feeling of the cool air lingers on my skin. It's not cold though. Instead, all I feel is blood rushing up to my face. My hands. My feet. *I can feel everything.*

Aiden clears his throat and looks out the window. Admiring the lanterns, I'm assuming. "So, does that mean I get to decide on my prize?"

I follow his lead and stare out the window, appreciating the scenery. "A deal's a deal. Just let me know what you want. As long as it's reasonable." I can't believe I managed to say that without stuttering.

He nods coolly. "Alrighty."

Maybe it's the way he smiles afterwards or the slight sound of air he makes with his mouth. But I swear— "Did you just . . . chuckle?"

Aiden stares me dead in the eyes with a bewildered look on his face. "No."

Such smoothness, no one would've suspected anything. Heck, they might've thought I was the crazy one. Well, that is until his innocent face breaks into a goofy smile.

"Reasonable!" I say, finding myself smiling at his mischievousness. My foot nudges his playfully. All he does is laugh and nod compliantly. I should probably be worried about his request but strangely enough, I'm not. In fact, I'm excited. I want to know what he'll ask of me.

I'm really happy right now. So happy, I wish this would last a little longer.

Kayla was chosen as one of the fall rally senior participants. She took the chance to tell me that it had been making her nervous all last week when our class headed for the gymnasium. So *that* was why she had been so anxious previously.

"No pressure. Just have fun out there. You got this," I told her.

She thanked me with a smile before everyone dispersed to sit with their friends on the bleachers. I hope that did the trick. I know she was nervous singing on stage last weekend—which was why I hid myself. Aside from the subtle shake in her voice at the beginning of the song, she sang the rest of it without a hitch. "Close to You" by The Carpenters is Mom's favorite song. Mom would've loved Kayla's cover of it. She sounded so sweet. She sang it well too. I'm not too worried about her in this rally. She can handle it.

The rally emcees—Cindy and Mike—starts to wrap up their little speech about the agenda and our upcoming football game.

"Alright, everyone! This is what you've all been waiting for! We're very honored to announce, starting this year, we're expanding our rally participants to members of our sports teams to play our games and spice things up! Woo-hoo!" Cindy cheers.

"You know who you are!" Mike points to the crowd and swiftly swooshes his hand down towards the floor. "Come on down!"

The selected four contestants from each grade start to make their way down from the bleachers. Kayla's seated a bit far from me, but I still watch her as she scoots out of her row and down the stairs. Reaching the bottom, she gathers around the other senior members.

Fuck. Emma got chosen?

Fuck! Kevin too?

Did they actually randomly pick these people? This is way too much of a coincidence. Either that or Kayla's got some funny luck. The emcees make their way to the four freshmen and splits them into two teams—Team A and Team B. Each team consisting of a guy and a girl. They do the same to the sophomores and juniors. When they reach the seniors, I start getting antsy. *I think I know where this is going.*

"Emma and Josh, you two are Team A," Mike says into the microphone.

Cindy pulls up next to him and gestures to the remaining members. "And that makes Kayla and Kevin, Team B!"

On my right, Nick nudges my elbow and points at the senior participants. "Bro, look."

As Emma and Josh high five each other, Kayla and Kevin look at each other in surprise. The vibe doesn't look too bad, thankfully. Kevin says something then extends a fist towards Kayla, who smiles and fist bumps him back. I had asked her about Kevin and the whole note issue during our last study session. She told me it was nothing. Kayla confronted him and said everything was all good. It's not like I don't believe her, but I know Kevin. He's not really the forgiving type. I wasn't exactly sure how to take it. But seeing him with her now . . . *maybe I owe Kevin an apology.*

"Well, I did not expect that," Nick says.

"Kevin's growing up!" Theatrical sobs follow the voice. I lean forward to peer next to Nick. It's Donny, sniffling back fake tears.

"Okay, everyone, listen up! We have two games for you today, in which all teams—both A's and B's—will participate. Do your best to rack up points, because they'll be added up in the end. The class with the most total points wins!" Mike roars.

"But like we said, we're spicing things up this season," Cindy continues after him. "Each individual team is gonna want to rack up the most points because that specific Team A or B with the highest score will be getting a little reward for their sports team!"

"Keep in mind that it's possible for a class team to win the total but not the individual," Mike says. "For example, let's say the sophomores scored the highest score of fifty, Team A and B both earning twenty-five. Following right behind them are the seniors with a total of forty-five points. Here's the catch! What if senior's Team A scored thirty and Team B fifteen? Thirty being the highest individual team score?"

Kayla sighs at the disrespect. I almost laugh when she covers it with a flat smile. At the same time, Kevin sneers, shaking his head. Mike doesn't see that he's offended Team B and proceeds on.

"So in this case, seniors' Team A, Emma and Josh" — he pauses as Emma and Josh raise their hands, smiling — "if your team scores the highest individual team point, girls' lacrosse and boys' basketball will be rewarded!"

Emma and Josh make celebratory poses as their respective teams cheer for them from the bleachers. Cindy—who's also in girls' lacrosse—claps for them before emceeing again. "As you can see, you can lose the class competition but still be the winning individual team. Now let's get to the games!"

While the emcees explain the rules of the first game, Emma ties her hair into a bun, smirking at Team B's direction. I know that look. *She does that when she gets competitive. And she's not one to play nice.*

Kayla shifts her feet, seeming to notice my ex staring. Shaking her head and paying that cheater no mind, she uses both her hands to take the hair around her face and carefully tuck it behind her ears. She repeats it a few times, making sure to grab all the baby hairs. Kayla always does this before we dive into a study session. My lips turn up. When she notices Kevin looking at her all weirded out, she shrugs. Suddenly, he imitates the gesture. Kayla shakes her head with a *so done* smile, and Kevin chuckles. *When did they get so close?* Their interaction seems to kill my excitement a little.

No, I can't— *Dammit.*

"Okay. Ready?" Cindy chirps as all the players get into position. "Go!"

The buzzer goes off and arcade game music starts to play.[2] Starting from their designated spots, each guy runs a lap within the borders of the rectangular area while the girls answer a question from their assigned teachers, each of whom are holding two rolls of tape behind their back. Answer it wrong, they get painter's tape. Answer it right, they get the duct tape—the stickier one.

Kayla paces around in her little area as her teacher waits for her answer. Nearby, Emma answers it quickly and receives the duct tape. Josh and Kevin are coming around the corner when Kayla shoots a hand up and gives her answer.

Duct tape. Yes!

Kevin runs past Emma, who gets a little distracted by her competition when Josh arrives. Unlike Emma, Kayla had already peeled the beginning tip of the duct tape while she waited for Kevin to finish his lap and return to their spot. So when she hands the roll to Kevin, he starts wrapping her with tape within seconds. She holds down the nonsticky side of the tape to her shoulder as Kevin circles around her to connect the tape—the sticky side facing out. Some of the other girls spin in place as the guys circle around them with the tape. Kevin gets the same idea and motions her to spin. Kayla gives him a despicable look and says something that makes him sigh and continue the mummification. This slowed their taping progress

---

[2] See Appendix B for more details

compared to the others but surprisingly, their taping had less spaces in between.

A give and take.

Occasionally, Kayla would help out in a slow spin or two. When the taping gets to her knees, she wiggles around until Kevin looks up. They exchange a few words. Looks like they're arguing until he sighs again and rips the tape there. Each team had their girl wrapped from shoulders to ankles—or at least they tried to because more tape meant a higher chance to collect the cards on the mat. I wonder why Kayla insisted on stopping the tape at her knees.

Around the same time, all the girls jump onto the big mat in the center of the gym floor. They roll around, their tape collecting the scattered cards. It seems easy until some of the girls get stuck in place and have to put force into it to roll from place to place. The audience starts to get loud, sometimes giggling when a girl gets stuck on the mat or stuck to another girl. There's even yelling and cheering when some girls are rolling like pros, collecting cards like a lint roller removing hair.

From the edges of the mat, the guys are yelling for their teammates and pointing at where to collect. Kayla's doing well. So is Emma. The crowd gets enthusiastic when all the cards are cleared except for a remaining two in a corner—they fell off a girl's painter tape earlier. All the girls are currently either in the middle or at the opposite end of the mat. Their teammates are all yelling for them to roll there.

"Only two more cards left! Who will reach them first? It's a battle among the seniors, Emma and Kayla, and junior Krystal. Though by the looks of it, Kayla's at a disadvantage being in the middle of the three. Emma and Krystal are getting ahead, closing her only path! Seems like Kayla's out of the ra—"

Mike stops mid-narration when Kayla stops rolling and forcefully sits up. Folding her knees to the side, she pushes herself up and manages to get onto her feet.

So that was why.

I break into a smile. Not missing a beat, she starts to jump. The crowd goes wild. Some of the seniors are yelling her name.

"I stand corrected! Look at her go!" Mike says.

Kevin's lurking around the border near the section of the remaining cards, aggressively gesturing to the cards as she leaps past Emma and Krystal. Her hair's flying all over her face, but that doesn't stop her. Several students spring out of their seats, cheering, unable to contain their excitement. Me included. Nick even swears next to me. Kayla's a few steps away from the cards when she—with no hesitation—plops herself down onto the last two cards.

The crowd erupts. Simultaneously, the music stops and the buzzer goes off. The sound of people cheering and clapping swallows the entire gym. I think I can even hear people laughing.

"What a game! That was so unexpected. That was allowed right? Not against the rules?" Mike looks over to some of the teacher supervisors. The crowd starts to boo at his question. I don't have a good angle at the supervisors but Mike's next words put my heart to ease. "They said it was okay! Rule was to get as many cards as you can *with* the tape. Didn't say how, so that will count!"

The booing turns to celebration. Eventually, everyone settles down into their seats again.

"Fellas, please help your partner up. Our team will be over with scissors soon. Please gather all your cards for counting," Cindy says.

All the teams do as they're told as student council members help the girls out of their tape, collect the cards, and take away the big mat in the middle. The two emcees do their small talk before someone hands them a piece of paper. Dramatically, they announce the runners-up one by one.

"And first place, with a whooping forty-five, seniors!" Cindy exclaims, finishing the alternative score telling. "Seniors, not only are you in the lead for the class total, you're leading the highest scoring individual team as well. With twenty-three points, Team A!"

Emma and Josh give each other a high-five as seniors start to cheer. To their side, Kayla and Kevin clap for them.

"Congratulations, Team A, but it's still too early to celebrate!" Mike says. "Because with just *one* point behind is senior's Team B and sophomores' Team A!"

"Fear not, other teams." Cindy brings a hand up and turns all directions to speak to every grade. "This second game is where you can catch up!"

The other student council members finally finish setting up the new props on the floor for the next game. Every team has a little section of their own. From left to right—laid in a straight line on the floor—is a set of red, yellow, and green Hula-Hoops, each around eight feet apart. A basket of balls sits next to the red hoop, a giant handmade spoon prop in the yellow, and a big empty bucket in the green.[3]

Mike and Cindy explain the rules: girls use their giant spoon prop to pass the balls to the guys and the guys shoot them in the basket. Girls can scoop and pass the ball however they like, as long as they don't touch the balls with their hands. As for the guys, they can receive the balls outside of their green hoop as long as they don't pass the blue-taped line in front of their hoop. Above all else, both players must stay in their circles when passing or shooting.

The buzzer goes off. Music plays again.

From the red hoop, Kayla dashes for the spoon in the yellow while Kevin—from the green—runs to place the empty bucket in the yellow. Both run back to their assigned hoops. The crowd makes some noise as the girls start scooping.

Emma scoops up a ball from her basket and tosses it to Josh with ease. *As expected.* She isn't the lacrosse team captain for nothing. Another girl places the ball on the floor and hits it to her teammate like it's golf. Some others throw it the best they can, letting it bounce and roll to their partner.

Kayla—having some trouble scooping her first ball—finally gets the scoop and tosses it. The ball flies, but that's not the only thing that goes up in the air. The top half of her spoon flies with it. It skids across the floor, landing somewhere near the yellow hoop between

[3] See Appendix C for more details

them. Kevin steps out of his green circle to receive the ball that went completely off track. He retrieves it and freezes in place when he looks over to her direction. Like Kayla, he looks at the broken spoon on the floor and then to the remaining half she's holding.

Nick curses next to me, taking the word out my mouth. Some of the crowd notices and gasps. "Oh my! Seems like Kayla from Team B just broke her spoon! Is this it for the fourth-years? Or will Team A's Emma and Josh carry the seniors?"

Kayla recovers quickly and sprints to take back her broken spoon, signaling Kevin to keep going.

"Man, what is with that guy? He really has it out for Team B," Nick says as the emcee starts to narrate something impressive about another team.

"I think he's got something for Team A, if you know what I mean."

Donny's not wrong. I've seen Mike around Emma before, and the way he looks at her . . . let's just say, I know that look. I grit my teeth, staying quiet as I watch. Kevin returns to his green hoop and shoots his ball as Kayla gets back in her red hoop with half of a spoon in each hand. Flipping the bottom half of her spoon, she uses the handle to push a ball onto the inside of the spoon. Holding the spoon by the neck, she preps herself with a quick count of three before tossing the ball up a little and hitting it to Kevin.

Like a tennis stroke.

I smirk. This ball passes faster than her first and more directly to Kevin, who catches it with surprise. Without delay, he shoots the ball. Scoop and hit. Catch and shoot. Repeat. They're doing great. Cindy and Mike circle around, emceeing remarks and descriptions about the competition. None of them comment on how impressive Kayla manages to work around the broken spoon. At least I hear some of the seniors cheering for her.

Emma's passes suddenly become more aggressive. Josh still manages to catch them and shoot. For one of the top basketball players, he misses a lot. Or should I say, he shoots straight into the bucket almost all the time but six out of ten times, the ball bounces out of the bucket. The music's loud so no one hears what Emma is yelling at him, but I recognize that face. Frustration. Anger. Impatience. *I feel bad for Josh.*

Kayla's holding her own no problem. Sometimes, she sends a thumbs-up to Kevin when he makes the shot in. He's making most of them, sometimes through hitting the insides of the bucket or bouncing the balls in. The timer counts down its last digits, initiating the buzzer to go off. The music stops and the players do the same.

The student council members retrieve the props accordingly while the participants move into position. Emcees do their small talk again before revealing all the runners-up and their scores. Second place gets announced, and we're cheering before the class winners get declared.

"And first place with a total of eighty-one points goes to the seniors!" We continue to celebrate. "Okay, okay, settle down. Let's not forget there's still a winning team for the highest individual team score."

"According to the scores we have here, it seems like the top two highest individual scores are both from the seniors! Wow, they're on fire today. What do you all think? Team A or B?" Mike's question starts a riot of people screaming "A" and "B."

Cindy laughs into the mic. "The leading team with a total of forty-one points is . . . drum roll, please!"

Everyone stomps their feet, causing a thunderstorm in the gym. Together, Mike and Cindy announce, "Team B!"

Kayla looks surprised and turns to Kevin, who shoots both his arms up in victory. Suddenly, they do a high-ten. Standing nearby, Josh nods and claps for them. Emma looks away, clapping against her wishes.

"Congratulations to the football team and girls' tennis. Ms. Nono will be relaying the prizes to your team. Great job!" Cindy says.

Mike wraps up the rally when all the participants return to their seats. Shortly after, the principal takes over to dismiss us class by class. The seniors make their way down the bleachers and out the gym. Donny and Kevin are walking ahead and are about to take a turn the other way when I jog up from behind.

"Kevin." He stops and turns to me. "I'm sorry about last time. It was wrong for me to assume."

His brow knits slightly, not giving too much of his thoughts away—unlike Donny. Kevin's always got something to say, but he's been pretty quiet as of late, so I know he's not going to say anything. I give him a nod before I turn the other direction to head back to class. Kayla arrives at her seat, seconds after I do. We grab our bags and when our eyes meet, she gives me a wide but embarrassed smile.

I grin. "You did great. What did I say?"

"Thanks." She looks like a happy puppy. If she had a tail, it'd be wagging right now. "I'm just glad it worked out, especially after that . . . spoon incident. That was nerve-wracking."

I nudge her arm. "*You* made it work. Did you hear everyone cheering? Your teammates were going crazy for you."

The comment gets a laugh out of her and it makes me feel fulfilled. We exit the classroom together, and she points to the opposite direction of where I'm going. "I'm heading this way."

"Alright. I'll see ya."

"See ya!" She beams with a pretty smile, then sends me a wave.

I return the gesture before we separate. Kayla would probably never know what that does to me. It's okay because she gave me the energy I needed for what I'm about to do. I make my way downstairs, through the hallway, and turn a corner.

She's alone. *Good.* When I draw near her locker, she finally takes notice and turns around.

"A-Aiden," she says in surprise.

"It was you, wasn't it?"

"Excuse me?"

"The rally. You put Kayla on the list and paired her up with Kevin, didn't you? As if tampering with her spoon wasn't enough, you even had Mike in on it."

Her left eye twitches before she scoffs.

Goddammit. I'm right.

"How could you accuse me of that? Do you really think I would go through all that trouble just to make her look bad?"

I grit my teeth, refraining from blowing up. Emma's the student council's second vice president. It's not hard changing up some names on a computer or even doing something to the props. The spoons were color coded for each specific team and out of everyone, only Kayla's broke. That was way too much of a coincidence to be an accident. And Mike . . . come on, even Nick and Donny noticed. *Did she think I wouldn't piece it together?* Her pettiness has always been her weak point. Luckily, my silence gets her rambling.

"She won in the end. *She's* the one who made me look bad at the rally. In front of you. Can't you see what's happening? She's tearing us apart! Are you really gonna let that she-devil use yo—"

"Don't call her that." My threatening tone makes her take a step back, swallowing hard. "There is no *us* anymore. Why don't you get that?"

"But—"

"I'm sorry I wasn't enough for you. I'm sorry you had to ruin us because of me. But don't blame it on her when it is *your* fault."

"Aiden, I said I was sorry."

"You're not sorry you cheated, Emma. You're sorry you were caught."

She gets quiet, and I let it sink in. It was easy to cheat because she didn't really care about our relationship. *She didn't care about me.* If she did, I wouldn't have felt so miserable around her, would I? Deep down, she knew that.

"And just so you know, if Kayla really was using me . . . I'd let her."

She's frozen speechless. I would've laughed if it weren't for the mood. She deserved it for spouting such nonsense. I only came here to confront her. Since I've done it, I walk away but suddenly stop. *How did I forget the most important thing*? With my back towards her, I turn my head to the side so she hears me loud and clear.

"Stay away from her. That's a warning."

I get out of the bathroom, having changed my clothes early. Tennis practice doesn't start until a little later, but I definitely needed the change after working up a sweat at the rally. The stairway's close to empty when I go down and exit the building to the outdoor plaza. From not so far away, I spot a certain someone sitting on one of the benches. *That's weird*. He looks almost . . . sad. I head towards him without a second thought.

"So, we totally did not just win the fall rally today." I take a seat next to him. "What's up?"

Kevin turns to me, smirking. "Nothing. Just waiting for Donny."

"Didn't know Donny could give you a face like that."

"It's not him." He looks away, watching other students walk around the campus.

"So . . . it *is* someone. You wanna talk about it? Sometimes, talking it out makes you feel better. Give you a new perspective, maybe."

His attention shifts back to me. There's an annoyed look on his face, but it's one of the milder ones. "Are you always this curious or do you like to pry into people's business?"

"Curious, yes. But I don't like to pry into anyone's business. I know it's hard to talk about your feelings, *especially* if you're a guy. I know the stigma with that. And before you go thinking 'You're a girl, what do you know,' trust me. I get it. Some of us struggle with that too. For our own reasons. My point is, it doesn't matter who you are. If anyone keeps it all bottled up, they're gonna explode eventually."

Kevin's face softens.

"What I'm trying to say is" — I clear my throat — "if you need someone to talk to, I'm here to lend an ear."

It takes a second for him to look away again. *Well, crap. Kevin's back to his silent game.* Can't blame him on this one though. I think I might've gone a little overboard this time. A little *too* personal. Just because we're good now, doesn't mean we're best buddies or anything.

"If you need some time alone, that's important too. I guess, I'll take my leave now." I get up and take a step away when I'm stopped by my backpack straps.

"Wait."

I realize it's him holding me—technically, my backpack—in place. Reversing, I sit myself down.

He sighs without looking at me. "It's Aiden. He . . . pisses me off."

I look at him blankly and stay silent as my brain fires off a bunch of why's and compliments about Aiden. *Quiet down, I'm sure he's got his reasons.* I mean, the guy's got *something* against Aiden—that's for sure.

I don't know what, but it must've been way before our little water fountain incident. A grudge maybe.

"I've liked Emma since sophomore year."

Ohhh. I think I know where this is going.

"We've flirted from time to time, and I've made a couple moves. Moves she never rejected. The team liked to tease me about it because they knew I liked her." He looks ahead to people watch, so I do the same. "That summer, she joined us for our training to prepare as our team manager. She got along with everyone. The coaches love her. She's pretty. Smart. What's there not to like?"

I nod.

"When I finally gathered enough courage to ask her out, every single time I tried to, Aiden was always with her. He was always in the way. Before I knew it, they were dating by the time junior year started. He practically stole her from me."

There's no way she could have been stolen from him when she was never "his" to begin with. Quotations on his, because again, she's not an object. But this probably isn't a good time to tell him that. And I know what he meant by that. "Kevin, did you ever consider that Emma was always with Aiden and not the other way around?"

He seems skeptical when he turns to look at me. "What do you mean?"

"I'm saying, instead of Aiden chasing Emma, it was her who was chasing Aiden. Maybe you were left confused because she was giving you mixed signals."

"She liked me back. She knew I liked her. Everyone knew. It was so obvious!"

"Did she tell you that?" He knits his eyebrows so harshly I have to clarify. "Did she say that she liked you?"

His frustration starts to simmer before looking away again. "No."

"I'm not saying she didn't like you. But she went out with Aiden in the end, so what does that say?"

"That I'm stupid for thinking she was into me."

"No." I sigh and look at the trees. "You're not stupid for thinking that. If she flirted back, then you have valid reason to think that the feelings were mutual. But maybe there's a lot of other guys who flirt with her too, and . . . maybe that's how she brushes them off?"

"By being receptive of our feelings?"

The tone of his voice sounds a little hurt, and it makes sense. I turn to meet his eyes. "By going with the flow. Sometimes it's easier to play it as a joke than to confront them about it. Let's say she does say it outright, there're two possible outcomes. One, the guy's cool about it. Or two, the guy gets embarrassed and starts saying hurtful things to her because his pride got stepped on. Things get awkward and . . . well, you get the point."

He looks like he just solved a math problem without knowing how he did it. It's silent for a moment as his focus shifts to the floor. "I didn't think about it like that."

It's my first time hearing him admit to something that he could've done but didn't do. I'm kinda shocked. His new sense of vulnerability makes me want to lighten his load a bit. "Hey, you know what? I don't think everyone knew."

"Knew what?"

"Your feelings." That grabs his attention again. "Feelings are always obvious to the person who's feeling them. But some of us . . . we tend to hide them better than we think we do."

He smirks. His mood, an improvement from earlier. "You speak from experience."

"We learn a thing or two, growing up." I laugh when I look away. It's quiet for a bit. We get to hear the beautiful sounds of nature.

"So?"

I look at him confused. "So what?"

"You're not gonna tell me your story?"

His question catches me off guard, I almost think I imagined it. But there's a hopeful look on his face. "You wanna hear it?"

"Yes, I would love to hear how *the* Kayla Summers got her heart broken. Leave no details, please."

"It's not like that, it's—" I realize I'm about to explain myself, but when he looks at me expectantly, my resolve breaks. "Okay, fine. I'll tell you."

Somehow, that causes him to smile. *What the heck? I haven't even told him anything yet.* Clearing my throat, I distract myself with the scenery. "So, before I came here—before freshman year—I liked this guy. For a really long time. We got along well and we had a connection, or at least I thought we did."

The memory feels so distant now. Yet, still so close. I chuckle. "I felt like I hit the jackpot when we were paired together for a team project. I liked being around him, but I was a nervous wreck. I was awkward. I stuttered. My face heated up. It was so painfully obvious that I liked him. There was just no way he or my friends didn't know."

Kevin snickers at the idea of young Kayla doing all that, and I roll my eyes.

"Somewhere along the line, my best friend at the time was added to our team because her partner transferred schools. And before I knew it, I found out that he and she officially became a couple. I felt betrayed. By him. By her." I take in a deep breath, preparing myself for what's to come next. "I was annoyed that she went after him when I had feelings for him. I was jealous that he picked her over me. But the more I thought about it, I was wrong. There's nothing wrong with her chasing someone she likes. Or him liking her more because . . . well . . . I mean, I wasn't an option to begin with."

I sigh, steadying my breathing before I can get emotional. Surprisingly, Kevin is understanding and stays silent. "Now that I look back at it, it all makes sense. The things she said, the things she did, how she played everything out when it was just the three of us. She wanted his attention. She wanted you to know she was this sporty, outgoing, fun girl you wanted to hang out with. By the time I realized what was happening, it was too late. He was falling for her. And I knew I had no chance because I would never compare to her." I clear my throat and try to laugh off the somber mood I just brought.

"Well anyway, he never treated me any different than before, so I guess he never noticed how I felt about him."

I finally have the guts to look Kevin in the eye again. It's not pity he's looking at me with, but something that makes me want to clarify it was all in the past. "Oh, I'm over it! If he didn't like me, he didn't like me. Feelings shouldn't be forced."

Kevin's expression loosens, looking away as he nods slowly.

"Y'know, I think the worst part was the way she would low-key compete with me or show him that she was better than me. That's what pisses me off the most. I honestly think that she *knew* I liked him," I say with a matter-of-fact tone. Feeling as if I had just let go of some dead weight, I lean back.

Next to me, Kevin does the same and turns to me with curious eyes. "Do they go here?"

"Really? After all that, that's your question?"

"Just wanted to see if I could put a face to them."

I sigh. "The guy, no. The friend, yeah."

"Are you still friends with her?"

Wow. He's completely invested in this, isn't he? I clear my throat. "Well, it's complicated. I've known her since we were kids. She's no longer my best friend, but yeah. She's still a friend."

"Even though she used you to make herself look better?"

"Okay, it's not as bad as it sounds. Really. That's just how I *felt*. I never confirmed if she knew about my feelings."

"So you're giving her the benefit of doubt?"

I don't like the tone of voice he uses. And is that disappointment I see in his eyes?

"No. I—" I take in a breath. "I'm highly suspicious of her. But what's done is done. It's in the past now. All I can do is be cautious and learn from it."

Kevin blinks in surprise. "I don't know how you can move forward just like that."

"Because it's easier. Constantly comparing myself to her wasn't healthy. Easier said than done, I know. To be completely honest with you, I'm still working on it."

Silence ensues after my statement. The thought of *that* being what ends the conversation makes me uncomfortable. "You know what's funny? They broke up after three months. I was still friends with the guy, so it was cool. The topic came up one day, and I asked him if he ever liked me." I chuckle. "He said he did. But then he admitted he started liking my friend after they hung out a bit more. So, I guess he didn't like me enough, 'cause his feelings changed just like" — I snap my fingers — "that."

Because it really did feel like that.

Kevin leans forward, resting his elbows on his knees. He looks deep in thought, staring hard at the concrete. "Do you think Emma was like that? She liked me first but then lost interest and went for Aiden instead? Or that she didn't know about my feelings and thought I was just playing with her? Maybe she was playing *me*?"

That last bit didn't sound like a question to me, and I know Kevin's really in a spiral now. "I don't know her enough to tell you, but I had one encounter with her to know that I get bad vibes," I say, keeping it short and brief.

Kevin doesn't need to know about that smug look on her face when she suspiciously wished me luck on that second rally game. That spoon breaking was no accident—it felt weird the moment I held it. Nor does he need to know about that little threatening incident that happened in the bathroom. Emma's clearly not over Aiden yet. If she does get with someone, she'll probably be using them.

I rest my elbows on my knees to lessen the distance between us. "Look, I don't want to tarnish your image of her. But if you're going to shoot your shot, just . . . be careful."

Kevin turns to me, surprised. "You worried about me?"

He's almost grinning now. *God, why is he making it so weird?* I scoff. "You wish. I'm just being a good person and giving you a heads-up. Sad doesn't suit you."

He laughs at that. I guess he agrees too.

"For what it's worth, I may be completely wrong. To be honest, I don't believe that this whole Emma thing is the reason you've got something against Aiden," I admit carefully. The idea got too big for me to ignore, which was why I had to say something. He averts his eyes, staying quiet. *All this hate can't just be about one girl, can it?* Guys have always been simpler than that. However, if Emma really *was* dating Kevin at the time, then that'd be a different story. But it isn't like that.

"Then what is it, genius?"

"I don't know. That's probably something you're gonna have to figure out yourself. But I do know one thing." He looks at me like I'm about to give him lottery numbers. "Holding a grudge is tiring."

Kevin looks almost taken aback by my words. *Seems like I'm heading towards the right direction.*

"You won't believe it. It was in my bag the entire time! I went to my locker, the classrooms, even the bath— Oh." Kevin and I look at his surprised friend. "Hi, Kayla!"

I smile. "Hey, Donny."

"Thanks for making the rally worth watching. That was quite something."

"Very funny." I chuckle a little and dig up something in my bag. When I grab a hold of it, I hand the tiny bag of gummies to Kevin. He takes it, confused. "Some food for thought. Don't think too hard about it, okay?"

Donny's approaching closer so I get up, letting the friends reunite. "I gotta head to practice. See ya."

The boys bid me a goodbye, and I start to walk away. "Wait, what about me? Don't I get a bag?"

Crap, I did not think that through. I stop and turn around, hoping my honesty can compensate. "Sorry, Donny, that was my last one. Ask Kevin to share some!"

Disappointed, Donny reaches a hand toward the now-opened bag of gummies but Kevin smacks his hand away and mutters a "Get your own."

I laugh at the interaction before waving at the both of them. Despite all the weird stuff that happened, today was a good day.

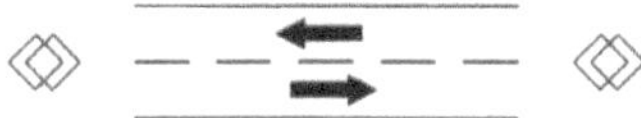

I finish typing the last bullet point and turn in my seat to look at my science partner standing a few feet away behind me. "What about this? You think this should go before or after the previous slide?"

Chris walks towards me. "Let's see."

I turn my attention back to my laptop screen to see what his thoughts are. Unexpectedly, Chris—standing right behind me and my chair—leans forward and rests his hands on the table in front of me; trapping me between his arms.

I stiffen. Seriously? First, our presentation gets pushed forward for no reason and now this? Never in my life would I ever imagine someone pulling a *kabedon* on me. A seat *kabedon*! Does that even exist? What the heck! Why did it have to be Chris? If it had to be anyone, why couldn't it be Aiden? For goodness' sake!

If I wasn't so bad at science, I would've pushed him off by now. But science is my worst subject and this guy has an ego. I can't risk offending him or making it awkward before our presentation. *Why are you doing this to me, Chris?* And why in the library? I know you recently broke up with Hailey so you're single now, but this is really weird! You don't do this to just anyone. Ever heard of personal space? Or is this . . . a difference in culture? Crap! How do I even say this nicely?

Chris is looking at the slide on my laptop over me. He's busy reading the material.

I try to scrunch up discreetly. *Maybe I'll just excuse myself to the bathroom.* Yeah, that sounds legit. "H-Hey Chris, can you exc—"

"Excuse me."

I freeze, confused. *That deep voice wasn't mine.* Chris's arms pull back and my rigid body finally manages to let my neck turn a little to my right. Holy crap!

Aiden's here.

Relief. I exhale, finally remembering to breathe again. Chris returns to a standing position again, backing up to a more comfortable distance behind me. Anxiety and worry start to disappear. Only now do I realize Aiden's got a hand on Chris's shoulder. D-Did he get him away for *me*? My cheeks get warm. I can finally feel my limbs again.

"Can you give me a minute?" Aiden nods to my direction. His grip on Chris's shoulder loosens to a pat.

"Okay. Sure?" Chris walks off compliantly to a nearby empty table and distracts himself with his phone.

Aiden swiftly comes to my right side with a hand on the table, and suddenly, he crouches down so we're eye level. Tender eyes stare into mine so intensely, I can't look away. It feels like it's just the two of us in the room. I think I'm melting into my seat. I have become the seat. Wait. What? *Crap, did I even say hi to him yet?*

"I'll meet you here after school?"

He asked you a question. Say something, Kayla. I swallow, but my voice doesn't seem to be working. *Just nod. Nod!* He smiles, giving me a little nudge on my arm.

"I'll be right there if you need me, okay?"

He points over to an empty table not too far away, his bag laying there peacefully. He said *if you need me.* Does that mean he's letting me call on him if I need him? My heart flips. Or wait, is that my stomach? He just told you where he sits. *Relax, girl!* I try to but it doesn't work. Aiden's stuck on repeat.

If you need me.

If you need me.

If you nee—

My lips stretch into a smile. *Dial it down, Kayla.* "Okay," I manage to say, but it only comes out as a whisper. Was that too quiet? Should I rep— *Oh man, please don't smile like that.* I'm kinda dying right now. My heart's going crazy!

Thankfully, Aiden stands up and nods to Chris. I hear my science partner get up and suddenly, I realize I've forgotten my manners. Aiden's hand hasn't left the table yet, so I take the chance to touch it. His attention's back on me.

"Thank you," I try to say, but no sound comes out. *Did my lips move at least?*

He chuckles, nodding like he understands what I just said—or tried to say. As he's about to leave, Aiden takes a step closer and puts a gentle hand on my shoulder. It's very nonchalant. Brief. But somehow, I finally relax. He takes it away and I start to miss it. *Uh-oh*. Quietly, I watch him turn around and head to his seat.

This is bad. This is really bad. Dang it!

Don't do that, Aiden.

Don't make me like you even more.

There was no precalc today, so I didn't get to see Kayla in her Halloween costume. I've been wondering all day what she dressed up as or if she even dressed up at all. I hope she did. She has to have. Unfortunately, I haven't been able to catch her anywhere around school today either. Now that the school day is over, maybe I'll bump into her somewhere on campus during this Halloween event.

I want to see her.

Someone nudges me on my right. It's Nick—dressed up as Flynn Rider from *Tangled*—pointing at the nearby stall of what looks like a candy-themed haunted house. "I want to save candy civilians, let's go!"

We head over to the station. There are candy props and decorations around a big poster reading "Candy Guy's Calamity." Next to it, a scoreboard of the top five teams with the highest points.

"It says a party of five."

Nick groans. "Where are those three when you need them?"

I chuckle. Evan, Jack, and Luke disappeared two games ago. They haven't responded to our texts either.

"Hey, guys! Do you want to play this game too? We'll join you!" Donny—dressed as one of Merida's brothers from *Brave*—and Kevin—a cowboy—approaches us from behind. "We've been wanting to assemble a team, but we haven't seen many seniors around. I think most of them are enjoying the teachers' section."

Nick and I exchange a knowing look. *So that's where those three went. They won't be going anywhere for a while.*

Donny turns to his left. "Kev, whaddya say?"

"Sure."

Nick and Donny celebrate while I nod, half expecting it. Kevin has been acting very strange since the fall rally. *Nice* is a bit of a stretch, but he doesn't ignore me now. He actually tolerated being around me this past month. It's a little weird. I'm still trying to get used to it. But Nick and Donny have finally been able to hang together with the both of us around. So, it was definitely an upgrade for them. I'm not sure if it's because of my apology or something else entirely, but I won't complain as long as he doesn't bring up the silver platter topic again.

"Well, we're gonna need one more player." Nick folds his arms. "Senior, preferably. I don't really want to do this with an underclassman. No hate, I just want to end it with our class, y'know? It's our last year here."

I nod in agreement.

Kevin shrugs. "Fine by me. Not a fan of underclassmen anyway."

"I think I found someone! Be right back!" Donny says, dashing off.

He zooms past the mass of people and finally slows down when he walks near a ringleader who had just stuffed the last of her ice cream cone in her mouth. She throws her paper into the bin before going back to watch her friends—an angel and a devil—playing another game. Donny approaches her and she turns around, her chin-length hair spinning with her. They talk briefly, and then Donny points over to us, making her look at our direction.

Next to me, Nick waves at them. "Oh hey, it's Kayla!"

From across the plaza, she waves back before returning her attention to Donny. I look away, a little bummed I didn't get to send her my own wave. Before I know it, both Donny and Kayla are coming over. They get closer, and I get to see her costume in more detail. A red ringleader jacket with gold tassels. Black-and-white striped pants. Black boots. There's a tiny whip keychain hanging on one of her front belt loops. I smirk. *That's one way around the no-weapons policy.* I've never been a fan of circuses, but I can see why it's so appealing now.

Donny and Kayla approach us, and she beams when she gets a good look at our costumes. "Wow, you all look so nice!"

Her praise is meant for everyone, but it still sends me butterflies. Good thing I'm wearing my aviators. Unable to keep my smile off, I look away and fix the collar of my air force pilot uniform. If it had been just me and her, I would've given her a compliment by now. But the other boys are here, so I keep my mouth shut. To my right, Kevin looks the other way with a smirk on his face.

"Thanks, and *you* look great! What a boss!"

Nick's comment makes Donny turn to him in excitement. "That's what I said!"

They do a high five, making Kayla laugh. Suddenly, her eyes are on me and her smile widens. I give her a grin before she looks away shyly. *Are ringleaders supposed to look this cute?*

Kevin clears his throat, grabbing everyone's attention. "Are we going to play or stand around here and talk about our costumes?"

"Right!" Nick claps his hands. "Let's go!"

We follow him and walk to the zombie attendant. He gives us a big empty box, a piece of paper, and a Sharpie. We put any loose belongings in the box for safekeeping. While another attendant—a peppermint girl—opens the curtains for Kevin, Donny, and Kayla, Nick doesn't miss the chance to name our team "Circus Animals" and hands the paper back. The zombie attendant takes it, puts it in our box, and stores it safely in their stash.

"Really?"

Nick shrugs at me. "What? I had to."

We join the rest of the team in a darker room, where Peppermint Girl gives a monologue and backstory of the game through slides. Candy Guy—Candy Republic's human savior and the final boss—recently lost his wife from sugar overdose and swore to eliminate all of Candy Republic. He's captured all the Candy Army Officers, having every ingredient to make the ultimate candy bomb to destroy all candies.

What we have to do is simple: (1) collect as many hidden candies as we can in his mansion, (2) show them to him to prove how much his wife loved candies and to dissuade him from destroying Candy Republic, all the while (3) avoid getting ghost-stickered by the mind-controlled henchmen—which meant point deduction. As for defense, we're provided small laser guns. Shooting the goons in the chest is a one-shot kill, but a shot in the knees would do the trick. Stopping Candy Guy would mean stopping the mind control. So, not killing them is ideal.

Peppermint Girl wishes us luck before sending us into Candy Guy's mansion. The "mansion" is carefully constructed within a series of classrooms, including the hallway. Partitions are set up to direct a certain path for us to follow. Most, if not all, of the rooms' windows are blacked out, sparing only minimal light to show some of the props laying around. The darkness also helps hide the surprise-attack goons.

After having found and collected some randomly placed candy plushies, along with a bag to put them all in; we go through a few brainwashed goons by shooting their knees. Donny and Kevin, being in the front, were attacked with a few ghost stickers. Halfway, we get into a bonus room where we need to open a treasure chest. A very conveniently-placed projector airs a video of Candy Guy's wife locking candies in the chest with a spell. After a few trial-and-error attempts, we narrowed it down to a spell that needed to be ten words, rhymes on the fifth and tenth word, and ghost-related. I randomly took a stab at the first five words without thinking the rest. And to my surprise, Kayla was able to bounce off mine and finish the last five words without a hitch.

Like . . . she's my missing piece.

To my sentence. *Ahem*, obviously. We collect a few more candies and shoot down some goons. Out of nowhere, I turn to see a goon about to stick a ghost on Kayla's back. Instincts kick in.

"Summers!" Kevin shouts.

She spins around and shoots down, but I'm already in front of her, stopping the goon by the arm. I don't think when I shoot him in the chest. The fastest shot. Light glows from his chest plate and knee pad when the goon pretends to fall down and die. On my left—a good few feet away—Kevin has his arm up aimed to where I had just shot, his gun glowing.

So, he shot too.

I turn to check on Kayla, but she's not behind me anymore. She's already walked around me to the pretend-dead goon and takes a fake rose prop nearby. Crouching down, she lays the rose on his chest, whispering, "Sorry, buddy."

Nick and Donny—who were watching from the sidelines—look at the goon pitifully and whisper something about our first death by casualty. Suddenly, a random goon comes from behind them and reaches a hand towards Donny with a sticker.

"Donny!" Nick jumps in front of him, taking the hit instead.

He clutches onto the ghost sticker as Donny shoots the goon in the knee. Kayla stands next to me as we watch the scene unfold. Nick dramatically falls, and Donny catches him in his arms.

"Nick! Stay with me, brother! You're gonna be okay!"

"Donny" — *cough, cough* — "I'm not gonna make it. Go on," — *cough* — "without me."

"No! You said we were gonna save Candy Republic together!" Donny grabs Nick's collar with a hand. "We made a promise! I'm gonna carry you there if I have to."

Kayla is giggling when Kevin clears his throat, interrupting the scene and points to a room with a piece of paper indicating Candy Guy's room. "Break it up, guys. Boss room's right here."

The boys recover from their soap opera and hurry over to Kevin while Kayla and I trail behind them. Out of the blue, I feel a tug on my sleeve. Kayla gestures me to come closer so I lower a little towards her.

"Thanks for the save," she whispers to me with a bashful smile.

My lips curve up. "Anytime," I whisper back.

Kevin opens the door and bursts in with the rest of us following close behind. "Give it up, Candy Guy. It's over!"

Candy Guy—a theater kid with a fake mustache and a lab coat on—laughs at Kevin. In front of him lays a big black cauldron with fake smoke flowing out of it. On the shelves behind him are carefully crafted cardboard cutouts of the Candy Army Officers he's kidnapped.

"You're too late, humans! I've already extracted Colonel Caramel's DNA. All it needs is a single drop and my bomb will be complete. I will destroy all of Candy Republic with this bomb! Nobody needs to eat candies anymore! No one needs to suffer!"

"Not on my watch." Nick shoots a little square panel near the cauldron, stopping the fake fire flames from going.

"No! My concoction!" The five of us watch Candy Guy silently, wondering if that did the trick, but he quickly smirks and pulls out a fake bomb prop from a nearby drawer. "Good thing I have this backup bomb! This one might not get the Caramels, but it can still wipe out the rest of them!"

Candy Guy is about to fake light it up but halts when Donny brings up a hand. "Stop! Don't do this, Stanley."

"Stanley . . .? How do you know my name?"

I clear my throat. "We saw an old video of your wife in one of the rooms."

"She was hiding candy from you," Kayla adds.

"Ah, yes." Candy Guy nods nostalgically. "Honey liked hiding candy around the house because I'd take the ones in the kitchen away."

"Here's a bunch of candy that we collected around the mansion," Kevin says awkwardly and gestures to the bag of plushies Donny's holding. "Look at how much your wife loved candy."

Nick inches forward to Candy Guy. "Think about it, Stanley. Ending Candy Republic and destroying all the candies out there would be the last thing your wife wanted."

Candy Guy—or Stanley—starts to break down, and Nick walks over to comfort him.

"You're right. She loved candy so much. She'd share them with everyone. I miss you, Honey!" The theater kid is sobbing for his lover and giving the performance of a lifetime when Nick manages to discreetly take the bomb out of his hand.

Suddenly, the lights go out. It's pitch black. I can't see anything.

"Woah, what happened?" Nick asks.

"A blackout? Should we ask Stanley?"

"Ah!" That was Kevin—somewhere on my left. "Stop it, Donny."

"Stop what? Stanley? Fine, I won't ask him then. It's probably part of the game anyways."

Candy Guy has been quiet the entire time, so maybe this is normal? Come to think of it, Kayla hasn't spoken anything either. *Is she okay?* She was on my left the last time I saw her. I blindly reach a hand out, taking small steps toward her direction.

"Hey, I put the bomb down," Nick says from a distance. "Maybe we're supposed to look for an exit?"

Donny and Kevin start throwing suggestions out when suddenly, something bumps into me. Not something, *someone*. The force isn't hard, but the surprise ends up tripping the person onto me. I grab shoulders and take a step back to support the extra weight. It's not heavy. *Is that velvet I feel?* Tassels.

"Sorry!" she murmurs.

"Kayla?" I whisper back as she finds her balance.

"Aiden? Is that you?" She speaks in a quiet voice.

I'm about to give her an answer when one of her hands pat around my torso, as if to feel it's me. It's very innocent, but I seem to have lost my voice. My heart begins to race. Body doesn't move. I swallow, trying to steady my breathing. Her small hand makes its way up and touches my chest. I accidentally grip her shoulders. It wasn't even that hard, but she stiffens.

"Oops, sorry!" she utters as she carefully backs away.

Just then, there's a loud pang. Kayla jolts, and instincts kick in again. I pull her into me. Her fingers curl, softly clutching my flight suit. The sensation of holding her close feels nice.

I think . . . *I like this.*

Donny apologizes for knocking down the cauldron, and Kayla relaxes in my arms, letting out a breath of relief. I clear my throat, reluctantly loosening my grasp on her. All of a sudden, something creaks. A ray of light shines through the room, interrupting the bickering of our team. The light gets bigger and then we see Peppermint Girl holding a door open.

"Hey, sorry, y'all! We were experiencing some technical difficulties." She waves us over. "You can come on out now."

Kayla immediately pulls away and follows the other guys out the door, not once batting an eye at me. Something heavy itches my chest. *Am I really that hard to be around? Why is she avoiding me?* I'm not exactly sure what I was expecting, but I tag behind, not liking this feeling one bit.

This feeling of . . . rejection?

I knew it. I should've been more careful. I should've kept some distance from this girl. Just because she looks harmless doesn't mean she is. I swallow. It's fine. This isn't enough to hurt. I'm fine. I'm in the clear.

We get into the other room where our team gathers into a half circle to face Peppermint Girl and her board. Kayla walks faster and passes Kevin a little. He makes room for her before standing in between us. Whether it was on purpose or not, it bothers me the whole time as the candy citizen tells us our scores and team evaluation. Too fed up, I take a glance at Kayla. She doesn't look at me, persistently keeping her focus on Peppermint Girl. I'm not even subtle at this point. She knows I'm staring right now.

But in a well-lit room, I realize I was wrong. I'm an idiot.

Her cheeks are flushed.

As if accidentally feeling Kevin in the dark wasn't enough, I had to bump into Aiden too? I didn't mean to touch him like that. It was dark and I needed to know my surroundings! It's not like I wanted to. I mean I do, but obviously not without his permission. That must have been so weird. *Did he hate it?* He got all tense but didn't say anything, so I had no idea what was going on. I just didn't want to trip again! Luckily, I didn't. But I still freaked out when Donny knocked over the prop. Aiden was nice enough to hold me still. The worst part is that I *enjoyed* it. It felt amazing. Geez! How embarrassing.

Aiden's staring at me. I can't even look at him right now.

Relax, Kayla. It was an accident. Exactly. Just like at the lantern festival, he caught me when I fell backwards. I'm sure he understands. Knowing him, he's probably worried, right? Right. Holy crap, that makes it the second time he's caught me. I hope he doesn't think I'm clumsy. I resist scrunching up my face.

"Picture time!" Peppermint Girl squeaks.

The five of us pose, and it's only when she posts our picture on the scoreboard do I find out we made the new top score. I must've completely spaced out! After gathering our things, Team Circus Animals—you're a genius, Nick—start to disperse with Kevin and Donny departing for another game. I'm about to take my leave and head back to Franny and Pat when Nick asks me a question.

"Are you going to the scare festival tonight, Kayla?"

"No. My friends aren't going, and I don't want to go alone either." I chuckle nervously, trying to hide my disappointment.

"Aiden and I and a few others are going later. You can join us if you'd like."

Nick seems excited about the idea, though I can't help but feel skeptical. Their other friends don't know about this yet, and I don't want to ruin it or make it weird if I joined in on their fun. But I also wanna go. There's gonna be carnival games, and Aiden's gonna be there. I can't say no to that. *This is your chance, Kayla. Take it!*

"Are you sure? Is that okay?"

"Of course! Evan, Jack, and Luke wouldn't mind. Right, Aiden?" Nick and I both look curiously at the dashing pilot.

"Yeah. The guys don't bite." He smirks. "You should come. There'll be a lot of games there. I think you'll have a great time."

Well, if he says it like that . . . I chuckle a little, nodding. "Okay, I'll be there."

"Great," Aiden says, grinning.

Nick celebrates with a fist pump, and I smile at the welcoming atmosphere. I hope Evan, Jack, and Luke are just as nice as them. I'm looking forward to tonight. Not wanting to take more of their time, I decide to head back.

"Cool! Then I'll see ya later." I send them a wave and walk away but remember something. *Mom and Dad never liked it when we stay out too late.* I turn back to them almost immediately. "I can't stay out too late though, so I'll probably leave a little early. Just letting you guys know."

"Hey, we respect that," Nick says casually before excusing himself when he spots a friend nearby.

Aiden gives me a reassuring smile before he clears his throat. "If you need a ride, let me know. You can leave whenever you need, I'll still drive you."

His offer touches my heart, and I can't help but smile. I'm so tempted to say yes, but I can't. I shouldn't. *You can like him. You can enjoy being around him. But don't rely on him too much. What if he thinks you're needy?*

Dad thinks I'm useless.

Tracy thought I was dead weight.

Right. And I'm not even sure if I can handle being in a car full of guys anyway. Where would I sit? Would they ask me random questions? What if we don't get along or they feel uncomfortable around me? Not to mention, I'll be raining down on the parade when I leave early. Aiden's got a heart of gold, so I know he would drive me just because he said so.

But I don't want to be a burden.

"I'll be okay. Thank you." I fidget with my sleeves. "I don't wanna impose or get in the way of you and your friends."

He looks like he's about to say something but decides against it. Thankfully, I don't have to come up with another excuse. *Don't be too bummed about it, Kayla. This really is for the best.* Aiden nods—looking almost affected by my decline. I'm probably reading into it too much. Bless his heart though. I brighten up in an attempt to assure him with my excitement for tonight. "Will you text me about it?"

He smiles and gives me an upward nod. "I will."

"Cool. I'll call you when I get there!"

And call him I did. Not just because I said I was gonna, but because I'm completely lost right now. Taking a vacant corner, I turn around and search the area.

"I don't see a big skeleton," I say through the phone. "Is that near the entrance? 'Cause I think I passed the gates already."

"Where are you?" Aiden asks.

"Next to the circus tent." The place is big. What if I can't find them? What if they can't find me? Am I taking too much of their time? I hope I'm not inconveniencing them. Maybe . . . Maybe I shouldn't have come. There's a lot of people walking around. Anxiety creeps up a corner. Not good. I really shouldn't have—

"Circus tent," he repeats, followed by his incoherent talking to his friends. "Kayla, stay there. We'll come get you."

"Okay" — I look down — "sorry."

"Hey. Don't worry about it, okay? I should've thought of a meeting place."

Aiden's voice is so calming, I remember to breathe again. My cheeks start to warm. Body begins to relax. If he said that to make me feel better, it worked. I smile, even if he can't see it.

"I should've taken you up on your offer earlier." *Wait, did I just say that out loud?* I hope he didn't catch that. The walking crowd is noisy and I'm sure I didn't say it *that* loud, did I? It's quiet on the other side of the line. *Good, he didn't hear—*

"You should've." He chuckles.

I don't know whether it's my anxiety talking or the way he says it, I think I really should've just accepted his offer. Something gets ahold of me, and I'm elated with a newfound lightness. Is this approval? Permission? Does that mean that it's okay to count on him once in a while?

Can I do that?

I like this guy. What am I holding back for? He's the one who suggested I come along too, remember? Even after all the hurt he's been through, he's still letting people in.

Maybe I should too.

The way she straightened up when she spotted me—*ahem*, us—and the way she scuttled over, she looked like an excited puppy. It was adorable. Evan, Jack, and Luke—who didn't see Kayla earlier today—complimented her on her getup. Kayla was generous with her words too. However generous she could be to their Ghostface killer, Jack O'Lantern, and Luke Skywalker costumes. Thankfully, the costume talk and some other weird jokes Evan makes, seemed to break the ice.

Going around as a party of six worked out better than we planned. Many of the rides were two-seaters, and the games required sets of two or three. Evan and Luke took turns fighting to get paired with Kayla—to my dismay. But I don't blame them, she's kind of a lucky charm. Everything was going pretty well until Jack suggested we go to the haunted house.

It was dark in there with minimal light. Sometimes, the actors would pop out and scare us. Jack, Luke, and I don't spook easily so it wasn't a big deal to us. In fact, it was kind of funny. But Kayla, Nick, and Evan were a different story. The three of them were either yelping or shrieking every other minute, even when there weren't any jump scares. Jack and Luke occasionally messed with the guys, which worked out for me because Kayla scooted towards me for safety. She probably thought it was a good idea to stay away from the jokers of our group. Or maybe—just maybe—she saw me as some sort of comfort because she trusted that I wouldn't scare her. I hope it's the latter.

The haunted house had everything—gory props, ominous graffiti, fake corpses, and even dangling hair. It was all very predictable. Looked pretty fake too. Neither the scary music nor fake smoke help drown out the smell of plastic. Even so, Kayla was buying it. She was so jumpy. I almost feel bad for having her go through this if it weren't for the way she hid behind me for protection. I love the way she clutches onto my suit. I was having the time of my life. The jump-scare actors were great. It was probably the fourth actor—a clown with a chain saw—that did it for her. One of her hands let go as she fell silent as a mouse. I turned a little to see that she had covered her eyes. I'd never seen her so scared before. She was a champ and never complained. I reached behind my back to take her hand into mine. She must've been pretty spooked because she didn't peek up at me. But the moment I felt her squeeze my hand, that was it. It was over.

I was unstoppable.

For the rest of the way, I—holding her precious hand—led the group out of the house. Evan came running out, with Luke jogging after him. Not far behind, Jack comes out with Nick clinging on his back. I was too distracted by Kayla shyly thanking me that I didn't notice Luke approaching from her backside fast enough.

He gives her a sudden "boo," and she cries out, jumping from the surprise and letting go of my hand in the process. My now-empty hand goes straight for her back to prevent her from stumbling backwards. One of her hands land on my arm for support. Kayla looks to me in shock. Then it turns to relief. It sends me into a whirlwind. It makes me ecstatic. After recovering and realizing it was Luke, she manages to laugh it off. Jack has the audacity to suggest another haunted house around the corner. I'm about to suggest something else when Kayla speaks up.

"I think I've had enough scary for the night. You guys go on ahead." She smiles, keeping it lighthearted. The subtle shake in her voice doesn't go unnoticed by me.

Nick raises his hand. "Yeah, I'm with Kayla on this one. I'm gonna sit this one out."

Evan is seconds from agreeing until Luke taunts him, causing him to change his mind. Jack looks to me in question. "Aiden, you coming?"

"I'll pass. We'll catch you guys later."

Evan, Jack, and Luke walk off as Nick, Kayla, and I go to other booths for entertainment. Thankfully, playing a few games seemed to help shake Kayla's jitters off. Or I thought it did. I notice her get timid again as I roll up my sleeves for our current game. *Maybe eating some sweets would help.* Hoping for the best, I grab the hammer and take my stance before giving the machine a hard smash. Ninety-one.

"I'm sure I hit harder than that. The machine's a little stiff." I don't know why I said that, but Kayla's watching and I . . . wanted a different score. A *higher* one.

"It's rigged." She giggles.

Nick scoffs. "Oh please. Let me show you how it's done."

I walk next to Kayla as he takes my place. Shaking his limbs, Nick takes the hammer and slams it down the machine. The three of us look at his score. Eighty-seven.

He taps the machine with his foot. "It *is* a little stiff."

"Okay." Kayla laughs. "I need to try this."

She takes her tassel jacket off, and I swallow a little at the sight. She's wearing a white long sleeve—it's not even that revealing—but her shoulders . . . are exposed. *It's just skin, dammit.* But she looks so good in it. I clear my throat before reaching a hand out. "I-I can take that."

"Thanks!" She sends me a stunning smile as she hands me her jacket.

I stand straighter as she walks to the machine. Nick—who's already made his way next to me—nudges me with his elbow. He's smirking, and I don't bother nudging back for him to stop because I'm too distracted by Kayla. The sweet and cautious girl I've come to know looks so different. In a very attractive way. It's like I'm seeing a whole new side of her. Kayla grips the hammer and practices aiming on the target before she takes a step back and smashes it. Ninety-five.

"Wow." I smile.

Nick throws his arms. "Oh, come on!"

"You loosened it up for me!" Kayla exclaims. She sets down the hammer and skips over to us excitedly, laughing. "Told you it's rigged!"

"Or you're just strong."

"Maybe? But not stronger than you or Nick! Nick, where are you going?"

"You two have fun! I need to grab a drink." He shakes his head as he walks away.

Before Kayla can think about feeling guilty, I nudge her elbow. "Don't worry about him. He's just sad he came in last." I send her a wink.

It makes her smile before she carefully reaches for her jacket. We go on to play a few more games until we decide to grab some sweets for the night. Fortunately for me, she hasn't put her jacket on yet. Kayla excuses herself for the restroom and I, not wanting to wait outside like a creep, tell her I'll line up at BooBoo's first. It's not too far away, so I don't worry too much. A few minutes go by, and I move up a spot in the line. Nearby, Kayla approaches me, looking a little shaken. Maybe even a little alert. Should I be alarmed?

Maybe I should've waited for her like a creep.

"What happened?"

"Nothing much." She laughs awkwardly, waving down a hand. "Some guy scared me when I came out the bathroom, and I accidentally kicked him. He got all worked up, but then Kevin came and told him to knock it off. I think he's a freshman from our school, Kevin seemed to know him."

Kevin did that? Does he—

No, that's not important right now. "Are you okay?"

"I feel like I'm forgetting something important, but yeah, I'm good! Thanks." Kayla searches her body, and when it seems she's got all her stuff with her, she flashes me a smile. I relax a little. She may be okay, but I should've been there. I could've done something.

This isn't the time to be jealous.

Jealous? No. I don't have the right to feel that. It's not even about jealousy. It's about her safety. Her well-being. Just like the other time at the library. I only stepped in because Chris was clearly intruding her personal space. She was going to get out of the situation with or without my help, but I don't know what came over me. He ticked me off. And I hated seeing her look so uncomfortable. I had to do something, and I'm glad I did because the look of relief on her face . . . That smile. It made everything feel right.

Is Kevin feeling that now? That expression that makes me all warm and fuzzy inside, did she show him that too?

We move up next in line. Before long, we seat ourselves in a small table after ordering. Kayla's got a bit of a sweet tooth. No surprise there. In the midst of enjoying our desserts, I don't know how we get to talking about my dad, but we do. "No, seriously. You were amazing, standing up to him. No one's ever talked to him like that before. No one dares to."

She chuckles. "Thanks. I hope I wasn't too rude though. I didn't like the way he talked to you. Actually, he . . . he kinda reminds me of *my* dad."

"You weren't rude. Don't worry about it," I say in hopes of reassuring her. It's my first time hearing her talk about her dad. Aside from the story of her grandparents, she never spoke about her family before. There's a little sadness in that casual tone of hers. "Is your dad tough on you?"

Kayla focuses on separating the cream from her lava cake. "Sometimes. Mostly when I do anything that disagrees with him. He's got a lot of expectations, and I don't really meet his standards, unlike my older sister. How I talked to Coach James that day, I can never do that to my dad. Every time I defend myself, he cuts me off and starts a lecture. I don't even speak up anymore, because I know he won't listen, and even if I did try . . . I'd just end up crying."

The thought of Kayla crying makes me still. *I don't want that.* I don't even know how to think for a moment. She takes a small bite of lava cake and stabs a few strawberries from her fruit tart to stuff into her mouth. The sweetness forms a smile on her face. I'm sure it would've been bigger if I hadn't asked her my question. "Thanks for telling me. I know it's not an easy subject."

"Thanks for listening." She looks at me and shrugs. "Honestly, it's nice to finally tell someone that. Not even my friends know."

Am I the only person she's told that to? She could've shared that piece of information with anyone, but she chose to tell *me*. I feel special.

Happy even. There's a wave of excitement that washes over me. Not exactly excitement. More like an urgency. A sense of necessity.

A want.

A want for *more.*

Maybe I want her to tell me more. To give me more. To open up more. I'm hazy on the details, but I know it's Kayla I want more of. The feeling is hard to ignore. It's almost frightening, so I take a bite of my cheesecake. We eat in silence for a moment.

Eventually, *desire* consumes fear.

"Hey, I haven't cashed in on that prize I won from the lantern festival yet."

Kayla's got on a look of recognition before she nods. "You haven't. Did you ever figure out what you wanted?"

"That depends."

"On?"

"Your plans this Thanksgiving break."

She looks at me strangely. "Well, my parents are taking a road trip to visit my cousins. Then they're gonna head over to my sister's after."

"Is your sister in college?"

"Yeah, a first-year. Only a year older than us."

"So you're going too, huh?"

"Don't know yet. She starts her break a little later than ours. If I tag along, I'm gonna miss a whole week of school. But if I don't, my parents are gonna send me to my aunt's. They just didn't want me to spend Thanksgiving alone. 'It's my choice,' they said." She snickers, as if recalling something ridiculous.

"Do you want to spend it at your aunt's?"

"Not really. I'm not particularly looking forward to it. Her sons are all married, and they always have their friends over. Everyone's on the older side. So I'll just be a loner there. But I'd rather be a loner at home." She sighs before cramming the last of her lava cake into her mouth, chewing with tolerated annoyance. Her expressions are so funny.

"How about joining me and my family?" I ask. Kayla swallows in surprise when I continue. "We're going to have a Thanksgiving gathering at a friend's house for the weekend. It's about a three-hour drive from here, so not too far. It's mainly family and friends. There's going to be a bunch of games and food." The last sentence was an attempt to convince her to come, I'll admit that. But I'm not ashamed at this point.

"Are you sure it's okay for me to tag along?"

"They said I can bring a plus-one. The more the merrier."

She grins before worry takes over again. "But I won't know anyone there."

"You know me. And my mom and dad. For all I care, you can stick by me the whole time if you'd like. I wouldn't mind."

She looks at me incredulously. "I can't bother you like that!"

"No, please bother me. I'm mostly watching over the kids anyway."

"Oh, so you need another babysitter, is that it?" she jokes.

"Something like that." I smirk. "But hey, games and food."

She laughs. Obviously, that's not why I want her to come. It's not like I was gonna say, *I want to spend more time with you, so I would like it if you came. It would be less boring if you were there.*

No. I can't say *that.*

I clear my throat. "You don't have to say yes. Just think about it. That's all I want—I mean, that's all I'm asking."

She smiles confidently, putting me at ease. "I *will* think about it, and I'll let you know after I ask my parents, but . . ."

"But?"

"This doesn't count. You're gonna have to rethink your prize."

"Why? That's not reasonable enough for you?"

She shrugs, grinning. "It's not."

"Okay, fine by me. I'm not complaining." It's me who's laughing now. She looks pleased I didn't put up a fight, and I feel like I've conned her—somehow getting more than I bargained for. Having her consider my invitation was all I needed. I could've called off the prize. After all, there's nothing I would ask of her. *Nothing reasonable.* In the end, I stay quiet and accept her terms. There's not even an ounce of remorse in me. I realize, *I'm quite selfish.* Kayla notices something and looks at me with a mischievous smile. "What?"

She clears her throat softly and points at my neck before gesturing to her own. "I think you got some spiderweb stuck in your collar."

The scene somehow feels very familiar. I swat the area and manage to grab a few cotton strings. "Did I get it?"

"A little bit, but there's still some kinda stuck." She chuckles when I attempt to grab it off some more and fail every time. "May I?"

I pause, a little confused but mostly stunned she's asking for permission. It's a first for me. The feeling is foreign. But it feels good. Like I have a choice. "Go ahead."

Kayla gets up from her seat and reaches over. Suddenly, the room gets warmer. *She's close.* I look the other way to make it easier for her. She tries to grab the fake web first without touching me but when that fails, she takes a careful hold of my collar. Pulling it back a bit, her fingers softly brush against my neck as she removes the web. It sends shivers up my spine.

I swallow, grateful she can't see my face. When she finally pulls away and sits back down, I thank her. As if she didn't cause chaos to my body, Kayla smiles as if happy to help before continuing to eat her fruit tart with satisfaction.

Goddammit.

Her fingers weren't even *cold.*

Is it even considered a prize if *I'm* the one who's benefitting from it? Either Aiden's one heck of a humble guy or he just doesn't know how to make deals. What a weirdo. But that's what makes him so charming. He is the same weirdo who held my hand through the haunted house and walked me to my car that night. A gentleman who knows how to make people feel safe. A generous and kind boy who invited me to spend Thanksgiving with him. Best day ever! That was so awesome!

I told him yes—of course—about a week ago. I'd be stupid if I said no. *Wasn't gonna make the same mistake twice.* It's gaming and eating at a big house for three days and two nights. And the best part is I get to be around Aiden! Who would say no to that? It took some time convincing Mom and Dad, but it worked out, thankfully—after I shamelessly confessed that I liked the guy and practically begged them to let me go. He's gonna pick me up tomorrow. I'm so excited!

Coach Aubrey dismisses us and that's a wrap for the last practice until break is over. I feel a smile on my face when I grab my tennis gear and walk out with Pat and Franny.

Pat grabs our attention with a giggle. "Franny, how are things with Alek?"

"It's getting there! I think I'm getting closer to the boy. I can feel it!"

A memory flashes in my brain. Oh my god. I freeze. So *that's* what I forgot? *My goodness, Kayla! You're in for a big one.* I swallow, catching up with them. "Franny, I don't know how to say this, but during the scare festival, I think . . . I think I saw Tracy and Alek together . . . holding hands."

The three of us come to stop. Franny turns to me and her face drops. "What? Kayla! That was three weeks ago! You're telling me *now*?"

Her raised voice makes me panic. "I'm sorry, I just remembered!"

"How can you forget something so important? You know how much I like him!"

"I-I only caught a glimpse before a freshman scared the crap out of me. It was dark and I'm not entirely sure if it was them, but it *did* look like them. I'm sorry, it totally slipped my mind."

Franny storms off.

"Franny!"

She continues to walk without turning back.

Sighing, I turn to Pat, who looks rather disappointed. "Pat?"

"I'll talk to her. See you after break, Kay."

With that, Pat jogs over to Franny while I watch them go on. Without me. The body heat from all the exercise seems to fade away when a breeze blows by. *It's cold again.* To avoid tailing them, I take another route to the parking lot. *I screwed up. How on earth did I forget about that? How do I always manage to make things worse without even trying? It . . . It's my fault, isn't it? God, I'm so stupid.*

"What the heck, Brandon? Don't just leave me here!"

Someone's voice breaks my trance, and I look up to see Kevin yelling at the taillights of a departing car. The Brandon he's calling for gives him the middle finger and drives off. I pick up on what's happening.

"Need a ride?" I ask softly.

Kevin spins around to see me and sighs. "Yeah, that'd be nice."

We get in my car, and I start driving with Kevin occasionally giving directions. I don't ask him about his Brandon situation, and luckily, he's quiet today. He hasn't asked me anything or tried any small talk since we left school so the ride to his house is mostly in silence. Good for me 'cause I'm not really in the mood to talk.

"You were right."

"Turn right?"

"No, stay straight. It's the blue house down the block. I said you were right."

"About what?"

"Everything. About Emma. About me. My grudge against Aiden. It was all . . . jealousy."

I stay silent, trying to listen intently as I focus on finding the blue house down the block. *Where is he going with this?*

"I was so blinded back then. I get why you called me narcissistic. Ever since we talked, I've been questioning so many things. Realizing so many things. I *am* arrogant. And ignorant. I see that now. I see so many things about me that I—" He sighs. "It's driving me nuts!"

His volume would've scared me, but I guess I expected it. I pull up in front of the blue house's garage and shift the car to park. He sounds frustrated. *Why do I keep messing up today?* "I'm sorry."

He sighs again. "I'm not saying it's your fault. I'm saying it's overwhelming. It's not a bad thing. I'm just not used to it. Being this self-aware almost makes me . . . hate myself."

His last two words put me in a frenzy. I'm not in a good mood already, and everything I've said so far today has been wrong. So, I don't say anything. *What is there even to say to that? I'll just make it worse.*

"It's been a while since someone actually cared about how I act."

I finally turn to him. *What the heck is he saying?* His statement confuses the crap out of me. I don't know if he's telling me he's struggling or if he's trying to give me a compliment. He's looking down, seemingly troubled.

"Okay, I'm just gonna say it." Kevin suddenly turns to me with a certain look. "I know I haven't been the best person since we've met and I might not catch on quick, but . . . I like you."

What on earth?

I did not expect that. Why the heck would he like *me*? I literally called him narcissistic to his face! Just how— What— Where is this coming from? I try my best not to give him a weird look. His gaze on me is so intense, I have to look away. "T-Thank you, but I-I can't. I'm sorry."

"Look, that guy from the water fountain earlier this year, I'm not the same person anymore. I'm better. *You* made me better."

He's earnest, and I know he means it. I turn to him. "It's not you, Kevin. I know you're a good person. It's just that I . . . I like someone else." My confession shocks him. Then his face hardens before he looks away. *Please. Please let it end here.* I don't need another person being mad at me today. He looks at me again.

"It's Aiden, isn't it?"

How did he—

Crap, my eyes give it away. As if his face couldn't get any harder, it does. I swallow. "Kevin, he doesn't—"

"Fuck, Kayla! If you were going to go for him in the end, you could've just left me out of it. You didn't have to pull an Emma and lead me on too."

His words come out of nowhere and smack me in the face. I think I feel tears forming. *Blink, Kayla, blink!* "L-Lead you on? What are you talking about?"

"You helping me out during the rally. Cheering me up that day and telling me your story?"

"I was being nice. I would've done that for anyone."

"What about that song at the lantern festival? Weren't you singing about me?" He gestures to himself desperately, as if referencing his own golden hair and blue eyes.

"Close to You" by The Carpenters? Oh my god, he was there when I sang that? I would be so embarrassed if I wasn't so angry right now. "That was a coincidence! I wasn't singing there voluntarily. I was covering for my aunt, and that was the only song I knew!"

Upon my explanation, his face falls flat. He turns away and I settle into my seat, trying to get my muscles to relax. It's finally quiet in the car, giving me the chance to collect myself and calm down a bit.

"Am I missing something here?" I ask softly. He doesn't answer me, but I let him be when I catch his chest heaving. "Kevin, I . . . I just wanted to be a good person. I never intended to send you the wrong message." I don't know if that made it worse, but I had to get it out there. There's a pause before he finally looks at me again.

"Clearly, I've misunderstood you." He sounds so adamant; I know it's the end of the conversation. "Thanks for the ride," he mutters before getting out swiftly. He closes the car door with a slam and walks to his house.

It could've been worse. He was holding back his strength, I can tell. But still, I feel like a chunk of my flesh had just been cut out. The words—if I even had any—catches in my throat, and I try to swallow them down. Shit.

They're back.

Go, go, go. Quickly shifting gears, I drive away as tears start falling. I only get a few blocks away when I pull over to an empty spot and wipe my eyes clean. It's quiet in the car. I take deep breaths in and out. A few minutes go by, and I think I finally calm down. The air feels chilly, so I put on my hoodie.

"You're okay, Kayla. You're fine!" I chant to myself. "Yeah, I'm fine!"

Oh, who am I kidding? First, it's forgetting to tell Franny about Tracy and Alek. Then, it's leading Kevin on? What is up with today? Oh my god. *You did it again, didn't you? You ruined everything. Why are you always doing something wrong?* Tears start forming again, and I wipe them away before they can fall. I wanna go home and curl up in my bed. Eat ice cream and binge-watch anime. I don't want to do anything during this Thanksgiving break! Yeah, that sounds nice. Mom and Dad are gonna be out so I have the whole place to my—Oh, hold on. I can't!

I'm spending the break with Aiden and his family! This is the worst! I mean it's great, but I can't be sad—not now! I sigh. Dad's always complaining about my attitude. I can't even imagine how it is when I'm *actually* sad. I'm gonna rain down the party, aren't I? This is bad. I wanna go, but . . . but I'm just gonna ruin it too. Don't do that to Aiden. He doesn't deserve all my crap. He doesn't need that. Maybe I should text him I can't make it.

Are you serious, Kayla? You told him you were gonna go. It's tomorrow! A little late for a notice, don't cha think? Don't flake out on him. And what's your excuse? You're sad and can't go because your friends are mad at you? That's not good enough. Just pretend like it's one of those family dinners. Smile and trudge through!

But I don't wanna do that. Aiden's gonna be there. I can't do that to him. I don't wanna be any less than my best when I'm with him. *It's not like you were at your best every single time you were with him.* I know, but if he sees me like this, he'll finally see that I'm just a . . . a screwup.

That I do things wrong. That I'm not worth being around. *You're ridiculous, you know that? You're throwing away a chance. A chance for you to be happy.*

I sigh. It's the right thing to do. I pull out my phone and scroll to my last conversation with Coffeebeans. Just looking at the nickname I gave him brings up a good memory. He doesn't even have to be here to make me smile. I need to do this. Five minutes go by and I'm still not satisfied with the draft I'm typing him. I don't wanna lie, but really? Is "I'm not feeling too well" the best I can come up with? Sounds pretty bad. Is this even appropriate to send? I try to come up with another draft, but my fingers are numb and aren't cooperating. Forget it. Maybe I should— Yeah. I press the call button. He picks up after the first ring.

"Hey, Kayla! What's up?"

His voice turns me to mush, and I take in a deep breath before speaking with my best normal voice. "Hey, Aiden! I— About tomorrow, I don't know if I can— I mean, if it's not too late, I . . ." I swallow the lump in my throat. *I called him and don't even have the guts to say it! Why did I think this was a good idea? What is wrong with me?*

"Kayla?"

"Hm?"

". . . Are you okay?"

"Yeah, I'm good!" My response comes out before I even think to reply. It sounded believable enough. Aiden doesn't say anything for a moment, and I wonder if I should ask him how he is. Wait, is that what he even asked? Before I can debate any longer, he speaks up.

"Where are you?"

I look around for the street signs. "Olive and Twenty-Seventh. Why?"

"Olive and Twenty-Seventh," he repeats quietly.

Then I hear something. *Is that a turn signal? Is he driving?* Sounds like he's on speaker so it's fine, but still, my timing could not be any worse.

"Stay there and don't move, okay? I'll meet you in a bit."

"Y-You're coming over? No, no! You don't have to do that."

"It's okay, I'm close. And I'd rather talk to you in person anyway."

I'm about to retort, but I have nothing to say. Seems like Aiden always know how to catch me off guard. Is this dread or excitement? I don't even know which one I'm feeling. This isn't good. *Does this mean I have to say it to his face?*

"Hold on, I think I see you," he says.

My eyes dart down the street. A car drives towards my direction. Nope, not him. Suddenly, a pickup truck comes from behind and pulls over at the empty space in front of me. Oh dear.

He's really here.

I hang up before I mutter curse words and run a quick check on myself in the rear-view mirror. It's not that obvious. He won't know. It should be fine. It *has* to be. Aiden gets out his car, so I turn mine off and do the same before meeting him in the middle.

"Hi," I try to say excitedly and smile it through.

"Hey." Aiden looks at me intently with those soft eyes of his. I want to avoid his eyes, but that'd be giving it away. *He can't tell, can he?* Suddenly, he clears his throat. "Before you tell me what you're going to tell me, I just want to say I thought of my prize."

That was random, but to my benefit, it kinda shakes my nerves away. "Sure, what is it?"

"If you're not uncomfortable with it . . . I want a hug."

"A what?"

"I want a hug from you," he confirms. I stare at him in disbelief—maybe in some confusion—unintentionally making the mood awkward. He seems to catch on and is quick to explain himself. "I gave Nick one the other day, but he pushed me away." He chuckles. "I guess he didn't know how to respond. You know us guys, we're touch deprived."

His joke cracks a small smile out of me. I would've laughed, but I get it. Physical touch isn't really a thing in my family. It's kinda sad, actually. I'm foreign with that stuff, so if he wants comfort, I'm probably the worst person he could ask. Plus, I'm smaller than him. *What kind of comfort is that? What if it doesn't work?*

I pull down my sleeves to cover my cold hands. "Are you sure you don't want anything else? I'm probably a bad hugger."

"I'm sure." He laughs before running a hand through his hair. "Actually, I want to hug you if that's okay."

He wants to hug *me*? I stare at him, speechless. There's a smile on his face when he opens his arms. Silence fills the air.

He inches closer. "I'm taking that as a yes?"

Oh god, heart! Answer him. Don't back away, stay still! Words. What—how words? Forget it. Smile. Nod!

He beams before he pulls me into him, embracing me with his bigger body. Engulfing me in his warmth. I wrap my arms around him and feel the full extent of the hug. Holy moly guacamole. Dear Nick, thank you for pushing him away. Sorry, Aiden. You might've been looking for your solace, but this . . . *this*. It seems like I found mine instead.

My body relaxes. If comfort and security were human, it's him. This is exactly what I needed. Suddenly, all my worries seem to fizzle away. *Everything's gonna be okay. I'm gonna be okay.* I want to stay like this forever, but I know it's probably been long enough, so I loosen my grip a little.

"Just a little longer," he says, not letting go.

I let out a small laugh and hug him again. Snuggling into him with my face pressed against his chest. I hear his heart beating. It's steady. Calming. I like this so much, I accidently squeeze him a little and snuggle in closer. He smiles, rubbing my back soothingly. That makes me *melt*. I relish the feeling until I realize something.

This is so unfair! To *him*. Right, I should return the favor. One of my hands starts to stroke on the wide surface area. Unexpectedly, he chuckles.

I pause. "What?"

"Nothing. That feels nice. Keep going."

I smile and continue. Hugging him makes me feel safe. It's reassuring. I wonder what hugging *me* feels like. Considering the difference in size, there's definitely no way he feels protected. The thought almost makes me laugh. I just hope he's getting the comfort he was looking for—if he even was looking for any. *Aiden really doesn't ask for much, does he?* He touches my head briefly before we eventually let go of each other.

"Thanks, I needed that," he says.

I smile, hoping he can't see the heat on my face. Geez! If anyone needed that, it was *me*. Looking away, I clear my throat before taking my chance. "I-If you want a hug, you don't have to ask me next time. I won't push you away." I chuckle nervously at the ridiculousness I just spit out.

"You can't take that back." I turn to him with a confused look and catch a smile form on his face. "I'm a hugger. I like hugs."

"Okay." I snicker.

Without warning, Aiden comes forward and smothers me with another hug. I jolt a little from the surprise, but I return it. *Warm. So warm.* I'm laughing when we break away shortly.

"Just making sure." He grins.

My cheeks hurt from smiling so much. "Satisfied?"

"Very." He clears his throat. "You can . . . you too, if you want."

I smile. "Good to know, thanks."

He returns my smile, and it's quiet for a bit. Wait. That was my chance at another free hug! Why on earth did I hesitate there?

He shifts his feet. "So . . . when you called, was there something you wanted to tell me?" he asks delicately.

The stress and anxiety from the situations with Franny and Kevin seem almost nonexistent compared to earlier. The terrible feeling is still there, but it's numbed down now. When I think about it, the problems aren't as problematic as I thought they were. I'm simply upset that my friends had such a negative reaction towards me without trying to understand where I came from. I never wanted to hurt them and it pains me that they're offended right now because they *think* I did it on purpose. I did what I could to apologize. I don't know what I'm supposed to do right now but give them space. There isn't anything I can do at this point but to wait it out.

Aiden's looking at me with concern, and my heart swells. That hug was exactly what I needed. It did everything for me. *Don't worry, I'm not gonna disappoint you too. I won't.* Giving him a smile, I shake my head. "No, not anymore."

"Are you sure?"

"Yeah." His stare is strong, I have to turn away—suddenly feeling embarrassed. Taking a step back, I clear my throat. "Well, I still got some stuff to pack up so I should get going. See you tomorrow?"

He nods. "Pick you up at eight. I'll text you when I get to your house."

"Okay," I say and we walk to our cars. "Oh. Hey, Aiden?"

"Yeah?"

He turns and I give him a smile. "Thank you. I'm really excited for tomorrow."

"Me too." He's got a charming smirk on his face when we separate.

I end up driving home grinning from ear to ear. The excitement doesn't go away; not when I arrive home, not during dinner, not even after I finish packing. In fact, I go to bed almost scared I won't be able to sleep because of all the anticipation.

There's a little part of me that's still saddened about Franny and Kevin lashing out at me today, but I'm not that bitter about it anymore. They were emotional. I should've expected it, to be honest. *Give it some time and it'll be okay. It's going to be okay.* I'm not afraid. Not anymore. Taking a deep breath, I cuddle in my bed and wrap the blanket around me some more. It's warm. It reminds me of Aiden. My heart skips a beat. He really is the best!

I like him.

I like him a lot.

Stop. No more thinking about him! My heart's about to burst. Taking a few more deep breaths, I try to clear my mind. But it's no use. It keeps replaying the same scene over and over again. Just hoping—maybe even wishing—that those hugs today . . . *that* hug . . . was for me.

She was crying. I'm pretty sure of it. I knew something was off the moment I heard her voice through the phone. And I was right. Right when she stepped out of the car, I could tell something was bothering her. The usual lightness she carries wasn't there, and worst of all, she wasn't smiling with her eyes. Even if she really did cry, she definitely didn't show it. Kayla was putting up a front and it made my heart ache. I blurted out the first thing that came to mind. Whatever I could come up with to give her some sort of comfort without being too obvious.

Honestly, I don't know if that was the right approach. But I'm glad it worked out in the end. She was holding up fine but whatever had made her so unhappy, I knew she was going to cancel on the trip. As much as I hated seeing her so sad, I wanted her to go. I thought that maybe I could change her mind.

I was being selfish.

I won't deny it. I like hugging her. And the fact that she *lets* me is a whole nother feeling itself. The way she relaxes into me when she hugs me back . . . it's indescribable. I was glad to be there. In the moment. Somehow, it felt rewarding. The funniest part is that the hug was meant for her. So when she rubbed *my* back, I was caught off guard. I was the one trying to comfort her but got comforted in the end. It'd felt so good. She's a small ball of joy even when she's down. I hope she's feeling better today.

Leaning against my truck, I shoot Kayla a text that I'm outside. Not a minute later, her front door opens. Out comes Kayla. Her hood's on like it's too early in the morning. I snicker as I walk up behind her when she locks her door. When she turns around, she greets me with a smile. "Morning!"

"Morning." I smile, enjoying the sweetness of her voice before gesturing to her duffel bag. "Can I take that?"

She looks a little taken aback. "Sure" — she lets me take it — "thank you."

"You packed light."

She shoots me a confused look. "It's only a few days."

I nod, chuckling. For a weekend getaway, I was expecting at least three giant bags. That's what E—

Never mind. Maybe I'm just . . . intrigued? We get to my truck, and when I open the rear door to put her bag in, she gasps.

"Pilly!"

My lips curve up at the sound of her dog voice. Pilly sits up excitedly when he catches sight of the girl behind me. He jumps down from his seat and out of the truck before pawing at Kayla. With no hesitation, she picks him up and cradles him like a baby. "Hi, buddy! How are you? Have you been good? Hm? You've been a good boy, huh? Yeah, you are."

There's a big smile on her face when she pets him. I can't believe I'm envious of my own dog. At least she seems happy. Much better than yesterday. I should just bring Pilly to her the next time she's sad. We get in the car, and not long later, I'm driving away. The radio is on but aside from that, it's a little quiet. "My parents left yesterday to help get ready for today. So it's just you and me. I hope that's okay."

"Are you kidding me? Of course that's okay. I wouldn't even know what to say if your parents were here too. I'm glad it's just us. And Pilly."

"Good." I clear my throat. "So, I know it was a last-minute text, but you remembered to bring a swimsuit, right?"

"Yup. Do they have a pool or something?"

"No. We're going to a water park tomorrow."

"A water park! Really?"

"Yeah." I give her a glance before shifting my focus back on the road. She looks like Pilly when he hears the word *treat*. I let out a snicker. "I didn't think you'd get so excited."

"I've never been to one before," she says shyly.

"Oh." A thought comes across my mind. I almost feel stupid for not asking earlier. "Do you know how to swim?"

"I do. Do you?"

"Quite well, actually."

She nods. There's a small pause before I hear her mutter, "Bummers."

Did I hear that right? I stop at a red light, and take the chance to turn to her. Kayla notices me staring and looks mortified. I smile. *Seems like I did.*

"I mean that's great! You won't drown a-and . . . and I don't need to save you!"

Her ramble makes me chuckle as I entertain the idea. "I might be too big for you to carry back to safety. I'll probably drown you too."

She chuckles. "At least you won't drown alone."

It was only a joke, but I liked it way more than I should have.

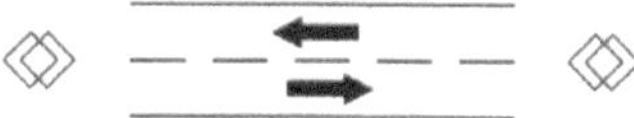

We arrive at the house half an hour later than I expected. There was traffic, but the car ride seemed so short with Kayla next to me. Mom lets us in and brightens up when she sees Kayla—as she does every time she sees her. A few other family relatives who are also staying the weekend have already arrived. Somehow in the midst of everything, Kayla gets introduced as my friend. I don't deny it because it's true, but I don't say it outright either. *It's weird.* Mom plays it cool so the other ladies follow her. They don't pay much mind as they're busy setting up everything.

Dad and some of the uncles are chilling in the living room, chatting away and watching football. They're distracted so I get spared from their knowing looks for now. Kayla notices the potluck dinner and looks at me, worried. Before she can even ask, I tell her my mom's already brought more than enough. I give her a pat on the back, and she visibly relaxes. *Fascinating.*

Giggling little girls are running around somewhere in the house when suddenly, there's a loud thump. Megan—Mom's friend and the co-owner of the house—stops our tour midway. "It's the two rooms in the west wing. Aiden, you know the way. I gotta go check on the girls."

I give her a nod. The next second, she's running towards the thump. Kayla follows me as we make it to our rooms for the next two nights, separating to get settled in. We're right next door to each other, which means I can check on her if she ever needs anything. This is good. Tomorrow's the water park. Day after is the scavenger hunt. I get so caught up thinking about what I'm going to do or say to her that I take longer than expected to settle in. I'm arranging a few things when my eight-year-old cousin comes running into the room.

"Aiden! Who's that girl? Did you bring her?" he asks, pointing out the door.

"Yes I did, Milo. Her name is Kayla."

"Kayla? What happened to Emma?"

His innocent question makes me pause. I forget kids can be so straightforward. Taking in a deep breath, I crouch down in front of him. "Emma and I aren't together anymore."

"How come? She was nice."

"She didn't like me enough, I guess."

"Why not? You're awesome, Aiden!" He gives me a big hug with those little arms.

I chuckle when I return it. "Thanks, pal."

"You're welcome!" Milo pulls away when his younger brother, Max, rushes in with a toy sword in each hand.

"Aiden! Aiden! We're playing swords! Wanna come join us? We're gonna be knights and you can be the pirate captain again! Captain One Eye!"

"I thought I was Captain Squid Beard?"

"We forgot to bring the beard," Milo explains.

Max takes out an eye patch from his pocket and gives it to me. "But we brought the eye patch! Here, Captain One Eye! Daisy, Kellie, and Mal are playing too. Daisy's a wolf. Kellie's our healer. And Mal's the plant controller. You know the drill!"

I laugh. "So what did Captain One Eye do this time?"

Milo jumps excitedly. "I know! I know! You kidnapped the princess! Kayla can be the princess, and we have to save her from you!"

"Yeah!" Max cheers at the idea. "Wait, who's Kayla?"

"The girl that Aiden brought!"

"Hold on, guys. You can't just make her play your games. What if she doesn't—"

"Let's ask her!" Milo says before rushing out to the next room. Max follows his big brother and I'm on his tail, hoping they won't overwhelm her.

"Milo, knock before you go in!"

"But it's already open." He points into room. "And no one's here, Aiden."

I get to the door and peek in. He's right. It's empty. Just then, Megan's three daughters run up the stairs, laughing. Daisy, Kellie, and Mallorie—who are all around the same age but smaller than the boys—run towards us with their props. Daisy with wolf paws. Kellie, a staff. And Mallorie, a flower plush toy with its bendable stem wrapped around her waist.

"Aiden!" they all squeal as they latch onto my legs.

I chuckle as I attempt to return their hugs with head rubs. "How are my magic girls?"

The sisters pull away, and Daisy howls enthusiastically. Kellie and Mallorie jump up and down, chirping, "Good, good!"

"Are you going to be Captain Squid Beard again?" Mal asks.

"He's Captain One Eye today, and we're going to save the princess he kidnapped!" Milo points at me accusingly, causing Max and the girls to cheer as I crouch down next to them.

"Let's not get too ahead of ourselves. We didn't even ask Kayla yet, and I don't think she'll feel like being kidnapped today," I say, worried they're getting their hopes too high. Kayla's always been capable of doing things herself. I've never seen her ask anyone for help before. The chance of her willingly play damsel in distress isn't high, but not entirely impossible. She does have a soft heart. She might just give in to the kids and actually go along with it.

"It's okay, she doesn't need to be kidnapped. She can be taken by you!" Max says, giving Milo a sword.

Before I can respond, Milo raises the sword in his hand. "Yeah, let's go find Princess Kayla!"

The kids charge downstairs, making war noises while I follow behind. Suddenly, they get quiet when they reach the dining room. *Seems like they found her.* When I turn the corner, I see Kayla setting the table. She turns around and freezes in place when the kids have her surrounded. Her back is facing me as they corner her to the table.

"Hi, are you Kayla?"

"Yes?"

"I'm Milo. Do you want to play with us? You can be the princess!"

"Hi Milo," she says politely. The rest of kids introduce themselves, and Kayla greets them.

"Come play with us! You get to see us use our powers and rescue you!" Kellie nags as Daisy howls from the side.

Kayla backs up a bit, bumping the table. "From what?"

"Captain One Eye!" Max answers.

Milo clears his throat. "Aiden's Captain One Eye! He's going to kidnap you, but don't worry, we're going to save you!"

At the mention of my name, Kayla looks around until she spots me. I give her an embarrassed smile and a shrug. She starts to laugh when I put on the eye patch. Clearing her throat, she tries to answer but looks to the kitchen hesitantly. Aunt Mel—the boys' mom—and Megan both stop cooking for a bit and turn to Kayla, quietly urging her to go.

Mom comes up next to her and takes the rest of the tableware from her hands. "Go ahead, Kayla sweetie. We got this."

"Are you sure?" Kayla whispers.

"Yes, we'll be fine. Though I can't say the same to you. You've got the harder job," Mom whispers back. She chuckles before she leaves the scene, patting Kayla with a "good luck."

Kayla turns to the kids and smiles awkwardly. "Okay, I guess I'm your princess for the day."

The kids cheer as Mal runs away somewhere. She comes back in a flash and gives Kayla a tiara. "Here, put this on. You can't be a princess without a crown!"

"Okay" — Kayla puts it on carefully — "thank you."

The kids bow to her, chanting, "All hail, Princess Kayla! All hail, Princess Kayla!"

I guess that's my cue. I sneak up on them and, with my best pirate voice, I give them a big, "Argh! It's Captain One Eye, and I've come to take your princess!"

The kids scream and run around. I quickly turn to Kayla, who's looking at me with an amused smile. She flails her arms, panicking calmly. "Oh no," she says sarcastically, trying hard not to laugh.

I snicker. *Seems like this princess isn't very scared of her captor.*

Kellie's the first to stop pretend-panic and stands with a power pose. "We're not going to let you take her without a fight!"

I turn and let out an evil pirate laugh. "Good luck, Healer! I slipped a slow-motion potion into all of your drinks earlier. You'll all be slow for the next two minutes or so. That's enough time for me to grab the princess and take her to my ship."

The kids take out their weapons and speaking in slow motion, mostly to react and respond to me. I don't have much time, so I turn to Kayla. She's scooting away discreetly but stops when she notices me eyeing her.

"What? I didn't drink anything at first!" She makes a run for it.

I'm on her tail, yelling after her. "Don't resist, Princess! You're only making it worse for yourself!"

She's laughing when she runs around the house. Fortunately for me, she doesn't know the terrain like I do. So I slow down a bit when Kayla unknowingly comes across a dead end. She spins around but stops when she meets me at her only exit. "Okay, you got me." She sticks out both her hands. "Arrest me, Captain."

I smile. "It's not an arrest. It's a kidnap, Kayla."

"That's *Princess* Kayla to you." She smirks, fixing her crown.

I chuckle. I'm about to take her hands when she grins, suddenly using the chance—when I have my guard down—to make an escape. But I'm quick. I take ahold of her arm, stopping her from going any further than a few steps. She doesn't struggle much when I lay my other arm to support her back.

"I was going to play nice, but you left me no choice. Hold on." I bend and hook her arm over my neck. She doesn't resist, confused with what I'm about to do until I get an arm under her knees. "Excuse me while I kidnap you."

Before she can react, I scoop her up in my arms. Kayla squeals a little but holds on. I take a glance and see her staring back with these humungous eyes, completely silent. I clear my throat. "I'll put you down if you don't like this."

Kayla looks away, shaking her head timidly. "Y-You're fine. Just don't" — she brings up her free hand to shield her face from my view — "don't look if you don't have to."

"Why not?"

She turns away even further now, and I catch an anxious smile behind her small hand. "Too close," she murmurs.

Am I making her nervous? Her answer does something to me. It's exhilarating. Maybe even, empowering. "Alright, deal. As long as you stop covering your face."

She nods, slowly moving her hand away and turning back. Her cheeks have become pink. I grin, casting her one last look before adjusting her to a more comfortable position and heading out. Kayla's utterly quiet when I maneuver around the house. I don't need to stare to know she's awkwardly finding a focus point—looking anywhere but my face. She holds on tightly and doesn't move much in my arms. This must be the most stress-free kidnap ever. Is it considered a kidnap if she's willing? *She really is making it too easy for me.*

I shift her a little, and she connects her hands to make sure she's got a good grip on me. Doing my best to look straight, I make a turn. The kids made it a few steps out of the dining room and are charging at us slowly.

Kayla watches them helplessly as we pass them. "Where are my warriors? Your princess has been kidnapped. Save me!"

She sounds desperate. I'm convinced she actually wants to be saved. *Is she that embarrassed to be carried?* Kayla's too shy to peek over my shoulder, so I turn to look at her warriors. From a distance away, the kids turn to our direction slowly.

"The slow-motion potion hasn't worn off yet!" Milo yells back sluggishly.

Daisy drags her howl as Max calls out like his brother, "Hang tight, Princess!"

"We're coming!" Mal and Kellie shout together, barely matching up in speeds.

Kayla chuckles a little, and I turn around and head for my "ship." I'm out of their sight as I turn a corner. We reach the stairs to the upper floor when she suddenly shifts a little, finally turning to me. *Is that worry I see?*

"Y-You can put me down now."

"I'm not going to drop you."

Kayla melts into a smile and shakes her head. "I know you won't. I just don't wanna make it hard for you. It's the stairs."

I let out a laugh. *Are the stairs supposed to be intimidating? What is she worried about?* She isn't even half of what I lift in the gym. "Don't worry. You're light as a feather. If you want to make it easier for me, just hold on tight."

Before she can retort, I walk up the stairs. She tightens her hold on me, scrunching her body even closer to me during the process. I am enjoying this *way* too much. By the time I reach the top, we hear the kids making noise and talking.

"I think the slow-motion potion's wearing off," she mutters.

"Hold on." I speed walk to my room, whispering, "Close the door. Close the door."

Kayla snickers and closes the door swiftly when I turn around. Turning back, I walk to the only chair in the room and gently set her down on it. Just then, the door bursts open and the kids charge in. Princess Kayla is back and pretends to be tied up.

"It's over, Captain One Eye!" Max roars.

Mal sticks up her flower plush toy in the air. "Vine trap! Get him, guys!"

That sets off a bomb. While Mal stands still to hold the spell intact, I pretend to be caught in her vines. Daisy charges forward, barking and pawing at me. Milo and Max are coming at me, swinging their toy swords. Kellie gets a few jabs at me with her healing staff. I pretend to break free and drag on the fight a little longer by sending my invisible pirate parrots to attack the children. It keeps them off for a little while until Kellie heals her teammates. They're back to using whatever tactics they can to take me down. It's all very chaotic.

The scene gradually shifts to me falling onto the bed where I pretend to succumb to their attacks and finally get terminated. I peek open an eye and see all the kids cheering. Kayla seems to have rotated herself in the chair to watch it all happen. She's got a smile on her face.

"Look, he's smiling! He's still alive!" Kellie points at me before holding her staff with both her hands. "Take this!" She pokes me in the stomach with her weapon.

For real this time, I fake my demise and stay still. The kids cheer again, and it sounds like Princess Kayla is no longer a hostage. "You saved me, warriors. Thank you!"

That was the end of round one. We entertained the kids for a few more rounds until Mom calls us down for dinner. The youngsters no doubt were having a good time. Kayla laughed a lot, so it's safe to assume she also enjoyed herself. And me? *I was having a blast.*

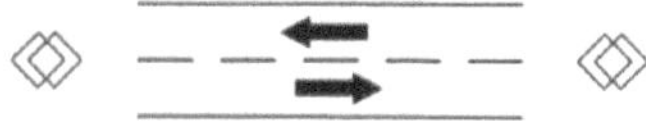

While I loiter outside the locker rooms with the guys, Mom and the rest of the ladies come out. Following behind Megan's daughters is Kayla. She's wearing swimming shorts and a . . . tankini? Is that what they call it? I wonder how someone who looks adorable in her pj's can look so pretty in a swimsuit.

I can't keep my eyes off her.

Kayla walks up next to me and gives me a smile that makes the sun hotter. She doesn't look at me much afterwards, which is a good thing. I would be more concerned about why she's avoiding eye contact again if it didn't give me the chance to silently admire her beauty next to me. She suddenly stands straighter and—

Fuck.

Her top isn't as long as I thought. It stretches up a bit, exposing some skin above her shorts. I swallow. There's a ton of girls walking around, showing more skin than that. But when Kayla does it, it drives me crazy. What's with me? This can't be—

No. No, it can't.

The whole gang huddles up. While the adults talk among each other, Ronald—a son of one of Dad's friends—notices Kayla and her swimwear. "Why are you wearing so much? You're so weird."

I'm stunned. Speechless. *How dare he?* Kayla looks at him strangely before looking down at what she's wearing. I can't tell if she's offended or not.

"This is much? You should see my other swimsuits, kid. I have a long sleeve and longer shorts than these, but I didn't want to wear them 'cause they're heavy. And this" — she gestures to her outfit — "feels secure."

Ronald looks at her, dumbfounded. "Who you calling a kid? I'm twelve and I'm taller than you!"

Kayla shrugs and looks rather unfazed after handling the boy perfectly. Even so, I can't stand by and let this slide. "Don't be rude, Ronald. She can wear anything she wants to wear. Apologize or I'll tell your mom to put a shirt on you."

Mommy's boy looks at me in horror. *That's right, Ronald. Imagine the disappointed look on her face when I tell her that her little boy was disrespecting my guest and telling girls what they should and shouldn't wear.*

"But, Aiden, I don't wanna wear a shirt!"

"Then apologize."

From the side of my eye, Kayla glances at me before looking at the boy again. I would've turned to her but I'm adamant about this. So I stay focused and give him a stare down.

He huffs and puffs before giving in. "Sorry."

I clear my throat.

He looks away grumpily. "Sorry for calling you weird."

I'm not satisfied with his half-assed apology, and I'm bothered that Kayla had to encounter this shrimp because of me. I'm about to make him apologize again—until he gets it right—but Kayla's hand on my arm sends electricity through me. It's like I don't know how to talk anymore.

"It's cool," she simply says to him. "Enjoy being shirtless. Don't forget sunscreen."

Ronald looks at her strangely before he walks away to join his siblings. *Goddammit. The next time I see him, I'm gonna teach that punk some manners.*

Kayla removes her hand, and I swallow before looking at her. "Thanks!" She gives me a genuine smile. "I appreciate it."

I stuff my hands in my pockets. "It wasn't good enough. His apology."

"It was more than enough. I wasn't expecting one in the first place. It's cool, really."

She's so indifferent about it. *It bothers me.* Maybe it's a feeling of responsibility to compensate the negative or something else entirely, but I try to channel my annoyance and use it as fuel to say something encouraging. Something positive that doesn't scream out *pretty.*

"You . . . You look good."

She brightens up, suddenly bashful. "Thanks, I think so too."

If I had water in my mouth, I would've spit it out. Of all the answers, I definitely did not expect that one. I don't know what kind of expression I was making, but she starts to snicker and I follow suit. The adults finally decide how to go through the park as a group and who should watch who. The older kids will go ride whatever they want while the parents watch the kids together and go on the rides their kids can go—the ones they reach the height requirement for. We'll all meet up after an hour and a half so we can play in the big pool together.

Kayla and I ride on the water slides with the younger teens, and I make it my mission to ensure Ronald doesn't get on the same floatie as us. Mission successful. Only three slides later, the younger folks didn't want to hang with us. So Kayla and I got to ride together by ourselves.

Things couldn't get better. I like splashing water at her because she'll splash back, and sometimes, if I'm lucky, she'll even playfully push me to stop. I love the feeling of her skin on mine. It's fun. It's fun seeing Kayla have fun.

Time passes too fast, and we're meeting up with everyone again. It's a shame I didn't get to spend more time with her by myself, but it's alright. It was nice seeing the warrior kids so excited to hang around her. As it turns out, Kayla's a great swimmer. She's probably saved the youngsters a handful of times when they floated away from their parents. And this includes the children of my other family friends that joined in for the water park trip today. For a great deal of the time, she was basically the kids' personal water engine.

I pretend to be swept away by the current and call out for her help, but she doesn't bother swimming to me. She only splashes water at me and laughs. I don't blame her. I can stand in the pool.

Before we know it, and much to the kids' disappointment, it's already time to leave. The adults distribute towels and some are packing up. Voluntarily, Kayla helps the kids with their towels and shoes. When she gets a towel for herself, I don't worry much and focus on getting Max to stay still so I can put one on him. Milo is fine, he listens to me, but his little brother likes to make things difficult when he doesn't want to leave. I finally get ahold of him and crouch down to tell him we'll come here again some other time. It does the trick. Instead of complaining, he goes on about the crazy wave that swept him away and the rides he'll ride when he gets taller. I finally get to wrap a towel on him. Unexpectedly, a towel gets draped over me, and I look up to my left.

Kayla.

"Don't forget yourself, big guy."

I only get a brief glance at her signature smile before one of the ladies call her over for help. She doesn't hesitate, and I watch her walk over to assist with a bag. Max taps my hand and I turn to him.

"Is she your girlfriend?"

"No." That came out fast and curt. Almost harsh.

Aunt Mel comes out of nowhere and scoops her son up into her arms. "Not *yet.*"

She walks away and I stand up with a newfound weight on my shoulders. I look at the girl working on a stuck zipper and adjust the towel over me. Her act of kindness leaves me with a feeling of reassurance I'm unable to shake away.

She cares.

It feels so nice to know that.

I must've been the happiest girl in the park yesterday. The water rides were all very fun, but the best part of it all was getting to spend the day with a shirtless Aiden. I really should've sneaked a few more glances, but it would've been so embarrassing if he caught me drooling over him. I mean, those arms! That torso! Ugh, so gorgeous. And when he pretend-drowned? Oh. My. God. I wanted to swim over and pretend-save him so bad. Except, I didn't know what I'd do being so close to him. Or more like, what *he'd* do.

I'd completely freaked out the other day when he carried me with that precious body of his. Did I save a country in my previous life? I'm like the luckiest girl alive. My eyes have been blessed. My soul has been blessed. Wow. He's so meaty, I wanna eat him up.

Okay, ew. Don't be gross, Kayla. Fine. But can we talk about how he treats us ladies with so much respect? He's like the greenest flag ever.

Emma must regret throwing away gold, huh? Yeah, she totally does. I would if I were her.

Aiden and I are accompanying the kids in the middle of town for a scavenger hunt activity. The other children from yesterday are in a different group, thankfully. Because I like the warrior kids better. Our squad doesn't end up winning, but at least we had fun. The kids were a little bummed out so we took them to a nearby pumpkin patch to cheer them up. It was Aiden's idea. As expected from the thoughtful cinnamon roll!

For the first time in what feels like forever, I'm actually *wanted* somewhere. Well, at least that's what I feel like when I'm around Aiden and the kids. With them, I'm not a screwup. They actually like what I can offer. What I say. What I do. They appreciate my presence. Not my sister's. Not Tracy's. *Mine.* I'm having the time of my life right now. Nothing can ruin this.

Nothing.

Aiden and I silently watch the kids ride ponies from the sidelines. When I turn around to do a little stretch, I see something unfortunate. *Maybe I thought too soon.* Did it really have to be now that I bump into a friend? Of all times! Why her? I didn't want to think about any of it on this trip. Her eyes stare me down, and I give her a wave to say hello, but she doesn't return it. Instead, she stays in the bakery line she's in and signals me to come over to her. There's a familiar guy next to her. *Is that Alek?* Not good. Not good at all.

I turn to my left and tap Aiden on the arm. "I'll be back. I gotta go talk to a friend."

He looks to the direction that I point, and his jaw slightly tightens when he spots her. "Is that Tracy?"

Oh god. He remembered her name! *Really, Kayla? This isn't the time.* Right, sorry. I nod. Aiden turns to me but keeps an arm leaning on the fence.

"Do you have to?"

His soft question makes me look up at him in surprise. Is it me or does he sound like he doesn't want me to go? *You're overthinking again, Kayla.*

He gives her a quick glance before returning his focus onto me. "I don't like the look she's giving you."

Okay, not overthinking. This is real. His words suddenly make me warm, and I turn to look at Tracy. Oh, wow. Look at that glare. Wait. Why is she angry at *me*? What did I do? I don't want to go, but if I don't, she'll definitely come over. That's the last thing I want right now. I'm not gonna let this whole Tracy drama ruin it for me. Or for them.

"It's important. I'll be back." Since he sounded like he was concerned, I give him a reassuring look. I think it works because he nods.

"Okay. I'll be here if you need me."

If you need me. I love it when he says that. It's like a confidence boost or something. Aiden always know what to say to calm me down. I give him a smile before I go. I'm walking to Tracy when suddenly, she steps out of her line and walks to me. Alek's holding their spot in line, so I guess there's no need to worry. When we reach each other, she takes me by the arm and drags me to a quiet corner. Still no hi. Before I can ask her why Alek is with her, she dives straight into it.

"Kay! How could you rat me out like that? No one was supposed to know that Alek and I were dating yet!"

They're dating? Holy. Crap. Hold on, what does she— "What do you mean 'rat you out'? You've never even told me you were dating him."

"Franny wouldn't have known if you didn't snitch on me. I wouldn't be in this mess if it weren't for you."

"Snitch? If you're talking about the scare festival, I only saw you two there by chance."

"Does that matter? Everyone knows now, and they're blaming *me* for it!"

Her voice is raised, but I remain calm. The wrong party here isn't me. "I was being a friend and telling it as it is. You two were holding hands and Franny should've known about it. It was wrong, Trace."

"Not this again. Franny gave me an earful already. I don't need to hear this *girl code* thing another time."

"Well, she's right. You knew she liked him, and you said you were gonna be her wing-woman."

"Alek doesn't even like her! What was I supposed to do? He can date whoever he wants."

"He can, but if you were gonna help Franny, you could've at least told her that he didn't see her that way. Or let him tell her himself. I can't believe you just dated him like that. *Behind her back.*"

"Why are you getting so mad, Kay? This isn't even between you and me!"

Why am I mad? God dang it. I had a feeling she was gonna do this again! I should've known better. I should've seen this coming. I should've warned Franny. But I didn't. I thought she would only do that to me. Looking away, I try to gather my thoughts and think of an appropriate response.

"Is this about Nathan? Are you jealous he picked me over you?"

I remain still—trying not to give her the satisfaction of my shock—before locking eyes with her. "You knew I liked Nate?"

"Yeah, so what? I liked him too. I didn't need to ask you to date him. He wasn't yours, Kay. I won him fair and square."

I can't believe it. *This changes everything.* She looks at me strangely when I start to laugh.

"I'm not jealous of what happened Trace, because . . . you're right. It was fair and square. He picked you 'cause you're better than me. Wherever we were, whatever we did, you just had to be the better one. You don't have to rub it in my face, I get it!" I sigh, getting my emotions under control. "I get it. To be honest, I'm glad he chose you. Because of that, I learned that my self-worth isn't determined by beating you or by getting the guy. It's about being proud of who I am. Of what I can do. I may not be perfect, but I'm trying to be the best person I can be. I'm trying to do the right thing here. Give it a try sometime."

She looks at me, flabbergasted. No. Not the crocodile tears. Anything but—

She sniffles. Eyes get glossy. A teardrop falls.

Oh, come on! Those weren't even insults. Are you kidding me? How does she even do it?

Tracy wipes her face, sobbing. "How can you say something like that, Kay? I thought you were my friend."

"I *am* your friend. But if being your friend means getting hurt and feeling like I can be thrown away at any moment, then" —*you can't hold it in forever, just spit it out*— "I don't wanna be your friend anymore."

It's silent between us, aside from her crying noises.

"Fine, if that's how you really feel." In an instant, her tears stop and dry up. "I have plenty of friends who I actually *like* being around. You weren't even that good of a friend anyway."

Her opinions get ignored. It's always been a one-way street with her. I know that. And I'm done walking on this street. I'm okay without her. Everything's fine because there are people who actually like being around me. And they're waiting for me. *It's time to wrap this up.*

"Best of luck with Alek." I walk past her. "Maybe you can last more than three months this time."

She scoffs. "Aiden McLaren."

I stop in my tracks. *No. Don't panic. I'm not gonna let her do anything to him.* I turn around with a fearless gaze and see her sneering at me.

"He's out of your league." She smirks, thinking she's done something to me.

I let out a laugh, relieved. She wasn't planning anything other than an insult to me. So these are her true colors. How refreshing. *So much for eight years.* I give her one last smile, a toast to the end of our friendship. "You don't get to decide that."

I walk away from a rather quiet and irritated Tracy. That might've hurt if I hadn't thought of it all before. But seriously, who cares about that? At least I'm not hurting anyone like she is.

I just really like someone.

What's wrong with that? Can't I enjoy liking this guy? He understands me and actually listens to what I have to say. I like him, and I like spending time with him. He's a mischievous goofball who's so fun to be with. He's what it feels like to be *happy*. I don't even know how I got this lucky to be around him. To have him open up to me and hang with someone like me—a nervous wreck who ruins things. Sometimes, I question if I even deserve this. Maybe I do. Or maybe I don't. I don't care anymore. If there's an opportunity, I'll take it. You don't have to ask me twice.

I'm greedy.

And it doesn't matter what I think. Because in the end, whether he's out of my league or not . . . that's Aiden's decision.

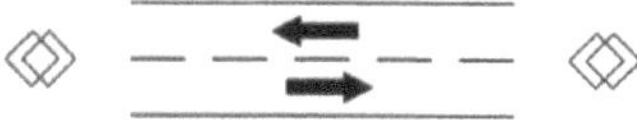

I told myself I wasn't gonna ruin it. I really tried, and I think I did a decent job engaging with the kids after my talk with Tracy. But I can't right now. The adults are handling the barbecue while most of the food's been served. I couldn't ask for anything better honestly. Aiden's family and friends are scattered everywhere, eating and chatting about countless things. I don't know how they do it. How do you not run out of things to say? The sliding door to the outdoor patio is open, and I go out to find a place to sit. Some adults are here and there. The kids got their own little area and are enjoying themselves with each other. I choose an empty and quiet seating area to eat.

After I left Tracy, Aiden met me nearby. He said he was gonna check up on me because I was taking a while and in case we got kidnapped. What a joker, he is. But then again, a lot of dangerous things have been happening in the world lately, so it's not too far from the truth. He's so caring. Strangely, but thankfully, Aiden didn't ask me anything about her. He's actually been pretty quiet since then, aside from entertaining the kids. I feel like he's giving me space, ever since the thing with Tracy happened. Though I don't know what for because I feel relatively fine. That insult didn't do much to me, and mostly, it's just that I broke up with a friend who ultimately wasn't really a friend. I'm not feeling fantastic, but I'm actually okay. Did I look that bad to need space?

It kind of feels like Aiden doesn't want to talk to me. Or even see me.

That's what's bothering me. Crap. I must've ruined the mood for him. Was it because I went and talked to Tracy even though he was kinda against the idea? Is he disappointed in me?

Well, this is not how I wanted to end the break. I've taken a few bites when I hear soft steps coming towards me. Pilly pulls up near me, drops his bone on the floor, and stares at me.

"Good boy," I quietly say, petting his head. He seems content, and I let him enjoy his dinner while I enjoy mine. Out of nowhere, someone decides to sit next to me. I prepare myself in case it's one of the relatives or family friends, but there's no point.

It's Aiden.

Oh my god, he's here. Why does it feel like it's been so long since I've seen him? Never mind that, I'm just glad he's not ignoring me. What should I do? What do I say? I take a peek at his plate as he settles into his seat. Perfect.

"Hey." I take the cup of Mrs. McLaren's potato salad on my plate and give it to him. "This is for you. They were running out, and I wasn't sure if you'd gotten the chance to grab any yet, so I got this in case." *What the heck. Why does he look so surprised?* He said he was looking forward to it yesterday.

Hesitantly, he takes it with a breathtaking smile. "Thanks. What about you?"

I show him my plate. A good chunk of potato salad takes up a section of my plate. Aiden looks impressed. Or amused? "One of your uncles thought I was crazy for potato salad."

He smiles and gestures to the cup I gave him. "What were you going to do with this if I had some already?"

"Eat it?"

That gets a chuckle out of him. Somehow, it feels like things are a bit closer to normal. We eat in silence for the most part, sometimes talking about the kids or the food. I'm finally finishing up my plate when he returns with dessert.

"You like fruits, right?" He hands me a bowl of strawberries, blueberries, and green grapes.

I nod vigorously and thank him when I take it like it's the most precious thing ever. Because it is. *Aiden got it for me.* My heart swells just thinking about it. I'm almost sad I can't keep this forever, but there's no way I'm letting it mold. Taking careful bites to savor the sweet and juicy fruits, I treasure it. Bite by bite. There's only so much, so I have to eat slow if I wanna preserve this feeling. This taste.

For some reason, he chuckles before he works on his cake. "I know we're leaving tonight, but I hope you've had a good time so far."

"Yeah, it's been great. Thanks. Everyone's been really nice and all. They're cool."

He stabs his cake and keeps the fork in there when he looks at me with a dubious expression. "I thought you said *I* was cool."

His almost-pout makes me laugh. "You *are*."

"But if I'm cool and they're cool, what's the difference? What makes me cooler?"

I look at him in disbelief before biting back another laugh. Never would I have imagined that Aiden would care about *this*. It's almost childish. But it's cute. And somehow, very flattering. Like my opinion matters.

"Is there . . . anything that stands out?"

"You really want me to answer that?"

"Yeah, I want to know what's good about me. Just one thing that comes to mind when you see me."

He's keeping it lighthearted, but it seems like he really wants to know. I look at him in silence. So many good qualities. It's hard to pick just one. What comes to mind when I—

"Your vibe. The feeling I get when I first see you. You make me feel comfortable. Safe." *Crap. That was a bad choice of word. Emma used that during their breakup.* I clear my throat in a hurry. "What I mean is, I feel like I can trust you. You're reassuring. If I was ever in trouble and you were there, I wouldn't be as scared as I would be if you weren't there. Kinda like that."

Oh dear, that was terrible. He takes a moment to come up with a response, and I wonder if he took my *safe* comment as a bad thing. I can't believe I screwed that up! And that attempt of a cover up wasn't any better.

"You get all that just by looking at me?"

I don't understand his confusion. I mean, does he not see how strong and reliable he is? "Yeah, it's like a sixth sense. I can pass out right now and trust you won't do anything to my unconscious body. Aside from saving me, of course." I try to keep it casual and playful, but it's still the truth. "It's a gut feeling, y'know what I mean?"

He has to put down his plate of desserts to laugh. It's like he's just heard his very first joke.

"No, I'm serious! And I know I'm right 'cause you treat people with respect. You're honorable. You keep chivalry alive!"

Aiden turns away and carries on with his laughing but this time, he waves his hand to me like he's telling me to stop. Like he can't take any more. Everything I've said so far is the truth and well, it wasn't exactly easy to say all that. It's kinda embarrassing actually, and I don't even think it's all that funny. For what it's worth, I'm glad he finds it amusing. I like hearing him laugh. When he's finally done with his cackling, he recovers himself in his seat and takes back his plate of cake.

"Hey, you asked and I answered."

"I was not expecting . . . *that*."

He's taking a breather, and my brow furrows. *What was he expecting?* Something about his looks? I'm sure he already knows he's a good-looking guy. He's seen a mirror before. "Okay then. What about me?"

Aiden looks at me and suddenly, I get all self-conscious. *On second thought, maybe I shouldn't have asked that.* I want to retract it but he doesn't take long to answer.

"Your smile. Because you always know how to brighten up the day. And . . . I can always look at you to feel better." He smiles, almost looking a little embarrassed. "Sounds cliché, doesn't it?"

He's rendered me speechless. I shake my head, unable to keep myself from smiling. Aiden pauses and looks at me carefully. He looks like he has more to say, so I do my very best to not look away.

"I also like your eyes."

I chuckle. "They're brown."

"They're beautiful. And honest. And . . . I like dark chocolate." He looks away before stuffing a bite of chocolate cake in his mouth.

Calm. Down. Heart! Did he just say—

He swallows before clearing his throat. "You should see them for yourself. They glow like honey in the sun."

My words get caught. All I can do is smile. I can't even say a thank you. God, this is so unfair. I can't even— I mean, I should— Geez! This is so frustrating. How can he just do that to me? He continues to eat his cake like he didn't just give me the best compliments I've ever received. I grip my fork. *Come on, Kayla. He really outdid himself with that one. The least you can do is pour out some of your feelings.* Say it. Before this silence drags on too long and it's too late. I gather up my courage and swallow hard. "T-The trees."

He turns to me, confused. "What?"

I gaze into his eyes. They're predominantly a lighter shade of brown and if you look at them closely, you can see flecks of green in them. "The trees . . . on a sunny day in the fall. That's what your eyes look like to me."

"Why in the fall?"

I think of tennis practice. The towering trees around the school's tennis courts. A clear day where the sun shines on them *just right.* When the trees are calm. Gentle. Warm. And looking at them makes me feel at ease. They're . . . peace.

But Aiden doesn't need to know all that.

"It's my favorite season." I focus on eating my fruits, too embarrassed to look at him. Suddenly, it gets quiet. *He must be weirded out, huh?* Maybe I said too much. I should really shut up next time.

"Summer's mine."

I glance at him. He's sincere about it. If I didn't know any better, I would've thought he actually meant something else. *Don't be stupid,*

Kayla. You should know where you stand by now. I smile and play it off cool.

The night wrapped up pretty fast after that. We bid the kids a goodbye and the next thing I know, we're on the road. Aiden's parents left in another car while he drove me home. He walks me to my door as I wave to Pilly who's watching us from the truck's rear window.

"Thanks for driving me and everything. I had a great time."

"Of course. I'm glad you came." We walk up the three steps to the front entrance, and I stab the key in the door when he clears his throat. "So, I'll see you on Monday?"

"Yeah!" I get the door open shortly so I can toss my bag somewhere in the house before I turn around. "Hey, Aiden?"

"Hm?" His hands are in his pockets when he looks at me in question.

Maybe because the whole trip feels like a dream, I don't want it to end. *Not like this.* The longing sensation becomes so overwhelming, it makes me daring. With a quick two steps, I get closer to him and then go for it.

I wrap him in my arms.

I have feelings for her. Goddammit, I think I knew it deep down, but I've been trying to push it away for some time now.

I like Kayla.

I *really* like her.

At first, I thought I felt protective of her because she defended me. Because she never judged me for my weaknesses. Because she understood where I was coming from. It was fun being around her. The way she'd always make time to say hi—to not only me, but her other friends as well—with such brightness and excitement. The way she's so considerate of other people's feelings. Of *mine*. She's a good person and seeing her troubled worried me. I like that smile on her face. But it's more than that.

I want to *keep* it there.

I'm not sure when it started, but it's only hitting me now. She's incredible. So capable. Honest and caring. I still can't believe she put a towel over me. Or the fact that she thought to save me some food. I can't believe she said *that* about my eyes. My heart must've flown out the window at that time. I never really had any impression on my eyes, but they're probably my favorite thing about my face now.

And that hug. Holy fuck. It's the first one she initiated. To say that it felt amazing is an understatement. I almost didn't let go. Never—not even in the one year I was with Emma—did I feel this cared for. This cherished. And here I thought I would hate the word *safe* forever, but I was wrong. If anyone could do it, count on Kayla to make it sound like it was something good. I had no idea *that* was how she saw me. She makes it feel good to just be *me*.

That I'm somehow enough.

But it's all over now. Tracy showed up and I shot myself in the foot. That glare she was giving Kayla bugged me like hell. It didn't feel right seeing Kayla go talk with her. So I stupidly decided to go look for her. Just to be close, in case Kayla needed someone to lean on. But dammit, I didn't mean to stumble that close. I didn't hear much. Just bits and pieces. It sounded like they were fighting over a guy. I only caught a few words from their conversation. I don't even have the whole context, but I can't help but wonder and make the worst assumptions.

Just who the fuck is out of her league?

Who can possibly be out of *her* league? I've been trying so hard to figure it out, I can't stop thinking about it. Is it Nathan? The Nathan they're talking about? But which one? There are three Nathans in our grade. I don't think I've ever seen Kayla talk to any of them. I even thought the guy hanging around Tracy was a Nathan, but he's not. His name's Alek, and I still have no idea what he's got to do with all this. Maybe I'm wrong and it's not Nathan they're fighting over. Maybe it was Alek. Is that the type of guy she likes? Or does she like someone else?

Who is it?

Because whoever it is, he's one lucky guy. I want to be him. I want to so bad but I know better than that. I know what I can offer. What my limits are. I've learned. And in the end, the one who gets hurt is me. As much as I want her, I know that.

Even so, I still yearn.

I can't act right. I can't even think straight. I don't know what I'm feeling anymore. I just know it's frustrating. That I don't like whatever is going on right now. If she has someone she likes, I don't think I can do this anymore. Why did I let myself get this close to her? It may be too late, but I can still save myself. As long as I don't go in deeper than I already am. This is where I stop.

I just need to draw a line.

Unfortunately, I have. I've been trying my best to keep things neutral, keeping things to a minimal. It's so hard to not care. To not do what I want to do, but I don't want to escalate my feelings any further.

I can't.

Aiden's been acting a little strange ever since school started. I'm not sure if it's because of all the embarrassing things I've said at the barbecue or the hug that scared him off, but either way, it feels like I messed it up. Like I've ruined my shot before I even tried to shoot. He still talks to me thankfully, but it feels like he's keeping his distance.

I swear something's off.

Other than that, some things have been looking up. A lot must've happened during the break, because Franny seems completely over Alek now. She knows he and Tracy are dating. It's official. Everybody within our circle knows. At least Franny's treating me like normal now. She even thanked me because if it weren't for me, she wouldn't have found out the truth until who knows when. There wasn't any mention about how she snapped at me last time. Whatever. I'm just glad the drama has been sorted out. Tracy doesn't visit our hangout area anymore, and from what I've seen, our friend group doesn't hang out with her anymore either.

Things seem a little less hectic ever since tennis season ended. Aside from the occasional club activities, there's not much going on anymore. Seeing Aiden in precalculus is always a joy, but then again, it's been weird lately. So I don't know how to feel about it. He doesn't seem to want to talk as much or come over to say hi or anything. Though that might just be because he's got a lot on his mind or that he didn't see me. *It's no biggie.* I push away the thought as I write Aiden's name and classroom number on the square piece of paper with my left hand. It's unrecognizable—just the way I want it. Completely satisfied, I give it to the student working at the table, thanking him before I turn away and leave.

"Wait! You forgot to write your name."

I spin around and give the boy a smile. "I didn't forget. Thanks though!"

He nods, slowly processing the information as I make my exit and turn to the left. Crap. I switch direction and walk out of there. *You're doing good, Kayla. That's it. Discreetly. Not too fast or he's gonna see you.* I reach a corner and turn, letting out a sigh of relief. One too soon.

"Summers!"

It was a call from far away. That wasn't too loud. I can just pretend I didn't hear that, right? Yeah, let's do that. *Keep walking, Kayla.* Footsteps squeak on the floor, and I realize they're not mine. Oh my god, is he jogging after me?

"Summers, wait."

I slow down to a stop and turn to meet him. He reaches me pretty quick and looks at me softly. It pisses me off. *What right does he have to look at me like that?* Yes, I'm still mad that he accused me of leading him on.

"What do you want, Kevin?" My tone is soft, as I don't wanna be rude about it. Even so, that doesn't mean I can't be straightforward. I wanna get this over with as quickly as possible. Surprisingly, he seems to understand that.

"I shouldn't have said all that in the car. I was upset and said a lot of stupid things. Things I didn't mean. I'm sorry."

His apology comes unexpected. The worst part is that he looks and sounds sincere about it. I honestly don't know what to say right now. *Am I supposed to forgive him?* I'm still hurt about everything he said to me. My silence makes him swallow before he speaks up again.

"You were right. *Again*. I got offended and lost my cool all because my pride got stepped on. And I blamed you for it. I messed up. Really. I'm sorry, Kayla." He looks at me—almost like he's pleading—and my heart gets soft. "Please say something."

"What do you want me to say?"

"I—" He turns away with a serious look on his face. "I don't know."

Wow, this is the first time I've ever seen Kevin look so . . . beaten? I guess there is one thing I've been wanting to know. "Do you really think I led you on?"

His attention instantly shifts back to me. "No! You didn't lead me on. I just thought you liked me back. No. I was *hoping* you did. Even if you didn't, I was hoping you would give me a chance. But I got angry . . . because Aiden beat me to it. Again."

I stay silent, appreciating his confession. The Kevin from months ago could never.

"I'm not asking for forgiveness. I probably don't deserve that. But more than anything, I want us to be good again." I look at him hesitantly. He softens his voice. "Don't avoid me. Please."

My face must've shifted because he sees through it.

"What? You didn't think I'd notice?" He smirks. "You're always turning the other way or pretending you're busy whenever I get near you. I see you. I don't want to but I can't help myself. I still like you, Summers."

"Kevin, you know I like—"

"I know." He sighs. "And that's okay."

His newfound understanding throws me off. I'm speechless once again.

"But I hope we can still be friends. It was nice when you said hi to me in the hallway. It was nice when I could talk to you. Honestly, I didn't think it would make such a difference, but it did."

Avoiding Kevin wasn't difficult. It was like reverting to my old ways before the whole water fountain fiasco. But I have to admit, it was kinda sad thinking about it. Plus, I still acknowledge Donny, so it's been pretty awkward lately.

"We're good." I give him a smile, and he suddenly brightens up. "And you don't need my forgiveness. You were upset, I get it. I do appreciate the apology though."

"Has anyone ever told you, you're too nice for your own good?"

"No."

"Well, you are."

"Okay. Did you want me to say something else then?"

"No." Kevin smiles. "Thank you. Truly."

I smirk and the next thing I know, we're walking to the parking lot together. "Honestly, I didn't expect that at all. What happened over the break?"

"Let's just say, Donny talked some sense into me."

I chuckle. If it's anyone, you can always count on that boy to keep Kevin under control. *What a funny duo.*

Kevin clears his throat. "So are you gonna tell him?"

"Who?"

"Aiden."

"About?"

"Your feelings." He looks at me expectantly.

I normally would never talk about these things with my friends—not even with my family. But maybe it's because Kevin knows already or maybe it's the open conversation we just had; I answer him. "I want to, but I don't want to ruin what we have." I sigh. "I thought he might've been somewhat interested but . . . I think it was just me who felt like that. I'm not entirely sure. He's not— He's been— I don't know, distant lately? What if I'm completely wrong and he doesn't even see me that way?"

Kevin snickers. "You don't have to worry about that. Trust me. I see the way he looks at you."

The way he looks at me? Doesn't he look at everybody with the same pair of angel eyes? He could make anyone feel giddy if he wanted to. How do you tell? I would ask Kevin but he looks confident. "Are you saying he likes me back?"

"I'm not saying anything."

God dang it. He can be so cheeky sometimes. What's the point in telling me that then? I wasn't actually thinking of confessing because it's probably too soon. I've had a crush on Aiden since sophomore year, but it's not like I really *knew* knew him. Until I did. These past months really just solidified my feelings for him. I like him. Even more so now. But that doesn't change the fact that he literally broke up with Emma this year. "What if he's not ready?"

Kevin doesn't laugh at my question, thankfully. Instead, he gives me a thoughtful look. "Are *you* ready?"

I knit my brow. Am I ready? For what? To tell him my feelings and risk ruining our friendship? No. To find out he doesn't like me and that I'm not the one? Again? No!

Kevin notices my inner turmoil. "If he asks you to the winter ball, are you gonna say yes?"

"Yes." My answer's immediate. I let out a laugh. "But he's not gonna ask me."

"How would you know?"

"I-I don't know. But I think he's avoiding me. I would ask him to the ball, but I don't wanna ask someone who's obviously uninterested."

There's a pause before Kevin speaks up again. "So, what are you gonna do?"

A terrible idea forms in my head. "I guess I can casually bring it up to see if he's going first. If he is and doesn't have anyone to go with, then I'll ask him?"

"If he doesn't say yes and you don't have anyone to go with, I'm here. I wanna go with you." I give him a knowing look and he laughs. "As friends of course."

Not knowing how to handle his bluntness, I look away. I was definitely not planning to go if I knew Aiden's going with someone else. I'm not even sure if I wanted to go if Aiden wasn't going to be there. Not to mention, Franny and Pat found dates to the ball. So if I were to go, I'd be going *alone*. And I didn't want that. Kevin's offer just now is tempting, but I really wanted to go to the ball with the person I like. I keep my mouth shut, knowing better than to say any of that to the guy next to me. Luckily, we come to a stop when we get near his car.

"Donny has a date and I don't. But hey, it's senior year. Winter ball doesn't happen twice. So I'm going anyway. Alone. If Aiden's not going with you, we can go alone together." He grins. "I promise I won't do anything funny. Just let me know."

That was somewhat encouraging. So I nod. "Okay."

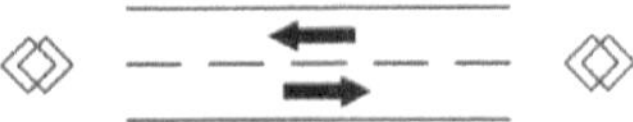

It's our first study session after the trip ended, and it's awkward. He doesn't seem like he wants to talk all that much. So, other than me answering his questions, nothing else is really being said. Sometimes, it doesn't seem like he needs my help at all. At this rate, we might not even be study buddies anymore. We finally call it a day, and I start packing my things.

I don't know what I did, but if things are gonna be this weird now, I might as well go all out and make it weird on my own terms. Right? Right. *You're about to leave and if you bring it up now, at least you'll leave right after. This is your chance, Kayla. You can do it, just go for it.* "I can't believe winter ball's next week."

"Yeah." Aiden closes his textbook and sets his things aside.

I stuff the last of my mine in my bag. Zipping it up, I try to keep it casual. "Are you going?"

Aiden pauses for a split second. I would've missed it if I weren't paying attention. That definitely wasn't my imagination. He gets up from his seat, and I do too.

"No."

"Oh, did you have something planned already on that night?"

"No."

Another one-word answer. Again. He doesn't even elaborate. Would it be rude if I asked? I wanna know why. *No Kayla, don't bother him.* If he doesn't wanna go, he doesn't wanna go! Can't force him. And he clearly doesn't wanna be asked about it. I push in my chair and Aiden seems to be waiting. It's like he wants me to leave. *I shouldn't have asked him. This is excruciating.*

"I don't like winter balls."

I turn to him in surprise. It seemed like that took a lot of effort. There's almost a sullen look on his face. I don't wanna make it worse so I smile and nod. "I see." Adjusting my bag, I walk towards the door with him. "Well, then."

Aiden seems bothered by something. Maybe I should ask him if I overstepped my boundaries during the break. I can give him some space if that's what he needs. I look up at him.

Or not. Maybe next time, when I'm more prepared.

"I'll see you in class." He nods, giving me a smile. As beautiful as it is, it seems forced.

Oh geez, you didn't have to. Really. I'll get out of your hair. The mood is so weird I only manage to get a small smile in. "Right, see you in class."

I turn and walk down the porch steps. He usually stays at the door until I'm out of sight. Should I check? I'm against it but when I'm almost out of his view, I turn and look at him, immediately regretting it.

The door's closed.

I swallow and head to my car. Okay. *Seriously, what the heck happened? Did I really imagine everything we've had so far?* Everything we've had? I mean, we hung out together and had fun. That's it.

I get in the car and let out a groan. It was the hug, wasn't it? I thought he said he was a hugger! Maybe it was because I said *safe.* That might've been it! Hold on, wait a minute. Things were a little weird beforehand already. Before? Oh right. Was it when Tracy and

I talked? That look on his face when he saw Tracy! Nothing good was gonna happen talking with her. I knew that. I knew *he* knew that. But it was a conversation that had to happen. Come to think of it, Aiden did get all strange after that. Is he . . . *Is he disappointed in me?* A heavy sensation latches onto my heart.

It's fine.

It's fine he doesn't want to go to the ball. I'm not upset he doesn't like winter balls. Personal preference, I understand. And if he said that just because he didn't want to go with me, it's also fine. It's okay because I never expected him to like me back. But we're still friends, right?

No.

We're not friends. *Friends at least wanna be near each other.*

I sigh before taking in a deep breath. Why is it that when I finally get comfortable and start opening up to someone, something always goes wrong? Like they don't want to be around me anymore.

Dad's been complaining ever since I started having opinions.

Tracy's completely tossed me aside when I had just started to rely on her.

Nate's feelings became nonexistent when someone better showed up.

And Franny doesn't even have enough faith in me to actually think that I would hurt her on purpose!

What's wrong with me? Am I really that *unlikable?*

No. *Don't do this, Kayla.* My vision gets blurry, and I blink them away. *You're not a crybaby anymore. You know better.* I grit my teeth. This is nothing new. I thought I'd get used to this by now, but I was wrong. I shouldn't have opened up to him.

Aiden . . . Aiden can like someone else for all I care. I'll get over it. But if it's something that *I did* that's making him like *that*, I wish he'd just tell me. Forcing himself to tolerate me is the last thing I want. I'd rather he just stop talking to me altogether. The guy can't even look me in the eye these days, and *I'm* the one who has a problem with eye contact.

I feel like shit.

I've pretended to be okay with all this but I'm not. I can't ignore it anymore.

This hurts.

Nick seems to think I'm the biggest idiot in this town. To some degree, I'm not gonna deny that. At this point, I don't care anymore. I have my reasons.

"What the hell, bro?"

"She asked me *if* I was going. She didn't ask me *to* go."

"And you told her you weren't? That was your chance! You could've gone with her. She obviously wanted you to!"

She already has someone she likes. Why would she ask me? She should've asked *him* instead. Besides, winter balls aren't a good memory for me. They're an opportunity to have expectations, and expectations mean that *I'm not good enough.* I'm not ready to put myself out there and let myself be a punching bag again. Emma showed me enough. I'm not that guy. I will *never* be that guy. If Kayla ever looked at me with disappointment in her eyes, I don't know what I'll do. Sighing, I lean back in my chair. "Nick, I didn't want to go the ball with her."

"Yeah, no kidding. It's over now."

"You seem more upset about it than I am."

"I am! You were acting all strange around her, and I was getting all excited, assuming you had some surprise planned, but you didn't. I thought you liked her, bro. You two look good together."

Nick probably knew I liked her way before I did, didn't he? Still, this is exactly what I'm talking about. First, it's Mom. Then, Max and Aunt Mel. And now, Nick? People thought Emma and I looked good together, and look how well that turned out.

But . . . he's not wrong.

"I do like her." This is the first time I've verbally confirmed it with him.

Nick sits on my bed and calms down. "I saw Kayla at the ball."

It's not a surprise. I assumed she would go. It's senior year. Who wouldn't? I try to push away the image of what she looked like. What kind of dress she wore.

"She went with Kevin."

My heart drops. *So it was Kevin?* I should've guessed it was him. I knew something was up during the fall rally. Even during the Halloween festival, he—

Nick clears his throat. "It didn't look romantic, if you ask me. Are you really not gonna do anything?"

"Can't I just enjoy what we have now?"

"What is there to enjoy when you don't even let yourself be around her? Don't think I haven't noticed you've been keeping yourself busy with us guys. You might've been with us, but you weren't *with* us. You look miserable, man. Probably as bad as you were with Emma. Maybe even worse. Even Kayla can tell something's going on."

"Nick, I can't. She likes someone else."

"Who?"

"I don't know. Kevin?"

"Bro, I just said it didn't look romantic. They didn't even hold hands!"

His remark brings some kind of relief, but that doesn't change things. I'm tired, I'm edgy—all the time. I don't feel good these days. And all because of what?

Because Kayla has that much power over me.

I need to stop now before I get in too deep. While I still have the chance.

"Okay, back the hell up. How do you even know that?"

I tell Nick what I remember about the bits and pieces of the conversation Kayla had with Tracy, and he flips.

"For god's sake, Aiden! Did you ever consider the person she likes is *you?*"

"Me?" I don't think I've ever been so dumbfounded. "No, it can't be."

"What?" Nick gapes at me. "Do you *not* want her to like you?"

"No, I do! I just— I don't . . . It's complicated." If she were to ever be something more than a friend, she'd have my heart. Emma was one thing, but if Kayla ever decides to break me?

I'd be destroyed.

"It's simple, Aiden. If you like her and she likes you, just get together and be happy already."

"Nick, I like what we are now. She can't hurt me." It accidentally spills out.

He gives me a soft look. "You're hurting now, aren't you? Because of her. And that's literally self-imposed. The funniest thing is, you don't even know for sure what her feelings are."

I look away, guilty. He . . . *He's got a point.* "What if I can't be what she wants?"

"Would she even like you if you're not what she wanted? Love isn't always sunshine and rainbows. There'll be rain too. Maybe you should ask yourself if the ups with Kayla outweigh the downs. If yes, I'd say go for it. If not, then there's always other fish in the sea."

I don't want other fish. I want Kayla. I want her to want me. I want her to look at me. With those beautiful eyes of hers. With that bright smile. I want to be the one she runs to when she's happy. And when she's sad, I want to be the one to comfort her. To hold her. For her to *let* me.

I want it all.

Nick's right. If she doesn't like me, then it's no different from what I'm feeling now. But if she does . . . what's the worst she can do? Ramble on about how safe I make her feel? Not tell me why she's sad?

Though the latter sounds pretty bad in itself, I'm sure she has her reasons. I understand. I have my reasons for not wanting to act on my feelings.

It's hard to know that I'm not good enough.

It's even harder to accept it when I *want* to be.

But Kayla's always been kind and caring. *She won't care about things like that, would she?* No. That girl accepted the sorry excuse of an apology that punk Ronald gave her. She still lights up and greets me with a smile, even when I've been a guarded jerk to her. If there's even a tiny possibility that the person she likes is me, then that would mean I . . .

"I messed up."

Nick gets up and makes his way towards me. "For the record, if she really does like you, that means you were acting all sad and jealous of yourself. That's kinda hilarious." He starts to laugh. I'm this close to pushing him away when he stops and spots something on my desk. "Ooh, is that a Christmas gram? Who sent you that, you lucky bastard?"

"I don't know. There's no name on it."

He picks it up and inspects it carefully. "Is it Kayla?"

"That's not her handwriting."

"Damn, that's too bad. Okay, well I'm gonna go grab a snack. Be right back." Nick hands the gram back to me and leaves the room.

I take another look at it. That's definitely not how she writes. Her letters usually connect, having a flow to it. But this? It's stiff and spaced. It kind of resembles a kid's handwriting.

But what if? *What if it was Kayla?* I've seen her write her numbers messy one minute and neat the other, so it's not entirely impossible. Excitement forms and for once, I let myself feel hopeful. If it really was her, then does that mean she likes me too? But why would she not put her name on it? Why go this far to hide your handwriting? I didn't pay much attention before so I take a look at the candy for any other clues. Maybe it's just a coincidence or maybe it's fate.

It's dark chocolate.

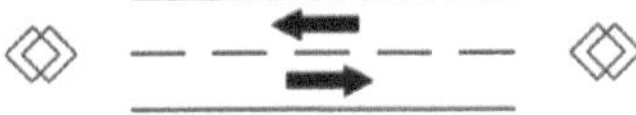

When I say I messed up, I fucking messed up. I've reached out to Kayla over the winter break twice to see if she wanted to meet up. She couldn't make it the first time, but luckily, she came through on the second.

We're bowling and it's mostly quiet between us. Occasionally, we'd exchange a few compliments and encouraging words. She looks like she's enjoying herself, but I haven't seen her in a while. I can't be sure. She looks a little stiff, not physically as she's the one with the higher score right now, but . . . emotionally. As if she's cautious. The few conversations I've tried to start doesn't go too well. It's like back when I first got to know her. We talk, but she feels so far away.

Kayla's wary of me.

I don't blame her. I've been such a dick to her since Thanksgiving break ended, giving her short answers and never engaging in conversation. I even avoided her at school sometimes. It took a lot of effort, and it was exhausting. I hated it. *I'm an idiot for doing all that.* It makes me angry at myself. Yet, Kayla's been nothing but a saint the whole time. She's been so patient with me, respecting my space and never pushing further. I'm honestly surprised she actually agreed to hang out. Her kindness isn't something I should be taking advantage of.

I need to fix this.

Our time is up, and we sit next to each other, looking at our scores. Kayla beat me by a few points and doesn't acknowledge it much. Instead, she says I did a great job before changing her shoes. Humble as always. I should bring her to bowl with the guys sometime. They'd be fighting to get her on their team, but I hope she chooses to be on mine—if she'd even want to go. I change into my shoes and finish up before she does. She ties her shoelaces and, without hesitation, grabs her bowling shoes. When she stands up, I lay a hand on her arm to stop her. She looks taken aback, but slowly sits herself down and puts the shoes back on the floor.

"Kayla, I . . . I know I haven't been the best to you lately. I had a lot going on in my mind, but that's no excuse for the way I treated you. I'm sorry."

Her expression softens. "It's fine. I'm sure you had your reasons."

"No, it's not fine. You don't deserve any of that."

"You're good. Really. If you need space, I get it. Just let me know. I don't wanna bother you."

"No, you're not— That's not—" I sigh. "That's not it. You're *never* a bother. It's me. I've been hung up on something, and I couldn't think straight. I was a mess and did some stupid things. I was running away when things got complicated."

Kayla must've really had her guard up because only now does her body finally seem to relax around me. "Are you okay?" She places a comforting hand on my arm.

Wow.

When was the last time she touched me? I look away and soak in all the glory that comes with it. I don't know if she does it on purpose, but she starts rubbing me softly. It brings a smile to my face.

"Yeah. I'm okay now. I think I figured it out." She removes her hand—unfortunately—and nods. "Still. I'm sorry. I don't know how I can make it up to you."

"It's okay. You don't need to—" She stops midsentence when I look at her. I don't know what kind of expression I'm making, but suddenly, she clears her throat. "Well . . . there is something you can do. Actually, two things."

"Anything. Tell me."

"First, I wanna know if you're still okay with me hugging you."

I furrow my brow. "Of course. Why won't I be?"

"That night during Thanksgiving break, when you dropped me off at my house, I gave you a hug and . . ." She swallows. "You hesitated a bit. I thought maybe I overdid it. Maybe it was the hug that—" She stops, looks away, not wanting to finish her sentence. *She probably doesn't want to mention the part where I was being an asshole. My words, not hers.*

"God, no! That wasn't it. I was just surprised, that's all." Kayla looks at me again, almost with an uncertain pout. "I'm serious. Don't think like that. Please." I clear my throat. "W-What's the second thing?"

"The second thing. Right." A wave of relief must've washed over her because she doesn't seem to be that anxious anymore. Instead, there's a familiar playful feeling to her. "We passed by an ice cream shop earlier. Buy me one and we're good."

"Consider it done." I grin, grateful there's something I can do to make this right. There goes her signature smile—the one that makes my day. It's been a while since I've seen it. Needless to say, it still works like a charm. Before she decides to pick her shoes up, I pull her into a hug. "Thank you, Kayla. You don't ask for much, do you?"

I feel her smile when she returns my embrace. "What are you talking about? Ice cream's expensive."

We both laugh. I'm not sure if she actually meant that or if that was a joke, but I'm not lying when I say most of the tension is gone now. She rubs my back gently before whispering, "I don't want to be greedy so . . . don't offer more than you need to."

If she's greedy, then I must be *insatiable*.

I hug her a little tighter, unable to come up with the words to respond to that. Relief comes with visitors but I blink them back. If this is what it feels like to be forgiven, this is a great feeling. I don't deserve it, but to be accepted in her arms again . . . I want this. I want this forever. As if I can't fall for her more, I do.

Eventually, we separate on good terms, return the bowling shoes, and walk out to that ice cream shop. It's as if time never passed after

Thanksgiving break. Letting myself be near her again really did it. I can finally joke around her again. Tease her. When we get there, she settles on a simple soft-serve twist and I a plain fudge sundae. We take window seats and eat our ice creams in a comfortable silence.

"I know it passed already, but Happy New Year's."

Her comment is so random, I can't help but chuckle. "Happy New Year's." I had actually wanted to call her up on New Year's Day but decided against it. I regret it now. It would've been a perfect chance to ease into whatever we're doing right now. It's a new year, I should've started it better. I should've done a lot of things better. But *should've* is for the past. I will do what I can *now*. I clear my throat. "Any New Year resolutions?"

Kayla thinks for a bit. "To take risks once in a while and to not be afraid of the outcome."

"Risks?" I snicker. "Never took you for a gambling type."

"No, not gambling!" She laughs as she elbows me playfully. "I've always been someone who just sits there quietly and wonder 'What if I did this' or 'I should've done that.' So instead of overthinking everything, I want to take the opportunity when I get it. At least try to. Because you only live once, right? And it's senior year. I want to spend it right. To end with no regrets."

"That's a great resolution."

"Thanks. What about you?"

I would've given it some thought, but I don't need to. "I want to confront my fears. Be honest with my wants. To not run away when things get complicated or . . . when I get scared."

She has a smile on. It looks more of amusement but I can't quite pinpoint what she's thinking right now.

"What?"

Kayla lets out a chuckle. "Sorry. It's just that, I didn't think anything scared you."

I smirk. *Funny how the person who says that is the one who has the ability to do so.* How ironic. Her little remark brings back an old memory. "There are things scarier than clowns with chain saws."

"Like what?"

"Spiders."

Kayla breaks into a laugh. "Don't worry, I gotchu! I'm a pro." She pats her chest with confidence. "I don't offer catch and release services though. I only squash. If you're okay with that, come to me and I'll take care of them for you."

I snicker. "You're kidding."

"No, no joke at all. I've got three go-to weapons at home. I even made one of them."

"Yeah? And what's that?"

"It's a fully taped, rolled-up magazine stick. Best for a short to mid-range attack. It's kinda shaped like a running baton."

"A baton . . . made of a magazine?"

"Yeah, a *porn* magazine," she says proudly, lifting her eyebrows up and down. I choke on my bite of ice cream. Kayla looks around before whispering, "Oh sorry, should I have said *adult* magazine instead?"

I cough a bit before looking at her in disbelief. I feel like laughing but I have to cough. I end up doing both.

She chuckles. "Hey, hey, don't get the wrong idea! It was just sent to the wrong address. I thought it'd be a waste to throw away such a sturdy magazine, so I put it to good use. No one can see it! It's covered in tape."

As she lets me continue laugh-coughing, she looks away and continues to lick her ice cream like she didn't just say the word *porn* with an innocent face like that. What were we even talking about again? Damn. How is she this adorable? Kayla swiftly gets up from her seat and fills a cup of water. She comes back and puts it in front of me as I recover.

It's these little things that she does. It makes my heart soft. I feel my cheeks get warm before I thank her.

As I take a sip, she clears her throat. "My cousin's getting married in April. I was wondering if you'd be inter— I mean if . . . if you would be my plus-one?"

She looks away in embarrassment as I stare at her quietly. *If you would be* is a big promotion from what she was about to say. The thought makes me thrilled. I swallow my last gulp and put the cup down. Before I can reply, she hurriedly continues on.

"Y-You don't have to say yes. I don't want you to feel obligated or anything."

Obligated?

She doesn't look me in the eye when she says it, but I don't need to see them to know she really doesn't *expect* much from me. I should've thought it through. I should've remembered. She'd never impose anything on me.

My heart sinks a little as guilt and regret start making their way in. I should've never run away. I thought I was protecting myself. But I was wrong. Not only was I hurting me, I ended up hurting Kayla too.

This is all my fault. I'm such an idiot. Her eyes connect with mine when I tap her lightly on the elbow. "I never feel like I'm obligated to do anything when I'm with you. If I do or say something, it's because I want to."

A pretty smile forms on her face before she lets out a breath of relief. "Okay."

"I would love to, by the way."

"Really?"

I nod. "Yeah."

Her grin gets wider and she giggles a little before looking away to focus on her ice cream. Kayla's swinging her legs back and forth with a happy expression on her face. Her excitement is contagious. I feel my lips curve up. My whole body feels lighter just by looking at her.

Damn.

I missed this.

I didn't want to go.

Aiden reached out during the break and it seemed like fun, but the thought of one-worded answers and me feeling awkward really put me off. Even though—for the first time since the break—*he* wanted to engage in something.

But then, he asked a second time.

Not gonna lie, I was hopeful. Funny and mischievous Aiden was fun to be around. I wanted that again. I told myself to just go, and maybe if the mood was right, try asking him if something was up. It was harder than I thought. He was actually trying this time. I was trying too. But my body wasn't cooperating with me. What did I expect? A month of aloof Aiden doesn't just go away.

I build walls too.

I couldn't even ask him about it like how I had practiced. Thankfully, I didn't have to. Aiden not only addressed the elephant in the room, he even apologized. I didn't even know how to take it. Turns out, he was going through something. Man, I should've been more open-minded. I feel so stupid. Geez! I'm glad it all happened the way it did though. Seems like we went over a big hurdle or something. Aiden's himself again and we hang out together like we did in the past. Maybe it's just me, but I think things are even better now. I feel more comfortable with him and he greets me with a hug almost every time I see him. His hugs are to die for!

Studying at his place pretty much became a new normal. Mom and Dad are used to it now and don't ask me about it every weekend. It's nothing new. But this is my first time staying for dinner. Dinner with his family should be normal, right? I don't know why I feel like this would be kinda weird. Is it weird to have a female friend over to eat dinner? I mean, technically, we're study buddies. And it so happens I'm a girl. It should be fine, right? I'm probably overthinking anyway.

This can't be stressed enough: Aiden's mom is wonderful. The lady is such a boss. She's generous and always makes me feel welcomed. I don't think Mr. McLaren likes me very much though. I mean, he seemed fine during Thanksgiving break, with his family and friends keeping him preoccupied and all. You would think he'd be okay with me by now, but I don't know. I feel like he's got something against me. It makes me nervous.

Mrs. McLaren made corned beef and cabbage. I'm enjoying it, but I would be enjoying it even more if we weren't sitting on the couch with the TV in front of us. Coach James is watching football.

Intensely. He's rooting for the team in white—I'm pretty sure. Every now and then, he reacts with a cheer or a complaint on how the tackle played out. I've stayed quiet during the whole time, not knowing what to say. Instead, I watch in silence. Occasionally, I catch eyes with Aiden and smile. I think he knows I'm clueless with football vocabulary.

I get up from the couch and walk over to the table to get seconds. But instead of going back to the couch, I sit at the table and eat. I still have a good view of the TV, so I hope that still counts as watching. Aiden notices me and comes over to do the same. He sits next to me and only now do I speak up in a low whisper.

"We're rooting for the white team, right? Sorry, I have no idea what's going on."

Aiden chuckles softly and nods. "That's fine. You don't have to."

We eat a bit as we watch football players tackling each other, coaches shouting aggressively, and enthusiastic fans cheering. At my side, Aiden's watching closely, as if learning what he can improve on.

"So, what position do you play?"

"I'm the tight end."

I nod like I know what that is. "Cool."

Aiden laughs a little before explaining what his position is and what he does. From what I understand, it's a hybrid of two positions—the blocker and the receiver. He can do both, depending on how they wanna play it. We continue to eat as he points out the tight end on the white team. When something amazing happens and they show replays of the act, Aiden elaborates in detail. I'm watching with a little more effort now, mostly to see and understand what he does during practice and games. Interesting. Aiden's strong enough to block and athletic enough to receive the ball. It makes sense. He really is versatile.

"How's the food? Is it to your liking, Kayla?" Mrs. McLaren joins us at the table.

"Yeah, it's really good. Thank you." I proceed, praising her for the tender meat and perfect seasoning to make sure she gets the compliments she deserves.

Mrs. McLaren laughs and details how she cooks it. I share some of the techniques my mom uses in the kitchen. We get so into conversation, I don't realize Coach James coming over until he's here. He looks rather disappointed and upset. I wonder if it's because his team lost a point or because it went to commercial. Did I laugh or talk too loud? Or is it because everyone's at the table except him? Did I do that? I hope he didn't feel left out. *Stop, Kayla.* There's no point in worrying about that anymore because we're all finished with dinner already. I bring my dishes in and offer to help with anything.

"That's okay, sweetie. I got this. Sit down and relax. I'm bringing out dessert in a few minutes."

Not wanting to nag, I nod and walk back out to the dining room. Aiden and his dad are silently staring at each other. Maybe even glaring because the air is getting thick. *Oh my god, I only left for thirty seconds. What on earth happened?* The cooler of the flames is in the kitchen right now. Not wanting to sit through minutes of tension, I take the chance to make an escape for the bathroom real quick. I don't really need to go, so I just wash my hands, coming back fully refreshed and ready to socialize again. They're talking now, and I hope Mrs. McLaren is out there too. I reach closer to the dining room but stop when I realize I might be interrupting something. It seems serious as Coach James speaks in a low voice.

"Why is she here on football night? She doesn't know a thing about it!"

"So what? She knows *me*," Aiden says firmly. "Kayla's here because she understands and appreciates *me*. That's all I care about. That's what you should too."

It not even a statement. It's an *affirmation*.

Feeling a little bad about Coach James's comment—but surprised and touched by Aiden's—I stand still. Unable to move. Unsure of whether I should walk in and pretend like I heard nothing, or maybe wait a little longer, for a good moment to walk in. *They must know I went to the bathroom, so they should be wrapping up soon, right?*

"Aiden, you know what Sunday football means. It's tradition, it's about bringing the family together."

A plate gets set down on the table. "Relax, darling! We're still together, just at the dinner table tonight."

"Honey. Everyone's supposed to be watching the game together over *there*. That's how it's always been. That's how it *should* be."

"It doesn't *have* to be." Mrs. McLaren scoffs. "She's our guest, you have no right to force it on her. Stop using tradition as an excuse. You're just upset because she's not as into the game as *you* are."

"That's an understatement. I bet she wasn't even watching. Of course, she wasn't. She doesn't get it because she's not—" He stops abruptly, the word catching in his throat. It gets quiet, and I finally notice the doors separating the dining and living room have glass panels on them.

"She's not *what*, Dad?" Aiden asks in a dangerous tone.

"She's not . . ." From the glass reflection, Coach James gestures a hand to his face before he speaks lowly, "One of *us*."

Mrs. McLaren gasps. "Richard!"

Well, this is weird. I probably should've walked in earlier.

Aiden's mom whacks her husband on the arm, yelling at him in a hushed tone, "I did not marry a racist pig like you!"

"Honey, that's not what I meant! You know that. I'm just saying we're different people," he yells back in a whisper.

"Did you think that about Tommy Lee when he tried out too? You didn't think he had it in him, but look at him now. He's one of the best receivers you've ever had."

"Honey!"

Mr. and Mrs. McLaren continue to bicker quietly, while I make up my mind to walk to the bathroom again and come back. At least then, I get the opportunity to *announce* my arrival. When I take a step back, some part of the wooden floor creaks. *Never mind then! Plan B, it is.* I make my way towards the dining room. Aiden's the first to snap to my direction, his face ghostly pale. His parents aren't looking too hot either.

"Kayla . . ." Aiden swallows before getting up from his seat.

"Hi!" Before he takes a step closer to me, I smile and walk to him. I remain cheery and give him a casual touch on the arm to sit him down with me. *I didn't hear anything. I didn't see anything. Nothing at all.* It's silent when I tuck in my chair, so I look at them in confusion. "Did I miss something?"

"Nothing important, sweetie. You came right on time. Here! It's apple pie, I made it myself."

I thank her as she hands me a plate of her perfectly sliced pie. You can always count on Mrs. McLaren to ease the tension. This lady knows what's up. She and I talk about the pie while the guys remain eerily quiet. The TV is broadcasting the football game again, but Coach James stays at the table this time. He's a little tense and Aiden isn't far from that either. Dessert is finished as comfortably as can be and finally, Coach James returns to the couch to continue watching his game. I bring in my dishes, and again, Mrs. McLaren doesn't let me help her with any of them. Aiden comes up and helps his mom put the dirty dishes in the sink.

"Then I guess I . . . I should probably head home now. It's getting late. Thank you for dinner, Mrs. McLaren. Everything was delicious!"

"Of course, sweetie. You get home safe now." She taps Aiden on the back. "Aiden, it's dark outside."

"I know. I was gonna walk her out."

My cheeks get warm all of a sudden as I turn away to grab my things. Mrs. McLaren calls out to me, holding a plate of the remaining pie. "Did you want to take some pie home, Kayla?"

"Oh, no I couldn't."

"Please do if you like! These boys don't appreciate my skills like you do."

Coach James is far enough to miss that but Aiden looks at her, offended by her words. "Mom, I love your food!"

She rolls her eyes, and I nod eagerly with a laugh. "Yes, please. I'll take some. Thank you!"

Happy with my answer, Mrs. McLaren packages it nicely for me in no time and bids me a goodbye before returning to the kitchen. For manners sake, I bid Coach James a farewell too. Surprisingly, he turns away from the TV and utters a small "bye" and a "get home safe." Before I know it, Aiden and I are out in the cold night—just a few steps away from my car. Other than the one car that drives by, it's crickets. I put Mrs. McLaren's pie in the back and when I close the door, Aiden breaks the silence.

"Did you . . . hear all that earlier?"

I turn to him casually. My face doesn't even get to make an expression before Aiden's worried look turns regretful. I don't even have time to decide how I want to play it before he sighs.

"I'm sorry."

"No! Don't be sorry. It's okay, Aiden."

"It's *not* okay. You don't deserve any of it and . . . I hate everything he said. My dad, he's—" Aiden runs a hand through his hair, unable to finish his sentence.

I take a hold of his free hand, giving it a little squeeze. "It's okay. *I'm okay*. Trust me. It's nothing I haven't heard before."

"That doesn't make it any better."

I chuckle. "You're not the one who said it."

"But my dad did."

He squeezes me back, so I give a him little caress with my thumb. "That doesn't matter to me. As long as *you* don't think that."

"I don't."

"I know. I heard you." A smile forms on my face. "Thanks for having my back."

Aiden looks at me with an expression I can't quite pinpoint. Suddenly, he tugs me forward and catches me with a hug. He doesn't even have a jacket on, how is he so warm? I try to push these silly thoughts away as I give him a comforting rub on the back. Maybe this will warm him up too? As if he read my mind, I hear him break into a smile.

I could stay like this forever.

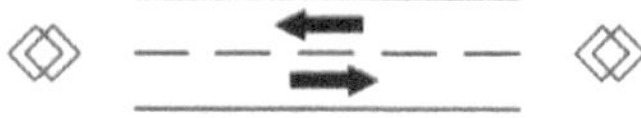

Forever seems impossible when time goes by so fast. Aiden was okay after that, thankfully. Study sessions continued as normal. However, Coach James seemed to have gotten nicer or something. He even personally invited me to join them for their spring break party. It was fun. The semester seemed to fly by. It's surreal. We even had our first graduation practice. I can't believe it. It's kind of sad, actually.

The bell rings and I make my way out the class. Coming down the last step of the staircase, someone catches up to me from my side. "Hey, Kayla, I need to talk to you."

Oh god. *Why him?* "Sure . . .?"

Jonah walks to the side to an emptier area, and I follow him. When he stops, he's digging up something from his backpack. Students pass by but are thankfully minding their own business. From a distance, I spot Rico. He looks at us, full of anticipation. No, this can't be—

"Here." He shoves a packaged bag of snacks to my hand. Not wanting to be rude or make things weird, I reluctantly take it. "This is for you."

For me? It's a bag of coffee flavored candy. Cool, but I don't eat this. Just as I hand it back to him, he speaks up again.

"Will you go to prom with me?"

What the heck? I hit a birdie at this guy's crotch, and he still wants to ask me to prom? Dread. Panic. I take a pause before I draw a clear line between us. Maybe that'll get him to say no? "As friends, right?"

"Y-Yeah, as . . . friends."

Crap, he *still* wants to go as friends? Why? This guy has only made me feel powerless and incapable—if not creeped out and uncomfortable. There's no need to think about this. I don't want to go with him. Even so, the definite answer doesn't come out my mouth. It's stuck. Ugh! Why is it so hard to say no? *Eighteen years of trying to please Dad and Mom will do that to you, girl. Just make up an excuse!* Well, is he still gonna go even if I say no? Will I see him there? That'd be so awkward! How do I say this? *Come on, Kayla. Don't panic. Think!*

I think of Aiden.

Clarity.

I know what I want. Wherever he is right now, I wanna run over to him and get out of here. The drive does something to me. Suddenly, a solution comes. "Jonah, sorry but I'm not going. Here." I give him back the bag of candies. "I can't take this."

"No, it's for you."

"Thanks, but I can't accept this. To be honest, I don't even eat this candy."

"You can keep it, it's a gift."

I take a deep breath before standing my ground. "Look, I'm not gonna go, so it's weird if I just take this. I also don't wanna waste it. So, please take this back."

"It's fine. You're not going to waste it."

That's it. No more Miss Nice Girl. I tried three times already, and he still doesn't get it? *Sometimes, you gotta say it straight to their face.* "I don't wanna be rude, but I'm honestly not going to eat this. So if you don't take this back, I'm sorry but I'll just give it away. And if no one wants it, I'm gonna throw it."

He looks shaken, shocked by this other side of me. I feel bad, but I absolutely hate being pressured into doing or taking anything I don't like. *Why does he keep insisting on giving it to me?* I hand it to him and he takes it back this time.

"Thank you," I say before walking past him to leave. Then realization hits me. *Screw it! Might as well go all the way, right?* I turn back and walk to him. "And Jonah?"

"Yes?"

"I appreciate the thought and effort, but I don't see you in that way. I don't like that you always push things on me when I don't want them. And it's probably a little late to say this, but it'd be great if you'd stop."

"O-Okay."

"Thanks." Now, I leave for good. It feels like a whole load of rocks have been tossed off my shoulders. Wow, if I'd known how relieving this would feel, I would've told him sooner. I should've! But then again, I never felt comfortable enough to. Why else was I always trying to avoid all contact with him for the past three years? We don't even talk aside from the few times we so happen to play together during badminton club. We barely even speak to each other. I didn't think he would ask me.

Man. That surprised me! I didn't even know I had it in me to say all that. Wow. I couldn't have done that without Aiden. He gave me the courage to do so. He makes me want to draw my boundaries clear and cut off any loose ends.

I might not know what the future holds but Aiden makes me sure of one thing. Scratch that, two things: I like him and . . . *I want him to know that.*

Light green might just be my new favorite color. Kayla's absolutely stunning in it. Her dress is simple—nothing eccentric—but she makes it look one of a kind. My gaze flicks to her whenever I get the chance.

Aside from being mesmerized by her, I've been following her around to greet her family and friends. There's a lot of them, considering they make up half the attendees. Most of them are so busy catching up with each other, Kayla and I don't converse with them apart from saying our greetings. Occasionally, there's a very curious aunt or two who notice me.

This time, I get introduced as her friend. I'm not exactly sure how I feel about it. Again, it's not wrong. I like being her friend. But now I can admit, I'd also like to be *more* than a friend. Kayla laughs off the suggestive looks of her relatives and denies anything of that sort.

I don't know if I should feel grateful or disappointed. She likes someone, that's for sure.

Just *not me.*

Nick thinks otherwise, but I can't say for sure. Before long, Kayla and I take a seat at our assigned table. I ask about her family and she points them out one by one, describing how exactly she's related to them. She doesn't expect me to remember them, just briefly going over them so I get a sense of who is who.

"And that's Simon, my sister's date."

I follow her gaze and spot her sister, Josslyn. The guy next to her—Simon—stands there awkwardly, occasionally nodding his head and giving his input as Josslyn engages with one of the cousins. "They don't look like they're dating."

Kayla chuckles. "You're right. Not yet, at least. My sister's been waiting for him to make a move, but he doesn't even know that she likes him."

"Does he like her?"

"Yeah. For two years now." She nods her head but looks at them with pity. "Worst part is, she's known since a year ago." My face contorts, horrified. Kayla notices my expression and laughs. "Yeah! I know, right? That was my reaction too, when I found out. I don't get why she doesn't just tell him already."

We turn to watch Josslyn and Simon talk to another uncle. As she talks, Simon stares at her with a look of admiration. He wants to hold her hand but doesn't. *I can relate.* "Telling someone you like them isn't that easy."

"I know. But *she knows* he likes her back. She's got nothing to lose." Kayla shakes her head in annoyance. "I've been telling her to just tell him how she feels, but she keeps insisting that if he likes her, then he has to make the move."

I turn to her, grabbing her attention. "So are you saying, if *you* liked someone and knew he liked you back, you'd confess to him?"

"Yeah, of course," she says without a second thought. "What? Why are you looking at me like that? You don't believe me?"

"No, I do."

"Well, what about you?"

I take a moment to think about it. *If I knew that Kayla liked me . . .* I smile. "I'd go for it."

"Yeah! Right? I'm not saying it's not hard. But if the feeling's mutual, then why not?" She glances to Josslyn and her pending boyfriend. "It's not about pride. It's . . . finally being able to open up to someone. To share your feelings to the other person. To finally look at him without having to wonder 'does he like me' or '*can* he like me?'"

"I thought you said she knows that he likes her."

Kayla turns to me, snapping out of her trance and clearing her throat. "She does! What I mean is, knowing that the other person feels the same about you, doesn't that feel great?"

"It does." I nod. "So are you gonna tell him?"

She looks at me strangely. "No way. I'm not gonna meddle in their affair. I mean, not gonna lie, I wanna tell him. But I really don't have the right to, so I'm gonna sit back and watch them pine for each other. As frustrating as that is. Give it a few more months, I think it might just happen."

I chuckle. "No, not Simon. I meant the person that *you* like."

Kayla freezes, her demeanor becoming completely serious. Slowly, she eyes me suspiciously. "How do you know I like someone?"

"I . . . do now."

A few seconds go by and she buys it, looking away with a defeated smile.

I let out a subtle breath of relief before playing it cool. "So, who is it? Does he like you back?"

"I'm not telling you and I" — she stares at me silently before looking away — "I don't know."

"Come on." I nudge her a little, "Do I know him?" *What am I doing? Grilling her for information?* I shouldn't. But I can't help myself. I need to know. Because if it's someone else, then . . . *I'll move on.* I have to.

There's a strange look in her eyes. For some reason, a teasing smile forms on her face. Instead of dodging my question, she nods. "You do know him. Pretty well, in fact."

Pretty well? It must be one the football guys then. A familiar sinking feeling creeps up on me. *I knew it. It's Kevin.*

"Don't bother asking, I'm not gonna say anything. Not yet, at least."

"Not yet?"

"I told you I wanted to end the year with no regrets, didn't I?" She looks away briefly and takes a deep breath before returning her gaze on me. "So I'm going to confess to him. On Saturday."

"That's six days away. You can just tell me now. What difference does that make?" I keep it casual, doing my best not to explode from curiosity.

"I . . ." Kayla looks away and adjusts the plate in front of her. "I'm not ready yet."

I swallow, nodding. Saturday, huh? That's not enough time. Maybe I should tell her how I feel before then. Maybe she'll give me a chance. But that might throw her off her game. *I can't mess up her plan.*

Kayla looks over at me and chuckles, patting my arm. "Be patient with me, you'll be the first to know."

Trying not to let our little conversation get into my head, the rest of the wedding goes by rather quickly. The bride and groom get married. We get served dinner by late afternoon. Kayla and I ate quietly for the most part while the rest of her family at the table talked about the news, jobs, or the economy. Mr. Summers was usually the one who instigated it. Sometimes, he'd talk about Josslyn's achievements. *Never Kayla's.* Occasionally, he brought up politics with the in-laws sitting with us. When there was some sort of clash in viewpoints, Mr. Summers casually interrupted them and started to explain his opinion. The uncle is stubborn himself but Mr. Summers is absolutely relentless. When the aunt knows her husband isn't going to win the battle, she steers the conversation to a new topic. Things got tense a couple of times, and I thought it was just my imagination until I saw Kayla's face.

She did warn me about this, even preparing me for it during the car ride here. So this must be what she meant when she said he'd cut her off and start a lecture. I can't imagine how it must feel to explain yourself when your dad doesn't even listen. At least my dad *tries* to understand after Mom's talked him down a bit.

It's no wonder Kayla rambles rather quickly. *She was never given the proper time to explain herself.* She's so quiet right now. Seems like this happens a lot. Her dad is a complete businessman. An intimidating one. I can see the resemblance to my dad now. Like her dad, her mom and sister are also quite serious people. They're all dressed up fancy with sparkly accessories standing out against their dark attire.

Kayla, on the other hand, is the only one wearing a soft, warm shade of color. Her jewelry is simple. They don't scream at your face. Instead, they decorate; bringing the focus onto the person wearing them. Her style is easy on the eyes. It's just personal preference, but I like it.

The contrast between her and her family is so different that it manages to keep my worries about Saturday at bay. While her family continues with their depressing economic talk, Kayla and I keep busy with our own conversations. By the time the food has been cleared, the DJ is hyping the crowd. Some people gather at the center of the dance floor. Kayla watches them in silence, smiling and slightly bobbing her head to the beat. Her family is still talking about business. I've seen enough to know that none of them will step onto the dance floor.

"Wanna dance?"

Kayla snaps her head in my direction with an excited smile and nods. We get up from our seats, momentarily grabbing the attention of the others at the table. Mr. Summers looks at his daughter, as if to warn her not to *embarrass* him. I don't know what I was going to do if Kayla didn't walk away.

I follow her to join the others on the dance floor. The DJ drops a beat and we rock to the music. It was a little awkward at first, but then disco slips in. I pull out a tacky dance move, hoping to get Kayla to laugh. It works. She copies me and does another cheesy dance move, making *me* laugh. I don't even know why it's funny. Maybe it's the silly faces she makes or how she's dancing like that in her dress; it should be illegal. The ice breaks and soon enough, we're grooving to the music. Doing ridiculous moves with and to each other. Just goofing around on the dance floor. There's a lot of laughing involved. I think some of the people around us were laughing too. It's wild and exciting.

It might be one of the last few times I get to have this much fun with her. So for today—at least in this moment—I let myself enjoy it while I can. Before Saturday comes.

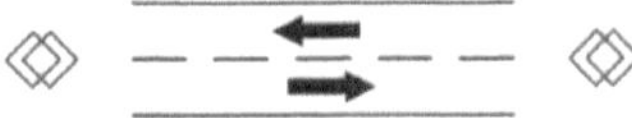

It's no surprise that Nick would be able to point out the obvious.

"Our farewell party with the football team! You said she was going, right? Your mom invited her," he said just a few days ago.

I should've seen that coming. Nick's right. It had to be there and then. *He* was going to be there. When Kayla said she wasn't ready, she must've been nervous. She didn't need to be. I've seen him during our little haunted house adventure at school. Kevin feels the same way I do.

He likes her.

From my seat, I look around. The team and their families are lounging and having a good time. Kayla's helping my mom refill drinks and set up some things. It's just a matter of time.

When?

Where?

How?

I don't know what to think. I don't know *how* to. During one of our conversations at the wedding, I found out she's going to Mayfair for college. That's a six-hour drive from where I'm going. In just a month, we'll be four hundred miles away from each other. I can't see her every day anymore. What's going to happen after we graduate? Will I see her again? Does she even want to see *me*?

It feels unreal.

Everything's coming to an end.

It's too late.

I should've cherished our moments more. I could've spent December with her, but I was dumb and pushed her away. Maybe *that's* when she fell for Kevin. *Damn, I'm such an idiot.* Nick slaps me on the back. It helps me stop tormenting myself for the moment.

"Bro. Relax, will you? She'll come through."

"The party's almost over. She doesn't look like she confessed to him yet."

"The fuck, man? I already told you it's not him."

"Then is it *you?*" *Damn. I let my nerves get the best of me.*

He gives me another slap, and it snaps me out of my misery. "Bro! Seriously?"

"Sorry. She said I knew him pretty well, so . . ."

He rolls his eyes. "Damn, Aiden. I don't get why you don't ever consider yourself in the race."

I stay silent. Emma and I had a good thing once, before she became someone I couldn't recognize. Waiting for her to change back—*wanting* her to—only ate me away. I want Kayla to like me back, but if I don't prepare myself for the worst, what's going to happen to me? *Hope is dangerous.* And . . . *I won't be hurt this time.*

Nick sighs, getting up from next to me. "Go grab a drink or something. You're making me nervous. And if you're that tired of waiting, just ask her yourself."

He leaves me to go catch up with the other guys. With him gone, it's just me. I take his advice and grab some punch at the drinks section. Surprisingly, I see Kayla sit at the table I just left from. Finally. This is my chance. Before I take a step towards her, someone stops me by the arm. I turn as they let go.

Are you serious? I *told* her not to touch me again. Resisting the urge to wipe away the area she'd just touched, I step back a little to create some distance between us. "What do you want?"

Emma swallows. "I just want to talk."

"About?" She's still not used to me being curt like this. It's not like I care anymore. *I have places to be.*

"I got into Whitwell," she offers with a small voice.

Whitwell. Her dream college. "Congratulations." That's probably the first nice thing I've said to her since the breakup. She smiles. It gets silent for a bit, so I think it's the end of the conversation. I'm about to leave when she speaks up again.

"I'm sorry, Aiden. I mean it. You were great to me, and I took you for granted."

I have nothing to say, so I stay quiet. I heard that she and Kai got together but broke up shortly after. Nick said he cheated on her. I'm not particularly happy about it. Nor surprised. *What goes around comes around.*

"I really am sorry," she says, looking down.

"I'm over it, Emma. It's in the past."

Blue eyes meet mine again, looking almost hopeful. "Then . . . can we still be friends?"

I sigh and look away, my attention subtly drifting over to Kayla, who's casually sipping cider while reading something on her phone. She doesn't look over at us, but something tells me that she's waiting. *For me.* I know it. Clearing my throat, I turn to the girl near me. "No."

Emma looks taken aback. She tucks a loose strand of hair behind her ear, recovering from the shock. "Y-You might not like me anymore but we're still gonna see each other in the future, whether you like it or not."

Dad and Robert are still friends. They catch up once in a while. It may not be as often as when Emma and I were dating, but their friendship hasn't ended after we broke up. If it's an absolute must, then we probably *will* see each other. I never ruled it out. "I know, but that doesn't mean we have to be friends."

Emma falls silent.

"Thanks for the apology and I'm glad you can finally admit to your faults, but that doesn't change anything. You still made me feel worthless. Pathetic. I don't need that in my life. I don't want it."

She looks like she's about to cry, but it's the truth. And frankly, I don't give a damn. I'm not responsible for her feelings anymore. *I never should've been.* "If we do see each other, so be it. But don't expect me to be friendly."

I walk away, leaving her behind. I may be over the whole cheating thing and the breakup, but the truth is I'm still recovering. There are things that I do—maybe even things I *don't* do—and say because of her. *I hurt Kayla.* Pushed her away and doubted her *because* of what happened with Emma.

I'll always hate myself for that.

Even after everything, I still haven't forgotten that little stunt she pulled at the fall rally. So troublesome. I don't want Emma's pettiness anywhere near me again. And *definitely* not near Kayla.

"Hey." I take my seat next to her.

She clicks her phone off and looks at me, smiling. "Hi."

We'd eaten together with my family earlier, but we haven't really had any time alone with each other. Kayla's been busy helping Mom out, so there's no helping that. "So you were going to tell me who you liked, remember? Did you confess yet?"

"Not yet."

She looks away bashfully, and I follow her line of vision. From a distance, Kevin's leaning against a wall, talking to Tommy. Their attention shifts when Emma suddenly comes into the frame. No longer interested, I look back at Kayla. She's watching them quietly. I resist a sigh. *Of all things, did I have to be right about this one?*

"You're hesitating." Her eyes return to mine, almost in a state of fear. She's uneasy. I smile, trying to give her some reassurance. "You should go for it. You have nothing to worry about. He's one lucky guy."

Her lips curl a bit. "You think so?"

"I know so."

"Aiden . . ."

"Yeah?"

Kayla looks down on the table, her fingers fiddling with her napkin. "It's . . . I mean I . . ."

I watch her swallow nervously as her eyes finally settle back on mine. She wants to tell me something, that's for sure. And it finally hits me. *She can't confess to Kevin if I'm here, right?*

"I get it. You take your time. You can do it." I stand up and she looks at me in concern. "Go for it. I'll be back."

"Then I'll— I'll tell you when you come back."

I turn to look at her and see a newfound certainty on her face. *Courage.* I force a smile and give a nod before leaving her.

It's really happening.

She's gonna do it.

I keep walking—briefly chatting with a few of my teammates when they approach me—before heading to the restroom. Running the water, I splash some on my face to clear my head.

This is it.

She's going to confess to him and I'm going to be okay with it. I have to be. I don't regret liking her. I don't. Kayla gave me great memories. She's made me feel like I'm worth being around. She cares about me. As a *friend*. And I will be okay with being her friend after all this is over.

Will I?

Kayla's going to bless Kevin with a smile every day. She's going to open up to him. Share things she's never told anyone before. She'll let him hold her. Kiss her. Envy boils inside me. Maybe I should've told her how I felt after all. At least then she'd know how I feel about her. She'd probably even *consider* me.

What . . . am I doing? Kayla's out there being brave and actually carrying out her New Year's resolutions. And what about me? Hiding in the restroom? What happened to confronting my fears and being honest with what I want? What happened to not running away when things get complicated or when I get scared?

I need to get it together.

I clean myself up before making an exit, quickly heading back to the table. Panic kicks in when I see her empty chair. Dammit. I scan around the room. No sign of Kayla. No Kevin either. Where did she go? Walking out to an emptier area, I walk towards the restrooms again. I peek over the corner, and there she is. She's in the middle of the hall with her back towards me. Hyping herself up. Waiting in front of one of the occupied restrooms—the one that *I* just left from. A glimmer of hope reaches me, and I don't push it away fast enough. Before I can step any closer, the door suddenly opens.

Just as he steps out, Kayla manages to croak out, "I-I like you. That's what I wanted to say."

Before any of them can spot me, I turn around and leave. I thought I prepared myself for this. I thought I could do this. That I could handle it. But I was wrong.

I can't.

And now it's too late.

It hit like a shot in the heart.

Holy shit! How did I screw *this* up?

"Kevin?"

"The one and only."

"What are you— I mean I thought—" Realization hits. "Oh my god, I am so sorry. That . . . That wasn't for you."

"Yeah, I figured."

Kevin smirks as I take a quick glance at the other bathroom door. It's green. Unoccupied. *Did Aiden take that one*? I swear I saw him walk into this one. I shake my head. That's not important right now. "I'm really sorry. I know you—"

"Kayla, we're cool." He nods. "You said feelings shouldn't be forced. And I agree."

"Kevin . . ."

"Go. While you still have the momentum."

I give him a relieved smile. "Thank you, Kevin. Really!"

With super speed, I quickly make my way back to the main room and search for Aiden. He's nowhere to be found. He wasn't in the bathrooms and not in the food area either. Just to be safe, I search the front entrance. It'd be weird if he left without telling me, right? He said he'd be back. Wait, is that—? I take a closer look through the window and spot a familiar figure walking outside. Without a second thought, I get out and run after him.

"Aiden, wait!" He suddenly stops at the sound of my voice. "Where are you going?"

He turns around. Woah. He looks . . . heartbroken. *What the heck happened?* Was it Emma? They talked earlier, and it'd looked serious.

"I'm sorry, Kayla. I have to go."

Where the heck does he need to go to when he's supposed to be at this party?

He's lying.

"Can you spare me a minute? It's really important. I wanted to tell you that I—"

"I know," he cuts me off. His voice is hoarse.

"Y-You do?"

"Yeah." He nods, voice cracking. "I've known for a while, but I was an idiot for hoping things were different. I . . . I have to go."

I stand there, speechless, as he gets into his car. I almost consider going up to his window and stopping him from leaving. But what if I make it worse? He looks miserable, and I'm scared he's coming down with something. Helplessly, I watch him drive off.

I was an idiot for hoping things were different.

Different? So he was hoping I didn't like him? Right. Of course. He only sees me as a friend. God, I should've known! Did he think I befriended him for the sole purpose of getting into a relationship with him? That I was taking advantage of his broken heart and attacked him while he was weak and vulnerable? He confided in me, and now I ruined our friendship. At this rate, he can't even trust girls anymore! Me liking him . . . really does ruin everything. I just made things weird between us, huh?

I sigh. I shouldn't have put it off for so long. I didn't think that seeing Emma with Aiden would make me doubt myself. That just the mere thought of them getting back together would make me *hesitate.* And when the time came, I struggled. I chickened out. But Aiden was so patient with me. Watching him leave was what helped me gather up the courage to confess. I was scared I'd lose the adrenaline and couldn't wait any longer so I followed him to the bathroom. I turn my back one second—just to rehearse a few lines—and I end up confessing to the wrong guy? I can't believe it. I just can't!

I didn't even get to tell him that I like him. *In person.*

No.

No!

This feels unfair. It doesn't even feel right. I don't like the way it played out. Unless I've said it directly to his face, I won't know exactly what he's feeling.

I need to try again.

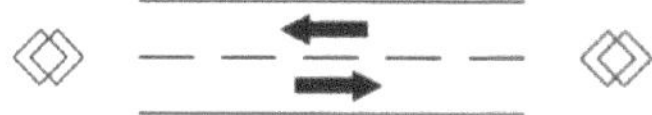

Aiden didn't respond to my text last night. I should've expected it because something's up. I can feel it. There's some sort of misunderstanding here. Unless he's that repulsed by the idea of me liking him, that's one heck of a reaction. Before I left the party yesterday, I even asked Nick if he knew anything about why Aiden had to leave early. He didn't. Or if he did, he didn't tell me. So what am I supposed to do when I can't reach him?

Wait outside his house, that's what.

Mrs. McLaren greeted me at the door ten minutes ago. She seemed normal. I guess she didn't notice anything strange about Aiden. According to her, he went out for a walk. She didn't know when he'd be back and even asked me to come in, but I kindly refused. I didn't want to be in his house if Aiden doesn't even want to see me.

So with Mrs. McLaren's permission, I settled down on their porch bench. I don't care how long I have to wait, I'm gonna see Aiden, and I'm gonna tell him the truth so we can clear this up *today*.

Or that's what I thought. Half an hour has passed, and I'm having second thoughts again. Maybe I should just go. What if he needs time? Space?

He didn't want to talk to me yesterday—I knew it deep inside. He was trying to be nice, and I was selfish for holding him there. Crap. I don't even know what went wrong. He seemed fine when we were at the table yesterday. It was okay until he left for the bathroom.

Should I wait until I see him at school? No. This can't drag on any longer, and I really need to tell him. But is it weird to wait out here for him? Does that seem kinda stalker-y? Maybe I should wait in the car instead. What if he runs away again? I should just—

Shit, he's coming! Making a turn, he walks onto the pathway to his porch. His eyes are on the ground the whole time, so he hasn't noticed me yet. He must be pretty deep in thought, because he doesn't even see me get up from the bench. When he reaches closer to the stairs, I get the courage to greet him. "Aiden."

He looks up at me in surprise. "Kayla?"

"Hey."

"What—" He gets up all the stairs and stops a few feet away from me. "What are you doing here?"

"I . . ." *I what? I was waiting for you? I was worried? I didn't get to tell you that I like you yesterday?* Crap. He doesn't look like he wants to talk. *Not yet, Kayla. Too soon. Ease it in.* "I just wanna make sure we're okay."

"We're good."

That tone. It's post-Thanksgiving all over again. And for some reason, he looks drained. I hope he's not actually getting sick. Gently, I ask, "Are *you* okay?"

"I'm fine." He rubs his neck, looking away uncomfortably. "Didn't sleep too well, that's all."

A minor explanation. Better than nothing, right? Does he *hate* me? *Stop it, Kayla. Stand your ground.* Just then, his eyes catch sight of the brown paper bag on the bench. "Oh, I brought you some mac 'n' cheese."

One of his eyebrows twitch. He stares at the bag quietly before looking back at me with these sorrowful eyes. I-Is he mad at me? Did I overstep his boundaries? Stop. *He doesn't like it. He doesn't want it.* I said stop. *Don't you get it, Kayla? You're nothing but a—*

"Why?"

I swallow as Aiden watches me carefully. "I thought you were maybe feeling under the weather. That's only if you want it." I clear my throat. "You left in a hurry yesterday. I didn't get the chance to talk to you."

He sighs before speaking softly, "I'm sorry, Kayla. Next time, okay?"

Turning away from me, he grabs his keys from his pocket and goes for the door. *Next time? What next time will there be when he keeps avoiding me?* Just as he gets the door open, I grit my teeth. "I know you know already. And I know that I'm probably making it weird, but don't run away."

The door opens a few inches before he stops. Crap. Was that too harsh? He doesn't move. He's . . . contemplating. Slowly, he closes it. His hand's still on the knob, body facing the door. *What are you doing, Kayla? Just tell him already!* I feel myself burning up. Heart racing. But I stay quiet until he lets go and turns to me.

"Kayla, I—"

"Aiden, I like you!" He freezes and finally looks me in the eyes. "I like you. I really do. And I should've told you earlier but I—" I swallow a choke. *Deep breath. Calm down.* I look away, unable to meet his eyes. "M-My whole life, I've always been the second choice. I've never been the one, not when I *want* to be. And I'm finally okay with that. I don't want to *want* anymore because . . . there's always gonna be someone better. I know that. I don't even try. But when I'm with *you*?" My voice cracks when I turn to him. "God, Aiden, I *want* to be."

My eyes get wet. *Stay calm. Keep it under control.* His jaw tightens, and I try to hurry it up before he sees something I'll regret. "You're a really great guy. Wonderful. A-And whatever I did to hurt you, I'm sorry. I don't wanna burden you with my feelings. So if you don't like me back, that's okay. If you just wanna be friends, I'm okay with that. Just don't . . . Don't shut me out."

Shit.

I turn, quickly wiping away the tears that escaped. I don't want him to see me cry. Not like this. *Screw it. It's too late now. Just own it, Kayla.* I face him. He's closer than I remember. His face softens and I finally see him again—the Aiden with no walls up. I don't know if I'm seeing right or if it's just my eyes getting blurry, but his eyes are tearing up.

"Don't cry," he says gently.

"I'm not crying, you're crying." I hold my waterworks in, breaking into a smile when he wipes his falling tears.

His lips curl up, but his eyes look uncertain. "What about Kevin?"

"What *about* Kevin?"

"Isn't he the guy you liked? I saw you confess to him last night."

"How did you— I-I thought that was *you* in the bathroom!" I take in a deep breath. "I should've waited till you came back. I should've. But you make me so nervous. I can't even tell you how much you mean to me without choking up."

Aiden starts to laugh.

I'm on the verge of another round of tears here, and he's laughing? "Why are you—"

Suddenly, he comes forward and wraps his arms around me. The solid force embracing me with warmth. *Relief.* My body doesn't hesitate to hug back.

"I'm an idiot, Kayla."

"What are you talking about? No, you're not." I rub his back, hoping it will dissolve any of his bad thoughts.

"I am." He holds me tighter. "I'm the worst."

I chuckle. "Don't say that."

"But I am."

He's so adamant, I give him a little squeeze. "Fine. If you are, then I must be one too. I followed you and *still* managed to confess to the wrong guy."

We start laughing in each other's arms, and occasionally, I take the time to stroke his back some more. He feels nice. When the laughter starts to subside, Aiden speaks quietly. "Can you say it again?"

"Say what?"

"Say you like me." He pulls away just enough so we can see each other. "Because I like you too."

"Really?" I ask, but no sound comes out. He grins, nodding. Then, he pushes back a strand of hair blocking my face, his finger grazing some skin. It tickles. This . . . *this is real.* My heart feels like it's about to explode.

"I like you." It comes out as a whisper. *Not good enough. Aiden deserves better.* "I like you," I repeat but louder now and with more confidence. "I really, really like you!" I chuckle as he literally beams. I don't think I've ever seen him so happy before.

Suddenly, he bends and picks me up with a hug. I wrap around him with everything I've got, clinging onto him like a koala. He snuggles into me. Holds me tight. Strokes my back.

Anxiety. Fear. Worry. They all seem to fade away, quickly replaced by something alleviating. Heartwarming. Solacing. I nestle in, quietly relishing this moment. One of his thumbs starts to do the caressing thing, and I turn to mush. I never thought I could hug him like this.

"You're the one," he whispers. "I want you. And I wanted you to want me too, but . . . I got scared. I thought you wouldn't like someone like me. I should've told you about how I felt sooner. I'm sorry."

I shake my head before I speak in a small voice. "Don't be. I'm just glad you like me back."

He laughs. "I should be the one saying that."

If it were possible, he pulls me in closer.

He's strong. And warm.

It's protected here, as if nothing can hurt me. As if my thoughts, my emotions, my being matters. As if *I matter*. Is this what acceptance feels like? Like I can exist without wandering anywhere. Without feeling lonely. Without worrying about my mistakes. My insecurities. Because all of that doesn't matter. Nothing seems to matter except this moment. Right now. Just the two of us.

Aiden likes me. Aiden wants me. He's a safe place. A place that I know will always welcome me with open arms.

He feels like *home*.

The only thing more comforting than mac 'n' cheese is mac 'n' cheese made by Kayla herself. There's nothing fancy about it, not the recipe nor the looks. Maybe it's because she made it especially for me, or that we ate it together, but it was the best I've ever had.

"I can't believe you remembered," I said, midway to finishing my bowl.

"It was hard to forget. I haven't looked at mac 'n' cheese the same ever since."

Her little comment got me sentimental, and I kept myself busy with eating. Kayla wasn't too hungry and ate only a little bit. But that wasn't a problem. I savored every last bite of it while Pilly was a good boy and kept her occupied.

We're sitting on the living room couch, casually playing with Pilly. Even though we haven't spoken much aside from talking about her mac 'n' cheese or about Pilly, it doesn't feel awkward. It's pleasant.

Once in a while, we'd look at each other. She'd smile. And I'd smile. Then, we end up laughing for no reason at all. It feels surreal.

Hell yeah.

I'm the lucky guy who Kayla likes. I can't believe she came all the way here just to confess to me. Come to think of it, she was about to tell me twice yesterday but I walked away, too blinded by hurt to see the truth. Damn, I told her I'd be back! I couldn't even keep my word. Kayla's done so much to show her feelings, I need to do better. I need to step up my game. Because she deserves better.

"Will you go to prom with me?" I blurt out. There's no flowers, no big sign with a funny pun. Just me and a question. It's not romantic at all. Not even the slightest. But she lights up like it is. I'm sure she's about to say yes until her face suddenly falls flat when she recalls something.

"I . . . I'm not going."

"Is it because of me? About winter ball last time? Because—"

Kayla quickly puts a hand on my arm. "No, I wanna go with you! It's just that someone asked me last week. I got so uncomfortable, I didn't know how to say no. Then I got scared that if I went, I'd see him there. So I panicked and told him I wasn't going."

"Was it Kevin?"

"No. Kevin's fine. I can at least say no to him." She sighs as she pets Pilly's head on her lap. "It was Jonah. Jonah Liu? I don't know if you know him."

"The badminton guy?"

"Yeah." She nods, looking at Pilly as she plays with his ears. "I don't want you to miss prom. So if you wanna go, you should go. Don't let me hold you back."

I chuckle. *She can be so silly sometimes.* "What's the point of going if you're not going?"

She looks at me, doubtful. "But it's prom."

"Yeah? It's *just* prom."

"It doesn't happen twice, Aiden. And aren't the guys going too? It's senior year. I don't want you to miss out because of me."

"They all have someone to go with and I don't. But if you want, I can still go. *Alone.* I'll make sure to bother the boys and credit you for it."

"That's not—" She huffs. Defeated. Kayla looks away with a small pout, something she does whenever I tease her. I get a kick out of it. "You know that's not what I meant."

"I know." I smirk, tapping her arm to get her attention again. "If you're skipping, then . . . will you skip prom with me?"

A smile forms on her face, slowly getting wider by the second. It's not a definite answer, but I start to do the same. Then she nods. Eagerly. "I would love to."

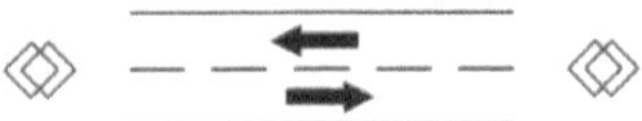

Things have only gone upward from there. School continued without a hitch. While everyone else was busy getting ready for the finals, we seniors had it pretty easy, finishing up the school year and continuing on with graduation practices. The year seemed to be ending so soon.

Prom's tomorrow. So for our skip-prom prom, I decided to take Kayla out to a nice dinner, then eat ice cream, and maybe watch the sunset together. Nothing too fancy or over-the-top, but she loved the idea. Kayla did say school dances weren't really her scene anyway. She preferred things less crowded. It's going to be great.

Ding! I grin when I look at the text notification.

Cookieface

Does dinner have dress code?

Or are you dressing up for prom day purposes? I need to know :)

Me

No dress code

I'm goin casual. Y?

Ok cool bc I have a dress

Winter ball dress?

If you want to dress up, I'll match ;)

Let's keep it casual, I like casual :D

No, not winter ball dress. I didn't like that one. I only wore that to fit school dress code lol

Oh ok :(

Why the frowny face? Did you wanna see it?

Yes pls

Typing bubbles appear and disappear. Maybe I shouldn't have said—*ding!* An image gets sent to me, and I finally see her in her winter ball dress. It's black and the only decorative thing about it are the long sleeves—made of lace. It looks nice on her. I wonder why she didn't like it. Right next to her is Kevin. They're both in a funny pose.

Ignore Kevin, we went as friends! Alone, together. I promise. I don't c him that way and he knows that. We didn't do anything funny and I thought of u the whole time

Not the whole time, but from time to time

What I mean is I only have eyes for u!

Ok, nvm. TMI, forget it

I actually laugh out loud. This girl. I really have nothing to worry about with her.

Lol ok I believe u

U look pretty though :)

Thanks <3 If u think that was pretty, just wait til tmrw

I'll be even prettier haha

Can't wait

Omg I was just joking, don't get ur hopes too high

I wasn't and too late

Aiden!

Kayla!

Hmph! Goodnight UwU

Goodnight Princess :p

I took a chance with that last text, and I try not to think too much about it. I hope she didn't hate the nickname. Maybe she'll even laugh. Clicking my phone off, I think of the fond memory. It brings a smile to my face. Just when I thought the conversation was over, another text comes in, and it sends my heart racing.

Sweet dreams Captain :p

Kayla wasn't kidding. She looks absolutely striking. I made sure I came looking sharp, but nothing can compare to her. It's a simple blue dress until she takes off her cardigan and I see her exposed shoulders. *Do I have a thing for her shoulders? Does she know that I do?* Or is it just the confidence she's carries in the dress that makes her stand out so much? It's like she knows she looks good. Beautiful. I think I was just staring at her during the whole dinner.

The day rolled out pretty smoothly. Until Kayla was about to treat me for the ice cream. I shot her a look—one that made her pull back and let me pay for it. So thankfully, everything went according to plan. We enjoy the sunset from the back of my truck, legs dangling over the tailgate. She eats her strawberry ice cream while I eat my chocolate. Being with her like this—in her company, by her side—it feels right.

This is something I want to last.

But we graduate in two weeks. We'll separate when we move for college. No one's addressed the elephant in the room so far. Four hundred miles isn't a short distance. We'll be apart, changing and growing without each other. But I'm sure about this. I want to be with Kayla. For a long time if possible. Even if it's long-distance, I want to make this work. And to do so, I need to be upfront about it. If I learned anything from this past year, it's *that.* And maybe that I don't hide my feelings as well as I thought I do. Either Emma never picked up on any of it or Kayla notices everything.

I'm weak. I get vulnerable.

But Kayla doesn't seem to mind.

I turn to my right as she stuffs the last piece of cone in her mouth and chews. I'd finished mine minutes earlier, but I wanted to wait for her to finish before I dive straight into something serious. Swallowing, she turns and gives me a questioning look.

"Kayla . . . I want to be with you."

She melts into a smile. A beautiful one. "I do too."

"But I'm not— I'm no Prince Charming. If you're looking for one, it's not me. I can't do grand gestures, public proposals, or anything very romantic."

Her brow furrows. "Good. 'Cause you know I have anxiety, right? Even if you wanted to, I'll beg you not to."

I break into a smile. "Kayla, I'm serious. I'm not capable of that. That's not who I am. That's not how I like to do things. So, don't expect that of me."

"I'm being serious too. You don't have to be or do anything. You're perfect. Just the way you are. I don't want Prince Charming. I want *you*, Aiden." She smirks. "Captain One Eye." That gets a chuckle out of me, but she doesn't stop there. "And you're wrong about one thing. You planned this whole date. You listen and you care. You're patient and understanding. You actually *see* me. For who I really am. For my thoughts, my opinions. That's romantic to me. I . . . I just wanna be around you."

If words could heal, it's *hers.*

I swallow, feeling like I've been put back together. "I want that too."

We share a smile. Kayla abruptly looks over at the ocean, thinking carefully. "If you're gonna lay it out there, then I should too." She looks down. Legs stop swinging. "I feel like I'm very easily misunderstood. Either that or I'm just really good at messing things up. I overthink and blame myself a lot even when I know it's not my fault. So, if you're ever fed up with me or if I do anything to hurt you, please just tell me. Have some faith and trust me when I say, I never intended to."

She doesn't look at me. I take her hand in mine and put it onto my lap. This grabs her attention. Soft honey eyes peer up at me. "I will. I won't run away again." I nudge her softly. "And I know you don't. You're the most kindhearted person I've ever met. I'm a blockhead, so if you're ever feeling troubled—*especially* if it's because of me—I want you to tell me too, okay?"

She nods, staring at me in silence. Her eyes start to glisten. "Last chance," she murmurs.

"For what?"

"To back out now, because . . . I don't let go easy."

I smirk, interlacing our fingers and giving her a squeeze. "You better hold on tight then. 'Cause I'm counting on it."

Kayla looks like she's about to cry, but she doesn't. My thumb strokes her hand to reassure her and she looks away for a brief second to laugh. When she does look back at me, it's with a strange glimmer of hope and uncertainty. "Then, does that mean we . . . that we're . . .?"

"Together." I chuckle. "Yes, Kayla. We're together."

"Okay, then." She smiles. A soft blush forms on her face. So does a newfound certainty. Suddenly, she gestures me to come closer and I lean in close so she can whisper something into my ear. "Can . . . Can I kiss you?"

Surprised, I pull back a bit to see her face. That wasn't my imagination. My heart starts to race. I admit, I've been wanting to kiss her ever since our confession. But I was willing to wait. I didn't want to scare her off or pressure her into anything. I grin, nodding. Kayla lights up a little before carefully leaning in. Slowly, she gets closer, eyeing my lips. Just when she's about a few inches away, she pauses. I remain still, desperately waiting for her to come at me. But she swallows nervously. As I debate whether or not I should make a move, she moves forward and places a soft kiss on my cheek.

Though that wasn't exactly what I was waiting for, it still sets me on fire. She retracts and looks at me timidly. I smile like a kid in a toy store, making her smile back. Kayla turns away with a blush, hiding her face behind my shoulder. I laugh and give her hand a little squeeze. I have her attention again. "May I?"

Her doe eyes freeze on me as I feel her fingers unconsciously twitch. My thumb caresses her in an attempt to comfort her. Eventually she nods, turning her head just a little—distracting herself with the sunset. It's the perfect angle where I can return her gesture.

But I have other plans.

I scoot in closer and with my free hand, gently take her chin and guide her until she faces me again. We lock eyes. No words are exchanged. But I know we're both anticipating it. I can feel it. So without further ado, I lean in. Our eyes close, lips connect.

Call it sparks.

Maybe fireworks.

Or even electricity.

Whatever it is, I don't want it to stop. I tilt my head more and lay a gentle hand on the back of her neck to pull her in closer, deepening the kiss. Kayla's a little stiff, but she relaxes into me seconds later. Just as I think she's opening up to me, I feel her hand on my chest, pushing me lightly. I pull away. Kayla looks at me all flustered.

How cute.

I slip in a kiss on her cheek before returning my position. "Don't ask me next time."

Maybe it's my remark or the kisses, but she looks away bashfully. I chuckle, moving her hand in mine. It gets her attention, and she faces me again—*as if I have her in the palm of my hand.* I shoot her a grin and she smiles at me. Before I know it, she scoots her body closer and takes my breath away with another kiss. This time with no hesitation. No question. This time, on the lips. I respond immediately, smiling as one of her hands takes me by my collar and pull me closer.

It's bold, yet kind and tender. Her care. Her desire. I revel in it. Everything feels right. In this moment, I'm not scared of anything. Not about what the future will hold for us. Not about her hurting me. Not about whether or not I am enough.

Because I am.

Because with Kayla, everything will be just fine. Whatever mountains we encounter, I know we'll conquer them together. Life can blow their hurricanes.

I'll always have my sweet summer breeze.

I turn the page and point at the photo of us sitting in the back of his truck—where we shared our very first kiss.

"And that's how your Uncle Aiden and I got together," I say softly, giggling.

The other pictures posted after that are of us during graduation, us visiting each other during college, post grad, and then to the latest additions to the photo album—our wedding pictures.

"Oh, look, Russell! There's your dad," I whisper, pointing at Nick in one of the photos. "He had a great best man speech. Maybe I'll show it to you when you get older."

From a distance, the bathroom door opens. Aiden walks out into the living room, fresh out the shower. "Is he finally asleep?"

I look down at the baby I'm cradling. "Yeah. I think I bored him to sleep."

Setting aside the photo album and getting up from the couch, I walk over to the dining table and put Russell in the car seat carrier resting on it. Aiden comes over and hugs me from behind, engulfing me with his warmth.

"You're a miracle worker," he whispers before pecking me on the cheek.

"I know, right?"

We both snicker as he watches me tuck Russell in his blanket. He sneaks in another cheek kiss. Another one. And another one before moving on to my neck. It starts to tickle so I try to sidestep and make my escape, but Aiden's got a firm grip on me. I have to stop myself from laughing too loud as I pat him to whisper-yell, "*SoGwa,* not in front of Russell!"

"But he's asleep," he whispers back, pausing and turning me around in his arms. "*SoGwa*? Did you just call me a silly melon again?"

"Yeah." I wrap my arms around him, grinning. "You're a *DaaiSoGwa.*"

"You married this *big* silly melon. Who's the real *SoGwa* here?"

I stare at him, flabbergasted. He pulled a reverse card on me in my native language and he knows it. Look at that smirk! I pout, pulling away and admitting defeat, but he pulls me back into him and kisses me on the forehead. Closing my eyes, I hug him back and enjoy his embrace. Just then, the doorbell rings.

"That must be Nick," Aiden mutters.

I let go of him and shake him a little to do the same, but he doesn't budge. He only looks at me with a small pout. "What? The faster we return their baby, the faster we can continue this, right?"

Realization hits his face. "You're right."

Quickly giving me a peck, he lets go of me. Aiden carefully puts an additional blanket on Russell and starts to pack the remaining things into the baby bag. I'm laughing as I make my way to the door and look through the peephole.

I swing the door open. "How was date night?"

"It was great! Thanks again for watching over Russell."

"Of course." I look around and spot his car. "Just you, Nick? What happened to Anna?"

"I dropped her off home first. She looked tired, so I told her to rest while I bring Russell back."

"I see. Tell her to take it easy for me."

"I will."

I nod just as Aiden comes up from behind me and hands the baby carrier to Nick. "Time to go home, Russell."

"Thanks." Nick receives his son graciously and then the baby bag. "Wow, he's sound asleep."

I chuckle. "Just keep him warm and fed. That'll do the trick."

"Okay, I'll keep that in mind. I should get going now or Anna's gonna start missing us. Thanks again, you two!" He turns to leave and right before he reaches his car, he turns around. "Oh, Donny's having a barbecue next Saturday. I heard Kevin's gonna be there, he just got back to town. You're going, right?"

"Yep. We'll see you there." Aiden waves at him and I do the same.

Nick gives us a nod before settling Russell into his car and driving off. The night air gets a little chilly, so I walk further into the house first. Aiden closes the door behind us, locking it. The next thing I know, I'm being lifted off the floor. I accidentally let out a squeal.

"W-What are you doing?" I laugh as I hold onto him.

"Kidnapping my queen. You said we'd cuddle tonight, remember?" He adjusts me and starts heading towards the living room.

"I didn't forget. But I can walk, y'know."

"I know. I just like carrying you." I roll my eyes, and he looks at me skeptically. "What? I can't carry my own wife?"

"Hubby can do whatever he likes." I give him a peck on his cheek and it gets a smirk out of him.

We get into the living room and he lays me down gently on the longer side of the couch. I take the TV remote and set it to the movie we'd planned for tonight while he grabs the nearby blanket and dives in next to me. Pulling the blanket over us, he scoots in close and wraps an arm around me. "So what story did you tell Russell anyway? I tried reading him the books Nick gave us, but I can never get him to sleep."

"I told him about how we got together."

He smiles. "Seems like it was just yesterday."

We get comfortable cuddling as the TV rolls the opening credits. Suddenly, a thought comes across my brain. "Hey, do you remember during our sophomore year, we had geometry together? I was collecting papers, and you wished me luck because I had a game that day?"

"I did?" He looks confused, and I look at him with a pout. Suddenly, he laughs. "I'm just kidding. Of course I remember. You thanked me twice, without saying anything else. I thought that was all you knew how to say."

I chuckle, playfully nudging him. "Well, I never got to tell you . . . I won."

He's a little quiet before he takes my hand into his. "You really are the *SoGwa*, you know that?"

"I know." Smiling, I scoot up a bit and place a soft kiss on his neck.

He grins and fiddles with my fingers. "That Christmas gram, during our senior year. That was you, wasn't it?"

"Yeah."

Aiden chuckles, kissing me on the head and squeezing me closer. I bury my face into his chest and hug him like I'll never let go.

"I love you," he whispers.

I smile. "I love you too."

THE END

Appendix A
Dead-End Breakup

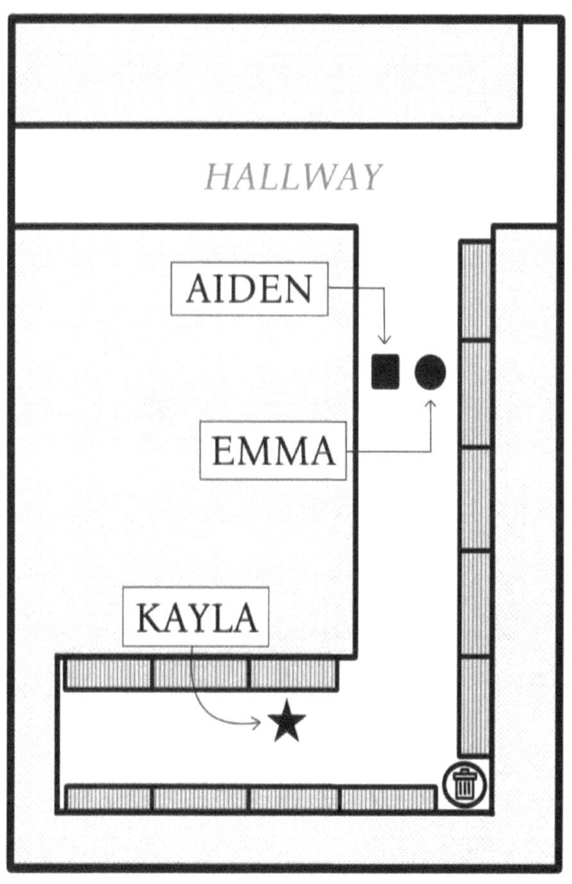
HALLWAY
AIDEN
EMMA
KAYLA

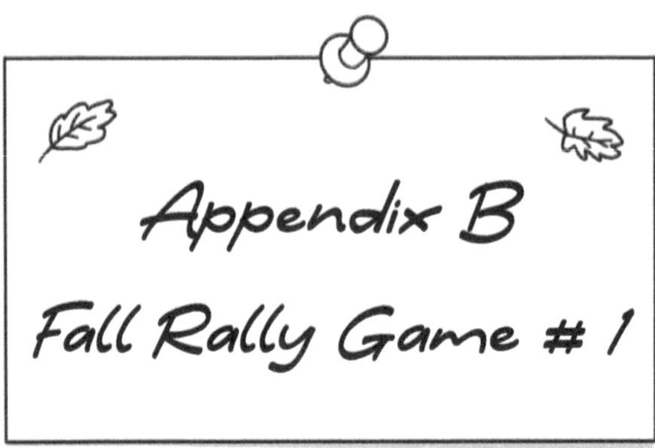

Starting Positions / Overview

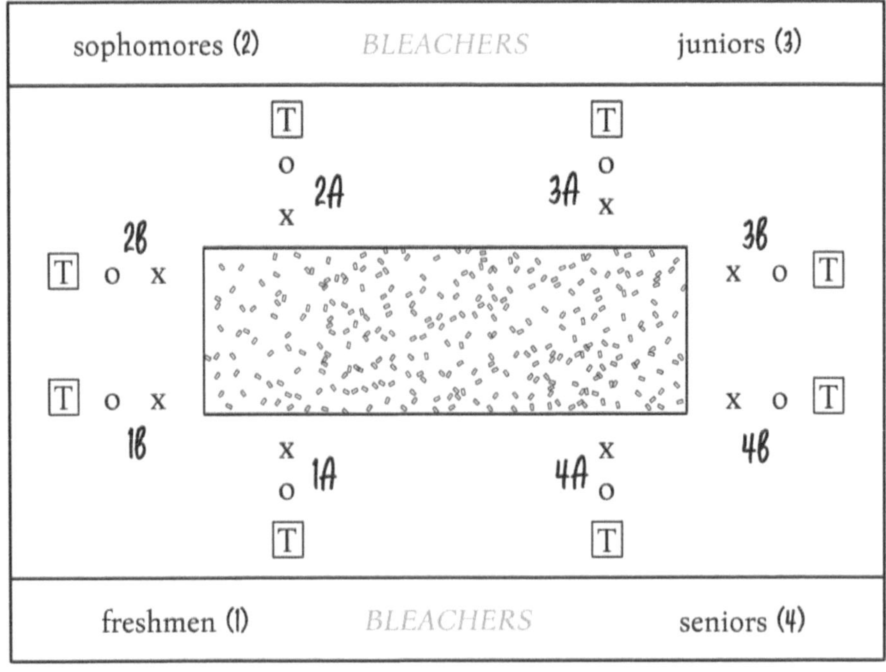

(1) X's run a lap around while
O's answer Teacher's question
(correct answer gets stickier tape)

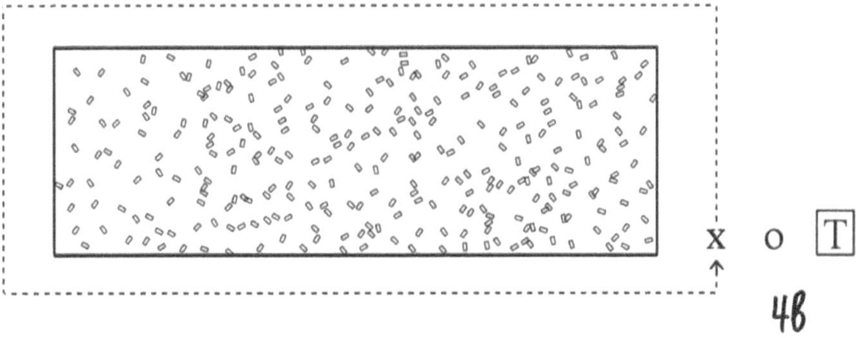

X O T

4B

X O

(2) X's wrap tape
around O's
(sticky side out)

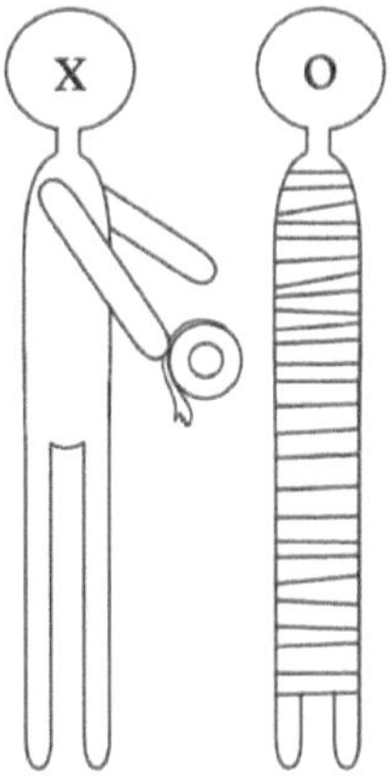

(3) O's jump on mat and roll
around to collect cards
until all are gone

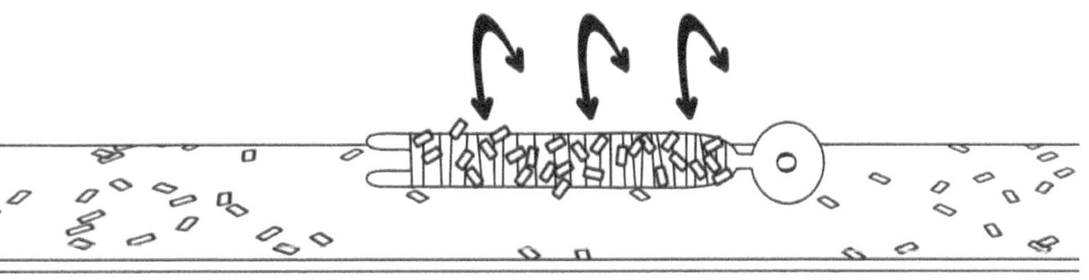

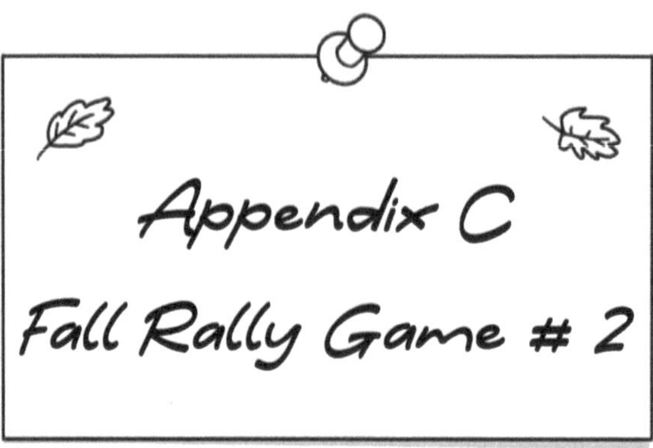

Starting Positions / Overview

MC – Emcees   x – Guys   o – Girls

sophomores (2)	BLEACHERS	juniors (3)

2A	x		o	o		x	3A
2B	x		o	o		x	3B
			MC	MC			
1B	x		o	o		x	4B
1A	x		o	o		x	4A

freshmen (1)	BLEACHERS	seniors (4)

(1) O's start in red hoop and X's in green (with empty basket)

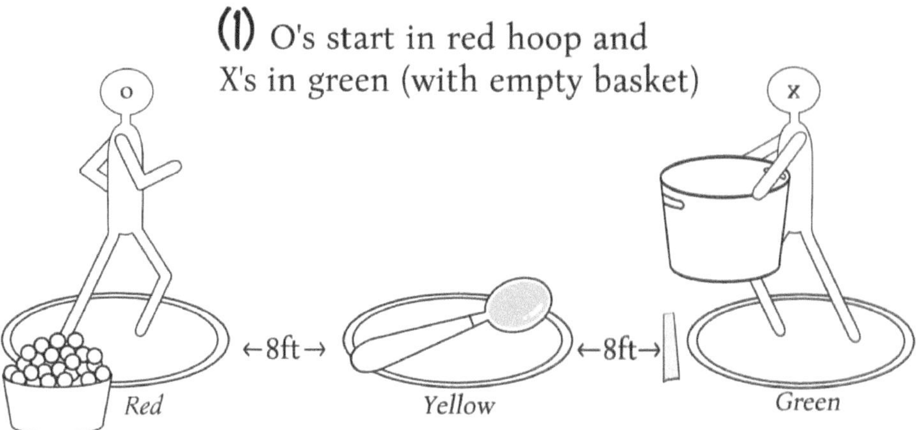

(2) O's grab the spoon while X's place the basket in yellow hoop

(3) O's and X's return positions

(4) Staying inside hoop, O's use spoon to scoop ball (no hands allowed) and toss to X's. X's must stay behind tape when catching

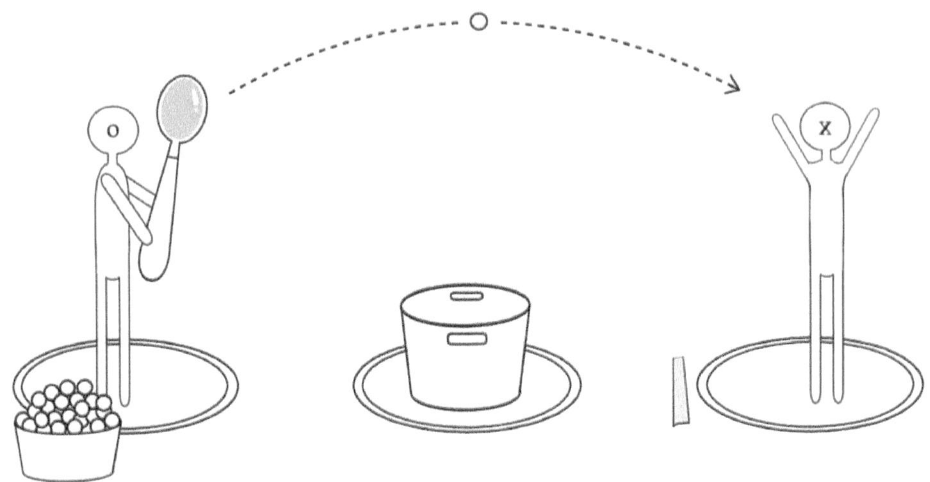

(5) Staying inside hoop, X's shoot the ball into the empty basket

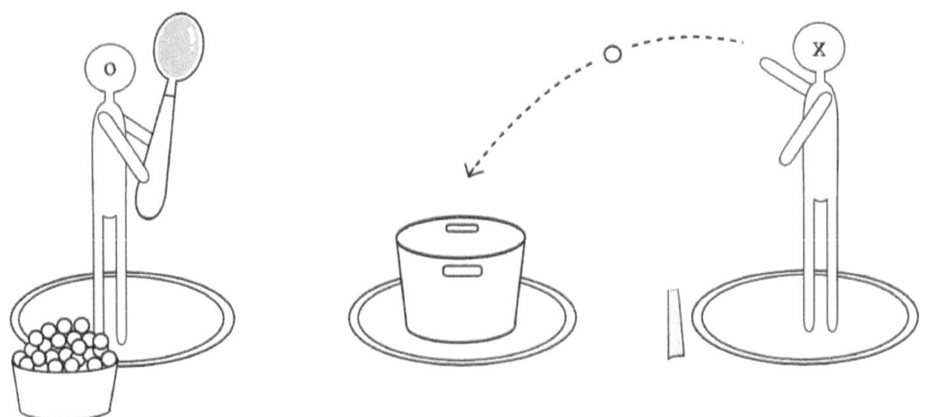

(6) Repeat (4) & (5) until all balls are used / time's up

Hi, Baylin here. Thank you for reading Seen Her Year! I've always been an avid consumer of stories since I was a kid, however they were presented—written, drawn, performed. I adored anything that made me laugh or cry. Anything that could convey emotions and feelings, in ways I could never express myself. Because in those moments, I felt understood. And little me wanted to do that too. To put out a message, touch someone's heart, make them feel like they're not alone. I wanted to create my own stories someday.

I did, eventually. As a hobby. It was fun. But creating stories wasn't exactly my priority at the time because of college and other important job decisions. Given my circumstances, pursuing a creative career never felt like a viable option. So I didn't know what I could do with my life, and at the same time, I did things I didn't want to do, because that's what was expected of me.

Fast forward to 2022. My job experiences weren't so great. I felt unfulfilled. Aside from consuming other stories, nothing brought me more joy and happiness than sharing my own stories to the world.

That seemed to be the one thing that came naturally to me. It's what I *want* to do. But 2023 had been a rough year. So much confrontation. Drama. Sacrifices. Blood, sweat, and tears—literally. Frankly, life-changing. Long story short, this is it. I'm going to do everything I can to make this hobby of mine—my passion, my dream—a real thing.

In case you didn't know, SHY was supposed to be a cute, lighthearted story. It turned out a little darker than I had originally planned. I'm not the person I used to be. I couldn't write SHY with the same outlook I had before 2023. Even so, I poured my heart and soul into this. I admit, I deleted a lot and hesitated writing some parts because it got too vulnerable. Old wounds resurfaced, some reopened. It took a lot out of me. But in the end, if SHY gets to see the light of day through one reader, I'd say it was all worth it. Of course, the more the merrier, am I right? LOL.

If you enjoyed this book, I would appreciate it a lot if you'd drop a book review. It would be super helpful to me in getting my book out there. (Also, I personally read every single one.) When you lend your voice, not only do you help authors gain exposure, audience, and credibility, but you also help influence other readers to pick a book up and determine its value from a reader's POV. Your opinion matters. If you don't know what to write, write anything you'd like; whether it's about the characters, their experiences, or even your own experience while reading it. It doesn't have to be long. I'd love to know. Whenever I'm feeling down or unmotivated, I'll be coming to your reviews for that extra dopamine!

If this book wasn't your cup of tea, I respect that. SHY's not perfect and everyone's got their taste. If you leave a review, don't be afraid to tell me why you didn't like the book. I'm interested in hearing your thoughts about it as well. Your honesty and effort in however far you've made reading this book is appreciated. I'll do my best to learn and grow from any feedback I receive.

Anything helps, whether it's sharing this book with others or leaving a review. Your support makes my dream a reality. For those who enjoyed my debut work, I'm excited to show you more of what I can and will do. Stay up to date with my future works when you sign up for my newsletter at www.baylinwing.com. It would be an honor to have you along my author journey. I look forward to seeing you, wherever you may be. Stay safe, stay healthy. Most importantly, be happy. Take care ☺

Kayla and Aiden, to think that I've been with you two since 2017 is unreal, even now. It's been a wonderful journey getting to know and grow with you two. SHY is nothing without y'all. So, thank you. I couldn't ask for a better duo for my debut novel.

Thank you, Mom. For supporting me in the ways you can, despite being so busy yourself. Dad, for your hard work and putting a roof over my head. My idea of love, my push to pursue my passion, and whatever you two have and will give me, I won't let it go to waste.

Thank you, Maxie. For being a reliable source and helping me kickstart what needed to be done for my author career. You have always been able to explain things I find so confusing. Bless that encyclopedia brain of yours. Your conversations, your way with words, your little scenarios you produce; they will never fail to ignite my creativity.

Thank you, Jaeon. For always supporting me and caring about what I have to bring to the table. You show up. You listen. You hype me up whenever I feel down. Your opinions and visions are beautiful, as much as they are valuable. Thank you, you book nerd/worm, for your abundance of knowledge, experience, and advice. I wouldn't feel as good as I do about this story without your continuous encouragement and reassurance. The boat is easier with you onboard. I'm very lucky to have a friend and fan like you. Cheers!

Thank you to my proofreader, Krista. From your promptness and professionalism to your eagle eyes and consistent thoroughness, you are absolutely amazing. SHY is as grammar-free and error-free as it can be because of you!

Thank you, H. For noticing me. For the feelings you gave me. For the hope and inspiration. SHY wouldn't be complete without you.

Shout out to younger me. For going through all that teenage angst. You put yourself out there and tried new experiences. Some were bad, embarrassing, and maybe even regrettable; but some were good too. I still hold onto them today. They give me hope. Strength. So thanks Boo, neither I or SHY would be here without you.

And lastly, thank you, Reader. For picking this up, giving it a shot, and making it this far. I hope you enjoyed this story and that it made you feel something. That would mean the world to me.

There were a lot of songs that captured the feeling I was aiming for. Whenever I was stumped, listening to these songs always made me picture a music video of Kayla and Aiden, which definitely helped me in writing SHY. Here's the main bunch that really sets the vibes for me:

1. "Good Things Fall Apart" – ILLENIUM, Jon Bellion
2. "Love Somebody" – Maroon 5
3. "Tall Trees" – (G)I-DLE
4. "I Just Wanna" – Amber Liu ft. Eric Nam
5. "Everything Has Changed" – Taylor Swift ft. Ed Sheeran (Taylor's Version)
6. "Kimi Ni Todoke" – Tomofumi Tanizawa
7. "Fallin' For You" – Colbie Caillat
8. "Youth" – Troye Sivan
9. "I Really Like You" – Carly Rae Jepsen
10. "Music Sounds Better With U" – Big Time Rush ft. Mann
11. "Angel Baby" – Troye Sivan
12. "A Little Bit Closer" – Babygirl
13. "Selfish" – Justin Timberlake

14. "Could I Love You Any More" – Reneé Dominique ft. Jason Mraz
15. "Make You Mine" – PUBLIC
16. "Someone to You" – BANNERS
17. "Want You" – Rynx ft. Miranda Glory
18. "One I Wanna Be With" – Trella

For the full playlist, visit: https://baylinwing.com/shyplaylist

Baylin Wing is an author of fantasy, contemporary, and romance genres. Touched by a variety of entertainment as a kid, she was inspired to create stories that provide a tangible experience to her audience—just as she was given. Baylin writes in hopes of sharing a safe space to heal, be understood, and feel represented. When not writing her next project, she's drawing, reading, or consuming other masterpieces.

Please visit www.baylinwing.com for more information.
Catch me on Goodreads, Instagram, TikTok, YouTube, X
—> **@baylinwing** or scan below:

ELH
Football

Bonus Content

What started Aiden and Emma's relationship?
What was Kevin's beef with Aiden really about?
What scene started this story?

Sign up for my newsletter at
www.baylinwing.com and find out!

Join The Wing and receive
free extra content, BTS, Q&A's, and
etc. regarding SHY and future works ☺

Coming Soon…

The Unholy Saintess (Book 1)

www.ingramcontent.com/pod-product-compliance
Lightning Source LLC
Chambersburg PA
CBHW030626310726
48979CB00003B/906

9781964680026